ACTS AND OMISSIONS

ACTS AND OMISSIONS

From a Single Act Judge Us All

Joseph C. Hoffman

Writers Club Press
San Jose New York Lincoln Shanghai

Acts and Omissions
From a Single Act Judge Us All

Writers Club Press
an imprint of iUniverse, Inc.

For information address:
iUniverse, Inc.
5220 S. 16th St., Suite 200
Lincoln, NE 68512
www.iuniverse.com

Any resemblance to actual people and events is purely coincidental.
This is a work of fiction.

ISBN: 0-595-22524-1

Printed in the United States of America

PART I

I was angry with my friend:
I told my wrath, my wrath did end.
I was angry with my foe
I told it not, my wrath did grow.

—**William Blake (1757-1827),** English poet, painter,
engraver. *Songs of Experience*, "A Poison Tree" st. 1 (1794)

CHAPTER 1

Watson Avenue in the South Bronx

A cold, wet snow was still falling. For the past week, freezing high winds had kept the wind chill well below zero, bracing the ugly oil-stained mounds of plowed snow from a recent storm that separated the city's sidewalks from its roadways. It was February at its worst.

In the basement apartment at 2506, Ramon Velez leaned softly over the bare shoulder of his Teresa.

"It's time for me to get up, sweetheart. Today is garbage pick-up and I want to make sure everything is OK. You know, lids on and all that stuff," he whispered.

"Mm, what? Oh, OK, Ray. How are the kids?" She had been in a deep sleep.

"They look fine from here, but I'll check them out as I leave," Velez said, looking over at the bunk beds against the wall facing the foot of their bed.

"My God, what time is it?" Teresa said, gently wiping the sleep from her eyes and looking at her watch lying on a bedside table.

"Six o'clock?" she said.

"Yes, yes, I know, but it's Wednesday—Morgan McCabe—his store?" Velez asked.

"Uh, huh, yeah, right," she said.

"Ray, it must still be very cold outside, please dress warm, *mi muchacho*," she smiled, blowing him a kiss, as he slowly closed the bedroom door.

He put on an old navy parka while pulling a blue watch cap from the pocket. He yanked the cap over his ears, opened the door and climbed up the steps to the sidewalk. Velez marched past the dozen or so overstuffed garbage cans that he had lined up in almost military formation, popping a few loosened covers back in place. He stuffed his hands into the side pockets of his jacket.

"Hey, man, pretty cold. Right?" he greeted two of his young tenants as they passed.

"Yeah, *mucho frio*, but you talkin' about *acqui en la calle*, or in *su casa, amigo?*" one of the guys laughed, blowing into his bare, cupped hands.

"Hey, man, *ingles, ingles*," Velez said.

The younger guy smiled, "Yeah, yeah, you right man—but my apartment—it's still colder than out here in the street."

"Hey, very good, my man, very good," Velez chuckled as the tenant shooed him away with a friendly wave.

As they reached the top step and were about to go inside the chilly vestibule, the guy who had spoken to Ramon turned to his companion.

"Hey, man, check this out," he said, pointing over the shoulder of his friend. His buddy turned and saw three young guys making their way along the badly cracked sidewalks of Watson. When they reached 2506, they stopped and looked up at the two young tenants standing at the front door staring down at them.

"Hey, you guys. You been hanging out with that big mouth Ramon, right?" one of them shouted up the concrete stairs as the other two laughed.

Ramon's friends turned to enter the foyer.

"Hey. We're talkin' to you, assholes. You tell Ramon to stop suckin' up to the cops. You got that?"

Ramon's young tenants looked back over their shoulders, stared at all three for a moment, and went inside the hallway. The two, who hadn't been talking, suddenly ran to the curb, lifted one of Ramon Velez's overstuffed garbage cans and heaved it halfway up the front steps, popping its cover and releasing its rotted contents. They started to howl loudly, and extended their stiffened right middle fingers as they took off.

The younger Latino shook his head.

"Let's clean up this mess for Ramon," his partner said, opening the vestibule door and starting down the steps.

Velez was still walking west on Watson Avenue. His five-feet five frame seemed weighed down by a pump-iron torso—tapered waist, over-developed chest and wide shoulders that thrust his beefy arms into awkward angles as if he were carrying two large bundles under each arm. At twenty-five, he had a full flow of silky, long, black and mostly uncombable hair that he lassoed into a foot-long pony tail. His more-square-than-round face played up what seemed to be a permanent impish smile made even more roguish by an unruly, black mustache drooping around the corners of his mouth and reaching halfway down to his chin.

As he reached the corner, he paused and looked up at a newly installed aluminum light pole. A large, plastic, temporary green and red poster encircled the pole, stapled in place at eye level. "Compliments of Consolidated Edison" it read.

"Yeah, right," he laughed quietly, "Tell it to Morgan McCabe."

Two vertical street signs, with chalk-white lettering against a bright, ultramarine background announced the intersecting of his block with one of Parkchester's busiest streets, Castle Hill Avenue. He smiled dryly, and shook his head from side to side.

"There would be no new signs or anything else happening for the good in Parkchester if it wasn't for Morgan."

As he reached Castle Hill and Westchester, he turned left, casually looking up at the sky, and squinting to glimpse at the sun's valiant attempt to rise on this brutally cold morning. It was very quiet; no people on the street.

He was thinking of the five winters ago that he and Teresa had been stretched out on the crowded, rusted deck of an anonymous oil tanker that finally neared an abandoned pier just below Hubert Street, on the city's West Side waterfront. Their eyes had never been opened as far as they were at that moment when they slipped over the side, using a rope ladder to reach the pier. As the tanker picked up speed and moved away they got their first glimpse of the huge fan-shaped harbor forming a semicircle around Battery Park. Later in the day their excitement would turn to fear as they got to the crowded and intimidating streets of the South Bronx. But then there had been the joyous day when he and Teresa carried their year-old son into their first home in this unfamiliar new land, a tiny, cold-water flat at 2506 Watson Avenue, and all else was forgotten. "And it's still a shithouse," he said to himself, but smiled this time.

He finally got to 2044 Westchester, between Pugsley and Olmstead, and walked up the concrete steps leading to the front door of a store. He was surprised to see that the front lights as well as those inside the store were off. He peered through the door's glass panels and twisted the large old-fashioned bronzed doorknob—the door was still locked. He went back down the steps and faced the structure. He scanned the outside of the aging three-story building and then looked at his watch. It was five minutes past seven, "Morgan McCabe would have been here no later than six-thirty," he said to himself.

"Morgan, are you in there?" he called out. He climbed back up the stairs to the front door and gave it a few whacks with the palm of his right hand. "Morgan, it's me, Ray Velez, are you OK, *hombrecito?*" No response.

Velez decided to try the rear entrance at the end of a long, narrow alley used by trucks delivering to Morgan McCabe's Parkchester Paint and Hardware, and a bodega next door. He walked briskly through the opening between the two stores. As he reached the rear of the building, he heard a crashing sound and, hearing it again, started running in the direction of the noise. As he got closer, he saw that a rust-stained aluminum combination storm and screen door that led to the rear entrance of the McCabe store was swinging wildly back and forth, banging against the side of the building.

Velez stopped running and started walking again—more slowly this time. "Morgan, Morgan, Mister McCabe," he called out softly. A naked red bulb over the rear door was still glowing in the cold morning shadows. As he got closer to the rear entrance, Velez saw a narrow streak of light springing from inside the otherwise densely shadowed storeroom that took up most of the space in the rear of the store. He hesitated, and then slowly stepped inside, closing the banging door behind him. The room temperature must have dropped below freezing, he thought. In fact, he felt colder now than when he was outside.

He began tracking the beam of light, starting from the doorsill he had just stepped over. My God! It was even darker than it was cold, he was thinking. He started to walk, slowly placing one foot directly in front of the other as he followed the narrow shaft of light. It was coming from a small goose-neck desk lamp leaning over the top of a wooden, mahogany roll top desk whose ribbed, pull-down top had been brought to rest on the edge of the desk. As he looked away from the lamp to the desk, he snapped back his head sharply, and felt a cold fear when he saw a large shadow outlined against the desk. He moved closer and saw a human form seated in a high-back swivel chair facing the desk. The chair was turned just enough so that Velez could not see who was sitting in it. His eyes narrowed as he peered into the darkened room and began walking slowly towards the desk and around the chair, "Morgan—Morgan, is that you?"

"!*Dios, mio,* Morgan!" Velez cried out, as he got closer to the chair.

McCabe was seated in an upright position, his handsome, perfectly proportioned gray-topped head sagging to one side, his chin buried in his left chest. The old man's clear blue eyes were open, staring, unblinking, under bushy, bright white, undisciplined eyebrows. His tongue was now a milky, pasty, white and protruding grotesquely from the left side of his distorted, open mouth in a twisted grimace as if he was choking. His long arms, sheathed in an out-of-style, long sleeved, pin-striped, green and white shirt with each arm adorned with an arm-garter, were hanging, motionless outside the curved armrests of the chair, and his glasses dangled precariously from his right ear and against his sagging chin.

Velez was trembling as he leaned over his friend and, placing his right hand against the top of McCabe's drooping left shoulder, pushed lightly against it, "Morgan, Morgan, please, *querido amigo mia*—my dear friend—can you hear me?" Velez quickly reached down to McCabe's right side lifting up his arm and gripping his right wrist. He first put his right thumb against where he thought he might find a pulse. Nothing. He frantically fumbled open the button to the old man's right shirt sleeve and pushed it back above his elbow. He then switched from his thumb to his right index and middle fingers—he didn't feel a thing. He'd never done that before and was sure he wasn't doing it right—"Morgan may still be alive, how would I know?" he thought. He was shaking uncontrollably as he reached for a telephone sitting on top of the desk.

As he lifted the black phone from its cradle, Velez heard the shuffling of feet coming from out of the dark, directly behind him. Before he could turn around, a heavy blow struck him in the middle of his back, just below the shoulders. It had the brute force of a sledgehammer, but he realized that huge, incredibly strong hands had hammered him. As he began falling forward, his own heavy arms were pinned behind him and his neck thrown into a death lock by two more powerful arms that were breaking his fall and pulling him backwards. He would either fall on to his back or choke to death, he was sure. He was gasping for air while continuing to fall backwards when suddenly his assailant removed an arm from Velez's neck and, while still holding on to his arms with the other, delivered another hard jolt into his right side, this time with something hard and cold. It must have been long and serrated the way it ripped at his flesh on entering his body and tearing apart the layers of skin as it went deeply inside his stomach, finally skewering Velez's small intestines.

He began screaming in pain, "Who are you, why are you doing this to me?" And at that very moment his attacker abruptly released his arm from around Velez's neck, letting him fall forward on to his knees, in a praying position.

His attacker had either withdrawn the blade or allowed it to slip out when Velez fell to his knees. He screamed again as the unendurable pain raced through his entire body. He instinctively reached behind him to the spot where the pain began and when he brought his hand back to a point directly in front of him, he saw that his fingers were drenched with blood.

He was still on his knees when he heard a whirling sound caused by the intense sweeping motion of his assailant's arm and felt the weapon plunge into him again, this time into his lower back. For a second time, it was quickly withdrawn and he could only cry out, "Oh, my God, please, no more," just before his mouth was forced open by a surge of blood billowing up from his throat. It gushed forth, a red vomit splashing on the floor in front of him. He slumped forward and fell into his own blood.

"Holy Mary, Mother of God, pray for us now and at the hour of our death," Ramon Velez whispered.

As he lay there, barely breathing, he heard an angry, grunting sound from the person who was trying to kill him—a sound more animal than human—and he was suddenly paralyzed by another thrust of the long blade into his back.

"*Dios mio,* bless my children and bless my Teresa, *Dios mio,*" he tried to shout, but he was choking on his own blood as his life drained away at the feet of his friend.

❦   ❦   ❦

Twenty minutes later the owner of the bodega returned from his pre-dawn trip to the Wholesale fruit and vegetable markets in Hunt's Point. He backed his badly sagging pickup to the rear of the store. When he heard the flapping of McCabe's storm door against the rear entrance of his building, he retraced the steps of Ramon Velez to the inside of the McCabe store. He nearly passed out when he recognized Morgan McCabe and saw a second figure laying in a fetal position on the blood-blanketed floor. He turned quickly and ran outside where he threw up in the alleyway. He finally got to his own store and was able to steady his hand long enough to dial 911.

Within minutes, Brian Joyce and Vince Savino were jumping from their police cruiser, 43 Precinct, Sector King, and running towards the store owner standing in the middle of the curb waving frantically.

"It's Morgan—Morgan McCabe, and someone else, *darse prisa,* hurry, please," he was shouting.

A blue and orange paramedic ambulance from Jacobi Medical Center, siren wailing, skidded to a stop just short of the police cruiser's rear bumper, its bright, rotating red-and-while turret lights bathing the three figures running through the alley. The cops and ambulance crew ran into the building, one paramedic rushing to the side of McCabe, the other falling to her knees and bending over Velez's body. They began examining the two victims for vital signs. It was obvious that there was no hope for Velez, but they still applied tourniquets to both his legs and arms to stem the flow of blood still draining from the gaping wounds. The two cops stood over the paramedics as they continued to examine the two bodies.

"Oh, my God, that's Ramon Velez. We know him too, right, Vince?" Joyce announced, as his partner nodded and then shook his head in despair. Joyce was clearly the younger of the two, just a bit over six feet, with a budding weight problem that stretched his gun belt to its last notch.

"It looks like he was stabbed at least three times—once in his right side and twice in his back," Savino added. Quickly they turned to Morgan McCabe. They lifted him gently from the chair and onto the floor, causing an audible groan to come from the rearranging of the contents of his stomach. They tried to stay clear of the blood still pouring from the body of Ramon Velez. The paramedics again fell to their knees, this time next to Morgan McCabe, and started a rescue attempt—defibrillation,   oxygen,   mouth-to-mouth.   "Start again—rotate—start again—rotate." But after fifteen minutes, there was still no sign of life.

One of the paramedics leaned closer over his body, and using her right thumb and index finger, softly closed his eyes.

"Hey guys, take a look," she almost shouted, pointing to what looked like a one-inch-wide, uneven red rash encircling Morgan McCabe's neck.

"Looks like some kind of burn, from a rope or something," said Joyce.

"Call the sergeant," he said, looking at his partner.

"I'm sure she's on her way. She heard the address as clearly as we did," Vince Savino said.

He was on the job for close to twelve years, all in the 43. He was a slim five foot-eight with beginning-to-gray, but still shiny, straight black hair that neatly fit in with his lineless, angular face. The uniform was strictly West Point.

Sergeant Jessica Munro arrived just as the paramedics were standing up, abandoning their life-saving efforts. She stood behind them, watching them in the faintly lit doorway. She had already called the local detectives, Bronx Homicide, and City-wide Forensics, and notified her precinct commander. At 30, she was close to six feet, her face youthfully sensual, her waistline slim, and her legs long and attractive. She wore her flowing black hair pulled back into a bun that raised her uniform cap another two inches.

She would supervise one of the cops, Joyce, as he examined every part of the store, while Vince Savino made notes of his companion's every move.

The paramedics had already covered the body of Ramon Velez, so Brian Joyce would start by looking carefully at the chair Morgan McCabe had been sitting in and the desk he had been facing. As he looked to the right of the chair—one of the few areas free of bloodstains—he saw what appeared to be a package wrapped in plastic, slightly crumpled and torn at one end. He bent down and, without touching it, saw that it contained a coil of lightweight hemp rope, the kind used for stringing clotheslines. He dictated his findings to his partner while he worked his way methodically up towards the main part of the store. As he approached the area closest to the front entrance where the store's checkout counter was located, he saw a piece of rope lying on the floor, directly below a cash register. It was clothesline replacement cord, similar to that which he had found in the back room. It was about two feet long and had been cut at one end. Savino made a note of that, too.

"This looks like the rope that could have put those burns on his neck," Savino said, looking at his partner.

He quickly turned and shouted towards the back room of the store where Jessica Munro was still bent over the bodies of McCabe and Velez. "Hey, Sarge, c'mere, quick, look at this, I think we may have found at least one of the murder weapons."

"But so far no sign of a knife or anything like that which could've been used to stab poor Ramon Velez, right?" Joyce asked. Both his partner and the sergeant shook their heads.

Sergeant Munro and Savino, with notepad at the ready, leaned against the counter and watched as Brian Joyce stooped over the cash register. He could see it was an old-fashioned type. "If you hit any key, the cash drawer jumps out," he said, continuing his running dictation. The drawer was open, obviously cleaned out. The rest of the store seemed to be undisturbed; apparently nothing was out of place. The merchandise on the shelves was neatly stacked and the floor displays meticulously positioned. The sergeant looked around one more time and said, "If anything had been moved it would have stood out like me at a meeting of the Klan."

The three cops went outside the store looking for any traces of bloody footprints or tire tracks in the driveway, at the back door of the store or at the curb in front.

Vince Savino noted that the front door seemed secure. It had probably not been used by the perpetrator to get into or out of the store. They circled the store three times. They stretched yellow "Police Crime Scene—Do Not Enter" plastic tape across the entrance to the driveway and over the front walk of the store. They were preparing for the usual circus.

The Blue Room in the West Wing of City Hall

"Mister Mayor, can you just go over those numbers one more time. I know we've all been handed a copy of the press release, but it sounds so much better coming directly from you," a reporter shouted, setting off a round of animated kissing and sucking sounds from his colleagues and a loud chuckle from the mayor.

"Yes, sure, Mark—my buddy," the mayor replied. "For the year just ending, violent crime was down in New York City by 11%; Murders were down 12%, Robberies 10%, Assaults 14% and Burglaries

16%. Ladies and gentlemen, they're stealing fewer cars, percentage-wise in our city than anyplace in the country."

"Obviously, Mister Mayor, you have the police commissioner and his community policing program, along with ComStat, to thank for those numbers. Right?" a young woman asked.

The mayor stiffened his back a bit. "Well, crime was down dramatically in our city for a number of reasons, and certainly community policing, and yes, ComStat, were among them."

"Among them? Come on, sir, what else was there?"

The mayor stood even taller. "What else was there?" You must be kidding. You guys are forgetting that my administration has provided more economic incentives for businesses to stay in—and to move into—our city than any other in history. That in turn has added more job opportunities for our young people and we've hired more teachers and extended our school year to meet those demands. The booming economy, triggered by our efforts, has lowered our public assistance rolls and our workfare program is the most successful of its kind in the country. And, hey guys, look at the numbers on Wall Street. They're making their way back, too. Right!"

"Mister Mayor, you're not taking credit for that, too, are you?"

"I was thinking about it—but then again, with the daily ups and downs that's happening lately, maybe not. Hey, Bruce what did the *Dow* do today?" He shouted to one of his aides. Some polite laughter from the press.

"Seriously folks, what I am saying is that we've been watching our three years of community policing and ComStat very closely. At this time, I would say it's too early to tell. On the other hand, I'm sure this type of policing and crime analysis has, and will continue to have, some impact on the control of crime here and in other cities," the mayor said, taking a deep breath.

"So you don't think that community policing is the primary reason for the big drop in crime in our city? As your police commissioner obviously does." A follow-up question from the assembled press in the Blue Room causing some nervous shuffling of feet amongst the mayor's aides standing in the usual semi-circle behind the chief executive.

The mayor smiled and stepped away from the lectern without responding to that question.

"But, hey, he's your friend, your buddy. What's up with you two guys?" the same reporter followed-up. Other members of the press began yelling questions above his Communications Director's blasé, "Thank you, ladies and gentlemen.

The Mayor's Office in the Northwest Wing of City Hall

The mayor was back in his office following the press conference. His phone rang as soon as he had settled behind his desk. He spun his leather high back chair around so that he was facing an antique credenza holding a bank of brightly colored telephones. He quickly picked up the one red line that was blinking.

"Mr. Mayor, it's the police commissioner, says it's urgent."

He gracefully whirled back around from the panel, both legs hoisted high off the ground and extended. Resting his heels on his desk, he put his right hand over the mouthpiece, and looked at a guest sitting in a comfortable chair placed at one corner of the desk.

"It's your friend, Chris Russo."

The older man screwed up his face while shaking his head from side to side. He was in his late 50's just over six-foot. A small potbelly protruded below the flaps of his Giorgio Armani vest. His thinning, gray hair was short, and carefully parted on the left side. An expensive cigar set off his unlined face, caught in an expression of slightly condescending agreeability. A pair of frameless, oversize glasses complemented its mid-winter tan.

The mayor waved a cloud of second hand smoke away, a reformed smoker's gesture of irritation, and spoke into the phone.

"OK, Janet, please put the police commissioner through."

"Chris, what's up?" the mayor asked, leaning back in his chair.

"Mr. Mayor—Tom. I—uh—. Are you alone?"

"No, I'm not. Gordon Halliday is with me. Why?" a darting look at his visitor.

"Yeah, OK, Tom. I just didn't know how to tell you this," the commissioner began, uncharacteristically awkward. "It's Morgan—Tom—it's your father."

"My father? What about him? Has he been hurt or something? What is it, Chris? What is it?" the mayor asked, sitting up quickly, his feet falling to the floor.

Halliday jumped up from his chair.

"He was found in the back of his store, about fifteen minutes ago."

"Found in the back of the store? Is he hurt? What happened to him, Chris?"

"It looks like a robbery or a burglary. He may have been surprised by the perp, or perps."

"My God is he OK?"

"No, Tom, no, he's not," Russo hesitated.

"Tom? Tom?"

"Yes, I'm here."

"I'm sorry, my dear friend. Your father is dead," Chris Russo said softly.

"Oh, no. Please, God, no," Tom McCabe said, groaning, closing his eyes and lowering his head close to the top of his desk, phone in his hand.

Halliday was now standing in front of the mayor's desk, shaking his head from side to side.

Tom McCabe slowly recovered and brought the phone back to his left ear. "How did he, Oh, Jesus, How did he die?"

"There was someone with him, too, Tom—possibly a customer."

"Oh my, Oh my," McCabe said

"Your father may have been strangled by a clothesline rope, taken from a shelf in the store. We found it on the floor near the bodies. We're not sure at this time. The other man seems to have been stabbed to death. We haven't as yet recovered a weapon."

"Where is my father now?"

"He's at the store along with the other man at the scene. Oh shit, they just told me, it's Ramon Velez, you know him right, Tom?"

"Oh, yes, yes. Of course."

"I'm calling you from my car. I just got the word. If it's OK with you, I'll send two of my chiefs to speak with your mother and bring her to the store."

"Oh, yes, my mom. Lord watch over her. Yes, thanks, Chris."

"I'll be at the scene in about three minutes," Russo said.

"Yes, of course. Thanks, Chris, I appreciate everything you're doing. I'm on my way, too" the mayor replied hoarsely and sat there holding the dead phone.

Thomas Jarvis McCabe leaned back and began to sob. He again lowered his head, shaking it from side to side in disbelief. He looked up, his tears obscuring the view through the window that overlooked the crescent-shaped plaza half surrounding City Hall Park. He slowly raised his head. The crying stopped. His guest stood up and stopped at the large pine double panel doors leading from the mayor's office.

McCabe stood up, white-faced and shaking. The phone dropped from his hand, dangling by its cord, forgotten. He glared at his friend through eyes still brimming with tears. In a strangled voice he protested, "My father. My poor, innocent, father. This wasn't supposed to happen. This fucking should never have happened, Halliday!"

Halliday started to turn around and leave.

"Please let me know if there is anything I can do," he said in a subdued voice. "Anything!"

McCabe made an obvious effort to control his emotions. Extracting a handkerchief from the breast pocket of his suit, he wiped his eyes with it and then slowly buttoned his coat. Then he looked up at his guest, waving at him to come back.

"Oh, no, Gordon. Please come with me. I want you to come. I'll need my closest friend at my side when I see my father and face my family."

"But what will your office staff think about me accompanying you?"

"Don't worry, Janet will take care of it," Tom McCabe said, placing the open palm of his right hand in the middle of his friend's broad back and escorting him through the front double-doored entrance to his office.

Tom McCabe's inviting his office guest to accompany him did take many of the mayor's staff by surprise, as Halliday had predicted. The staff member who usually gave instructions to the mayor's personal security cops and driver had always followed clear priorities about who would—and who would not—accompany the mayor to emergencies and any other events likely to draw media coverage. It was usually the first deputy mayor, the mayor's chief of staff, the mayor's press secretary, or a favored elected official who would be with him at such moments—and no one else.

"Janet, you didn't seem surprised. How come?" one of the younger inner-office administrative assistants asked, as her fellow workers stopped what they were doing and looked at Janet.

Janet Mullins turned slowly, drooped her eyelids halfway and stared coldly and unblinking at her inquisitor. Everyone fell silent and went quickly back to work.

The mayor's black Mercury, police Communications Section code "NORDIC," with one detective behind the wheel and another riding shotgun, was waiting for them at the foot of the concrete steps that led to the main entrance of City Hall. The cop in the front passenger seat jumped out as the mayor and his companion approached. He opened the oversized rear door for them.

The mayor's car looked no different than many of the chauffeur-driven town cars passing the Civic Center district in lower Manhattan each day on their way to the city's Financial District, just to the South, and off Broadway, except that the Mayor's car had specially tinted, shatterproof glass in all windows, a bulletproof exterior, a souped-up engine and two red lights and sirens buried inside the car's hood. These were now clearing the East River Drive as the car hurtled towards the Bronx and 2044 Westchester Avenue.

Tom McCabe slumped into the left corner of the rear seat, his usual perch. However, on this ride, the mayor wasn't about to indulge in the small talk he customarily initiated with his detective crew when alone or with one of his frequent guests. The passengers, in turn, respected his need for private reflection. Mayor McCabe gazed out the small, paneled window, gently nipping his lower lip as the moisture slowly gathered around his eyes.

The gymnasium at Cardinal Hayes High School, 1975

"Hey, Tommy, your old man just called from the store. He wants you to call him back. Now!"

"Yeah, right OK, coach. One more scrimmage, and then I'll call him," shouted a short-waisted, long-legged kid, with flaming red hair, from the gym floor. "Chris, come on, let's practice that feed into the key play one more time," he called out.

"You mean where I bust my ass getting the ball up court and then, when I'm about to be clobbered by their defense, I deftly pass off to you and you easily slam-dunk the winning basket? Is that the one?" answered a just-under-six-foot, wiry, but muscular guy with a closely cropped head of jet black, stubby hair.

They both smiled. "Come on buddy, it's for good old Cardinal Hayes, we gotta beat those sinners from Regis next Friday. Right?" Tom said.

"Dad, what's up?" Tom was calling from the pay phone outside the locker room.

"Great news, Tommy. You just got that call from M.I.T., and they accepted you. Isn't that wonderful?"

"Wow, super! What about the tuition, Dad?" Tom inquired.

"They'll pay half and pick up all room and board expenses," Morgan McCabe answered.

"That sounds great, but can we afford that? Even at half, the tuition is awesome."

"Don't worry, Tommy, we can swing it. We have to. It's your dream and we're going to make sure it happens," he responded, with increasing excitement. "Besides, your mother and I have already invited all the neighbors over to the house tonight, to celebrate. It will make an Irish wake look like a prayer service, Laddie."

Later that night, following a succession of off-key harmonizing, poor imitations of Irish jigs and reels performed by the Irish Ramblers from Cardinal Hayes, and even some embarrassing line dancing by some of the older guests, Tom McCabe leaped onto an empty table, placed his two pinkies just inside the corners of each side of his mouth and whistled loudly.

"I'd like to make an announcement," he told the quieted room. "Mom, Dad, my dear sister and my little brother, I know you didn't expect this, but maybe I didn't either," he began, noticing that some even put down their drinks.

"A lot of things have influenced me over the past year or so. Not the least of which has been my family's commitment to Parkchester and to the people who live here—and to those who want to live here," he said, becoming serious and capturing the full attention of his audience.

"So, I'm not going to M.I.T. I'm going to miss not going. I had my heart set on it," he confessed. "Chris Russo can tell you that," he went on, making a poor attempt to smile.

Morgan and Ellen McCabe were now holding hands, nervously, with counterfeit smiles, waiting for the next skyrocket to be launched by their oldest son.

"I'm going to stay in Parkchester, work with my family at the store, and get as involved in community matters as they are," Tom said excitedly.

The people who filled the room were still shocked, leaning back in anticipation—of something.

"Oh, yeah, and I've decided to got to City College, you know, C.C.N.Y., in Washington Heights, and take political science, and start working part-time for State Senator Monahan," he announced.

"And, of course, in time, I plan to study *the law*," he boomed out in his best-exaggerated Irish brogue.

Tom felt the thud of his heart as he waited for their reaction.

They sat motionless.

"Go for it, Tom," someone finally shouted, and then everyone stood up and began to applaud.

"Tom, Tom, Tom, he's our man," they began to chant.

Chris Russo just shook his head in disbelief.

Morgan McCabe was almost sobbing, while Ellen McCabe was hastily making her way to where her son was standing.

Later that night, long after the party was over, Tom McCabe and Chris Russo were standing and talking on the sidewalk outside of 200 McGraw Avenue.

"OK, Tom. What's this all about? You told me, not too long ago, that you wanted to get the hell out of this neighborhood no matter what. Now, you're making a big deal over staying," Russo felt a kind of baffled anger.

"Chris, you are, and always will be, my closest friend. But, please believe me, I can't tell you why, because I don't know myself—it's like—it's like, it just happened. Some day, buddy, maybe just some day, we'll both know," Tom smiled faintly.

"Yeah, yeah, right. But I won't hold my breath till then," Chris answered.

"But, hey buddy, we haven't talked about you. What is Cardinal Hayes' star play-maker gonna do after graduation?"

Before his friend could answer, Tom McCabe laughed and said, "Why don't you go to City College with me? Then you wouldn't have to hold your breath."

"I'm not sure what I'm going to do. You know my father—the cop," Chris said in an exaggerated caustic tone. "He's always telling me war stories about his days in the Marines and how it helped prepare him for what's he doing now—or for whatever else he would have decided to do with his life. He says that the new cops coming on the force who haven't had some kind of military training—you know, discipline and all that shit—are really not fully prepared to deal with the kinds of things that are happening in our city—or our world for that matter—today," Chris went on.

"You're not really serious, buddy? The Marines? The Cops?" Tom interrupted.

"I don't know. Could be. I'm not as sure, as you say that you are, about what I want to be in this world. Maybe a couple of years away from home will give me time to think," Chris finished.

"OK, my friend, but then you're going to have to play catch up with me," Tom McCabe winked. "That is, I think you will," he added. They both laughed.

❧   ❧   ❧

Tom McCabe looked up just as his car screeched to a stop in front of the store, a lonely survivor among the many boarded-up buildings on Westchester Avenue. They were met curbside by the police commissioner. The mayor cleared his eyes, rubbing them with his right index finger and thumb. He ignored the others in the car as he jumped out.

Chris Russo reached out for the mayor's hand and gently grabbed his shoulder, then said "Hello, Gordon," as he saw Halliday get out of the car.

"Commissioner," the mayor's passenger responded coldly.

They ran up the front steps and into the store. They walked past the checkout counter on the right and this week's promotional display on the left. They instinctively slowed down in anticipation of what they were about to witness and hesitated for a moment as they approached the back room. Russo had cleared everyone from the room as he escorted the mayor inside. Halliday deferentially stayed a few steps behind.

The sight of the covered bodies, and the deep red pools of now-dried blood were shocking, even to hardened law enforcement professionals still arriving at the scene. To the mayor and his companion it was worse. After several minutes of inconsolable crying and some inarticulate mumbling by Tom McCabe as he viewed the lifeless form of his father, Chris Russo began a detailed rundown where the investigation stood. McCabe half-listened. He couldn't stop staring at his father.

Suddenly he turned to Russo. "Chris, would you excuse us for a minute or two?" interrupting the commissioner in mid-sentence. Chris Russo was momentarily stunned. Was he being asked to leave a crime scene? But he reluctantly left the room. "Extenuating circumstances," he rationalized to himself, as he reached the front of the store.

As Chris Russo walked outside, he saw Ellen McCabe stepping from an unmarked police car and in between a pair of middle-aged men. They reached out to help her. She motioned to them that she was OK.

"Mother McCabe, Mom, I'm so sorry," he rushed down the steps and threw his arms around her. She was not crying, but was clearly shaken and welcomed his strong embrace. The Ellen McCabe that Chris Russo had known while growing up in Parkchester had seemed to gently float her way through middle age and now, at sixty-two, was more energetic and unmistakably more confident than ever in what she was to do with her life. She was not the dutiful housewife from County Cork who honed her domestic talents only to support her husband's struggle with life. She was at his side, his greatest supporter, his unflinching loyalist, but clearly by her own choice. She can handle this, he was thinking.

"Yes, thank you, Chris. I appreciate your sending Chiefs Hughes and Lombardo to fetch me. They were wonderful," Ellen McCabe said as she stepped back from the police commission-er's hug.

"Good, good, Ellen. Are you ready to go in?"

"Yes, yes, of course."

She turned to the two men standing at the foot of the steps, "Thank you, gentlemen."

They walked through the store towards the back room. Ellen McCabe did not look to her right or left—straight ahead, and Chris Russo did not try to escort her.

As they reached the doorway leading to the office, Chris saw that Tom McCabe was crying, his face pressed against a wall on the side of the room opposite from where his father was still seated at the roll top desk. A white sheet covered most of Morgan McCabe's body; only his head showed. McCabe's pure white, full head of hair looked almost iridescent, giving off a halo effect to the area around him.

Ramon Velez was covered by another white sheet his body rimmed by pools of dried blood. Russo grimaced as he looked at the crime scene again.

Gordon Halliday had his arm around Tom McCabe, his head resting against the mayor's back. Suddenly, McCabe pulled away from his friend, staring at him with red, swollen eyes.

"Well, what the hell are we going to do now?" he snarled at Halliday.

"Everything OK, Mr. Mayor?" Chris Russo interrupted, for the moment forgetting that Ellen McCabe was at his side.

"Oh my God, Mother," Tom McCabe cried out, rushing to his mother and throwing his arms around her. Chris Russo saw her pained expression and a light trickle moving down her cheeks.

Tom McCabe looked over his mother's shoulder.

"Yes. Yes, thanks, Chris. Everything's OK. Just fine," he stammered.

Chris Russo stared at the mayor and then glared at Gordon Halliday.

Russo motioned to Halliday.

Morgan, Ellen, and Tom McCabe needed some time together.

Her daughter and youngest son soon joined Ellen McCabe. She turned down a ride for them back to their home and they walked slowly, hand-in-hand, back to the two-story, semi-detached, brick Tudor on McGraw.

Tom McCabe, Gordon Halliday, and Chris Russo all shook hands, walked back through the store and down the steps without saying a word. The mayor and Halliday got into the Town car and sped off, sirens blasting.

"I hope he's all right," Russo asked himself, standing at the curb and looking at the magnetically attached turret light on top of the car whirling madly, bouncing its red-and-white splashes of light off the walls of the aging buildings of Parkchester.

Chris Russo called out to two guys standing on the sidewalk wearing matching trench coats and identical fedoras.

"Terry, Chips, come back inside."

"Hard to believe," Russo shook his head and looked down as they climbed back up the stairs "What a tragedy. Morgan McCabe fought so hard for his community, and now this."

Once inside, he spoke directly to the smaller of the two, his chief of detectives, Terry Hughes, a man with a wiry, greyhound's physique, rough, openly Irish features and brillo-like kinky red and gray hair mashed down by his hat, which were covering part of his long sideburns.

"How do you feel this should be handled, Terry? Chips and his guys taking the lead?"

"Yes. Yes, sir. Special Investigations Division, definitely. I'll have the activities of everyone involved in the investigation cleared through Chips' guys."

Deputy Chief Chester "Chips" Lombardo, C.O. of the S.I.D. was at least three inches taller than his boss, and close to fifty pounds heavier. His dark, Neapolitan features, black bushy eyebrows, black straight hair was overshadowed by the same kind of hat worn by Hughes. He had a noticeably ungainly way of walking. Lombardo nodded his head at the police commissioner and then looked over at Hughes.

"But remember," Russo, added, "I want the CPOs—community police officers—who cover this area to be involved as the case progresses. They've been trained by you guys to be preliminary investigators and they're closer to the sources in this community than anyone else, which may be the key to coming up with some real leads."

Both Hughes and Lombardo nodded in assent. The chief of detectives added a thumbs up sign.

"By the way," Russo asked, "Where are the cops and their sergeant from the 43 who were first on the scene? I didn't see them," the commissioner said, scanning the army of cops now at the scene.

"Joyce and Savino, one young, the other's been around, and their boss, Sergeant Jessica Munro, a young black woman, Commissioner," Lombardo volunteered.

"Good, OK Chester, thanks. I want you guys on the forensic reports, now. Got that?"

"Yes, sir."

"Wait, hold it. Better yet, even though Chips and his people will be the clearing house for the murders, I want you, Terry, to be personally involved in certain aspects of the investigation, starting with the ME's report." Before Hughes could respond, Russo added, "I want you to be there standing next to the CME in the examining room when he gives you his preliminary findings. I know it's unusual for you to be there, but—"

Yes, sir, of course, Commissioner, you're right," Hughes responded, turning to look at Lombardo. "We'll be on our way once the bodies are released from here—I'll take Lombardo with me."

"Good, give me a call from there. Don't wait until you get back to your office."

"Chester! Shit, I wish he wouldn't call me that," Lombardo mumbled, as he and his boss began looking for the three cops.

The sergeant and her two cops were rushed to police headquarters in Lombardo's car. They knew that it was a politically explosive case but were still surprised at being abruptly pulled from the scene. "Why the hell are they kidnapping us like this?" Savino whispered to his sergeant in the back seat. Lombardo didn't say a word during the entire trip.

They exited from the East River Drive at the Brooklyn Bridge. Lombardo had ordered them to enter the rear delivery entrance to the building, and to use the stairs to get to his eleventh floor office. "Why don't we take the elevator?" Joyce asked, but Savino and Sergeant Munro ignored him and kept puffing up the long concrete steps.

He persisted. "I thought they only took suspects and prisoners up these stairs."

"Well?" the sergeant looked over at him.

They opened the seldom-used stairwell door on the 11th floor where most of the Detective Bureau's specialty squads were located. They'd never been there and had to ask the receptionist, a bored, overweight, uniformed cop lounging behind a half-circle, four-feet-high desk, to direct them to Lombardo's office.

They knocked on the glass door of Room 1106. No answer. They knocked a second and third time. Finally, the door was opened by a huge, ugly cop—"He looks like a fuckin' frog," Joyce hissed—in street clothes, no jacket, open collar shirt, and a mismatched tie with the tail longer than the tie, and hanging one third of the way down the front of his coffee-stained shirt. He didn't say a thing, but from the disgusted look he gave them, and the preemptory gesture in the direction of an office in the far corner of the room, the cops knew that they shouldn't have knocked, but just opened the door and walked in.

They walked into Lombardo's office standing just inside the entrance. He didn't acknowledge their presence and they didn't speak.

Finally, without looking up, he pointed his right index finger to three chairs in front of his desk, and motioned for them to sit. They seated themselves on the edges of the hard, straight-back chairs, which must have been hurriedly brought in from the outer office.

"I know you responded about the same time as the paramedics and that the 911 call was made by this guy, let's see, what the hell's his name, Badillo, Padillo?" Lombardo asked, while squirming around in his black swivel chair and shuffling mounds of paper covering his desk.

"Mantilla, Chief, it was Fernando Mantilla," the sergeant answered.

"Yeah, right, Mantilla. All those Spick names sound alike, right, sarge?" Lombardo smiled, but got no response from the cops.

"OK, how long was that PR there before he called, and how long did it take you guys to get there?"

"I made notes, chief," Munro said, turning the pages of her memorandum log.

Lombardo couldn't wait. He reached over his desk and grabbed the sergeant's notes from her.

"Let's see that fuckin' thing," he snapped, and began reading aloud, "The call came over the air at 0830 hours, directing Community Police—I hate that name—43 Precinct, Sector King, to a possible past robbery at 2044 Westchester Avenue, in the rear, injuries reported, EMS paramedics dispatched."

Lombardo slammed the sergeant's notebook closed and slung it like a Frisbee back at her, just clearing the top of his desk.

"So how long did it take to get there?" he asked again.

Jessica Munro gave him an estimate.

"Then the crime scene and homicide guys, the chief of detectives and me arrived. Is that correct? And the PC and the mayor shortly thereafter?" Lombardo asked.

"Yes, sir," the sergeant responded sharply.

"OK, guys. I'm now directing you to end your investigation of the McCabe case. It's clear to me that Ramon Lopez, Mendez, or whatever, was a customer who was in the wrong place at the wrong time. My office, the Special Investigations Division—S.I.D.—will handle everything from here on in. If you get any information relating to this case you are to call me directly. I'll give you a number so you can get hold of me at any time of the day or night, seven days a week. You are not to discuss this case with anyone, not your bosses, not your family, not anyone. Refer anyone and everyone to me, if they ask. Understand?" Lombardo stared as if he was a drill instructor dealing with a bunch of recruits.

"Yes, sir, I think your orders are clear," the sergeant answered.

Lombardo stood and stretched.

"You did an excellent job at the scene. A credit to the investigative training we detectives gave you uniformed cops, and ladies, too, right?" Lombardo grinned at the three cops—all of whom were now hurriedly leaving their chairs and heading towards the door.

"Anything you say, sir," the 43 patrol supervisor turned back and smiled, then rejoined her two cops in their mad dash to get through the open door.

"By the way, Sarge, is that guy, you know, Cortez, or something," Lombardo began, grabbing the back of the young sergeant's gun belt, causing her to swing around and face the chief.

"Velez, Ramon Velez, sir."

"Yeah, yeah, whatever. Is he a *wetback* or something like that?" Lombardo asked.

"Wetback? What do you mean, chief?" she asked.

"Stop the shit, Sergeant, you know what I mean, somebody who swam ashore to get into this goddamn country. Swim, water, *Wetback*," Lombardo said, while flailing his arms as if he were swimming. "Is it possible this guy is an undocumented alien?"

"I'm sorry, chief. I never checked."

"Well, check the fuckin' thing out and report back to me, and *only to me*."

The sergeant led her two cops briskly down the long hallway toward the indifferent receptionist stationed in front of the elevators. He didn't even look up from his *Marvel Comic* book, Brian Joyce had commented later.

Lombardo followed them.

"Don't take the elevator, use the stairs again. I got an old unmarked Highway Unit Number 4 car waiting to take you guys back to your precinct. Remember, no one knows you were here."

Lombardo had sprinted from his office and was shouting at the sergeant who pulled nervously at the heavy fire door that was creaking open.

They were back in the dark, damp stairwell. Joyce jumped in front of his partner. Munro was now ahead of them, holding the cold, steel banister and swinging herself so that she could take two steps at a time.

"The stupid fuck," Joyce mumbled. Savino and Sergeant Munro didn't bother to look back.

CHAPTER 2

⚘

On the drive up First Avenue to the Chief Medical Examiner's office, Hughes turned to Lombardo.

"Chips, this case is a fucking political time bomb. The media is already in a feeding frenzy. They're going to bust our balls no matter what. Now, listen, I want this to be a textbook investigation. We'll explain everything we're doing—why we are doing it—when we are doing it," the chief said.

"No devious bullshit, and you know what I mean. *Capece*," Hughes frowned

He didn't wait for Lombardo's reply.

"There are plenty of vultures out there just waiting for Russo to step on his cock and for the mayor to rip off his balls. But it's not going to be because of something that you and I do, or don't do. I've been waiting a long time to work for a PC like Russo and I'm behind him all the way," the detective boss looked straight into Lombardo's eyes.

"I got you, boss. There'll be no fuck ups in this case."

At that moment, the voice of Lombardo's Exec, came over the car radio.

"Chief, are you on the air?" he inquired.

Before his driver, could pick up the receiver to hand it to his boss, Lombardo screamed, "Gimmee that fuckin' thing—ah, I mean

Detective Biscardi would you please hand me the phone?" he smiled. So did Hughes.

"Yeah, go ahead, Norman," a subdued Lombardo said into the handset.

"Chief, I got a call for you from some guy calling himself, *Virga*. He says it's urgent—actually, he used the word 'imperative'—but left no number."

"Ah, ah, oh, OK, Norman, OK. If he calls back tell him, tell him I'll call in a couple hours," Lombardo came back, clearly shaken by the message.

"Everything is urgent with that fuck—a typical confidential informant, CI, you know, chief. Right?" He smiled nervously at an obviously puzzled Terry Hughes.

❧   ❧   ❧

When Hughes and Lombardo arrived at the CME's office they were immediately escorted to Dr. Sam Gershowitz's office. He wore his usual white office coat, clean and crisp, no unsightly stains. Hughes always found the ME's fastidiousness a bit strange given the grim nature of his work.

"Doc, you know Chips Lombardo who runs our Special Investigations Division. Right?" Hughes asked, looking sharply at Lombardo

"Yes, yes, of course. How are you, Lombardo?" Sam Gershowitz said. He could count the times Lombardo had been in his office on the fingers of one hand but he extended his hand to a relieved deputy chief. Lombardo then ripped his hat from his head and stood as erectly as he could, moving closer to Hughes.

"I just finished working on poor McCabe. A fine man, what a tragedy," Gershowitz began.

"Yes, yes, he was, and we'll get the bastards. And Ramon Velez?" Terry Hughes asked.

"My First Deputy CME, our Director of Forensic Toxicology and I completed our preliminary examination of Mr. Velez first because the cause of death was so obvious. It was a goddamn slaughter, Terry," the C.M.E said.

"Yeah, you're right, Doc. OK, we really want to do this by the book. Can we get a stenographer or someone to take notes, in addition to you taping your findings, maybe first on Mr. McCabe and then Mr. Velez, as we view the bodies with you?" asked Hughes.

"No problem, Terry," the doctor responded, pushing a tab on his intercom with the latex covered index finger of his left hand. "Sherri, can you get someone to watch the phones and then you come in here and take notes?"

Sherri wasn't what the two cops had expected. She was tall, maybe five-ten, in her mid-twenties, with a scandalous pair of long legs, enshrouded in an obviously expensive one-piece green dress, about four inches above her knees and dipping about two inches between her breasts. As she walked through Sam's door, some strands of her long black hair played peek-a-boo with her left eye while the rest bounced off her back. She was hardly the bored, underpaid drudge that usually filled such civil service positions, they thought.

"Sherri, these gentlemen are Chief Hughes, the chief of detectives, and Deputy Chief Lombardo, the head of the police Special Investigations Division," the C.M.E said. She gave them a smile as the two cops clumsily got up from their chairs.

"Well, let's get on with it," the C.M.E said. "I'll begin with some general principles involved in performing an autopsy that can be applied to both victims in this case. If some of it is old hat to you two, please bear with me," Gershowitz began.

While Sherri scribbled notes, Gershowitz launched into a brief lecture on lividity and the use of body temperature in determining time of death. The CME kept looking back and forth from Hughes to Lombardo, to make sure he wasn't losing either of them. He noted that Lombardo was closely examining the backs of his hands, while

Hughes absent-mindedly rubbed his wiry red hair and looked out the window.

"The condition of the stomach, when the autopsy is performed, may also permit the drawing of certain conclusions as to the time when death took place. These conclusions are only approximate, however, because the stomach continues to digest food for twenty-four hours after death. If death takes place immediately after a meal, the postmortem digestion will be found to be very slight if the amount of the stomach contents is small and it may signify that the person has been dead for a considerable time. The stomach of a living person empties into the bowel tract in two to six hours. An empty stomach therefore indicates that death has occurred at least two to six hours after the last meal."

He thought he saw a glimmer of life before when he mentioned "strangulation" and "stabbing" and just now with the "two to six hours" comment.

"Oh, boy, Doc, I remember getting that lecture from you at Bellevue while I was in homicide training—about fifteen years ago," Hughes groaned.

"Yes, and nothing more sophisticated has come along in those intervening years in determining time of death," Gershowitz replied. "Homicide Training?" is that what they call that thing I teach to those thick-headed detectives of yours?" he joked, looking at both Hughes and Lombardo. "Let's go into the examining room, gentlemen, Sherri," he said, nodding first to them and then to his assistant. Chips couldn't resist a caressing glance at Sherri's hips. What he thought was a furtive look, wasn't. His boss glared at him and pushed him firmly towards the door.

It was a long rectangular room with a low ceiling and tile floors, painted in a faded blue. It held three examining tables, two of which were occupied by the nude, pallid bodies of the victims. The somewhat disquieting low gurgle of running water sluicing through the table's drains was the only sound in the room apart from the faint hiss of cold air that flowed through the air conditioning vents in the ceiling. Pinkish fluorescent lighting added minimal warmth to the cheerless space. An assistant stood by the first table, an overweight young man in green surgical coveralls who gave the CME and the detectives an incongruously cheerful grin.

Gershowitz turned around and looked at his secretary. "On second thought, Sherri, there's no reason to put you through all this. Just type up the comments we've made in the office and then on the tape as usual."

Both Hughes and Lombardo felt even more depressed than the surroundings warranted when Sherri made a quick and obviously relieved exit.

"I'll go over my preliminary findings, while observing each of the bodies, as your commissioner has asked you to do, starting with Mr. McCabe, as you asked, Terry," Gershowitz said, waving for Hughes and Lombardo to follow him.

"Sad, very sad, what a great man, a compassionate man, from what I've read and heard from others," the C.M.E lamented, as they entered the East Morgue. He used his hands to draw out the slide of the white-sheet-covered cadaver of Morgan McCabe.

"In any event, let's go down the list," Dr. Gershowitz started, pulling down the thin sheet and exposing the full corpse of the mayor's father.

A slight, but audible gasp escaped from Terry Hughes, who had known the mayor's father. He had met him at many community, as well as political, functions. The finely sculptured features of this extremely well liked, almost beloved man were now gaunt, the skin of his face so tightly stretched by rigor mortis that his hollow cheeks gave him an expression of eternal fright. "Oh, Lord, what must Morgan McCabe be thinking as we look at his naked, repelling, ugly remains," Hughes thought. You never get used to that moment. And when you know who it is, it's hard not to puke. He swallowed hard and stood next to the ME.

"According to our log, Mr. McCabe, as well as Mr. Velez, were brought in at eleven fifty-eight hours," the CME was dictating while leaning over and physically examining the body. "I began the examination as soon as the body was prepared—about 12:30 hours. The body temperature was 91.8, 6.8 degrees below normal. I considered Mr. McCabe' body structure—he was a rather lean person. He was dressed in a pair of slacks, heavy, thick woolen socks, winter long johns for underwear, and a long-sleeved shirt. The outside temperature had been about twenty degrees, cold but not abnormal for this time of year. There had been no unusual humidity or precipitation that would have affected his body temperature," he continued, still probing, talking simultaneously for the benefit of the mike that was hanging over the table, as well as the two detectives. "He was also a slim, thin-boned person, therefore tending to show less pronounced signs of rigor mortis. There were signs, however, of stiffness in his head, neck, shoulders, chest, abdomen, and upper legs. There was almost complete rigor mortis. Again, I considered his temperature and his muscle strength in developing my findings," Gershowitz began pointing at different areas of McCabe's body.

"Postmortem lividity was quite advanced. And surprisingly, quite diffused throughout the body. There were no signs of decomposition," The CME was stepping up his cadence, as if anticipating some climactic ending. "I examined the contents of his stomach. The amount of postmortem digestion was found to be very slight," he said, and momentarily stared at the two cops.

They were asking with their widened eyes, "So?"

"So, here are my findings," the doctor announced. Hughes and his number two both leaning forward so as not to miss a word; at last the CME had their full attention. "Mr. McCabe's body temperature, taken some two hours and fifteen minutes after he was first discovered, apparently dead, in his store in the Bronx, had dropped close to seven degrees. Considering all the factors that I've already explained to you in my office, it is my opinion that he died six to eight hours before I examined him. That would put the time of death between four and six in the morning. Probably closer to six."

Gershowitz stopped deliberately at this point, allowing Hughes and Lombardo to gather their thoughts.

"This finding is supported by examination for the progress of rigor mortis that was beginning in his upper legs. Again, the rigor was close to completion, indicating a six to eight hour interval between death and my examination," he continued. "The advanced stage of postmortem lividity supports the evidence of strangulation by rope or similar method. The level of lividity also supports the six-to-eight-hour theory," he said, hesitating. "But, a new twist, here," he said, stepping away from the body and looking directly at the detectives. "From the diffusion of blood to other parts of the body, it is my opinion that the body had been moved, and that probably the place of death was not in the store."

The two cops looked at each other trying to absorb the full implications of the ME's reasoning.

"So, he died much earlier than he usually gets to the store, seven-thirty each morning, which means he was probably killed before he got to the store and may have been taken there by his killer, or killers," Lombardo said thoughtfully.

"Doc, Are you sure your postmortem lividity examination supports the theory that the body may have been moved?" Hughes asked hesitantly.

"Yes, that is correct," the doctor confirmed, raising his voice to emphasize the importance of his finding. "And, *finally*," Gershowitz said, stopping them as they were about to turn away from Morgan's body.

"There's more?" Terry Hughes said, rubbing his deeply furrowed brow.

"Yes. As you may recall I stated that the advanced stage of post-mortem lividity supported the evidence of strangulation by rope or similar method. I closely examined the, quote rope burn marks, end quote, surrounding McCabe's neck, and found them to be unusually light in texture. In fact, I noticed secondary markings inside the predominant marks, and they were quite different in appearance from those produced by strangulation."

"Holy shit, Doc, what the hell are you saying?" Hughes asked, his eyes widening. He leaned so close to Dr. Gershowitz that their noses almost touched.

"Please, let me continue," Gershowitz replied, with a slight smile at Chief Hughes's confusion.

"During the act of strangulation, the arteries of the neck which carry blood from the heart to the brain are compressed. This immediately shuts off the blood supply, causing almost instantaneous unconsciousness because of the resulting anoxia in the brain," Gershowitz began. "Comparatively little pressure on the neck is necessary and this accounts for the peculiar positions in which strangled persons are found," the doctor was saying, when he saw Lombardo almost raising his hand for attention. "Yes, Lombardo, what is it?" he asked.

"Mr. McCabe was found sitting in his chair, at his desk, almost as if he had been working and fell asleep. He looked so peaceful, it's crazy when you think of what must have happened that was the cause of his death," Lombardo remarked.

"Yes, yes, of course. Although he probably suffered only for a short time, the anemia of the brain was almost immediate," Gershowitz pointed out. "In any event, strangulation proper, asphyxia, then sets and causes death. Where a rope is used, the signs of the rope will be found around the neck, with an interruption in the mark at the place where the perpetrator held the rope," Gershowitz said, stopping for the moment as Hughes then started to say something.

"There *were* clear red-colored marks on Mr. McCabe's neck," Hughes reminded the ME.

"Yes, because if he was garroted from the side, the face is often found to be red because of the complete compression of the arteries and veins on that one side only. If the pressure was applied at the nape of the neck, the face will be pale. In the case of Mr. McCabe, there were no such interruptions, and the markings are much deeper than on those found in strangling by rope," Sam explained, looking intensely at the two detectives.

"You're saying that Morgan McCabe was not killed by the rope we found, or any other rope, but was choked to death, strangled by a pair of hands?" Hughes asked incredulously, while Lombardo sat down on a metal chair and gave the CME a glazed stare.

"Make sure your Lab and Forensic people look very closely at the evidence gathered at the scene. I think the rope and the packaging for it were planted by someone who wanted you to believe Mr. McCabe was strangled at the scene by rope picked up in the store. It was meant to look like an act of spontaneous, impulsive violence," Dr. Gershowitz said, stopping when he now saw Hughes raise his hand.

"Whoever did this wanted us to think it was a burglar or burglars that McCabe surprised in his store—but he was really choked to death at another location, and then the body was transported to the store, as part of a premeditated plan to kill him."

"Precisely," the doctor confirmed.

"A fuckin' hit," Lombardo blurted out. "He was murdered two goddamn times," he said, unable to restrain the horror in his face.

"I don't know about that, but I'd guess it was premeditated, as opposed to an impulsive act of violence," the forensic pathologist said, slowly, precisely, as if testifying in court. "In any event, you're absolutely correct, Terry," he added, acknowledging his theory. "And, if you want me to look at the rope found at the scene, I will be glad to, but I'm sure your police lab folks will find that the fibers in that rope are not disturbed sufficiently to have been used to bring about the death of Mr. McCabe," Dr. Gershowitz said.

He pulled at the long white sheet that had been at the feet of the mayor's father and brought it up until it covered his head once again. The chief medical examiner tucked the top of the sheet behind McCabe's head, hesitated momentarily and then turned to face the two detectives.

"Yes, ah, thanks, Doc. Oh boy," Hughes said weakly, sighing deeply and shaking his head. "Doctor, can we break for about a half hour, so Chief Lombardo and I can compare notes and start assembling our report for the police commissioner? Hughes asked.

"Of course. I'm sure you want to get a bite to eat, too," the doctor responded.

"No, sir, not really," the chief of detectives sighed wearily. "I don't think either of us is up to that right now. Maybe we'll grab a cup of coffee."

"I understand. Why don't you and your assistant use the Doctor's Lounge down the hall from my office, it's quiet and they always have some coffee going," Dr. Gershowitz smiled. "We'll meet you back here in say, forty-five minutes?" he asked.

"And now to poor Mr. Velez," Gershowitz walked over to the covered body of Ramon Velez.

The ME followed the same procedure for Ramon Velez as he had for McCabe. Velez's body temperature had only been about three degrees below normal, while Morgan's was close to seven. Gershowitz concluded that he had died more than two hours later than McCabe, shortly before his next-door neighbor at about eight-thirty had discovered him that Monday morning.

"That finding supported by the lack of any demonstrative rigor mortis in his upper legs," Gershowitz said.

"Due to the lack of diffusion of blood during the postmortem lividity stage of death, I draw the conclusion that Velez, unlike the other victim, had been murdered where he was found," Dr. Gershowitz said. "That fits in with the shape and position of bloodstains taken from the scene." The ME paused, and then chose his words carefully. "However, it's not possible to arrive at definite conclusions on the question of exactly *how* the wounds were inflicted. The pattern of spattering may differentiate to a certain extent, and therefore can be of some help in reconstructing the homicide," he was saying.

"Hey, look, Doc. Are you saying that you can't tell exactly from the wounds what kind of weapon was used? And, that the different patterns of blood on the floor can help in IDing such a weapon or weapons?" Lombardo asked.

"Yes, yes, just listen," the ME snapped, as Lombardo slid back in his chair.

He went on in a firm voice. "Blood drops and blood sprinkles will have different appearances according to the height from which they have fallen or even spurted. If the distance is short, they appear as round drops, provided the surface on which they fall is not rough. If the height of the fall is greater, the blood drops have jagged edges, the jaggedness in relation to the height. The greater the height, the more jagged the blood drops will appear. If the drops fall from a considerable height, say two or three yards, the contents of the drop will be sprinkled in many small drops. While there was a great "pouring" of blood from Ramon Velez—we call it exsanguination, the draining of blood—because of the massive wounds in his back and on his side, there were also considerable blood droppings, caused by the initial thrusts of the weapon used to inflict the wounds."

It was his opinion, the CME explained, that given Velez's height and calculations based on blood patterns, the first of the three wounds on his body was inflicted while he was standing, the second while he was kneeling, and the third as he lay on the floor. "He probably had already expired before the third wound was inflicted," Gershowitz added.

Hughes grabbed the CME's arm and growled, "Don't talk to anyone until you hear from us. We'll have our public information people and the mayor's communications director coordinate the release of an official statement. I'll give you a call as soon as I get something that will guide you in this matter," the chief of detectives said.

"Yes, of course," he said, wiping the perspiration from his bifocals.

After briefing the police commissioner by telephone, Terry Hughes beckoned to Chief Lombardo and they both started down the long, echoing hall leading from the offices of New York City's chief medical examiner. As they reached the front entrance on First Avenue, they instinctively turned and looked back. Both were uncomfortably aware that more than just their lives would be changed forever by what had happened at 2044 Westchester Avenue. Then they saw Sherri Douglas dash from her office at the far end of the hall. She froze when she saw them, but quickly regained her composure, smiled, and waved at the two detectives. Somehow her having been there helped.

❧   ❧   ❧

"Dave, please, get me the mayor, forthwith," Chris Russo told the deputy inspector who ran his office.

When Tom McCabe came on Russo said, "I'm sorry to disturb you, Mr. Mayor, but we just received the medical examiner's report, and I wanted to quickly give you some of Dr. Gershowitz's findings."

He waited. "Hello?" Russo said.

"I'm here, Chris," McCabe said, solemnly.

"The ME is convinced that your dad was killed much earlier than he usually got to the store—around six that morning," Russo told him.

"Why was he in the store so early?" the mayor asked softly.

"That's just it. Gershowitz says—it is a little technical, but—that because of the diffusion of blood caused by what's called postmortem lividity—gravity pulling the blood to its lowest level—he feels that your father was moved from some other location to the store," Chris said.

"What does that mean, Chris? Is he saying that my father may have been held up on his way to the store?" McCabe asked.

"Or outside his home, Mr. Mayor," Russo offered. "And there's more, sir. I know it's difficult for you to hear these details, but they are very important to the investigation. According to the chief medical examiner's findings, the markings found on your father's neck," Chris Russo was interrupted by a muted sob. "Mr. Mayor, Tom, are you OK?"

"Yeah, yeah, I'll be all right. Just go on, please, Chris," McCabe responded.

"The markings indicate that he wasn't strangled by rope taken from the store's shelves, as we first suspected, but probably by some unknown assailant who—" he hesitated.

"Who, yeah, who what?" McCabe pushed.

"Killed him with his hands," Russo said almost inaudibly.

"Oh, Lord Jesus, is this ever going to end?" the mayor said.

"I know, Tom, I know. But you know nothing is more important to me than getting all the facts and catching this bastard, or bastards," his old friend told him.

"You think it might have been more than one?" the mayor asked.

"Well, our Forensic Investigations people are still combing the scene and possible routes from McGraw to the store, but so far there are no physical signs of dragging, moving, and so forth. The body was moved very carefully, we believe, and therefore it would seem that there was more than one perpetrator involved, and that it was a planned assault."

"OK, Chris, thanks," McCabe said abruptly and not waiting for Russo to answer, he hung up.

Russo put down his phone, while glancing at the huge Black Forest oak grandfather's clock facing him from the rear wall of his office. It had been a gift to the department from the West German—at that time—government for the security arrangements provided to Chancellor Willy Brandt when he visited New York City some years before. It was four o'clock.

For the first time, Chris Russo was able to reflect on what had happened over the past twenty-four hours. Morgan McCabe, was gone. Some thirty years of visiting, listening, talking, and laughing at the McCabe house on McGraw—a few blocks from the Russo's who lived in the 1500 block of Unionport Road—with Morgan, Ellen, Tom McCabe and his brother and sister. It went on even after Cathy Klinger, who at one time had dated Tom McCabe, and Chris were married and after the birth of their two sons—they all spent time at the McCabe's. Now it was all over. During the last two years, Tom, his father, and Chris had been particularly close with the introduction of community policing in the city. What a horrible personal tragedy for Tom and his family, he thought. What a terrible blow to the Parkchester community, and Morgan's legion of friends on Westchester Avenue. And what about poor Ramon Velez? He certainly worked as hard as Morgan to restore pride and security to their community, Russo thought, banking his face to one side so a few involuntary tears rolled away.

He thought about Tom—the young Tom, playing basketball in the gym, then the Tom on the phone. Something felt wrong to him. He sat there lost in thought for a few minutes. He then got up and walked towards a closed door leading to the washroom he shared with his First Deputy, Bob Coleman. He knocked lightly and, getting no response, opened the door to Coleman's office.

His boss had conditioned Coleman to such unannounced, almost spiritual incarnations.

"Ah, ha. Would you like to lie on my couch and tell me what's bothering you, commissioner?" he smiled at Russo.

"Yeah. I guess your right, Bob. Well, it's this damn thing with Tom McCabe. He's always been a cold fish. I don't know if you knew that, or not?"

Coleman shrugged his shoulders while shaking his head.

"Well, believe me, he is. But his attitude toward the investigation into his father's murder is kinda strange—even for him." Russo went on.

"Attitude?" Coleman asked. He and Russo had met when they were both patrol sergeants in the 32 Precinct in Harlem. They both were intense students, spending many of their off-duty hours together, studying and attending whatever schools they could find that would give them an edge in the civil service exams. Their near-obsessive pursuits would take them through the ranks of sergeant and lieutenant and, finally, to the most coveted of non-appointive positions, captain. From there on, it was no-holds barred politicking. When Russo jumped from Deputy Chief to Police Commissioner, complements of his days at Cardinal Hayes with McCabe, he immediately chose Bob Coleman as his first deputy. They knew each other's every move.

Russo didn't respond. He was looking out Coleman's window, chin resting on the knuckles of his right hand.

"Chris. Attitude?"

"Yeah, right. It just seems that he doesn't seem to want to hear about the investigation. I mean he sounds almost bored with whatever details I do give him."

"Well, you gotta give him a little slack on this, boss. He's been through a lot. I know you've taken this personally, but it is his father," Bob Coleman suggested.

"Yeah. You're right. As always, but—," he hesitated and then said," Thanks."

He had never sat down, and just turned and went back into the washroom.

Just as got back to his office, Dave Rothman knocked and opened the large wooden door to the office.

"It's the mayor back on the phone, Commissioner," he announced.

"You mean, Janet Mullins. Right?" Russo asked.

"No, it's the mayor himself, sir," Rothman shook his head and grinned.

"Chris," McCabe said before Russo would say "hello." "Listen to me. I don't want to go public with the medical examiner's report at this time, you understand?"

"What do you mean, sir?" Russo asked sharply, unable to mask his surprise.

"I don't want to start a stampede by the press. I'm not up to that kind of shit right now. Besides those ME's make mistakes all the time. How about that O.J. debacle and that DNA shit? Those doctors couldn't agree on the fuckin' time of day."

But, Tom, we'll only make it worse later on if we don't play it straight now," Russo pleaded.

"Straight? What the hell is straight? I just told you that Gershowitz could be wrong. He hasn't done the full autopsy yet, anyhow. I'm getting a statement put together now," he said. "I'll have a copy faxed to you."

"No, no, Mr. Mayor, please let me come over and talk to you first," Russo persisted.

"Goddamn it, Chris, I'm going to do it my way. I'm the fucking mayor, and that's all there is to it," McCabe snapped.

"You know you don't have to say that to me, Tom. I just want you to hear me out before you make a final decision."

"No, Chris. I've already made my decision. I'll fax you.

"Before you send it out?" Russo pressed, speaking to a dial tone.

"Now how does he know the ME hasn't done the full autopsy yet?" Russo wondered.

Things were getting curiouser and curiouser, just like Alice in Wonderland.

❧   ❧   ❧

Russo put down the phone and pushed back on his swivel chair so that he was staring straight up into the skylight that allowed the pale late afternoon sunlight to illuminate part of his office. Rothman pushed open the door without even knocking.

"Commissioner, I just got a call from Matt Reynolds at the 43," he began.

"Hey, how's my old Planning Division buddy doing?" Russo responded, for the moment distracted and twirling around to look at Rothman.

"Great, boss, but he wanted to tell me about some possible problems with the Ramon Velez situation," he replied in an unusually hesitant manner.

"Problems? Situation? What do you mean, Dave?"

"Well, Matt told me that Chief Lombardo had apparently 'kidnapped'—as he put it—the 43 sergeant and her two cops from the crime scene and brought them to his office. After hearing their version of what they had investigated at the McCabe store, he ordered the sergeant to determine the citizenship status of Ramon Velez."

"Citizenship? Why did he do that?"

"I'm not sure, sir, but in any event, Captain Reynolds called a friend of his, who just happens to be a supervising agent with the INS here in the city, who told Matt that Velez was in the country illegally," Rothman went on.

"You're kidding! I'm sorry, go on, Dave."

"Well, not only is he an 'illegal' but Velez has been, and I guess still is, the subject of some kind of investigation by the INS, the details of which Matt's contact couldn't discuss, of course. However, he did give Matt a hint by asking him if he had ever heard of the New York City Association for New Americans, Inc. Reynolds didn't answer that question—he wasn't expected to, he thought. Matt then asked his contact where Velez's family stood. He made it clear that they could be subject to deportation."

Russo shook his head from side to side. "Did Matt give that information to Lombardo?"

"He gave it to his sergeant and told her to call Lombardo. Yes, Commissioner, Chief Lombardo was given the information," Rothman answered.

"When?"

"Just before Reynolds called me, sir."

Russo called Terry Hughes and filled him in.

"Have you heard from Lombardo, as yet?" Russo inquired.

"No, sir, not yet," he said, somewhat solemnly.

The next morning, Russo was looking out of his office window at the usual back-up of city-bound traffic on the Brooklyn Bridge, with the WCBS Radio-88 Traffic Chopper hovering over—"With Neil Bush at the controls. What a guy! I love him, if he ever retires we'll have instant gridlock in the city," he was thinking. A faxed copy of the mayor's press release was on his desk. Before he could begin reading it, Rothman was peeking around the edge of the half-opened door. Russo smiled and waved him into the office.

"Chief Hughes calling from his car, boss," he said softly.

"Yes, Terry, what's up?"

"I got a call at six this morning from Chips. He told me about the telephone conversation with Matt Reynolds. Obviously, I didn't tell him that I already knew about the Velez thing," the chief of detectives reported.

"Aha, and?"

"And, sir, I told him to let Matt Reynolds work on his friend at the INS and try to get more information before we do anything with it on our own."

"Good. Thanks, Terry."

He got back to the mayor's fax.

"Look at this Dave. Wait, let me rephrase that. Inspector Rothman, have you read this? And if you haven't, you disappoint me," the commissioner said.

Rothman nodded and smiled.

"OK, then, can you believe this? Not only did the mayor ignore all of my suggested changes, but now Ramon Velez is described as a customer of his father's rather than a close friend, and fellow community activist, of Morgan McCabe's."

"I don't know, Dave, I'm worried," Russo, said, "My instincts are giving me some strong signals—the murders might be just the tip of a very dangerous iceberg."

Rothman shook his head, turned and left the office.

*   *   *

"And I thought Joe Majors' funeral was depressing," Chris Russo said, turning to Cathy. He was referring to a friend of his father's—a longtime cop—who had killed himself with his service revolver over marital problems. Cathy and he had been married only a short time, and Russo was a rookie cop. Both of them had never forgotten the day of Joe's funeral.

Now they were sitting in the second row of pews in the same church, St. Raymond's, at the casket of Morgan McCabe who lay at the head of the church's narrow center aisle. Russo couldn't help thinking about how uncomfortable the old man would have been with the solemn pomp of his requiem.

Cathy Russo leaned close to her husband and whispered, "Do you see Eve Halliday sitting next to the mayor, holding his arm? She must be shocked by Morgan's death, too."

"Yes, I guess she would be. I see Gordon Halliday is in the row right behind them, too."

Among the crowd of mourners were two elderly women who had come early in order to get good seats. One of them and her husband had lived on Zarega Avenue just two blocks from the church and had attended every funeral mass at St. Raymond's for the past 25 years. There were other parishioners, mostly elderly couples, who had done the same thing, some longer. Her husband had died two months ago, but she and other members of the funeral-watchers' club continued their vigils and, like their counterparts who went to watch the free entertainment in courtrooms and never forgot a trial, a defendant, or a judge, they had total recall of the details of every funeral mass, procession, and burial they had witnessed.

"I've never seen anything like this," she confided in a hoarse whisper to her companion, also a recent widow whom she was "breaking in."

"Even a couple of Victor Albanese's *ginzaloons*, you know," she took her left index finger, pressed it against the right side of her nose, twisting it to the left, "didn't have as many flower cars and limousines as this."

"Victor who?" her companion asked.

"Victor Albanese. You know, they call him "Victor the Wheeze—He's got a tracheotomy so he's down to only three packs of cigarettes a day," she said, proud to be so well informed about mob affairs.

Her friend still looked perplexed.

"For Chris sake, Emma," she whispered, "He's been the biggest bookmaker and loan shark in this neighborhood for years. My God, he's the *don* of Parkchester," she added, shaking her head in frustration.

"See, Matilda. *Pazienza*—patience. Now you've seen the biggest funeral of all, just because you took me under your wing," Emma chuckled, sticking her elbow into her mentor's right ribs, and ignoring her glare.

Monsignor Daniel Bustore, pastor of St. Raymond's concelebrated the mass with Joseph Cardinal Mullaney, Archbishop of the Archdiocese of New York. Tom McCabe gave the eulogy.

He did not speak from the pulpit but stood next to his father's casket.

He recalled how his father, an Irish immigrant, had worked hard to be accepted in his adopted country, how he had reached out to later immigrants from other countries

"He and his Irish comrades, along with many other newcomers, Jews, Germans, Italians, and others, eventually made their way into the hearts of those, who at first, had denied them. While my father never doubted the assimilation of his generation's émigrés, he was always very concerned with what he saw as an unusually high level of community resentment and resistance to the recent wave of new arrivals in our communities, the black and Hispanic families. He was deeply troubled."

"While he was always someone to be called on by his community and his neighbors, he was never a leader, that is, not until things got worse. There were those residents and businesses that just pulled up stakes and left, many with great bitterness towards those whom they believed had forced them to leave their beloved communities. Others had no choice, they thought, but to remain for family and economic reasons, but they were more despondent over their situations than they were antagonistic towards the new families. Then there were those who believed that the incursion by these people was a temporary aberration; they would leave and 'We'd go back to the good old days.' It was in this group where my father sensed the most hostility."

"As you all know, he became the founder and president of the Parkchester Community and Business Coalition. He dragged in my Mom as treasurer and secretary, while my sister and my brother ran our hardware store. I was in Congress at the time and I can assure you that my most active constituent was Morgan McCabe. When he made his daily calls to Washington, my staff would call out, 'Tom, Parkchester calling.'"

McCabe's voice quivered and he gripped the side of the casket, fighting back tears.

"I think that kind of sums up the last five years of my Dad's life, Parkchester *Calling*. He had no interests other than his community and his family. When my old friend Chris Russo first began talking about community policing, my father was one of the program's earliest supporters—long before me—teaming up with Councilwoman Linda Wright to get Parkchester as the pilot neighborhood and taking a seat on the first Police Community Advisory Council or PAC. He remained one it's staunchest supporters even in the face of growing criticism of the way we were using our cops. Even I spoke to him about my concerns. But he remained dedicated to the idea, and worked at it. How he ever had time to help with my campaign for mayor will always be a mystery to me."

The mayor recalled how pleased his father had been with the revitalization of Westchester Avenue, how he believed that he could now look to others to become leaders and devote more time to his family and to his business.

Once again Tom McCabe paused to choke back his tears.

His ending was surprisingly heartfelt and personal as he asked the congregation to pray not only for his father but for Ramon Velez as well, to honor their memories by supporting the causes they had fought for so long and so passionately. Many eyes filled with tears as he made a final plea on behalf of the late Morgan McCabe.

"My father would ask us to go back to our communities and work harder than ever to bring the love, the understanding, and the compassion to each other that he knew we were capable of giving."

The mayor slowly stepped down from the altar, walked to his father's casket, patting it softly as he walked away. "Good-bye, Dad," he said, not looking back.

Tom McCabe, his mother, brother and sister, along with Gordon and Eve Halliday, were in the first stretch limousine behind the huge hearse parked on Castle Hill Avenue in front of the church. They did not look back as the cortege began slowly moving towards Tremont Avenue. Nor did they pay any attention to the haunting, mournful skirling of the New York City Police Emerald Society's bagpipes.

If they had looked back, they would have seen that many of the mourners who had attended the services for Morgan McCabe, and who had been standing on the sidewalk to see him placed into Mulligan and Reilly Funeral Chapel's most luxurious hearse, were now going back up the steps and reentering St. Raymond's, followed by what seemed to be hundreds of new mourners, many of whom wore the traditional funeral dress of their respective countries.

The two young assistant pastors of the church concelebrated the mass for Ramon Velez. He, too, was accorded a eulogy, but this time in both Spanish and English. And tears that needed no words.

Teresa Velez, a young, rather frail woman, wearing a simple print dress that reached down close to the top of her low-heeled shoes, her long hair pulled around her neck and falling in place over the front of her left shoulder, walked quietly to the spot where the mayor had just stood. She looked at the casket in which her beloved husband was now resting at the head of the aisle where the casket of Morgan McCabe had stood just a few short moments before.

"My friends," she began in halting but clear English, "I have never been in front of so many people in my life. Please excuse my being so nervous," she began, trembling somewhat and looking out from her dark-circled eyes that showed both her sorrow and loss of sleep since the death of her husband.

"Ramon and I and our children once led very quiet, but happy lives. Although some of you who have seen my husband's passion for pursuing his work in the community might say, "Quiet? Ramon? Ha!" She smiled and her audience responded warmly with their smiles as she began to cry. She took a small lace-edged handkerchief she had been secreting in the right sleeve of her dress, and wiped away the tears.

"Morgan—my husband called him that; I always called him Mr. McCabe—had been Ramon's hero. He stood for everything my husband knew was good about our new country and the community in which we lived. Mayor McCabe said earlier that his father was well-known to people in his Washington office because of the daily telephone calls," she said, smiling and looking out at the crowd, many of whom were now standing on the outer aisles and in the rear of the church and some having made their way to the choir loft.

"But I can assure Mayor McCabe that his father probably made half those calls with my husband at his elbow saying, 'Go ahead, Morgan, call your son, he can help us,'" she said, lighting up the church with laughter for the first time that morning. "And it was Mr. McCabe and his English language courses that were held above his store on Westchester Avenue—in a lovely apartment that he did not rent out because he made it available for community activities like those that gave me the courage to stand before you today and speak to you in the language of our adopted country," Teresa said slowly and deliberately.

"Finally, I thank you for being here this morning. But I thank you, Ramon, more than anyone else, for giving me the most wonderful, loving life that anyone could imagine. I love you, my sweetheart."

She repeated these words in Spanish, stopping for a moment, before saying, in a voice full of sadness, "*Adios, mi corazon.*" The possibility of massive, uncontrollable weeping caused the nervous shifting of hundreds of pairs of feet and the incessant opening and closing of handbags, as Teresa went to where her two children were seated, took the oldest by the hand and led him to the casket of his father. They each kissed the side of their father's coffin. Teresa's kiss would be his last.

"*Buenas noches*, my prince, *hasta manana*," she said, weeping softly.

The pallbearers were all friends of Ramon Velez and his family, including police officers from the Forty-third precinct. A contingent of the New York City Police Bagpipe Band stayed behind, too.

"God bless America, land that I love—" the pipes groaned as Ramon's casket was placed into a hearse, overflowing with *florero brillante de color clara*, brightly colored flowers, *encarnacion, livio de los valles y rosa de te, carnations,* lily of the valley and tea roses, and followed by two limos, all donated by the Mulligan and Reilly Funeral Chapel. Ramon Velez, his family and a few friends, would be taken to a new family plot presented to Teresa by the administration at St. Raymond's Cemetery. The two friends would still be as close as ever.

CHAPTER 3

❀

$\mathcal{I}$t was close to midnight as they sat in the comfortable breakfast nook of their West 246th Street brick Tudor. A good night's sleep was not in the cards following the funerals of Morgan McCabe and Ramon Velez, so caffeine all around.

"I don't know, I'm really worried about Tom," Chris Russo said, taking a small sip of coffee and shaking his head.

"Yes, I know. Clearly Morgan's death is a horrible nightmare for him and the family but, as you've said, he does seem more out of it than I would expect. You know, like in a trance or something. That's not him," Cathy said.

"And it's pretty clear to me that he is leaning on Gordon Halliday—and even Eve, to some extent—for solace or something, more so than on Ellen or his brother or sister. That in itself is scary," Russo continued.

"Scary?" Cathy asked.

"Well, I guess from what I know about his relationship with Gordon—maybe in my naiveté—I always thought that it was pretty much business—you know, big fund-raiser, influential advisor, and so on—rather than being personal."

"And possible father-in-law, I would suppose," she jumped in.

"I doubt that," Russo responded.

"Really? How come?" Cathy asked.

"Well, she's two husbands down and, as you well know, Tom McCabe is a skillful dodger of long-term relationships. Needless to say, with this shared lack of commitment, they didn't hit it off at first."

"Wow. Go on, Liz Smith."

"Yep. From what I could see, she wore her Fieldston royalty too well for Tom, and he was too Irish and Catholic for her, and therefore must surely have missed his calling to become a priest and had instead settled for bachelorhood."

Cathy Russo just smiled when her husband hesitated. He was clearly anticipating another interruption.

"Tom himself once told me, in jest—he insisted—that Eve shouted out to him during a lover's quarrel, 'And besides, your whole damn family still lives in Parkchester—on McGraw Street, of all places!'"

Cathy shook her head in disbelief.

Chris went on to explain that Tom and Eve had first met when Gordon Halliday agreed to raise some money during Tom's bid for congress. During that campaign Tom and Eve's contacts were few and short-lived, again according to Chris Russo. It wasn't until Gordon Halliday actually ran McCabe's mayoral campaign that Tom and Eve would have more than chance meetings.

The campaign, of course, was Tom McCabe's life for almost a year, while Eve Halliday was between one of her sporadic, semi-permanent, flings, according to what Tom confided to him. In this unusual but timely setting, they somehow decided to explore the remote possibility that they might enjoy spending some time together, Russo went on.

"And?" Cathy asked.

"Well, from what I saw—from a distance, of course—it may have just been well-timed, opportunity sex in the beginning, but soon it became clear that they looked forward to their frequent high level socializing, compliments of the Hallidays, and their very public appearances, compliments of Tom's world."

"Oh, Yeah. We just have to follow them in the 'Evening Hours' page of the Sunday *Times's* 'Sunday Styles' Section, of course," Cathy said.

"In any event, they've been inseparable since Tom's inauguration. But lately I've noticed some signs that their romance might just be cooling off a bit," Chris said.

"Really? That's something I wasn't aware of," Cathy commented.

Chris Russo was clearly concerned with what he saw as Gordon Halliday's undue influence over Tom as the mayor, while Eve seemed to be messing up his personal life.

"So, what do you think you should do about it, Chris?"

"Nothing, yet. At this point, it's probably still none of my business."

Brian Joyce and Vince Savino asked to work an extra midnight to eight, hoping to find anyone who might have seen Morgan McCabe in the hours prior to the murders. Their CO decided that Lombardo's "keep out" order should not preclude the usual background investigation, even though the Special Investigations Division detectives would probably cover the same ground.

The two cops would take the same route that Morgan McCabe traveled six days a week for the past twenty years—from his house on McGraw Avenue, left to Pugsley on the North side of the Parkchester Met Life Housing Development, left from Pugsley past some private homes, St. Helena's Elementary School, and Temple Emanuel on Benedict and Pugsley to busy Hugh J. Grant Circle and Westchester Avenue where the Lexington Avenue El's #6 train stopped, and to Bickford's at the foot of the El station, where he got his morning coffee.

Morgan McCabe had not been seen the morning of his death either by the usual breakfast crew at Bickford's, the last of Parkchester's all-night cafeterias, or at the newsstand where Morgan bought his *New York Daily News* every weekday morning. Joyce and Savino got to Bickford's at five fifteen and spoke to the same characters who always had the cops' coffee waiting for them whenever they worked nights.

"We didn't know you two were working tonight," an older, but frisky woman was cleaning the counter.

"No, no, we're on our own time, Ang," Joyce said, as she handed each of them a large cup of steaming black coffee.

"Oh, OK then, since it's almost morning," she laughed and quickly took the two cups back, spilled some coffee from each and poured in some milk, to the amusement of the two cops.

"If you're on your own time, what're you still doing in uniform?"

They ignored the question. Savino ordered a danish. When Angie came back with it, Brian asked her if she'd seen anything unusual going on in the early hours of the morning the killings went down.

"No, not really, honey, but it was so slow that I went home a bit early. Ask Andy Rahn," she replied.

Andy was the night manager at Bickford's. They finished their coffee and went over to the register where Rahn was totaling up the nights' receipts.

"Well, we get the same winos and skels coming in every night to eat. They cash in their deposit bottles and cans and whatever's left over, and after buying booze, they use it to eat with," Rahn said, scratching his head underneath his not-too-white, not-too-starched, counterman's cap.

"But, last night, there were a coupla' new faces, come to think of it," Andy said.

"Holy shit, Andy, what did they look like? Where did they go? Come on, man, talk to us," Joyce asked excitedly.

One of the busboys chimed in. "They looked kinda young to be bums, but they was real dirty, their clothes all ripped and everything. It looked like they didn't shave for a long time."

"And boy, were they bombed out, or high, or something, and they smelled awful," Rahn remarked. The busboy nodded his head, "Shit, man, you got that right."

The two cops got the same story from the newsstand operator at the East 177th Street-Parkchester entrance to the elevated train station, and then from some cabbies using the hack stand in front of Bickford's.

It was nothing solid, but it was a lead all the same. When they got back to the Fteley Avenue precinct at eight that morning, Captain Reynolds was sitting in his small office, just off the muster room of the station. They filled him in on what they had turned up.

"I'm not sure you've got anything, but I'll pass it on up to the borough and SID. We'll see what they all make of it."

Joyce and Savino left Reynolds' office and waited around for Sergeant Jessica Munro who was due in at nine that morning.

"Do you think Chief Lombardo's going to cut off our balls?" Vince Savino asked the sergeant, when they found her in the small coffee room, just off the main desk area of the station house.

"Don't quote me but I think the chief was acting on his own," Munro told them. "I don't think he had any authority whatsoever to pull us off the case."

She thought for a moment and said, "I think he's looking to make this his ticket to somewhere, you know, breaking the case himself. You guys watch out for him. He's a big, nasty fucker."

The cabbies and news truck drivers, who loiter in the early hours at Bickford's near the El, miss nothing. One of the cabbies made a phone call. *The Daily News* would scoop the *Times, Post* and *Newsday* with an early edition headline:

TWO HOMELESS MEN SUSPECTED IN DEATH OF MAYOR'S FATHER AND PARKCHESTER COMMUNITY ACTIVIST

*Morgan McCabe, father of Mayor Thomas J. McCabe and promi-
nent longtime civic leader, and Ramon Velez, a well-known community activist were found dead early Monday morning in the
storeroom of Mr. McCabe' store on Westchester Avenue. Two uni-
dentified men sought.*

Brian Joyce and Vince Savino were quoted extensively in the article. Not from their own words but from other sources.

"What the fuck was that?" the old cop shouted, as he leaped from
his desk and ran towards the office of Deputy Chief Chips Lombardo. He slowly opened the door at the same time something again
crashed against the inside of it, this time followed by the sound of
glass hitting the chief's hardwood floor. The captain closed the door
softly, ran back to his desk, and hit the intercom.

"Yeah, what the fuck do you want?" his boss inquired.

"Are you okay, sir?" he asked.

"Of course, I'm okay. Get your ass in here," Lombardo ordered.

Lombardo was furious. He had specifically ordered the sergeant
and two cops from the Four-three to clear anything to do with the
McCabe investigation with him, he told the captain.

"And here they were out on their own, coming up with two
fuckin' winos," he said. "These goddamn lowlifes couldn't possibly
have been involved in the case, and here these two uniforms are
shooting off their mouths to the media. Norman, get me that fucking captain in that animal house he calls a police precinct; he's got no
control over his goddamn cops."

The captain used Lombardo's personal telephone line. When Captain Matthew Reynolds got on, he said, "Hold on for Chief Lombardo, Captain." Lombardo grabbed the phone, put his hand over

the mouthpiece, motioned to him to get out and said, "And close the fuckin' door behind you."

"Captain, what the hell is going on in your precinct?" Lombardo began.

He didn't wait for a reply.

"I gave a direct order to those goddamn cops of yours, what's their fuckin' names, again? I don't even remember," he roared into the phone.

"Sergeant Jessica Munro and Community Police Officers Brian Joyce and Vince Savino, sir," Captain Reynolds said quickly.

"Yeah, whatever. I told them that they were off the fuckin' case and that if they came across any information about it they were to call me, and only me," he roared into the phone.

"So what's the fuckin' story, Reynolds?" he seemed to be ready for an answer at this point, the captain thought.

"My understanding is that they were having a cup of coffee in Bickford's near Westchester Avenue when they were given this information by some employees at the restaurant. The CPOs are extra friendly with those who live and work on their beats and, apparently, the Bickford's people were very anxious to tell the community cops about those two guys they saw the night before the McCabe and Velez murders," the captain said.

Reynolds heard a low growl whenever he said CPOs or community cops. He would use the term a few more times.

"Closely following our Rules and Procedures, the CPOs reported the incident to me in the morning, after they finished their tour of duty, and I sent it on up. I'm sure your subordinates filled you in this morning, sir. Didn't they?" Reynolds asked.

"Captain, don't you dare ask me whether or not my people are doing their job. I'm asking you why those two fuckin' cops talked to the newspapers," the chief was now speaking and growling at once.

"To the best of my knowledge, and I've talked at length with all three officers, they deny having had any contact with anyone in the media. There were several employees who gave information on these two guys to the cops. I guess one of them might have gossiped with some of the customers, who spoke to other customers, who—," the captain was interrupted.

"Gossipers, my ass. Those cabbies, bus drivers and lowlifes that eat that slop at Bickford's would rat out their fuckin' mothers for an open bottle of JD. They probably got paid by those pricks at *The Daily News*," he yelled.

"That could be, sir. But my cops didn't talk to anyone in the media or anyone else for that matter. Of course, except to me as their commanding officer as per rules and procedures," the captain stated firmly.

"Yeah, yeah, rules and procedures, my ass," Lombardo slowed down a bit.

"I repeat, 'Those two fuckin' derelicts. skels, winos or whatever the fuck they are, couldn't possibly have been involved in this case.' And I'm telling you, Captain, that I'm going to be keeping my eye on you and those three cops of yours. If you or they step over the line again, no matter how slight, I'll have all of you up on charges. Do you understand that Captain?"

"Yes, sir, I understand," the precinct commander replied.

The captain put his phone down gently after Lombardo clearly slammed down his.

Special Investigation Division detectives followed up on the information supplied by Savino and Joyce. They spoke with the same people the cops did, and others. The two suspects had not been seen since that night in Bickford's and there was no reason, at this time, the detectives concluded, to believe they had any connection to the McCabe case. In fact, Hughes told some reporters, "You guys jumped the gun by saying the mayor's father and his companion had been killed by two homeless drifters. Pure, unadulterated bullshit."

⚜   ⚜   ⚜

The McCabe-Velez murder investigations went on and for Russo so did the everyday affairs of running the country's largest police department. Another week passed.

"Mayor's on the phone, boss," Rothman announced over the intercom.

"Himself or Janet Mullins?" asked the police commissioner, in a light-hearted tone.

"Mullins."

"Hi, Janet, how are you?" the commissioner said, attempting to sound more friendly than he actually felt. Janet Mullins wasn't married, was in her middle to late forties, looked like Jay Leno in drag, and her job was her life. She was, for better or worse, a major player in the McCabe administration. As far as Russo knew she had no real social agenda. Her private life was a total mystery.

"OK, Commissioner, how have you been? Haven't talked to you lately," she was unusually informal and at ease. Russo sensed that she was aware of the strains in his relationship with Tom McCabe, and prepared to exploit the situation for her own ends.

"Yeah, come to think of it, that's right. I've been so busy, I hadn't noticed."

"Yes, I guess we've all been busy—hold on, the mayor wants to speak with you."

"Hello, Chris. How's the investigation going?" McCabe's tone was cold and distant.

"Plodding along, sir. Those two witnesses are proving to be more valuable than we first thought. We'll be coming up with something shortly, I'm sure," Russo said. He had learned, as a matter of policy, not to make predictions, but which did not preclude the stretching

of the truth a bit to infer a prognosis. But, once again, he found himself puzzled by the mayor's lack of passion.

Had their roles been reversed, Russo would have been on the
phone every day, riding his police commissioner's ass, demanding
action, results.

"Good. Listen, I've been thinking about that thing you and some
members of the City Council have been talking about, you know,
civilian complaints against cops, and so forth," the mayor began.

"Yes, yes, sir. Amending the Civilian Complaint Review Board legislation." Russo wanted neighborhood people, as part of the Community Policing program to get involved in reviewing, at the very
least, verbal abuse or disrespectful behavior on the part of cops in
their precinct. He had expected McCabe to endorse the proposal that
he and Councilwoman Linda Wright had drafted.

"Well, I've been talking to my staff people who have been working
with you and Linda and members of that special group from the
public safety committee that looked into the Maynard case. That was
the woman's name, right?" asked the mayor.

"Yes, sir. Right. Christine Maynard," Russo answered quickly. He
was surprised that McCabe wasn't even sure of the woman's name.

"Well, Chris, I've decided that now is not the right time to consider amending legislation before it has been thoroughly reviewed
and signed off by me."

"What do you mean, Tom?"

"I mean I'm going to go along with that special committee's rec-
ommendations to expand the CCRB from its present seven members, four appointed by you and three by me, to nine members. I'll
appoint three, you three, and the city council gets to pick three," the
mayor said.

"But you know that compromise is just bullshit," Russo pleaded.
"Just a political hand job—not a real solution. Besides, it was developed before community policing really got off the ground in

Parkchester. Getting ordinary people involved is critical to the long-term success of the program."

"Yes, yes, that's right, my friend. But have you forgotten, that's what I do for a living."

"Come on, Tom, be serious. The C.C.R.B. was formulated long before community policing was ever thought of. Now with the program in place, getting local people, not just cops, involved is critical to the success of what we're trying to accomplish in our neighborhoods—trust in the police and confidence in what we they are trying to do."

"Not so, Chris. Don't forget, the real value in this change will be that representatives from the city council's public safety committee will review all findings of the CCRB, and I will have the final say. Period. What's wrong with that? After all, they, as well as I, represent all neighborhoods, including Parkchester—just as much as your advisory group—or whatever you call them," the mayor said.

"Police Community Advisory Councils. Your father was chairman of the first one—in Parkchester."

"Well, that's it, Chris. I wanted to tell you first. My next call is to Linda Wright. We'll announce it tomorrow at a press conference. You can attend, if you'd like."

"No thanks, sir, I think I'll pass."

❧❧❧   ❧❧❧   ❧❧❧

"Yes-s-s, Yes-s-s, Yes-s-s!" Bruce Solnich cheered, clenching his right fist and making three short, jabbing motions in front of his chest. It was he, at an early morning staff meeting in the mayor's office, who had suggested that the citizen complaint issue could provide an opportunity for the mayor to take a politically advantageous stand on community policing. After all, the cops certainly didn't like the idea of having local activists investigate allegations of police misconduct. Besides, most city council members didn't like the idea of Linda Wright getting credit for moving the issue along without their input. Finally, Solnich argued, virtually all of the city's business leaders, the corporate community, most of whom lived in the suburbs of New York City, thought that inner-city local community groups were already getting more city services than them and not paying their fair share. They would probably support the mayor's strategy. So why not begin cutting Russo down to size? He also felt that McCabe would agree, which wouldn't have been the case a few months ago, Solnich had reasoned. He strongly urged the mayor to confront the police commissioner on this issue, see what his reaction would be.

Nevertheless, some of the mayor's people at that meeting had warned that the move could backfire if the police commissioner decided to do one of two things. First, he could take the position that the mayor had previously committed to the idea and was now backing away from it, and he'd go public with that, either at a press conference of his own or in a statement to the press. He could also show up at the mayor's conference and say nothing, tacitly registering opposition to the mayor's move.

"Or he could quit, right?" Solnich looked around at the surprised expressions on the faces of the staff and the mayor.

"And what's wrong with that?" he demanded.

No one dared to follow up on Solnich's suggestions. But McCabe surprised all of them by making the call that Solnich had suggested in front of them all. When he reported that the police commissioner showed no indication that he would openly oppose the mayor, Solnich knew he'd rolled the dice and won.

Russo's absence from the CCRB press conference in the Blue Room didn't go unnoticed. In fact, it would be the lead story the next day. The press seemed to believe that the reorganized Civilian Complaint Review Board was, as Russo had said publicly on more than one occasion, a lot of political chicanery.

"Does the police commissioner go along with these changes, Mr. Mayor?" a TV reporter shouted.

"Commissioner Russo has always felt that the present committee, dominated as it is by police officials, was justifiably unacceptable to many of our citizens. He therefore was interested in some kind of realignment," the mayor responded.

"Was it 'realignment' or was he looking for a more drastic over-hauling of the whole civilian complaint review process?"

"Eventually, yes. But Commissioner Russo knows that changes like this must be eased into place. By adding two more members to the committee and giving the city council and the mayor important roles in the process, we are taking significant steps towards what the commissioner wants," the mayor continued, looking impatiently at Solnich, who was standing in the back of the room.

"But I was under the impression," a particularly dour-faced reporter stated, "That Russo and Councilwoman Wright were trying to carve out a role for Police Community Advisory Councils, you know PACs, like looking into beefs against cops. More community control, that is."

"Yes, that's true," the mayor said, grinding his teeth, and thinking to himself, "I know it's a PAC you stupid bastard."

"But it was my decision to move ahead quickly with this reorganization of the CCRB while continuing to look at the possibility of future PAC involvement in the process," the mayor continued, keeping his temper in check.

"Then you haven't slammed the door on their proposal," the same reporter asked.

"He's really squeezing our balls, the prick," Solnich whispered to the deputy mayor.

"No, there is a lot more work to be done in this area and there are, incidentally, other proposals to be evaluated," the mayor said firmly.

"I didn't know there were other proposals. What are they?" he pressed on. His colleagues were smiling. Solnich, the first deputy mayor, and the rest of the mayor's people standing in the room were scowling.

"I don't want to get into that now, Ben. I'm confident that the police commissioner will give his full support to the reconstituted board and he will be part of any future discussions relating to the overall process."

"But Mr. Mayor, that's not what I hear. I'd like to ask—"

"Thank you, Ladies and Gentlemen," the mayor concluded, seething, and bolting from the room to return to his office.

"Great fuckin' move, eh, Solnich?" he was glaring at his pint-size assistant who had dashed out of the conference ahead of his boss, and was now standing just outside his office, nervously awaiting his return. Many of the mayor's staff were also waiting at the entrance to the mayor's office to watch him give Solnich a chewing out.

Later in the day the mayor got a call from Gordon Halliday.

"Hey, Tommy, great move on that CCRB shit. My informal poll of the most important people in town says you did good—standing up to all these damn poverty pimp pressure groups."

McCabe felt reassured and called Solnich into his office to give him a little stroking. "You made the right call. On this one, anyhow."

"Thanks, boss, I needed that," Solnich said. "And by the way the cops I've spoken to are 100% behind you on the issue, too," he added.

CHAPTER 4

*A*t the heart of the growing conflict between mayor and police commissioner was a case that dated back to the previous administration—and the police commissioner who had preceded Russo, Dan McCourty. It had been hanging over the police department like a dark thundercloud. The Maynard affair, as it became known, was directly linked to Russo's pushing for both community involvement in local police matters and what he saw as a need to put into place a more effective system for the handling of civilian beefs against cops.

The Maynard affair flared up one day halfway through Mayor Williams' term. Eighteen year-old Christine Maynard, who lived with her year-old son, her grandmother and five assorted relatives and ringers in Highbridge Gardens. a city-owned housing project on University Avenue (Now Dr. Martin Luther King, Jr. Boulevard) in the 44, was smashed on the left side of her face by a detective. He held his gun in one hand and whacked her with the other. It turned out that the night before, two of grandma's boarders had held up a bodega down the street and shot the owner. The next morning someone knocked on Christine Maynard's apartment door. She squinted through the door's peephole and saw two men. She asked who they were and what they wanted. When one of them told her "Never mind who it is. Open the fuckin' door," she screamed that she was going to call the police. "We are the police, you fuckin' cunt. Now open the door," and with that the door was shattered and more cops than she had ever seen, in uniform and out, stormed into her apartment. With her grandmother, her son and three other children screaming, she asked again what they wanted and that was when she was belted and knocked to the ground.

Christine Maynard had called the Civilian Complaint Review Board, CCRB, saying that she wanted to file a complaint against five members of the Four-Four precinct. The processing of her case took over six months. There was never a formal hearing. She was told that the seven-member board had decided that the officer in question was telling the truth when he denied striking Christine Maynard or making statements attributed to him. Besides, after the cops bagged the two homicide perps, he had been awarded the department's second highest medal for bravery and courage for his part in the episode. The police commissioner, Dan McCourty, at the time, concurred with the committee's findings and the case was classified as closed.

❧   ❧   ❧

Failing to attend the annual dinner of the Guardian's Association of the New York City Police Department—representing the department's black officers—was tantamount to resigning from public office or never achieving it. This year it was held at the New York Hilton. As the evening wore on, Linda Wright finally made her way through the crowd to the side of Chris Russo.

"What's this prick up to?"

"Hi, Linda. Hope you're enjoying yourself," the police commissioner laughed.

The mayor had called her after speaking to Russo. When he told her about his decision, she was predictably incensed, but somewhat mollified by the mayor's promise to keep the door open on the proposal she and the commissioner had made. She had been at the press conference.

"Then I almost jumped from my seat to punch the son of a bitch in the mouth when he said there were 'other' proposals besides ours to be evaluated. What other proposals?" New York City's most prominent black councilperson snapped. "And, I just told him now, in person."

"OK, OK, Linda, don't get excited. But I can't talk about it right now," Chris Russo pleaded. "I'll tell you when."

"Bullshit," she replied and threw a punch at the cummerbund under his tuxedo jacket.

On the Monday following the funerals, Russo was conducting his regular weekly staff meeting. They were about midway through the agenda. As always, Rothman was seated not at the conference table, but against the wall, directly behind the police commissioner. One of his staff knocked softly, entered the room and whispered into Dave's ear. Rothman shook his head, got up from chair and leaned over Russo's shoulder.

"It's Monsignor Bustore, boss. It doesn't sound like something urgent, but he seems more than anxious to talk to you."

"Keep going guys," Russo stood up. "Terry, take over. I'll be right back."

Danny, *gizza deech*. To what do I owe this pleasure," Chris Russo began.

The pastor of St. Raymond's laughed loudly, "No, no James—I mean Chris—it is I who have the pleasure. I'm calling to thank you for having encouraged the 43 cops to step in and help with the arrangements for Ramon Velez's funeral. That was great. And I'm sure you know that they raised money for the hearse and limos, too," he went on.

"But, Danny, Monsignor, hold on a—"

"And getting St. Raymond's cemetery to donate a family pot for the Velez family. God bless you," he added.

"Dan, we've played some great practical jokes on each other, but this may top them all," Russo laughed.

"Commissioner, I can assure you, I'm not kidding. I guess I'm telling you something you don't know," the priest said.

"Uh, huh, *monsignore,*" Russo said.

"Well, let me enlighten you. Tommy made the original funeral arrangements, I mean Mayor McCabe, and were to include Ramon Velez as well as the mayor's father. In fact, Tommy and me met at the church. We measured the space at the had of the church's aisle, just in front of the low railing before the altar, to make sure that two oversized caskets could be placed side by side."

"No shit!" Russo blurted out. "Oh, I'm sorry, father."

"No, that's OK. In any event, I was therefore surprised by a telephone call I got just two days before the funerals," he went on.

"From Tom?"

"No, that's what's strange about this whole thing, Chris. It wasn't Tommy, but from some guy who identified himself as the mayor's executive assistant or something like that, uh, uh, Bruce Polnick, I think he told me that was his name."

"Solnich. Yeah, Father, he works for Tom," Russo laughed.

"Whatever. He told me that the funeral mass would be for Morgan McCabe only," the pastor stopped.

"Yeah, yeah. Go on, Danny."

"Well, when I asked, 'What about the arrangement for Mr. Velez?' he said, 'I really don't know any more than I'm telling you, Father,' and he hung up."

"So? Then what did you do?" Russo asked.

"Naturally I called Teresa Velez who was understandably upset. The same Mr. S had contacted her—you know whatever. So anyway, it seems that the day following the murders he had called her and assured her that the mayor's office was going to take care of the entire funeral arrangements. A few hours after this man called, I got a call from the president of the Parkchester Community and Business Coalition. He told me that his association and cops from the Fteley station were going to take care of everything and that I should be prepared to have the mass for Mr. Velez immediately following the one for Morgan McCabe."

Russo didn't want to allow his voice to convey his astonishment.

"Dan, that's wonderful, but believe me, I had nothing to do with it. They must have all done it on their own."

"Well, they certainly bounded your name around a lot."

Russo laughed, "Well, as long as it worked."

"Of course, they threw in the mayor's mother's name, just as much. That didn't hurt either."

Three weeks later, Chris Russo and Terry Hughes were at the Second Avenue Deli. Russo had been often playfully scolded for his unusual interest in Jewish deli. "I've never seen an Italian kid from the Bronx so mesmerized by pastrami, corned beef and brisket," he was reminded more than once. One of his closest advisors had reminded him that one of the former police commissioners would eat only in the most chic Manhattan night spots, and in that way became a celebrity of his own.

"A Police Commissioner's First Commandant is: "Thou shalt not upstage thy mayor, nor make thy self an idol," Russo would reply, adding, "That 'idol' stuff—appropriately for a police commissioner—is found in the book of Exodus."

Besides, he would go on, in a good Jewish Deli the only celebrities were the chicken in the pot, matzo-ball soup, chopped liver, and *cholent*—a central European Jewish dish of meat, bean, and grains.

"Terry, you know the Morgan McCabe/Ramon Velez murder investigations seem to be going nowhere. As far as I know, there's been no new developments since the SID guys hit a brick wall with

the community cops' leads about the two drifters. Could we be suffering from 'too many cooks?'" he asked his top detective.

"Well, as you know commissioner, sometimes these things move
real slow. But, I can understand your concern about coordinating
what's being done," Hughes responded. "Let me get back to you with
some ideas."

Good. Finish your brisket and let's get back to work."

Hughes called an early morning meeting of his detective commanders. He looked over the sleepy group, "I want you guys to come
up with the department's two best homicide investigators, and when
you identify them I'll give them the authority, the resources, and the
ability to dip into special funds set aside to support their efforts.
They, in turn, will be solely responsible for solving the two murders.
And don't forget," he added, "I've spent most of my life in the
bureau, so I have my own ideas about who's the best. So let's see who
matches me."

Hughes got a call at six o'clock the same night.

"We've picked Steve Covelli from the Manhattan South Homicide
Task Force and Roger Horan from the same outfit in the Bronx, sir,"
his executive officer was speaking for the group.

"Steve Covelli's got twenty years in Homicide. He's worked on
some of the city's biggest and most difficult murder investigations.
You remember him from the Fred Pollard murder case out in Jack-
son Heights, near La Guardia, right, Chief?"

"Yeah, I remember that one."

"Steve is methodical and patient," the single-star chief continued.
"He's an unusually modest guy, for a detective that is. Bottom line,
he's probably the best technical investigative professional in the
department."

"OK. And, Roger Horan?" Hughes asked.

"Yes, yes, sir, chief. He's relatively young, been working Homicide
for only five years. He went directly into Bronx Homicide after we

broke a big case in Bathgate on information given to us by then-community police officer Horan. I'm sure you remember that case, too, chief. A young, white girl, raped and shot in the head in Crotona Park near Boston Road, a section of the part used almost exclusively by blacks, according to the local uniforms," the chief explained.

"Even though we had evidence that she may have been killed somewhere else and dumped into the park, we somehow focused our investigation in the Bathgate and East Tremont neighborhoods around the park. For over a month the media had a field day playing up the racial angles, giving us a hard time for assuming she was killed in that community, meaning the murderer or murderers were black."

"In the fifth week of the investigation, Horan got a call from a wise guy he knew from the Victor Albanese mob. He gave Horan a name and an address, and hung up. Horan gave it to the local squad detectives. He went along for the arrest of a young guy who worked in construction. A guinea," he said and stopped. "Oh, sorry, I mean Italian-American. The white guy confessed when he realized that Roger's information had him nailed—and, of course, it was obvious where it came from."

"Horan's got a big stable of snitches, most of whom he's busted, or maybe not busted when he should have. His network is terrific."

Hughes thought it over and said, "I'm not going to tell you guys who my choices would have been—could just as well have been those two. But then, I'll soon find out just how good they are because they're both going to be reporting directly to me and to no one else."

When Lombardo heard about it, he was crushed. "And besides, they're going to be working with those fuckin' uniform losers in the 43? They'll never crack this case. You watch and see."

Covelli and Horan took over a small office in the community police storefront on Westchester Avenue—a former laundro-mat—with the approval of the Police Community Advisory Council,

PAC and the precinct's commanding officer, Matt Reynolds. The two detectives had read the "Unusuals"—the initial reports prepared by local supervisors of a serious incident that requires the attention of downtown or any office in between—and the more detailed reports on the same occurrence prepared by detectives from special units, such as Homicide Task Forces, Joint Robbery, Major Case, Forensic, etc. They were surprised by the clear differences in the two reports. Those prepared by Reynolds seemed to show the responding community cops playing a major role in the early stages of the investigation. Reports submitted by detectives never even mentioned them.

"I'm used to detectives playing down the cops and bullshitting about themselves, but this is ridiculous," Covelli said to Horan when they first saw the reports.

"Hey, what's new, baby?" his new partner laughed.

When they got Captain Reynold's permission to move into the storefront, they also asked to talk with Joyce, Savino and Sergeant Munro as soon as possible. On the day following their assignment, Covelli walked into a small meeting room in the rear of the renovate store. He began going over the files made available to them by Lombardo. The two cops and their sergeant came in just after 8 AM.

Horan was close behind, carrying two huge shopping bags.

"Steve, baby, *paisan*?" he greeted his new partner. They'd worked together on a couple cases. Horan was a big man, running to fat, with sandy hair carefully combed over an early-blooming bald spot. He wore an expensive tweed sports coat, gray flannels and carefully shined wingtips. He smiled at the three local uniforms.

"Hi, good morning, Roger. How are you doing? Good to see you again," Covelli replied, standing up and shaking hands with the young detective, but ignoring the two shopping bags. Covelli, like most detectives, also dressed in expensive, well-cut clothes. This particular morning he was wearing a plaid jacket that made him look even shorter than he in fact was. His brown, wary eyes missed very little.

"Rog, this is Brian Joyce, Vince Savino, and Sergeant Jessica Munro," he introduced the cops by waving his right hand at them, and giving each a squeeze on the shoulder as they stepped up to shake hands with Horan.

"Yeah, yeah, good to meet all of you. Now we got to talk about those guys that were seen out in Bickford's. Right?" He turned away and asked, "How about some coffee?" opening one of the shopping bags, holding five large containers, along with assorted Italian pastries from Covelli's favorite bakery on Arthur Avenue.

While the cops ate their continental breakfasts, Horan left the meeting room and went back to the outer office. He lifted the other shopping bag up to his waist and gently set it onto a desk that was covered by official forms. It held five more containers of coffee and more high calorie pastries. The cops and some community workers pounced on it like a loose ball on Monday night football.

Well, after we finish, why don't we go back to the store and start from there?" Horan suggested, as he drained his own container of coffee. "We're coming from behind here-to to make up for lost time." Joyce and Savino looked at each other. This might be a guy who could get the job done.

Parkchester Paint and Hardware was a few blocks west and across the street from the Police Community Service Center. It had been closed since Morgan's death, although Ellen and her children checked the store each day and, in fact, were talking about reopening it for business in another week. Covelli and Horan had a set of keys to the store given to them by Ellen McCabe, who was delighted when she was told that they were now exclusively assigned to the case. Chris Russo called Ellen and gave her their backgrounds. As they walked the few blocks to the store, the three cops went over their actions on the morning of the killings. It was about 9:30 when they arrived at the store.

"Hey, the outside lights are still on!" Covelli exclaimed.

After fumbling through the set of keys—they were Morgan's duplicate set, the original was at the police lab, of course—Covelli finally selected the right key for the front door. He stepped in, followed by Horan and the three cops. Horan reached for the light panel to the right, just inside the front entrance and, locating it, began flipping the lights on and off on each side of the front entrance and at the corner of the building leading to the alley.

They went over the entire store, eventually focusing their attention on the back office where Velez had apparently found McCabe. Horan and Covelli had the forensic team photos, along with transcribed notes from the police lab, homicide task force detectives and the chief medical examiner's autopsy report, which they shared with the cops.

"It's interesting that nothing seemed out of place in the store or the office or that there were no signs of a struggle," Covelli said.

"They sure must have been neat guys," Horan commented.

"Yeah, or it was so well planned that they knew the layout of the store, having cased it and therefore had no need to stumble around," Covelli retorted. "Something tells me we aren't going to get to the end of the road anytime soon. It's one bitch of a case."

CHAPTER 5

"Two weeks and zilch, right?" Gordon Halliday asked while sitting in a clearly uncomfortable chair in a far corner of the mayor's office.

"Why are you sitting over there, Gordon?" I can hardly see, or hear you. Besides it's not your usual roost," Tom McCabe called out, while hitting at the top of a pack of cigarettes and popping one into his mouth. He lit up.

"What the hell are you doing? Is that a cigarette? I thought you gave up that habit over five years ago?" Halliday said, moving up in his chair and staring at McCabe.

"Yeah, yeah, I know. But I just got to do something with all this shit going on."

"Well, let me know when you want to hit the *cubanas*. To answer your question, I'm sitting in this chair so that I can look out this window facing the parking lot so I can see who's driving up to the plaza and coming in and out of this building," he replied.

"You're kidding. What for?"

"My friend, you've only got one more year as mayor. If you want your ass in that chair come next November, we'll have to smoke out your potential stalkers, and put a price on what it will take to cut off their balls. Sooner or later one or all of those pricks will be climbing up those steps leading to your front door. I don't want to miss him—or her for that matter," Halliday responded.

"That's right—Hillary—I almost forgot," McCabe smiled weakly.

Halliday got up from his chair, flexing both shoulders in a sign of having been in the notorious chair too long, and walked towards McCabe.

"So. Who—no, I'm sorry, whom—have you seen so far today, J. Edgar?" the mayor asked.

"Never mind the bullshit. I asked you a question: Two weeks and shit. Right? What's going on with your asshole buddy at Police Plaza and the investigation into your father's murder? Is he too busy rounding up Souvlaki pushcart peddlers in midtown?"

"I don't recall such intense criticism of community policing when we were running for this office?" the mayor said.

"Stop the bullshit, McCabe, you never believed in it either, but it got us what we wanted, right?" Gordon snapped.

"No, you're wrong. I did believe, and I still do, with some concerns, of course," McCabe said.

"Yeah, right. Remember, you're talking to me, Gordon Halliday."

The mayor dismissed his comment with a wave of his right hand.

"What about the investigation? Any progress?" Halliday was relentless.

"Do you really want to know? I thought you said that you were sure it was a robbery or a bungled burglary?" McCabe asked.

"Well regardless of what happened, we will have to do more than having you do one of your usual, silly, theatrical, flip-chart presentations, showing how crime is about to disappear in this fucking city. You can't say that your father's murder was an anomaly because homicides were down over 25%, or some shit like that. That's Com-Stat horseshit—or whatever they call that silly fucking program with all the numbers. Who gives a shit about the reductions in crime when it hits home? Perception, Tom. I've told you before you can't off-set people's perceptions by throwing numbers at them."

"So, now crime statistics are getting to you, too," Tom shot back.

"OK, then forget it. But, back to the subject of your reelection or inglorious defeat. We've got to take a good look at this community policing shit and make sure how it might—and I'm sure it will—affect the running of your campaign," Gordon started again. "Let's look at Mister Community Policing, Chris Russo, your friend. I really don't know that much about him, except what little I had to know to get you elected mayor," he smiled wryly.

"Well, you know we both grew up in Parkchester, and played basketball together in high school. Then I went on to City College and, after two years in the Marines, and some time in Vietnam, Chris joined the cops. While I was taking political science courses at CCNY, Russo, on his off-duty hours, was going to John Jay. He wanted to get some quick promotions, and taking college courses would help get them," McCabe started.

"So, he's got a college degree?" Halliday interrupted.

"Actually, two. He's got a masters in public administration. So, after I got my law degree from Fordham and worked in State Senator Hughie Monahan's office for a while, I was elected to represent the Bronx's 16th Congressional District in congress."

"Yeah, yeah, I know all that bullshit about you, but what can we exploit in Russo's past to our advantage? For example, besides this community policing social work shit, wasn't he pushing to kick cops off that board that listens to beefs against cops and replace them with local political hacks?"

"Yeah, right, the C.C.R.B.—Civilian Complaint Review Board. Yes, he's still pushing that," the McCabe acknowledged.

"Well, you'd better wake up, pussycat. That fuck Russo is capable of screwing up this election for you. Either you get him out of the way, or you're another one-term mayor."

"Whatever. I can tell you that from the gitgo, I supported Russo on both fronts, and when I left the city for congress, I told Chris, a deputy inspector, that I was coming back to the city someday—as its mayor. By then he was touting community policing and was bending my ear about it every weekend while we hoisted a few Guinness' at Hoffman's Brauhaus," Tom McCabe started again.

"While I was in Washington, Russo was moving up in rank and his pet program along with him. We were in close touch, so I was hearing it all—over and over and over again," McCabe admitted wearily.

"Then Community Policing stalled when the mayor at that time, you know, Gordon, Paul Williams, reacted to pressures from some CEOs whose corporations were among his party's major political contributors—"

"And are now yours," Gordon Halliday said.

"Yes, Mister Halliday, I understand that, so let me continue. In addition to the CEOs a lot of affluent voters—read big contributors—were convinced that the building up of police presence in poorer communities came at their expense, in the numbers of cops and in actual dollars—"

"As a business man in Manhattan and a home owner in the Fieldston section of the Bronx, I couldn't agree more," Halliday said.

"OK, OK. Community policing became the most divisive issue facing the city since the 70's street riots. The police commissioner at the time, Mike McCourty—you know him, too, right, Gordon?" he smiled.

"Mike McCourty threatened to quit because he hated the idea of cops getting into what he saw as social workers' duties. As far as someone other than he or his cop appointees looking into civilian complaints—forget it! The police unions and many of the cops themselves supported his positions on both issues. The mayor was ambivalent. He accepted McCourty's resignation while putting a hold on expanding the program. No one really knew what his own feelings were."

"McCourty sounds like my kind of guy" Halliday said.

"You asked for this, Halliday, now let me go on. While all this shit was going on, Russo and I were both unhappy in our jobs; me because I believed that my 'no balls' colleagues in congress were turning their backs on some badly-needed federal legislation that would keep cities like New York, plagued with fiscal problems because of a shrinking tax base, from going under; Russo, an assistant chief by now, because he was pissed at what he saw was the beginning of the end for community policing. We continued to commiserate at Bauer's—it was actually Hoffman's, but Cathy Russo's family really owned the place, and before she married Chris, she kept their books."

"No shit! I didn't know that."

"Whatever. The two of us finally agreed that our frustrations were in sync. I would run for mayor with community policing as the centerpiece of my plan to bring New York City back to life. Russo would cool it and, if I won, he'd become police commissioner and carry out the new mayor's promises."

"But, I ask again, were you ever really sold on Community Policing, Tom" Halliday asked.

"I guess I was. On the other hand, Chris Russo saw community policing as a calling, while I saw it as a good thing in getting to where I wanted to take the city. You were in this thing by then, Gordon, getting me elected."

Gordon Halliday showed a rare display of humility, looking down at his super-shined

Mario Bruni's.

He regained his composure quickly. "And then the voters of New York City handed the city over to a couple of jocks from Cardinal Hayes."

Tom McCabe glowed, for the first time in weeks.

"Well, my friend, as you know, the controversies over community policing and how we use or don't use our cops—knockin' down doors instead of worrying whether some asshole has heat or not—and the CCRB—keeping the fuckin' civilians out of it—have come complete circle. They're big—maybe bigger—problems again for anyone in or looking to get into elected office, and how you—we—handle them may decide whether you succeed yourself or you have a successor," Gordon Halliday said, with a methodical tapping of his right index finger on Fiorello La Guardia's desk. "Besides, Eve will never forgive you if she stops getting her picture taken with governors, senators, congressmen, Hollywood liberals, and so forth—she even has one with the two of you and Bill Clinton, for Chris sake."

"Don't worry about it, Gordon, or about Eve, either. Just keep looking out that window."

Gordon Halliday was satiated, adroitly rolling his unlit *Cubana* around the outer surfaces of his lips.

CHAPTER 6

❀

*I*t was a minute before eleven when the call came into the Westchester Avenue storefront. Maria Fernandez recognized the voice. It was the same guy who had called and asked for Horan earlier that morning. Horan had a hunch that it was going to be his lucky day when the caller identified himself as Mikey Lanza, a small-time thief who had been a useful CI or "confidential informant" in the past—which was a fancy way of saying that Mikey would often drop a dime on, and rat someone out, if it served his purposes.

"Yeah, of course, Mikey. How ya been?" Horan said.

Vince Savino, who had just walked into the room, stopped in front of the detective and whispered, "Mikey? If it's Lanza, I know him," he said, pointing to the telephone and back to himself. Horan nodded and grinned.

"OK, I guess. I think I'm gonna get a job with a guy who's doin' some carpenter work or some shit like that for the city jails. That's funny, heh? They never fixed 'em while I was in," Lanza said, with an attempt at humor, but really trying to cover his nervousness, Horan thought.

"I'm glad to hear that, Mikey. I knew once you got away from that crazy gang at Randall and Rosedale, you'd be all right." He rolled his eyes at Savino, who smiled.

"Well, Rog, you know the *guinea* and Irish kids had to band together to protect our turf from the Spicks, you know, the Latin Kings and Netas from Archer and Beech, right?"

"Yeah, yeah, I know Mikey. So what's doin' *paisan?*"

"Well, irregardless of what I just said, I can never pay ya' enough for settin' me straight, Roger. That's why I'm callin'."

"Where are you calling from, Mikey?" Horan asked instinctively. It was a routine query used by experienced investigators when getting a call from a "squeal." The idea was to make the caller relax and spill out his story. At the same time, the cops could use the location factor to determine the urgency and motive for the call. Horan and Covelli had Bell Atlantic install a Caller ID on their phone in the back room of the storefront. They got the caller's number brightly displayed on a mini-monitor on the base of the telephone and quickly entered the number into their computer, where a "reverse" directory, a numerical listing of telephone numbers matched up with addresses determined the exact location from where the call originated. But Horan asked anyway.

"In a booth just outside the Carpenters' Union Hall at Middletown Road and, uh, let me see, it looks like, Jarvis, or some shit like that. Yeah, Jarvis Avenue," Lanza responded.

"Good, Mikey. What's up?" Horan asked, as he entered 325-9658 into the computer. By then Covelli was looking over his shoulder and patted him on his right shoulder when the location was confirmed.

"I was shapin' up at the union hall before I got this break with the jail carpenter. I was talkin' to this kid, he does *bazuko*, you know 'little devil' the Colombians call it, and he starts spillin' his guts about this guy he knew who knew somebody who knew somebody else who was supposed to have 'offed' some famous guy," Lanza said, deliberately lowering his voice.

"Yeah, Mikey. Go on, speak a little louder, please," Horan asked.

He put his right hand over the phone, and shouted to Covelli, "Hey, *wallyo*, wait'll you hear this."

Covelli gestured towards his phone asking if Horan wanted him to pick up the extension? Horan shook his head and told Lanza to meet him that night, in the Ferry Point parking lot under the Bronx-Whitestone Bridge. "Behind the old watchman's shack," the detective suggested. "You know where that is, right, Mikey?"

"Yeah, sure, see ya then."

Horan gave Savino and Covelli a quick rundown on his CI. Lanza's father had been an old-line soldier in the Albanese family. Victor Albanese never really was a true "Boss" in the old Genovese crime family that controlled the Bronx rackets. Horan explained that he was more of a *Cognoscenti*, a time-tested, loyal and smart super capo, who even sat in for Vito Genovese and then his successor Vinny the Chin Gigante on the much heralded "Commission" that settled disputes among New York's five major crime families. "Mikey's old man was nothing more than a gofer for Victor," Roger Horan commented.

According to Horan, young Mikey decided to become an independent contractor, hooking up with two black guys and a Latino who pulled off a liquor store robbery on Fox Street in the 41. Mikey, not the brightest guy in the world, had supplied the wheels for the heist. He was still sitting in the car he had stolen two hours before the armed robbery when the store's owner hit a silent alarm, the cops pulled up and his new-found buddies bailed out of the back door. He pulled a short term in prison before he was paroled—and his father disowned him.

"That's when I got friendly with him, after he got out of Attica," he concluded.

"Roger, for Chris sake, is he reliable, or isn't he? Covelli demanded.

"What's reliable? I think he is. You're coming with me tonight, right?" Horan asked.

"You bet your ass, I'm coming with you. I'll meet you here about midnight," said Covelli.

"You can use my name, too, buddy," Savino volunteered. "I think it would help."

"Thanks, Vince. We'll do that," Horan responded.

They used Covelli's second car, an incredibly beat-up, rusted, Ford Mustang. A convertible, no less, with the usual temperamental top that worked intermittently. Covelli refused to tell anyone the year of the car, but Horan guessed late sixties. They made their way through the damp and poorly lit streets on Brush Avenue, a road seldom used by anyone using Ferry Park. It was early March, and the bristling wind was pushing the temperature down to well below zero.

"I'm glad this fuckin' top worked," Covelli said proudly.

Lanza was right on time, shivering uncontrollably. He had nothing to cover his head, and no gloves for his bare hands. He was wearing a light, summer, basketball warm-up jacket that was obviously too small for him, so that he couldn't pull the zipper up to cover his exposed neck.

"Get in the car, get in the car, before you freeze to death!" Horan shouted at him.

He started with his life story as the detectives began yawning and fidgeting. He finally reached the part where a friend of his father got him a carpenters' union card and the day he heard this guy talking about "somebody he knows who killed some big shot. It was in all the papers." Covelli and Horan popped up from their slumped positions in the front seats of the car. Mikey was in the rear, leaning over the space between the two front bucket seats. He told them he had seen the guy before at the shape-up hall. He thought he might have been a joiner's helper, "or somethin' like that, you know, you get to know who does what by the way they dress. He does the shit work for the carpenter's."

"No Pierre Cardin's, right, Mikey?" Horan smiled.

"Who?"

"No, just forget it, Mikey," Covelli said.

"How did you know he was talking about the McCabe murders, Mikey?"

"Because I asked him. I said, 'What the hell you talkin' about? What famous guy?' So he says, 'this friend of mine knows the guy who made the 'hit'."

"When you called me, Mikey, you said this guy knew somebody, who knew somebody else, and so on. Right?

"Yeah, yeah, Roger. That's right."

"Good, great, Mikey. It's worth a shot anyway, *goombah*, and we're going to keep you out of this. You don't know this guy's name, right?" asked Horan.

"No, he didn't offer, and I didn't ask," Lanza replied with a grin.

"OK, good. When do you go to the union hall for shape up again?" Horan pushed on.

"Well, I'm startin' that job with the carpenter next week. You know, the jails. But I can go into the hall and look for this guy, tomorrow, if you want me to."

Horan reached into his right pants' pocket and took out two twenty-dollar bills. He grabbed Lanza's hands and stuck the money between them.

"No, no, Roger. I didn't tell ya' this for no money," Lanza protested, dropping the money back onto the seat.

"I know, Mikey. I'm not givin' you anything. It's just a loan till you get started on that carpenter's job." He picked up the money from the seat and held it out to Lanza. He reached out slowly and with a sheepish grin took the two bills and put them into a slit pocket in the left side of that terrible jacket he was wearing. He jumped out of the car and headed down the street.

"Great lead, Rog," Covelli said without much conviction in his voice.

"Yeah, yeah. Great, my ass. You owe me half that forty bucks and I want it now!" his partner bellowed, and they both laughed.

The chief of detectives was dressed in a strange combination of clothes. He was still wearing the brilliant white on white shirt he had worn in the office that day but which was now covered by a well-worn brown, tweed sport jacket. He had thrown on a pair of heavy, woolen red jogging pants. He was wearing brown, unlaced Florsheims, with no socks. Covelli and Horan were sweating in the chief's overheated office. Horan knew that he had gone out on a limb by requesting a meeting with Hughes in the middle of the night.

"You guys went pretty far down the food chain with this guy," Hughes said in a skeptical tone. He wanted some assurance that Lanza wasn't a flake. The magic words Hughes wanted to hear from Horan—"the informant is reliable and has been used by me on previous occasions that led to the arrest of numerous persons"—came right out of the affidavit that cops had to swear before a judge before getting an arrest or search warrant based on "information that has come to the officer's attention."

Horan started spooling out Lanza's background but Hughes impatiently broke in and said, "Yeah, sure. The kid's a loser. Why should we believe him? He hasn't even given us a name—and the guy he's talking about does *Bazuko* for Chris sake?"

It required a lot of reassurances from Horan about Lanza's reliability and past track record as a CI before Hughes finally gave in.

"Well, he's all we've got." He looked over at Covelli, "You got more time in grade, and you're the senior guy here. You buy this?"

"Chief, as you know, half the cases we clear would still be open if it wasn't for shit like this, ratting out somebody, anybody for a quid pro quo from us," Covelli responded.

"Yeah, Steve, I hear you," Hughes smiled, then yawned and stretched, "I don't know about you two, but I'm going back home and grab some sleep." He pulled his overcoat over the odd assortment of clothes he had thrown on and muttered. "I'm getting too old for this shit."

❧   ❧   ❧

While Lanza went inside the United Brotherhood of Carpenters and Joiners of America, Local 2710 Union Hall that morning, Horan and Covelli were sitting in the Mustang, parked about a block away at Middletown Road and Crosby Avenue. They were dressed to fit in with the crowd filing in and out through the hall's main entrance. And, of course, the battered car was a perfect cover, too. After an hour or so Lanza came out, walking slowly, almost casually, east on Middletown towards where they were parked. He was lighting a butt. Horan rolled down the window. As Lanza reached the intersection of Middletown and Crosby, he walked past their car and spoke softly, from the left side of his mouth, "Meet you around the corner." They took off slowly, and he soon followed. Mikey jumped into the back of the old convertible. He reported that his friend was inside. According to Lanza, there didn't seem to be much work for carpenter's helpers that day, and he should be coming out shortly.

It was another hour before the budding carpenter-joiner showed up. He was of medium build, about five-foot nine, one hundred and fifty pounds, black hair, obviously had an eczema problem, and walked with a slight limp. Covelli guessed he was about twenty-five. They drove around the corner again, dropped off Mikey, and swung back onto Middletown Road. The carpenter's helper was walking slowly, heading west towards the elevated station of the #6 Line at Middletown Road and Westchester Avenue. Covelli and Horan quietly jumped from their car and stepped behind him, walking at his pace. As he reached the corner of Middletown and Ericson Place, he stopped at the side of the curb. They split, and rushed to his side.

"Hi, buddy, can we talk to you?" Covelli said in a calm, low voice. The man bolted, bad leg and all, scrambling across the intersection and on to Westchester Avenue—against the oncoming traffic. He reached the other side of the street just before Horan, by darting between cars now traveling in both directions. Covelli got trapped in the middle of the narrow street, a minivan and a compact car both brushing against the back of his lumberjack coat. Horan caught him halfway down the street next to the Subway Shops and Yard just to the west of Westchester Avenue, grabbing him from behind by both shoulders, and throwing him against the wall of a vacant building. Covelli caught up, panting, and pointing to his rear end, "Holy Jesus, I almost got killed back there."

He didn't ask who they were or what they wanted, but seemed scared. He didn't struggle, and accompanied them back to their beat-up Mustang. They all went back to the Westchester Avenue storefront. He was clearly a kid who never got beyond the first year of high school, hit the streets, and never worked at a job for more than a few days. Crack was a natural for him and he had been using it for about six months, he told the two detectives. He had two vials of crack cocaine in his pocket. He was convinced that Roger Horan and Steve Covelli were narcs.

"Who else would dress like that? And drive such a piece of shit," he explained. They went along with it. He said his name was Johnny Farina and that he was twenty-two, younger than the detectives had guessed.

"We're not on you, Johnny. You know who we're interested in, your dealer. You know, what's his name, Pete, Dom?" asked Covelli.

"You mean, Sal."

"Yeah, yeah, Sal. They're all alike, right, kid?" Horan smiled.

"Ah, shit, you didn't know his name. Right?" the kid asked, looking down at the ground and despondently shaking his head, as the detectives grinned.

"OK, but I don't know nothin' about what he does, other than with me," Farina responded coldly. Both cops knew he would play it cute, figuring that they wouldn't waste their time in court on a small-time user. But Horan and Covelli spent the next two hours talking about crack and how the city was going to start sweeping down on known drops and hassling everyone in sight. Everybody was going to go—dealers, users, hangers-on—everybody, and he should jump on the bandwagon now and tell them more about Sal. Farina didn't budge, although he was getting visibly nervous. "Don't you need to get on the sheet?" cop talk for making a certain number of collars each month, Farina finally asked them.

"OK, so you fooled me into givin' ya' Sal's name, but I'm not doin' anything else to help you guys," he declared. "So ya' might as well let me go, cause you got nothin' on me. I don't know where those vials come from, and you guys gotta get on the sheet today, right?" Farina pressed. He was staring at Covelli, and then he turned to Horan as the two cops looked at each other.

"Johnny, we're not narcs. We're from Homicide. Special Homicide," Horan began, looking first at Farina, and then to Covelli, who nodded to show he agreed with his partner's tactic.

"We're investigating the double murders of the mayor's father, Morgan McCabe, and another guy, and we have witnesses who saw you and your buddy Sal, who you're covering for here, in the vicinity of the store on the morning he was killed," Covelli stated flatly.

"What the fuck you guys talkin' about? You got no witnesses that seen me do nothin'," Farina said, regaining his bravado.

"Well, we'll see Johnny. We'll just put you in a lineup and if our witnesses don't pick you out, fine, you walk. But if they do say it was you, you're dead meat, man," Covelli assured him. Both cops knew that if the kid went for the lineup this lead might be a dead end.

"Fuck you guys, I didn't do nothin'. Gaw ahead, put me in a fuckin' lineup."

Both Horan and Covelli lucked out; they made it home for dinner that night.

❦   ❦   ❦

Almost a year had passed since Victor Albanese stepped from the rear of the spotless, white stretch limo in Pelham Bay Park. It gleamed even in the dimmed lights coming from I-95. A barrel-chested, tall young guy, well over six feet, wearing a custom-made suit, held the huge car door open. He slammed shut the door with a cocky, sweeping motion of his left arm just as Albanese began talking to a man standing in the soft, wet grass, his face concealed by shadows.

"How much does this fuck owe us now, Rossetti?"

"Charlie, please, it's Charlie, Mister Albanese. Please call me Charlie—Close to two big ones," the guy answered stepping from the shadows and extending his right hand.

"Two fuckin' million dollars?" the diminutive, gray-haired Albanese shouted, ignoring Rossetti's offer of cordiality. His stooped shoulders and frail body were wrapped in a cashmere topcoat. He wore a size-too-small homburg on a head of white hair. Albanese had walked haltingly from the limo, holding a cigarette in his left hand. When Rossetti told him "Close to two big ones," he began coughing so violently that the younger guy was about to go to his assistance.

"Get the fuck back, ya *ginzaloon*," he said, covering his mouth and shooing away Rossetti. He took another drag on the cigarette. "How the fuck did ya let 'im get into us so far?"

"Hey, Victor," Rossetti began, smiling and extending his arms while holding out his two hands, palms up.

The old man stopped coughing and stuck the cigarette back into his mouth between his teeth.

"Mister Albanese, come on," Charlie Rossetti started again, putting his arms at his side and looking pleadingly at his boss. "You know this guy is good for it. He's one of the biggest investment guys in town. Ya know, from Wall Street."

"Yeah, yeah, bullshit. Wasn't too long ago you told me his tab was about 1 mil," Albanese growled, and before Rossetti could respond, added, "And, you put 'im on an installment plan, without asking me," he went on, taking a big draw on his cigarette and coughing again.

"Yeah, yeah, ya right, Mister Albanese, but remember the vig was over 20 a week, remember?" Rossetti begged.

"Vig, vig, my ass. He couldn't a run it up that much by just not payin' vig—you been lettin' him keep playin', too, right? I also hear you're socializin' with this guy and his family, too".

Charlie Rossetti was sweating despite the twenty-degrees chill. He was just over thirty, medium height, a bit paunchy, with classic Sicilian features, long nose, thick lips, a very lightly oiled, almost handsome pockmarked face, and heavy, bushy eyebrows.

Albanese jabbed a bony finger at Rossetti's chest. "That's it ya fuck. Well, *sera, sera,* but I told ya at the time, you made the deal, you collect the fuckin' money. Right, Charlie?" Without waiting for a response he snarled, "And ya ain't collectin' and ya lettin' him play, and all the time you're livin' it up with them in their big house in Fieldston. So now, I gotta collect the fuckin' dough, right?" Albanese's voice was raised as high as his physical condition would allow. "So now we—you Charlie *Pazzo*—are gonna collect. All of it!"

Suddenly the square white cloth that was hinging from the front of Victor Albanese's expensive suit flapped open, and a missile of phlegm headed straight at Charlie. He twisted aside, just avoiding it. Albanese didn't look embarrassed. He made sure the cloth was back in place and took another deep drag on his cigarette.

"You *capece,* you fuckin' *jabon*?"

"Yeah, yeah, Mister Albanese, I understand," Charlie Rossetti answered, trying to keep the fear he felt out of his voice.

"So, here's what we're gonna do with this fuck. What's his fuckin' name again, Holiday, or somethin' like that?" the old man began.

"Halliday, Mister Albanese. His name is Gordon Halliday."

"Yeah, yeah, whatever."

       ❧   *❧*   *❧*

Chris Russo reached for the Metropolitan section of *The New York Time's* early edition. At the same time he began sipping hot coffee from a mug only to choke when he read, in a brief side-bar item, *"Prominent Investment Banker, Gordon Halliday, Will Not Head Up Mayor's Reelection Campaign."* It had been a strategic leak from City Hall, according to the report. The demands of Halliday's business the reason given for the surprise move. A successor was not named.

"So, Halliday's finally been dumped. Good. He's been running the city long enough. Now we'll find out if he's been behind a lot of this silly shit that Tom's been handing out lately," the police commissioner said to himself with a sigh of satisfaction.

Russo hadn't spoken to the mayor since the Civilian Complaint Review Board flap three weeks ago. He picked up his red phone and called the mayor's office. Janet Mullins was as unflappable as ever, and sounded like she was trying to discourage Russo from getting to the mayor as quickly as he would like.

"Janet, put the fuckin' mayor on the phone, or I'll come over there and kick your big, fat ass," said Russo. His three and a half years of patience was at an end. Terry Hughes, who was in the office waiting to start a meeting with his boss, slid down as far as he could in the big, comfortable chair directly in front of the commissioner's desk.

There was no answer from the "Secretary to the Mayor." He didn't know whether he was on hold or not, but didn't get a dial tone and presumed he was holding for the mayor—or somebody.

"Wait 'till you hear this. Your friend Russo is on the hot line and told me he was going to kick my big, fat ass if I didn't put the fuckin' mayor on the phone," Janet Mullins informed the mayor. She was unfazed—even using a rather pleasant tone of voice.

McCabe laughed uproariously. "OK then, put the fuckin' police commissioner on, Ms. Mullins."

"Hello, Chris. What's up," the mayor asked, showing no reaction to his caller's strong "request" or the fact they hadn't talked for nearly three weeks.

"Mr. Mayor. I see that Gordon Halliday is not going to head your reelection campaign. Congratulations, great move."

"Oh, ah, Thanks, Chris," a somewhat surprised McCabe responded.

"Bye, Tom," Russo said abruptly and put down the phone.

"That son of a bitch," Tom McCabe murmured as he sat back in his chair after cutting off the telephone call from his police commissioner. "He never, ever, liked Gordon." He directed Mullins not to disturb him for the next fifteen minutes.

"No matter who calls," he emphasized, obviously rebuking her for letting Russo's call go through. "And have my car ready. I'm leaving for the day.

"Going to the Halliday's—again?" Janet Mullins asked.

"Just get the fuckin' car or I'll come out there and kick your big, fat, ass," the mayor laughed. She didn't.

❦   ❦   ❦

Gordon Halliday would be a bit late.

"Mister Halliday, it's a Mister Reiser on 0421," a youthful voice announced on the intercom. It was late and Halliday's executive assistant had left for the evening.

"OK, put him through," Halliday said, a bit weary. It had been a long day and, contrary to what the *Times* had reported, he had to chair a campaign strategy meeting for Tom McCabe's reelection at his home that night.

"Gary. How are you? How's good old Westport Trust doing with all that cash I'm sending through?" He greeted Reiser with as much enthusiasm as he could manage this time of day.

"I'm great, Gordon, my friend, and old Westport Trust is delighted with that account you—and I assume my, son Wes—brought in last year. Caribbean Moorings, Ltd., looks like a real winner for you, Gordon," Reiser exclaimed.

"Yes, yes. Good. I told Wes that if you and those zombies at the bank could get excited about something, it would be something like this," Halliday shot back and laughed.

"Cash flow always gets the adrenaline pumping. You're an old banker. You know that feeling," Reiser answered. "Of course, as you also know, we have this silly rule about money coming in from outside the country, particularly the Cayman Islands whose secrecy laws prevent us from determining the ownership of the company we're dealing with. You know we audit these accounts more often than others," Reiser got serious for the first time in their conversation.

"Oh, oh. What are you saying, my friend?" Halliday asked, also turning serious.

"Oh, come on, Gordon, I know you'd never do something shady, particularly if it would embarrass your old employer," Reiser said nervously. "But under the rules I've been asked to sit down and discuss it with you, and report back to our executive committee. Bottom line, buddy."

"Yes, yes. Sure, OK, I understand," Halliday laughed, half-heartedly. "I'll be glad to explain it to you, your committee or whoever. But I'll have to ask you to hold off for a while. I've got more irons in the fire than I usually have. I'm sure you read about me being too busy to run Tom McCabe's reelection campaign."

"Yes, yes, I did. In this morning's *Times*. Quite a surprise!"

"Yeah, well I'm really stretched to the limit, Gary. How about me calling you in about a month or so?"

"A month?"

"Gary, hold on, my other line is lighting up," Halliday cut off his caller without knowing whether or not he would hold on.

"Another call on your other outside wire, Mister Halliday," she announced, obviously excited by the chance to be noticed by the big boss twice in one night.

"Oh, shit. Find out who it is, and buzz me again," Halliday directed.

"Yes, sir."

"Gary, I'll have to call you back. Perhaps tomorrow," Halliday blurted, as the blinking light on his hold line stopped, and then began flashing again.

"OK, Gordon, tomorrow, but please remember. I realize it's a pain in the ass, but you know the bank," Reiser signed resignedly.

Halliday hung up without replying.

"Yeah, so who is it?" he asked as he hit the incessant blinking button.

"Oh my, Mister Halliday. He just told me to tell you to get on the—ah, ah—fuckin' phone, sir." Halliday felt a wave of depression roll over him. He knew who the caller was.

"Hello, Charlie. What's up?" he said, sounding as exhausted as he felt.

"We gotta talk, baby. We gotta talk," the caller insisted.

"Talk? Come on Charlie, things couldn't be better for you guys. Relax, will you," Gordon Halliday wasn't relaxing. He knew what Rossetti was talking about.

"My boss don't let me relax. There's a coupla things we gotta talk about—and soon. I'll set up the meet. Ya understand," Rossetti's tone was still guttural, but was now clearly threatening, too. "And I'll call you, when and where, ya understand? Don't leave that fuckin' phone."

"Hey wait a minute. Who the hell do you think you're threatening with all this 'do I understand' shit?" Halliday shouted to a dead line.

❧   ❧   ❧

The meeting at Halliday's in Fieldston was scheduled to begin at seven o'clock. Tom McCabe was already sitting on an antique deacon's bench in the foyer. The host arrived a few minutes before the first guest was escorted in. The meeting ended well after midnight. Later Tom McCabe was sitting with Gordon Halliday in the expansive library sipping the banker's single malt Scotch. In these frequent, late-night sessions, they would discuss their own lives and careers. McCabe's, of course, was largely public property thanks to his years in the city council, two years in Congress, and three and a half years as the city's mayor. While Halliday did get some exposure in the media, The Wall Street Journal, CNN financial news, etc., there was a good deal to tell Tom McCabe. The mayor found himself the listener this night.

"Tommy, I think you know that I went directly from that fancy graduate business program at The Wharton School, to stodgy, conservative, old Westport Trust," Halliday began.

"Not really, Gordon. I know a little from what I read about you in the papers."

"Well, each year the bank would pick two people from the top graduate schools of business in the country, Harvard, Columbia, Stanford, the University of Chicago and Wharton at the University of Pennsylvania." He smiled a moment, his face relaxing as he recalled the early part of his career.

"This particular year they picked me and coincidentally my closest friend, Gary Reiser."

"Hey, you both came from Fieldston, too. Isn't that right?" McCabe interjected.

"Yes. Yes, that's right. Anyway, I don't know to this day how he did it, but Gary went directly to private banking while I got a number of nondescript jobs, mostly as a financial analyst," Halliday pinched the bridge of his nose and rubbed his tired eyes. "And then somehow, in some mysterious way, Gary was able to get me into the same division as he was in," he added smiling.

"Private banking. I'm not sure what that means," McCabe asked, arching his eyebrows and taking another sip from his half-filled glass. Before answering, Halliday downed his drink.

"Gary and I used to joke about our assignments to private banking. It's where you spend most of your time walking your client's poodles, while your boss grabs the bread. These very wealthy clients who had the bank do everything for them from taking care of their checking accounts to doing their investments to hiding their fortunes from a series of divorce-minded wives," he laughed.

"But isn't that how you met Mrs. Halliday?" McCabe asked, hoping to impress his friend with a bit of unexpected knowledge.

"Oh, so you know? Well, one day while 'Daddy Warbucks'—I called her father that to Mrs. Halliday, but never to his face—was in the bank for a meeting. While the vice president in charge of my division was ripping him off, my boss, I volunteered to walk their dog. Not a poodle I assure you, but the biggest, meanest, Rottweiler I ever saw. That damn dog had either taken on the personality of my future wife's father, or the old man got his temper from the dog," Halliday's face displayed some of the anger and resentment that he felt, even after many years. He poured himself another drink and asked McCabe if he wanted his topped off. The mayor waved him off.

"Anyway, when I get near the mutt he lunges at me. Luckily, Georgia, the future Mrs. Gordon Halliday that is, is sitting next to him, and pulls him back. 'I guess if you want to walk him, you have to take me, too,' she said in the most seductive tone I imagine she could muster. That was it, the start of our courtship, Tommy, my boy. After we got engaged I was mystically assigned to a venture capital company, WestVen, that shared the same holding company as the bank."

"Oh, I'm sure it was strictly on merit, Gordon. Right?" McCabe laughed.

"Yeah, right. Well, the first few years were a little too slow for me. In the meantime, of course, I married my Georgia and we eventually had our son and two daughters. And, then the VC, Venture Capital, 'boom' began—that was ten years ago. In the next three years the markets were fighting over Initial Public Offerings, IPOs, and venture capitalists were practically standing on street corners soliciting business plans from potential customers. The fees were enormous and once a new venture went public we raked in even more. Granted, a lot of fast movers got into the capital-raising business, mostly guys who didn't really give a shit about the success or failure of the companies they were touting, but we, WestVen, played it straight—or as straight as anyone who risks other people's money could play it," Halliday smiled, but it was a relatively mirthless expression.

"You were really making a lot of money at that point," McCabe asked rhetorically.

"Oh, yeah. There were commission, bonuses and stock options for all of us involved. I made $300,000 my first year in the VC gold rush."

"Wow!" McCabe exclaimed, sitting up from his slouching position in the corner of the huge couch and perching on the edge of the enormous cushion he was sitting on.

"That was nothing. Tommy. After the third year, and our most successful year, I was 'looking back'—as they say on the 'Street'—at one million per. By the way when I told my old buddy, Gary Reiser, who was still walking dogs in private banking he almost shit," Halliday's words were gushing out of him. Excited by the memory, he suddenly leaned forward and poked the mayor's right shoulder.

"Then I moved into Westport's corporate headquarters at 44 Wall and got involved in 'recaps'—the recapitalization of mostly large, well-established conglomerates. I stayed in that area for about five years, but eventually got bored working for someone else and talked to my wife's father and told him I wanted my own business. Again, as in the VC business, timing was on my side, because some of the companies the bank had provided with start-up funds were having serious financial and management problems."

Tom McCabe slipped back into the corner of the couch. He started to yawn.

"Come on, Tom, this is exciting isn't it?" Halliday asked as he saw his audience losing its concentration.

"Oh, yeah. Sure. Go on, Gordon," the mayor said, shaking off the drowsiness and stiffening his back.

"Good. OK. Since the bank was a creditor in most of these cases, they had a special interest in keeping these companies alive, at the very least, and hopefully making them thrive once more. Westport Trust brought in consultants to deal with these companies. There were turn-around experts, hired guns who usually took over management of the company to carry out a predetermined rescue strategy. Work-out experts, who, working with or without current management, would sell equity (stock) or borrow to secure needed capital to keep the business afloat while stripping away the fat. Then there were those financial geniuses whose specialty was making a last-ditch effort to salvage a potential big loser. They were known as distressed business experts and they would try to salvage the best parts of a company and sell them off to get some kind of return for the investors. The alternative was filing for bankruptcy, in which case the investors would get a few cents for each dollar they put up, or even lose it all. I called them vulture capitalists," Halliday chuckled.

"Vulture Capitalists—VC—get it, Tom?" he hesitated, making sure his still less than enthusiastic listener got it.

"Yeah, well those birds plucked a lot of chickens," McCabe remarked sourly. He had more than a few friends who had taken big hits on their investments in the greedy 80's. "What did you think of sleaze bags like that in your line of work, Gordon?"

Halliday ignored him; he was caught up in his own narrative. "I wasn't impressed by all these lawyers, accountants, and finance types the bank was paying to rescue its investments. So I approached my boss, who was on the bank's executive committee, and suggested that I form my own company. My idea was simple—the bank would give me a couple of failing businesses in which they had significant amounts of money at risk and let me take a shot at breathing life into them. I was convinced that I could do a better job than the specialists the bank had been hiring over the past few years. My boss took it to the board and they signed on—I'm sure my late father-in-law had a lot to do with that."

"In any event, I got a very handsome severance package from the bank, along with some start-up capital for my new venture—convertible bonds that could be cashed-in somewhere along the line for 15 percent of the new company. I also got some money from Georgia's family and Halliday Associates on Broad off Wall was on its way. The rest is history," Halliday gave a big sigh and fell back into his chair.

"You took a hell of a risk, Gordon. I admire you for that," the mayor said, waving his still half-full glass of scotch in the direction of his companion. Then he looked at his watch, "I gotta go," he added as he struggled from the depths of the massive chair.

As both McCabe and Halliday were standing next to the huge coat closet in the front hall retrieving the mayor's coat, Eve Halliday came down the stairs of the serpentine marble staircase in the mansion's foyer. She wearing a bright, red beaded, Calvin Klein cocktail dress, very snugly covering her almost perfect body from just beneath here shoulders to a nip above her knees, displaying her long, shapely legs.

"Hey, Eve. Isn't it past your bedtime?" Tom McCabe said to her as she reached the last step of her long journey from the second floor. She walked softly up to him and kissed him playfully just as the corner of his lips. He didn't return the affection.

"Hi, Tom! Leaving already? And without me?" Eve asked.

"Oh, how I remember when all that affection was meant for me," Gordon Halliday was smiling at her when his wife, Georgia came into the front hall, wished them all goodnight and slowly climbed the stairs.

Halliday looked at his daughter and his friend, thinking what a handsome couple they made, matching her stunning five foot eleven to his six feet four.

Eve gave her father a distracted kiss on his cheek and said, "Come on Tom, the night is young—how about a nightcap in the city?"

"No, really. I have a long day ahead of me tomorrow. I think I'll pass," McCabe responded. His voice was hollow with fatigue.

"Yeah, right. We can take my car," Eve answered, throwing him his coat.

They ended up having three drinks, one each in a succession of different hotel bars, starting with the Sheraton at 37th and Park. It was in the Marco Polo cocktail lounge of the Plaza Hotel at 58th, looking out on to Central Park South that Eve finally brought up what was really on her mind. "Baby, what about Russo? He is hurting your chances for reelection pushing this community control of cops shit. Right?"

"Community policing, not control, Eve," the mayor said. "While that sounds like a petty distinction, the radicals on each side, those who want the cops to get more involved in the neighborhoods in which they work, and those want the cops to kick down doors and bust some heads and to forget about being close to the communities, are far apart and very vocal about it. And, as you would expect, the arguments always run along racial and economic lines."

"Whatever. Is it a problem for you?" she persisted.

"I guess it could be. But what's that got to do with you?" McCabe said somewhat annoyed.

"Oh, forget it, Tom," she whispered in his ear. Then she used her long right leg to best advantage by placing it between McCabe's legs and rubbing against him. They barely made it up to the penthouse suite they had reserved earlier in the evening.

❦   ❦   ❦

Harry's of Hanover Square was already a legendary pub in New York City's financial district. The boom in both stocks and bonds over the past two years had now forced the owners of the small bar to take over an adjoining building and almost double the number of tables available.

"Great food, Gordon," Charlie Rossetti grumbled, while continuing to remove pieces of the corned beef from between his teeth.

"Good, glad you like it," Halliday said cheerlessly, all too aware of the purpose of their meeting.

"Well, *paisan*, you owe us a lotta money—about two mil, for Chris sake."

Halliday started to speak but Rossetti cut him off.

"OK, here's the deal. We are gonna let you spread out some payments, say for a year."

"Charlie, that's pretty reasonable. So I can pay monthly, quarterly, twice a year, right?"

"What the fuck is this monthly, quarters, or two times a year shit" We're talkin' about a weekly pick-up—by me—of twenty grand, plus the vig, of course."

"Twenty-thousand a week? My God! Vig, what the hell is vig?" Halliday burst out, and then remembered where he was and looked around nervously to see if anyone was looking at them.

"Vig, you know, interest on the loan. Cause that's what it is, right? Hey, you're the fuckin' banker in this deal, Gordon," Rossetti said, sticking in the needle.

"How much?" Halliday asked in a shaky voice.

"Twenty-five a week."

"Percent? Twenty-five percent a week?" He leaned over the table speaking just above a whisper. Wiping his mouth, he said pleadingly,

"Charlie, Charlie, for God's sake that's five thousand dollars on the first payment alone."

"First payment, whatta you mean?" Rossetti inquired.

"Well, the interest is calculated on the unpaid balance. So if I pay you twenty thousand dollars the first week it reduces the principal owed accordingly. For example," Halliday took out his expensive pocket calculator. "The twenty-thousand reduces the one million to nine-hundred and eighty thousand, twenty-five percent of which, let's see, my next interest payment. I'm sorry; Vig payment is four thousand eleven dollars and thirty-nine cents. And it goes down each week I reduce the principal," Halliday put his calculator away and looked at Rossetti expectantly.

"What the fuck are you talkin' about? The payment is twenty thousand a week and the vig is five thousand a week. Period. Until it's all paid up," Rossetti explained.

Halliday began to sweat, "Twenty-thousand, plus five-thou-sand—a WEEK." He felt sick to his stomach.

"There's nothin' I could do, Gordon. Believe me, nothin'," Rossetti told him firmly.

"I understand Charlie. Thanks. But like you said, 'I'm the banker.' Maybe we can work out a side deal that I can show you will get you guys your money back even faster, and take some of the load off me."

"No fuckin' good, Gordon. It's our deal or nothin', you under-stand. Our deal or else," Rossetti came back.

Halliday pulled himself together. "Look, Charlie, don't threaten me. Just let me show you and Victor what I have in mind. I think you'll like it. If you don't, then we'll talk about your deal. But no ulti-matum, my friend. I'm not afraid of you or your boss," Halliday looked at Rossetti with all the assurance he could muster.

"Twenty-four hours. That's all you got."

✤   ✤   ✤

The *Times* story on Halliday's decommissioning was confirmed by City Hall. Nevertheless, Gordon Halliday was still spending more time than anyone else with the mayor in meetings, usually held at Halliday's offices or at his home. But occasionally they were forced to meet at the mayor's residence at Gracie Mansion or at City Hall, where they were meeting today.

Halliday was sitting in what had become his regular chair, a big, comfortable, leather armchair tucked into the deeper recesses of the mayor's room. McCabe was sitting behind his desk, one long leg draped over the right arm of his chair and the other propped on the edge of the desk, facing his campaign manager.

"What do you think of *The New York Post* article? What a title, eh? **HERO COP SAYS HE'S NOW A SOCIAL WORKER**," the mayor asked.

Before Halliday could respond, the door leading from McCabe's office to the office of the First Deputy Mayor suddenly burst open and Bruce Solnich rushed towards them.

"Mr. Mayor, have you seen *The Post* article?" he exclaimed, tossing a copy of the afternoon paper onto the mayor's desk.

"It's dynamite, Jesus, dynamite," he said, before either McCabe or Halliday could respond.

"Look at this great headline. It's exactly what we needed to stick it to Russo," he said.

"Calm down, Bruce, for Chris sake," the mayor laughed.

Gordon Halliday looked at Solnich with contempt.

"Mr. Mayor, this could be the launching pad for your reelection plan," Solnich insisted.

"Oh yeah? Why?" the mayor was still smiling at his aide.

"Well, as you know, I think that the issue with the most potential for causing damage will be Community Policing and what impact, if any, its had on the huge decrease in major crimes in the city," he said. "The people in the shitty sections of the city, where the percentage decreases are overwhelming, dig it. Not only do they get a sympathetic ear from the cops when they have no heat or their kids are sick, but the cops are kicking the shit out of crime, too. Big businesses in town and wealthy residents think it sucks, because they say they don't see the few cops they had anymore, and that from what they read in the papers, crime didn't go down as much in their neighborhoods as it did in others—Of course they didn't have much to begin with, but that's another story," Solnich said. He was proselytizing at the lectern and the mayor and his advisor were a captive audience.

Gordon Halliday's unresponsiveness puzzled the mayor. He was listening to his aide with only half an ear as he tried to figure out what was going on in his friend's mind.

"Now this story about how the cops really feel about Community Policing gets the mayor 'off the hook' so to speak," Solnich said. "Whatever good comes out of Community Policing, you can easily take credit for it," Solnich explained, "any downside could be attributed to Russo's stand on the CCRB. And now we have the cops opposing it."

The mayor and Halliday stared at Solnich and said nothing.

"I know you've heard me say this before, but I still think there's a possibility that Russo could resign. That would settle a lot of this shit," Solnich said. "And then again, maybe you shouldn't wait for him to 'pull the pin'—maybe you should fire him."

Halliday looked startled by Solnich's suggestion and started to say something but McCabe forestalled him by saying, "Ok, OK, Bruce, thanks. Let Gordon and me read the whole article when we get a chance."

Solnich knew he was being dismissed so he nodded respectfully and left. As the door leading to the First Deputy Mayor's office closed behind him, Halliday said, "You know I'm not a Solnich fan, Tom."

McCabe sat up straight in his high back chair.

"Well, Mister ex-Campaign Manager, I can tell you that just last week you and he were the only ones who thought my press conference on that civilian complaint shit was effective. You and he must have something in common," McCabe said.

"Yeah, bullshit," Halliday said.

"OK, OK, I'm sorry. Look, Gordon, I know he's a bit of a loose cannon, but he does have his redeeming qualities," the mayor said, smiling broadly. "Like you must have yours."

"Well, fuck you, Tom. In any event, I honestly can't imagine what that pushy little jerk's qualities could be. We don't need a—what did you just call him?—a loose cannon, in the upcoming campaign," Halliday said, not returning the mayor's smile. "I would be very careful when considering his advice, particularly when it comes to how to get you reelected. But we could use him for one dirty little job and keep him busy until the election is over." Halliday said. He got up and stood directly in front of the mayor.

"What do you mean?" McCabe asked.

"Assign him to work exclusively with our mole at police headquarters. I couldn't think of two more despicable pricks deserving each other more than those two. Besides, Solnich's always talking about Russo resigning or getting fired. Let him dig up the dirt that we need to bury Russo."

Across Park Row and Pearl, on the fourteenth floor of 1 Police Plaza, Dave Rothman was also preoccupied with the story in the *Post* and his boss was trying to reassure him.

"I haven't met a cop yet that doesn't have a strong opinion on anything and everything," Russo laughed. "That's why I love them, and why I love this job."

He looked at Rothman's troubled expression and tried again.

"We'll get 'em back in the fold, you wait and see."

"You're right, boss," Rothman said, but he didn't really sound convinced.

"The Patrolman's Benevolent Association and the Detectives Endowment Association presidents are making the round of talk shows, too," Rothman said. "They're really good, but you can see they're going through the motions for some of their constituents, as they should."

There was a quick knock at Russo's half-open door, and the "first dep" looked in.

"Just heard that Marvin Grim had some nice things to say about you, this morning," Bob Coleman said, with his glasses resting near the tip of his rather generous nose.

Grim was New York City's "Shock Jock" who had endeared himself to a strange assortment of morning rush-hour commuters and others. Construction workers, cops, teachers, stockbrokers, elected officials, lonely, bored or bitter retirees, and incapacitated and entertainment-starved shut-ins. He had his own talk show on New York City's affiliate of Alliance Broadcasting, WRHS. His program was carried to a half dozen cities outside New York City—Boston, Buffalo, Cincinnati, Cleveland, Pittsburgh, and Detroit.

Grim didn't fit into any categories, had no political allegiances. He never missed a chance to say that he was pissed off at the entire political structure in our country and had a deep distrust of most politicians. He blamed the riots in Detroit, Chicago, and Los Angeles on the lack of support of the police by the political leadership. Ditto, street crime. He was unsympathetic toward black communities who lamented the deterioration of their lives and their homes-but he had little to say about the drug dealers and criminals that preyed upon those neighborhoods. He was against what he called, "scandalous scams" such as welfare benefits without work; was in favor of cutting off such benefits for women who continued to have babies with no identifiable father; and he believed the cops should be tracking down the fleeing fathers of children on public assistance programs and "beat some sense into them." Even the cops, many of who were devoted followers of Marv, cringed at that one.

Coleman ducked out for a moment and then returned, holding a tape recorder. "You gotta hear this. It's vintage Grim."

Coleman put the tape recorder down on Russo's desk and pressed "play." A voice identifying itself as "George" from Mott Haven" came through clear and strong.

"Marv, I'm a city cop—been one for ten years all up here in the Bronx and I wanna tell you I've made hundreds of arrests, taken a lot of bad guys off the streets. Now I'm a CPO. You know what that is, Marv?"

"Yeah, sure—a community cop. So, you're doing a lot more walking these days, right Big George?"

But today "George" was doing a lot more talking than walking. He bitched about having to "nursemaid some of the punks I used to collar" and having to listen to complaints from people on his beat, people who it was obvious had skins that were the wrong color, people who were not much better, from "George's" point of view, than the criminals he was so anxious to take down. He wound up by placing the blame for all his unhappiness ("And there's plenty of cops who feel the same way, Marv") on the man at the top.

"It's Russo, you know, the PC, the Police Commissioner, who's doing all this," George complained.

"Yeah, yeah, I know," Grim responded. "But, just to be fair, I gotta tell you that I've met Russo a couple of times. He's a likable guy, and seems sincere enough, and a guy who's trying to put cops back on the beat. But he's such a goddamn phony liberal at heart that he's bleeding all over the department. He wants to save the world, like all pseudo-liberals, and believes that everyone can be rehabilitated, including cop killers and child molesters. He's dead wrong—and I think he knows it, but he's stuck with his own lousy ideas of makin' cops into nursemaids, as you call them, George. Russo knows goddamn well that there's a criminal element out there that must be obliterated, and our only hope for that happening is putting nightsticks back into the hands of cops, and letting them use 'em. But he never will."

"Right on, Marv. I knew you'd understand, thanks," George signed off.

Bob Coleman hit "stop" and looked at Russo, who grinned.

"I've really never listened to Marv Grim," he told Coleman and Rothman, who were now both standing in front of his desk.

"On the other hand, my oldest boy Jack is a faithful listener and ardent admirer of Marv's. Come to think of it, my other guy is glued to the TV every Monday night watching the World Wrestling Federation, The WWF. Where did I go wrong?"

"Well, whatever. Come on guys, finish your lunch and let's head back downtown.,"

There was pressure on Russo to meet with the editorial board of *The Post*, and to appear on *New York City This Week* that had a *Face the Nation* format and was televised live on Sunday mornings at eleven on Fox News' Channel 5. He was particularly sought out after a surprising comment he made about ComStat, at a conference at John Jay College. This program, started with great fanfare by his predecessor with the timely support of a mayor hoping to stay in office, placed all police commanders on notice that if their crime statistics didn't meet certain goals, they'd be looking for new careers. After he successfully implemented community policing citywide, Russo had made the dismantling of ComStat, his next priority. He hadn't spoken out on his dislike of the program or his intent to deep six it, so that John Jay comment received wide coverage. He compared the program to the introduction of Health Maintenance Organizations, HMOs, in the health care industry—Managed Care and Managed Crime; he called it—services to the consumers suffering in order to reach some unrealistic statistical goals.

As always, the department's public relations office reported all such requests to the mayor's communications director. These were routine notifications, indicating whether or not the department would grant the interview, and who would do the talking. The mayor's people usually acknowledged such communications and either gave an approval that wasn't "officially" needed or strongly "recommended" against such activity by an "appointed" official. They didn't this time. Clearly, Russo was on his own. He turned down both requests.

"Screw him," the city's police commissioner said to Dave Rothman. "I don't have to defend my position. He's the one that's got to get reelected."

         ❧   ❧   ❧

"I can't believe we're in here ordering shepherd's pie and smoked ham chop," Cathy Russo whispered to her husband. She didn't want their waiter to hear.

Attending daily mass at St. Barnabas R.C., on McClean Avenue and West 241st Street, and an occasional dinner at Rory Dolan's on McClean off Kimball, gave the local Irish brethren a glimpse of the heavenly life that awaited them all.

"It's to further confuse all those who think that a *paisan* who spends too much time in Kosher delis and fraulein who can't say away from scaloppine al marsala, are both weird," Chris Russo smiled, as he emptied the last half of a bottle of Murphy's ale into his mug.

"All I can tell you is that the first time I came to Rory's was on a date with Tom McCabe," Cathy explained, as Chris held his neck to keep from choking on the Murphy's.

An hour later, after finishing their dessert, they were back to discussing the tension that was consuming the relationship between Tom McCabe and Chris Russo.

"I think my friend may be abandoning me on a lot of issues, and it may no longer be just something between me and him. I got to go after him."

She looked away from her husband, and awkwardly smoothed out some imaginary wrinkles in the red and white-checkered tablecloth.

❧   ❧   ❧

"In the name of the Father, Son, and Holy Spirit. Amen," they chanted.

"The Lord be with you," Monsignor Bustore smiled at the congregation.

"And, also with You," they responded.

The 10:30 mass at St. Raymond's was always a sell out; no seats, no standing room. On this biting cold Sunday in March, they were out the doors and onto the steps leading to the front entrance. The mayor was attending mass at the church in which he was baptized and confirmed. His family, and Eve Halliday were with him. It was nothing special for them; Tom McCabe just wanted to go home for a day. But someone heard of his possible appearance and the rush was on.

There were always a few, very few, who were "not of the faith—non-believers, if you will" according to Parkchester's ruling Irish and Italian families. These outsiders would attend, from time to time, for the sake of a mixed marriage or dating, visiting family or friends, or one special occasions such as weddings, funerals, etc.

As Tom McCabe, Ellen, his sister and younger brother, all made the sign of the cross, Eve Halliday abstained.

"Before we end this mass, I would like to acknowledge the return of one of our own, the mayor of the City of New York, Tom McCabe, along with St. Raymond's ubiquitous worshiper, Ellen McCabe, and Tom's sister and brother."

Standing and applauding.

Eve Halliday was clearly pissed.

After a quick lunch at the McCabe's on McGraw Street, following the mass, Tom turned to Eve Halliday.

"Come on Eve, I'll drop you off at your house."

"What do you mean, 'drop me off?' I thought that we could spend the rest of the day together—away from here—just the two of us."

"No, no. I have to get back to Gracie Mansion. I have an important meeting scheduled for three o'clock this afternoon," he answered.

"An important meeting? On Sunday? Who the hell do you think you're kidding," she replied.

"Let's go, Eve. See you, Mom, see you, guys," he said, picking up Eve's expensive Burberry from the back of a chair and throwing it in her direction. She fumbled it, the coat falling to the floor. Eve Halliday looked at the others, waiting. She reached down and picked it up herself.

"Goodbye, Eve," Tom McCabe waved from the rear of his car. Only the detective who had held open the door could see her raised right middle finger.

"Home already, dear," Gordon Halliday shouted from the heated atrium facing one of Fieldston's most exquisitely manicured lawns, surrounded by a series of rare hanging gardens.

"Yeah, yeah. Up yours, too, Papa," she said, throwing her coat at her surprised father.

"What, what's—" he tried.

"Your friend, that fuck, Tom McCabe. He's really trying to dump me. Right?" she demanded, standing directly in front of her father, arms jammed into her sides, legs spread and heels dug in.

"Come on, dear. Please, sit down and let's talk," Gordon Halliday said. He didn't stand, but gently patted the seat of a large comfortable chair next to him. As she pounced down into the chair, he leaned over with lips puckered. She backed away.

No, her father didn't think that the mayor's behavior was a sign that he was ending their romance. Tom McCabe was clearly distracted by the death of his father, his upcoming reelection campaign, and the most recent flack he was getting on this community policing "shit"—was the way Gordon Halliday characterized it. He put most of the blame on Chris Russo.

"Bullshit. I'm telling you that Tom McCabe is blaming me, and you, too, Dad, for his problems with the cops and Russo, and probably for the death of his father," she countered.

"But, Eve—" he tried again.

"Never mind the 'but,' it's because you and I have both told him, over and over again, to get the cops back to kicking ass rather than trying to schmooze the welfare crowd in this city. It's none of the cops' goddamn business," Eve Halliday growled.

"No, no, Eve. I'm sure that you're wrong. I don't like Russo for what he is and for what he stands for, and I've made that clear to Tom more than once. But, blame for the death of his father? No way," her father was sitting up in his chair by now.

"So? So? Why? Why?" she bristled.

"Well, I don't exactly know how to ask you this. However, I do know that you're still out of the house most evenings, just as you were when you and Tom were apparently going at it hot and heavy," Halliday began.

"What are you saying, Father?" Eve Halliday narrowed her eyes and moved her face closer to his.

"I'm not saying anything, dear. I'm merely trying to answer your question about why things seem to have cooled between you and Tom McCabe."

"Well, screw you, old man. Maybe you should look at what's been going on in your life for the past six months or so, for the obvious answer to that question," Eve Halliday snarled, running from the room and giving the front door a contemptuous slam.

PART II

And I waterd it in fears,
Night & morning with my tears:
And I sunned it with smiles,
And with soft deceitful wiles.

—Blake, st. 2

CHAPTER 7

*V*ince Savino had no idea that his life would somehow cross with that of the mayor yet again as he stood at School Crossing #24 at Castle Hill Avenue and Randall Avenue on a bright winter morning. The community cops had replaced the civilian school crossing guards who had done the job for the previous thirty years. The idea was that it gave the local cops another opportunity to connect with people in the neighborhood.

Savino had arrived around 8:20 that morning. The school day started at nine with the first kids arriving at his corner between eight-thirty and a quarter to the hour. For some reason, Mondays always seemed busier than other days, although Vince reminded himself that he had no proof of that.

"Maybe they've had it with their parents over the weekend," he reasoned, "And it's not that there are more kids on Mondays, they're just noisier." He had only been at that crossing about three or four times since the Community Cops made their "comeback," he told one of the parents who had remarked, "Gee, it's great to see an officer on the crossing. My kids are thrilled."

He wasn't, as yet, familiar with any of the school's students. But he couldn't miss this one. She was about five minutes late and stood on the northeast corner of the intersection, impatiently waiting for the light to change, and for Savino to wave her across the street. As she dashed towards him, he saw that her face, around the right eye, was swollen and badly discolored—black and blue. He grabbed her right arm, as she tried to avoid his look, while darting around his right side.

"Hey, slow down, the teacher won't start without you," Savino smiled, but not letting go of her arm.

She looked down, saying nothing, while squirming to get loose from his grip.

"Hi, what's your name?" Vince Savino began.

"Please, I have to go. If I'm late again, they'll make me stay after school. Please, let me go," she cried.

"OK, sure. I'll see you at three, OK?" Savino answered, releasing her arm, and waving to her as she raced towards the double front door of the school. She didn't answer him, or turn to see his wave.

Savino was anxious for three o'clock to come around. While the kids seemed eager to get to school that morning, their obvious exuberance while blasting open the school's door as the echo of the dismissal bell lingered, made their real feelings quite clear. The afternoon crossing was more hectic, to. After all, they stored up their energy by kind of meandering in, almost casually, in the morning. At three o'clock it was a well-planned, meticulously timed evacuation from the school and reinvasion of their neighborhoods. Stormin' Norman would have been proud, Savino had thought.

She was one of the last to leave the school. She walked alone. Most of the kids walked with other kids or were met by their mothers or some adult. She knew that Savino was looking at her. She kept her head down, just enough to avoid his scrutiny and still see when he would start waving for her to cross the street. When she reached the middle of the street where the cop was standing, he put his arm around her and walked with her to the adjoining sidewalk.

"Well, you made it. How was school?" he asked, hoping to get a conversation going with her.

"OK, I guess," she said without any enthusiasm.

"Look, I'm kinda' new here, and I want to get to know the children at good old P.S. 138. Can I start with you?" he was hoping.

She actually smiled, while half looking up. "My name is Laurie Mitchell."

"Great, that's better. Hi, Laurie, my name is Vince Savino." She looked up a bit more. There was no doubt that someone had punched her in the left eye. It was clearly not an accident. But, he wasn't about to push it. She knew that he knew, he surmised.

"See you tomorrow, Laurie," he said, taking her across Randall Avenue.

"OK" she said softly, as she headed south on Castle Hill Avenue towards Lacombe Avenue and the Castle Hill Houses, a city housing project.

Vince Savino saw her the next two days, and then moved on to the late night shift, midnight to eight. It would be two more weeks before he'd be back on "days." His first day tour was on Wednesday, and he didn't see Laurie Mitchell that morning. She wasn't in school that afternoon, either. On Thursday she was late again, standing at the opposite corner, waiting for Savino to say it was OK to cross the street. She was holding her head down again. He was hoping to be greeted with a wave, a smile, or something to acknowledge that they made some progress two weeks ago. As she approached him, she looked up at him and stopped, knowing that he would have halted her on seeing her face. This time her face was bruised and her left jaw swollen. Savino didn't say anything, at first. He put his arm around her, and they walked slowly to the nearest sidewalk, almost directly in front of the school.

"Laurie, are you OK?" he asked.

"Yes, thank you. I just want to get to class. I'm late again."

"Sure, see you at three," Savino patted her one shoulder, and waved to her. As soon as Laurie opened the front door of the school and went in, the CPO took off for the "storefront."

He went over to Maria Fernandez and waited for her to get off the phone. Maria had been a civilian crossing guard at Laurie's school until the cops took over. He reckoned she might remember the girl. Even though hundreds of kids swarmed in and out of the Depression era crumbling red brick building, Savino was willing to bet that Laurie stood out from the crowd. Abused kids usually did.

"I've seen a little girl, she's probably about nine, who is obviously being beaten by someone. Two weeks ago she had a horrendous shiner, and today her face was all bruised and her jaw terribly swollen," Savino told her.

"I didn't see that too often, Vince. Do you know her name?"

"Yes, Laurie Mitchell. I haven't talked to anyone yet, except you, now. So I don't know where she lives. When I cross her, she seems to head towards the Castle Hill Houses project."

"Oh, yes. I remember her. She's a cutie. And I've seen her like that before," Maria said. "I reported it to the school, I'd say about six months ago, but nothing seems to have changed."

"Laurie wouldn't confide in me, either. I tried," she added.

Savino questioned other cops who had been assigned to School Crossing #24. They hadn't recalled seeing Laurie Mitchell, or any young girl who seemed to have been beaten, as he described. It may have been coincidental with his tours of duty, or maybe none of the other cops noticed Laurie, or maybe she had such a lousy attendance record that no one saw much of her, he thought. He wasn't going to let it go. After his morning school crossing the next day, and not having seen Laurie, Savino went to the Assistant Principal, Clarence Carlin. Yes, he knew of the problems with Laurie Mitchell. Yes, he remembered Maria Fernandez reporting her concern to him.

"So, Mr. Carlin, what did you do about it?" Savino asked, impatiently.

"I called Laurie's mother. She denied that Laurie had been abused or neglected, but agreed to come to the school to speak with me," Carlin responded.

"Well? What happened?" the cop asked, incredulously.

"She never showed up," he said.

"And then what did you do?"

"I made an official report of what Maria Fernandez told me, and my attempt to communicate with Laurie's mother."

"But what about the city's children's services, what about the goddamn courts?" Savino's voice was rising.

"I reported the case to children's services, after Miss Fernandez made a second report to me," he explained.

"A second report? And then what did you do or not do, for God's sake?" Savino was furious and shouting.

"Hold on, Officer, I don't have to take this from you. This isn't a police matter in the first place. Why are you so interested in such a purely social and domestic issue? Do you have the training to pursue this case?" Mr. Carlin got up from behind his small desk and began backing away from Savino.

"I'll tell you why I'm so interested, Mr. Carlin," Savino began, getting up from his chair and moving towards the assistant principal. "I'm so interested because a very young child needs some help from someone, anybody, and you're playing a fuckin' 'cover your ass' game. Besides, if it's not my job, as you say, who the hell's job is it?" he screamed. Savino had tried to restrain himself, but suddenly he crashed his clenched fist onto Mr. Carlin's glass-topped desk. It splintered into very neat and equal radial and spiral fractures.

"I don't believe this, Officer. I'm going to report you to my principal and your superiors," Carlin was now running for his office door.

"Good, and make sure you tell them that if I find any city agency, ANY, I repeat, was negligent in this case, I'm going to the fuckin' DA and whoever else should know about this," Savino shouted.

Savino looked at the assistant principal with amazement as the rage drained out of him. Here was someone directly responsible for the welfare of children—and when he saw a child who was obviously endangered he simply shuffled papers and walked away. Savino turned his back on Carlin and stalked out of the office. He waded through the small crowd that had gathered outside the assistant principal's office. He stopped at the desk of Carlin's secretary and demanded the girl's home address.

By the time he reached the Castle Hill Houses, he was in a state of barely repressed fury. When he arrived at 630 Castle Hill Avenue, Apartment 9A he knocked on the heavy metal, gray door. No answer. He closed his hand, and pounded on the door two more times.

"Who is it?" a male voice growled.

"Mr. Mitchell?" Savino asked.

"Who the hell are you? What do you want?" the man in the apartment responded.

"I'm a police officer, Vince Savino. I want to talk to you about your daughter, Laurie."

There was no response from inside the apartment. Savino took a deep breath, turned the knob and pushed the door open. Standing in the reeking, dimly lit hallway, he looked inside.

"Come in," a hulking, round-shouldered man motioned Vince Savino into the apartment. He was about forty, unshaven, strangely uncut hair, and wearing an athletic shirt, exposing unbelievably ugly hairy arms and an equally unsightly upper chest.

The front entrance led into a long, narrow, dark hall. There was no bulb in a ceiling fixture halfway down the hall. There was a bathroom on the right, along with a closet and small room, possibly a child's bedroom, on the left. The hall was strewn with dirty clothes, soiled towels, and piles of worn socks. A small kitchen was at the end of the hall with an oval Formica table, with four or five chairs, each of a different color. The remnants of what Savino had assumed to be part of breakfast—stained dishes and mounds of bread-crumbs—were on the table, under and around some scattered pages of *The New York City Examiner*. As Savino and the guy who opened the door reached the kitchen, a woman came in from what must have been another bedroom, off to the right of the kitchen.

"Henry, what is it? What happened?" she was obviously alarmed at seeing a uniformed police officer in her house.

"He wants to talk about Laurie, he says," Henry responded.

Savino was shaken at the sight of this woman. She was covered by some kind of tattered robe that must have been white at one time, but was stained and discolored, in addition to being ripped in several places. She seemed not to be wearing anything underneath and her hair was a mess, tangled and knotted at the ends. She was barefoot. Both eyes were swollen so badly that they were almost completely shut. Her nose had been broken some time ago, and more than once, Savino had guessed. He could hear voices, young voices coming from the back of the apartment.

"No, Mr. Mitchell, not just Laurie. I was going to ask about her, but after seeing Mrs. Mitchell, if that's who you are, ma'am, we're going to talk about a lot more than that."

Ten minutes later Savino, fighting back tears, walked out of the filthy apartment carrying the limp form of Laurie's little brother. He was four years old, feather-light from malnutrition. Timmy Mitchell's eyes were closed. He had found peace in the deep sleep of coma, a refuge from the horrors he had endured and a place somewhere far beyond the grim confines of the housing project, a place from which he would never return. When the NYFD-EMS ambulance Savino had summoned finally arrived, the paramedic began to examine the child and then looked up and slowly shook his head.

In the investigation that followed that day, perhaps the most harrowing hours in all of Vince Savino's 42 years, the appalling details of the Mitchell case emerged and shocked the entire city. It was, according to newspaper stories and TV accounts, the most shameful, shocking, and blatant example of the total uselessness of a social system that mishandled this case at every level of authority.

Mark Blaine wrote a long story that ran in the Sunday magazine section of The New York Times. It was a scalding attack on all the responsible city agencies and officials—including those who kept Henry Mitchell on the city payroll (it turned out that he worked—whenever he decided to show up—for the pot hole division of the Department of Transportation) and in city subsidized housing while he was abusing his wife and children. He excoriated those at her school who failed to report the obvious physical battering that Laurie was enduring and the cops who had been called by neighbors who reported what they suspected was going on in the Mitchell apartment. The police had responded only once, talked to the father and took no action. Blaine also highlighted the political and social aspects of the case—community policing vs. traditional policing and those "of us" who did nothing to avert a human tragedy. "Only a cop, one of our cops, maybe the last cop our town will ever see—saved us this time, by doing something while others just stood by, doing nothing," he wrote.

He concluded the piece with words that would come to haunt Tom McCabe, "Come on Mr. Mayor, tell us how we can live with our consciences-and our responsibility. Because we are all responsible."

Parkchester Paint and Hardware on Westchester Avenue reopened for business on Monday morning following Blaine's story. Ellen McCabe opened promptly at eight, thirty minutes later than Morgan had done for over twenty-five years. "A month, my God, Morgan, its been almost a month," she sighed, as she got to the front door of the store.

Ellen McCabe looked at the old sign that took up most of the space in front of the building between the store on the first floor and the second floor apartment that they had never rented out so it would be available for community meetings. She was hesitating; she had never opened the store without Morgan at her side.

"Come on, lassie, get with it," Ellen admonished herself. She knew that's what Morgan McCabe would have said.

After opening the front window blinds and flipping the lights in the small back office, she went into her bag, took out the thermos, and grabbed the Sunday Magazine section of her paper.

"My goodness, it's Vince Savino," she exclaimed. One of the pictures in the article showed Savino, in uniform, standing in front of the community service center, just down the block from her store. She devoured the story once and reread it with more attention to detail. She had powerful and mixed reactions to the story. She didn't like the way her son came across, and she wasn't blaming Blaine. She finally decided to call Tom McCabe. It was ten o'clock by then.

The phone was picked up on one ring, as always. "Hello, Janet, it's Ellen McCabe. Is Tom available?"

"He's got the president of the city council in his office. But I'll buzz him, if you wish," Mullins offered.

"Yes, please, I think it's important that I talk to him. Now!"

There was a predictable pause, but a bit longer than usual. It was Ms. Mullins' job to give the mayor an early warning when she saw a storm brewing.

"Boy, is your old lady pissed. Should I put her through?" She asked McCabe.

"Do I have a choice?" the mayor replied as he hit the key on his phone.

"Hi, Mom. What's doing? First day back at the store, right?" the mayor came on the line smoothly.

"Yes, that's right, Tom." She didn't give him a chance to respond, but continued, "Unfortunately, I didn't get to all of Sunday's *Times* yesterday, as usual, and got to the magazine section, just this minute."

"Oh, yes, Blaine's piece. Since when did he become such a great fan of his?" Tom McCabe laughed.

"Tom, he's saying that you're listening to the same, old crowd—including Gordon Halliday—he IS still around, I would imagine—that have been out to discredit the Community Cops Program, from the beginning. It's pretty clear to me and others that you're no longer a real supporter of the program," she continued, "Or of Chris, for that matter." McCabe could hear the hum of anger in her voice.

"Mom, can I call you back on this? I'm really tied up right now?" he asked. He needed to buy some time, let her calm down.

But Ellen McCabe wasn't about to be put off so easily and demanded a response from her son. She wasn't happy with what she heard. McCabe told her that the article was unfair to him and ignored the fact that critics of community policing had some legitimate complaints. When Ellen reminded him of his father's passionate commitment to the idea of cops working closely with the community, he responded

"Sometimes he listened to Chris Russo more than he did to me—and I think that may have been a mistake. There's a lot more coming out now about community policing that may even have had Morgan McCabe backing off a bit."

"The hell you say—Morgan McCabe was his own man, and no one else's—you know that. If anyone's been listening to the wrong people—and not being his own man—it's been you!" For the first time in her life she hung up on her son and then burst into tears. However, it wasn't the first time she cried over a family matter in recent months.

"Mom. Oh, Mom. Please, I'm sorry. I shouldn't have said that." McCabe realized that he had been insensitive but his apology was too late. He was talking to a dead phone.

The next day, Ellen McCabe put in a call to Russo's office. Rothman told her the commissioner was at a community meeting in Brooklyn's Crown Heights, but would return her call as soon as he returned. Just after noon, she got her call back.

"Hi, Mrs. M, how are you and the business, this fine, bright, and unbelievably warm day?" Russo greeted her.

"Oh, fine, thanks Chris. But I'm calling about the article in Sunday's *Times*. It really disturbed me," Ellen McCabe responded.

"Chris, I think that Blaine's right. Tom is no longer an enthusiastic supporter of the Community Police idea. And he's taking it out on you."

"Look. You shouldn't get upset over this thing," Russo tried to reassure her. "Tom is under a lot of political pressure. After all, the election is less than a year away—and opposition to Community Policing is just one of those pressures." He made a quick sign-of-the-cross with his free hand, following that declaration.

He was happy to see that she wasn't buying it when she said, "I know you will always be his friend, Chris. But I'm concerned that if this keeps up, he may no longer be yours."

"Please, I don't think we should talk like this. Have you discussed the matter with Tom?"

"No. I tried to. In the past, I never hesitated to have frank conversations with him. Now I get the feeling that I can't," she said, a forlorn note in her voice. "In any event, you're obviously right, Chris, and I will talk to him. But I wanted you to know that I will use whatever influence I have to support you and the cops," she said.

"Thanks, Ellen, I appreciate that," Chris Russo said, while he thought, "Now Tom's really in trouble. I wouldn't want Ellen McCabe on my ass."

❧   ❧   ❧

The four-story, wooden frame house on Beach Avenue just about midway between White Plains Road and the 43rd Precinct Station House on Fteley Avenue was probably built just after World War II. At any one time, New York City's Family Support Administration, FSA, had eight families in the building, two on each floor. No one really knew who the owner was, but the FSA was mailing eight rent checks each month to someone. The place was in shambles. The toilets, among other things, never functioned properly. Repairs of plumbing, heating, electrical wiring, and the building's structure had been made by incompetent contractors who cut every possible corner and paid the building superintendents to turn a blind eye to such dangerous and illegal practices. All under the auspices of an unknown landlord and financed by the taxpayers of New York City.

The unexpected indictment of Fred Thorne of Greenwich, Connecticut, the actual owner of the troublesome structure on Beach Avenue, along with many other similar properties in the Bronx and Washington Heights in Manhattan brought down an avalanche. Then one of his pigsties in the Longwood Section burned to the ground, taking the lives of two small children. A grand jury impaneled by the Bronx District Attorney targeted two inspectors. They were easily "turned"—given a deal in return for cooperating with the DA's investigators. They ratted out Mr. Thorne. He took the fall for manslaughter and negligent homicide and got life, with no chance for parole.

When the United States Attorney covering New York City also prosecuted and convicted Fred Thorne for violating Title 18 of the Federal Criminal Code and Rules, Chapter 95, known as the RICO, Racketeer Influenced and Corrupted Organizations statute, for depriving his thousands of tenants of their civil rights, all of his properties were forfeited. But even under the management of a federal agency the conditions at the Beach Avenue house got worse.

New York City was forced to relocate eight families to a crumbling welfare hotel on East 13th Street and Avenue B in lower Manhattan. The former tenants of Thorn's firetrap were delighted with the slow-running water, lukewarm radiators, hallway toilets, and 25-watt bulbs in rusted, but workable light fixtures. In the meantime, the building they left remained abandoned for over four months. Then the crack heads moved in.

Brian Joyce and Vince Savino hassled the junkies who took over the first two floors, the only ones that weren't about to collapse. The cops made detailed notifications and countless numbers of written reports to New York City's Buildings, Health, and Fire Departments, while they went on rousting the addicts. But nothing happened. Linda Wright, as a member of the City Council's Housing and Buildings Committee, also banged away at the city's slow-moving machinery. Four more months, and nothing.

The two cops finally ran out of patience and decided to make one more report to someone they knew could help them. They went over to Engine 64/Ladder 47 on Ellis and Castle Hill Avenues. Fire Fighter Bill Morrell was on duty. Joyce asked, "Who's working tomorrow night, Billy?"

"My squad, plus two other squads with Teddy Shidel and Louie Espinosa. You know them. Why, Brian?" Morrell responded.

"Would a coupla' you guys give up your meal period to supervise a small fire on Beach Avenue?"

The people living on Beach Avenue are still talking about how quickly the fire trucks got to the scene of the fire. In fact, they seemed to get there before anyone called. It wasn't really a big fire. Just enough structural damage for the Buildings Department to declare the structure unsafe. The Feds gladly gave it over to the city that demolished the house and replaced it with a small playground. Urban renewal had never been so quickly accomplished in New York City history.

CHAPTER 8

※

"You'll be late for your four o'clock meeting, Mr. Mayor," Janet Mullins warned him.

"Right, I'm on my way," Tom McCabe responded.

The mayor's schedule for the day showed "4:00 p.m. to 5:00 p.m-Personal." He left his office by the rear door, walked down the enclosed metal stairway leading to the grassy section between the north side of City Hall and the south side of the Tweed Courthouse on Chambers Street, and got into his waiting limousine. He usually left by the main entrance, where his car would be parked at the foot of the marble steps leading from the City Hall's main entrance, facing Park Row.

"Where to, Mr. Mayor?" asked his police chauffeur.

"We're going to Staten Island, Harry. Head that way. Hit the Staten Island Expressway to 440, The Richmond Expressway, and exit just before the tollbooths for the Outerbridge Crossing. I'll fill you in when we get off," the mayor directed.

"Wow, secret mission, eh, boss?" the cop asked, looking in his rearview and side view mirrors. "No security either, I see. Just you and me against the world, right Mr. Mayor?"

As they approached the intersection of Outerbridge Avenue and West Shore Parkway, McCabe told the cop to make a right on to Veterans Road then a left on to Arthur Kills Road and head North. They drove to the rear of a Knights of Columbus Hall, Stolzenthaler Council, on Kreischer Street, where the mayor got out.

"I'll be back in an hour," the mayor began.

"If you need me, Harry, knock on the side door twice, then hesitate, and knock once more. I'll come out—don't you come in," the mayor instructed his aide.

The hall was not in use at that time of the day. The custodian had already left. McCabe entered through an unlocked rear door, and climbed the short flight of wooden stairs to a room marked, "Chapel." He opened the right side of the double door, and went in. A very tall, slim, gray-haired man, wearing a dark, pinstriped suit, white-on-white shirt, and a maroon tie with blue stripes greeted him. He had been sitting in one of the pews, facing the altar, but rose and turned towards the mayor, as His Honor entered.

"Mr. Mayor, how are you?" the very erect, distinguished gentleman inquired.

"Good, fine, Dan, and how have you been?"

Dan McCourty hadn't been New York City's police commissioner for over four years, but he still had the authoritative and patrician presence that served him so well during his thirty-five years as a cop. It was not clear who really initiated the clandestine meeting but the timing of the meeting was right for both of them. McCourty had been advising some of those critical of Community Policing, and the mayor was being criticized for listening to them—and was making some changes, i.e., the new Civilian Complaint Review Board, and challenging the roles of the PACs. It seemed that the mayor was not only listening to the program's dissenters, but also seemed to agree with them, on some issues, at least.

They spent the full hour, discussing the movement of New York City's police department into the CPOs concept. McCourty blamed former mayor Paul Williams for starting the program. The former commissioner had tried to dissuade him from implementing the program. He regarded Harold Bartels, his immediate successor, with contempt. McCourty felt that he would have done anything to become police commissioner. Williams had asked McCourty to step down because of his continued opposition to the CPOs. The old PC remembered when Russo started making a name for himself by pushing "team policing" to the new chief of planning, Neil Nelson. They both had the same "inane ideas," he told McCabe. In fact, McCourty was not critical of Russo's motives. "He's almost perverse, when it comes to this social service proffering to fighting crime in the streets. It's tormenting our city."

McCabe smiled a bit at McCourty's obvious delight in displaying his legendary talent of throwing out rarely used, and at times, archaic words. Anyone who spent more than a casual moment with McCourty was soon endowed with the revelation, by the ex-commissioner himself, that he unfailingly completed each Sunday *New York Times* Magazine section's difficult Crossword Puzzle IN INK—and that he was a major communicator with that same paper's premier lexicographer, William Safire.

Yes, he told McCabe he had been asked to advise some cops, mostly their unions, and some community groups, by and large those in the outlying areas of the city's boroughs and others who were as unhappy with the CPOs idea as he was. McCabe asked McCourty how he would handle the situation.

"First, I want to tell you that you're doing the right thing, Mr. Mayor, with this CCRB dunnage. Get the social work amenability out of the hands of the cops altogether, although I'd rather see them retain it than give it to those community boards, or whatever in the Lord's name Russo calls them," McCourty began.

"And second, be resolute in eradicating those Advisory Councils altogether. They're divisive and are nothing more than an attempt to levy community control over the police—like the local school boards did with the Board of Education. Look what a mess that has been." He knew that McCabe had been feuding with the president of New York City's Board of Education over that very issue for years. "There is no *sine qua non* in those situations—the communities or the schools, and now the police," he argued.

McCabe heard him out and then said, "Good. Thanks, Dan. But what about the CPOs? What's your advice on what to do about them?" he asked.

"Mr. Mayor, I don't have to tell you an election is coming up, shortly. I'd move more charily in that area. The CPOs have a lot of support in certain areas of the city. And they're backed by a daedal of politicians, local, as well as state," McCourty answered.

"I'd let the program wither away. Don't do anything that would look like you're trying to purge them. As cops retire and you hire replacements, give them conventional assignments. Priority can still be given to foot patrols, but they should be used only to cut down on street crime. It is mandatory that they answer those radio calls for help coming into 911!" McCourty suggested.

"And pull them off those imbecilic school crossing assignments. Relieve them of all other non-police functions. Then put all those old women school crossing guards, now sitting on their fat *derrieres* in those storefronts Russo opened, back where they belong. You start getting rid of all these people, and then the storefronts will wither on the vine. Handle it through attrition. It wouldn't be attributable to anything you did or didn't do," the old, gray fox smiled. "Blame it on the chronic budget squeeze," he added.

McCabe made a move to get up from his chair. Dan McCourty put his right hand up to stop him. The mayor sat down again.

"Mister Mayor, I'm going to tell you something I've countenanced to very few people. Community Policing, as we know it, can never be successful—in New York City or anyplace else. The young cops coming on the job in the last ten or so years are the offspring of the baby boomers," McCourty said.

"Yeah. So?" the mayor asked.

"The cops in my time came from families that went through the 'depression.' They could relate to the personal and financial hardships suffered by people. They served in WWII. Later, some saw combat in Korea or Vietnam. So they had some real life experiences. They understood what life was all about. These kids today—these cops today, just don't get it," he said in a contemptuous tone. "Today's society, today's families, are not capable of producing the kinds of kids who can be real cops." he was forlorn at that point.

"Community policing is about two generations too late," he added.

"So let it whither away, Mister Mayor—just let it wither away," he concluded, lowering his head and actually closing his eyes.

McCabe sat there without responding, lost in thought, his eyes scanning the room. Finally he looked at the former police commissioner and smiled, and slowly got up.

"Mister Mayor, we used to say that 'only a cop stood between a civilized society and anarchy' And, it's just as true today—and maybe even more so—make no mistake about it, Mister Mayor, Chris Russo knows that as well as I do. But it's his legacy and obviously he's going to stick with it no matter what. Even if it means running the department—and your administration, I might add—into oblivion."

"Well, that's heavy stuff, Dan. I admire your courage in taking a position and telling me what you really think."

"Well, as always, if you ever have need me Mr. Mayor for anything, don't hesitate to call," Dan McCourty called out as McCabe walked toward the door. The mayor stopped and turned to the former police commissioner, "Yes, thank you, Dan, you've been very helpful in the past few months, on at least two occasions," the mayor said, looking unsmilingly at McCourty. "I assume your source inside the police department is pretty high up?" he asked.

"Yes, sir, and very vicinal to the investigation of your father's death."

❧   ❧   ❧

Westchester Avenue, from the Bronx River to the Hutchinson River Parkway, was the focus of intense canvassing by S.I.D. and homicide task force detectives, while the two uniformed cops were pulling in all their snitches. By week's end the cops got a break. The two homeless guys, who hadn't been seen since the killings, walked into the all-night cafeteria. The night crew had been told by both the homicide and local cops to call if they came back. But Andy Rahn, the restaurant's night manager, didn't call the special hotline number that had been set up by the detectives, he dialed the Parkchester Police Community Service storefront, and asked for Savino or Joyce.

They had just gotten to the center when the call came in. They called Munro, who notified the Bronx Homicide Task Force as required by department rules and procedures. The sergeant also called Andy Rahn, explained to him what the cops intended to do, and said they'd be there in ten minutes.

"How are you going to finger these guys for us, Andy?" Munro asked. Andy said he'd wait until the two got their food and picked out a table. He'd then send one of the busboys to get the cops. Munro said OK and told Andy that they'd be parked in marked cruisers on the northeast corner of White Plains Road and the Hugh J. Grant Circle, just one block away from Bickford's. Munro told Joyce and Savino to meet her there.

Ten minutes after they arrived, the cops saw a busboy charge out of the restaurant heading towards their blue and while.

"*Los cabritos de dos*—I mean dee two keeds—they are way over on de left side of front door, against de wall and lookin' outside the window," he said breathlessly.

"Perfect. Good, thanks kid. *Gracias*," the sergeant replied.

A minute later the 3 cops burst through the front door, guns drawn and rushed towards the corner table, scaring the shit out of the two-in-the-morning crowd, most of whom were eating their only meal of the day. Many had their life's belongings sitting on empty chairs next to them.

Panic broke out; tables were knocked on their sides, chairs skidded across the aisles, coffee sprayed against walls and rolls of rags and clothing sliding along the floors as everyone hit the deck and began rolling out of what they feared would be the line of fire.

"Freeze, don't get up! Don't do nothing!" shouted Savino at the two guys who were still sitting at their table, apparently dazed by what was happening.

"What the fuck's goin' on?" one of them croaked, his mouth almost obscured by the wild beard covering most of his face.

"Just don't do anything stupid. Get up from the table and lie down on the floor face down, spread-eagle. Both of you. Come on, get moving," Joyce ordered, while Savino and the sergeant stood aside.

"Phew, these guys fuckin' stink. Get the paddy wagon up here and we'll cart them back to the storefront," Munro said, after they patted down the two early morning diners and read them their rights.

She called the 43 Squad detectives, who called S.I.D. The latter notification a CYA—cover your ass—strategy.

Joyce and Savino were more than happy to interview the two drifters in the storefront's basement where the smell probably wouldn't make it to the upstairs offices. The younger of the two told them he was twenty, but he looked at least ten years older. His matted, tangled, scraggly, hair crawled down his back and looped around his neck on both sides. He still had acne on a face half-covered with a light blonde beard. Close to six feet, he towered over his friend, who, at twenty-five, he said, was shorter than his buddy by some six inches. Like the younger one, his face was drawn and bony, but his red beard was full and wild. He was already losing his hair, so that it barely reached down to his shoulders. He seemed less sullen and more open than his partner.

They said that they had arrived in the Bronx from Toronto about a week before the cops grabbed them. Both were from foster homes in the Midwest, the younger guy from Iowa and his companion from Indiana. They claimed to have met in Toronto's Covenant House.

They had stayed in that Toronto shelter for about a month before deciding to make their way to New York City. The truck driver who picked them up had dropped them off in front of Bickford's in the Bronx and given them five bucks to get a decent meal. But first they had bought a bottle of cheap gin and eventually had dined at Bickford's with the remaining two bucks.

"Where did you go after you finished eating?—You—tell me your name and answer my question," asked a lieutenant from S.I.D. jabbing his finger at the younger one.

"Jack—Jack Adams. We slept in the doorway of a flower shop, you know, a florist, just a coupla doors down from the newsstand," he said.

"Did anyone see you sleeping in the doorway?" asked Joyce, joining the investigation, to the obvious annoyance of the detective lieutenant.

"Yeah, the guy that opened it, in the morning," Adams replied.

"Where is this store?" the detective boss asked.

"It's called White Plains Road Florist—I know the owner. I'll get his home number out of the business file and give him a call," Joyce volunteered.

"At three in the morning?" asked a surprised lieutenant. He thought they could hold off on the interrogation until later that morning after everybody got some sleep. He looked at Adams and his partner and said, "Throw them in a cell overnight; for them it will be like the Ritz."

Joyce said that the storeowner wouldn't mind being called, even at this early hour.

"Sure, Al's a good guy," Vince Savino added, to the obvious disappointment of the lieutenant. "We saved his ass on more than one occasion. Al's got a problem with the horses and gets in over his head with the "books" once in a while. They had him worked over a few times, but we put a stop to it."

"These local cops with their community police shit—knowing everybody on their beats personal business—drives me crazy," the lieutenant whispered to one of the detectives who had just joined his boss and the cops in the basement.

Joyce called the station and got Al's home phone number. Al told him that he got to his store about eight that morning, and "I saw these two fuckin' winos stretched out in my door-way." He had to wake them up. He didn't know how long they were there, but "they pissed all over the place, even on the newspaper they were layin' on," Al complained.

The lieutenant pressed ahead. "You—what's your name and where have you been for the last week?"

"My name is Wayne Berlinger. We went into—Times Square—you know where all the movies are," he replied.

"We've been sleeping on sidewalks—you know, over those gratings where the hot air comes out," Adams added.

"Why did you come back here after all this time?" asked the detective, finally making his contribution to the investigation.

"New York sucks. We thought maybe we should go back to Toronto. It's better than this fuckin' dump," Jack said. "We thought that maybe we'd see the same guy drivin' the truck who dropped us off here."

"You're going to wish you had left town," the lieutenant said, ending the interrogation. He put in a call to his boss, Chief Lombardo.

"No one fuckin' move until I get there, *capece, you bunch of jabons?*" was Lombardo's admonition.

"Those goddamn cops. I'll kill 'em," Lombardo was screaming at his driver. "I warned them to stay away from the investigation and the detectives should know better. They shoulda called me," he shouted, stuffing a half-smoked cigar into his snarling mouth.

"Yeah, I heard you say that, Chief. I heard you myself," the driver piped in, stiffly turning his head adorned by a crumpled Rocky Stallone-style porkpie hat, towards the back of the car.

Lombardo stood shivering in the unheated basement after the briefing was over, asking the lieutenant follow-up questions and ignoring the Four-three cops. Finally, he said, "OK. Let 'em go."

"Uh, Chief? Excuse me, sir. Before you let them go, can I ask these guys a question?" Joyce requested.

Lombardo glared at him for a moment; the other cops nervously crossed and uncrossed their legs and shifted uneasily in their chairs.

"A question?" the chief bellowed. "What the hell do you mean? What's your name, again, officer?" Lombardo growled.

"Joyce. Community Police Office Brian Joyce, my partner, Vince Savino, along with our Sergeant, Jessica Munro were the first on the scene at the McCabe and Velez homicides" he responded.

"I know who you are, and who your partner is and who your patrol supervisor is, I had you in my fuckin' office—Remember? And I know who was fuckin' killed. So cut the shit," the chief snarled.

Horan nodded and said, "Yes sir," and smiled.

"Sir, I'd like to ask them about, about McCabe's store."

Lombardo didn't say no.

"Thank you, sir."

Lombardo and the rest of the cops marched back to the kitchen upstairs where Adams and Berlinger were still seated at a table. After introducing Lombardo, Joyce smiled at them, trying to put them at ease, and asked "Do you realize the two of you are suspected of murdering two guys near the location you mutts were at, the night you stayed in the Westchester Avenue neighborhood?"

The detectives and their chief gasped. "Holy shit, what's he doing?" the detective whispered to his lieutenant.

The two young drifters looked at each other for just a moment. Finally, Berlinger nodded an OK to Adams who said, "We didn't go right from the restaurant to the flower shop," he began, and Berlinger nodded in agreement. "We went looking for a place to sleep till morning. We walked about two blocks before we found a nice, open space, you know like a hallway or somethin' in front of a store."

"Yeah, and on the way we picked up some old cardboard boxes and newspapers from a garbage basket we found on one of the street corners," Berlinger added. "You know, we flattened the boxes out so we could lay on them and covered ourselves with the papers. It was great."

"We didn't remember what time it was, but was were woken up—I'd say it couldn't a been more than a coup'l a hours or so—by car doors slammin' across the street," Adams went on, looking for confirmation of the time from his partner, who nodded his head. "We saw these two guys get out of a car and start walking towards our side of the street. They stopped right in front of the store, next to the one we flopped in," he said.

"We was scared shit they would see us and maybe rob us, you know," Berlinger explained. The cops looked back and forth at one another, smiling and raising their eyebrows.

"They went up the stairs to the front door of the store," Adams started again.

"Yeah, the only reason we didn't flop in that doorway was the high steps," Berlinger laughed. When no one else did, he slumped back into his chair.

"It looked like they tried the front door and I guess it didn't open because they turned around and went back on the sidewalk, and started walking to their car," Adams continued, giving Berlinger an annoyed look. "They went to the side of the car, opened the door and it looked like they were wrestlin', you know grapplin', with somethin' they were pullin' from the front seat next to where the driver sits. We couldn't hear what they were sayin' until one guy yells, 'Oh, shit, is this heavy'," Berlinger was getting into it now. "By this time, we was wide awake and so scared we ducked our heads low so that they wouldn't see us," he went on. "But we still raised 'em enough so's we could still see what was goin' on. We got scared again, 'cause holy shit, it looked to us like these guys were carryin' a body, or somethin'. The two of them and the guy they was carryin'—yeah, now we could see it was a old guy, gray hair and everything—went into the alley in between two stores. 'Let's get the fuck out of here,' I said."

"Holy shit," Lombardo exclaimed. "And then you went to the flower store?" he said, looking intently at the two men seated directly in front of him

"You don't remember the time, or anything like that, do you?" Savino asked.

"Nah, but we was only asleep maybe a half hour when this guy, I guess who owned the store, kicked us out," Adams said.

"The guys carrying the body and their car, can you give a description of any of that?" Joyce asked, with the chief still scowling at him as he continued the questioning. Lombardo was clearly annoyed by Joyce's taking the lead.

"Yeah, it was strange. The two of them was dressed in the same, black, dark clothes, with the same color heavy jackets. And they both wore black, woolen caps. You know, like for skiin' or somethin'," Adams replied.

"Navy pea jackets and watch caps?" Joyce asked.

"Yeah, yeah, that's it."

According to Adams, one of the men was about six feet and heavy, "Boy, he musta been three-hundred pounds," Berlinger said, "but the other one was a little shorter and had like a wrestler's build or somethin'."

"What about the car"? Joyce asked.

"Hey, man, that I know. I used to fix cars, ya know. It was a Chevy, yeah, a Chevy," Adams answered.

"What kind of Chevy?"

"A Cavalier, yeah, it was a Cavalier," Adams threw out his chest. "And it definitely was just two doors, because the guy in the back had to push the front seat forwards to get out and help with the body."

"Clean 'em up before you bring them downtown to my office," Lombardo ordered. "Book them as material witnesses and throw 'em into holding cells."

"Chief, could they be booked at the Four-Three?" Joyce asked, standing up and facing Lombardo. "I think we can get an OK from an Assistant District Attorney friend of ours up here and a High-bridge judge we know pretty well, to have these two released, you know, on their own recognizance and placed in our custody. You know, Savino and me. This way we can keep pumping them."

Lombardo was heading towards the two cops, cigar in mouth and fists at the ready when the lieutenant stepped in and asked the chief if he could speak to him outside.

"In the kitchen, sir?" he asked.

Lombardo paused for a moment, burning a hole into the lieutenant's forehead with his eyes. He bit down harder on his unlit cigar, turned and stalked into the kitchen.

"This better be good, you prick. I don't like to be second-guessed in front of people."

"Chief, look, our chances are piss poor for making a collar based on what these two losers just told us," the lieutenant started out. He was aware his life depended on explaining his reason for interrupting Lombardo.

"But these fuckin' guys, they shouldn't have allowed the local cops to get involved in the investigation," Lombardo snapped.

"I know, sir. But why not let them do what they can with some small-time Bronx ADA and a political-hack magistrate, and we can get on with the real investigation," the lieutenant suggested.

"Maybe, but I don't like those two cops snooping," Lombardo said, but he seemed to be relenting.

The lieutenant was encouraged and suggested, "Besides, Chief, these two dirt bags will probably jump bail and all of them will be left holding the bag."

"I like it. I like it. Turn Royce, his *guinea* partner, and their two fuckin' wino witnesses over to Captain Rollins or Rowland, or whatever the hell his name is."

"Reynolds, chief. Captain Reynolds," the lieutenant said crisply, "And the loud mouth cop's name is JOY—." He stopped when the chief actually spit a piece of his cigar stump against his chest.

"Yeah, whatever. He's a wiseass, too," the chief stomped out of the kitchen, brushed past Joyce, Savino, Munro, and the detectives, glared at the two witnesses, kicked open the door leading to the station's outer office, and walked towards his big black car parked half on the sidewalk. He spoke to no one on his way out.

Chris Russo picked up the now-three week old copy of the *New York Daily News* from his desk. It would stay there as a reminder, until they cleared this case. He looked forlornly at the headline: **TWO HOMELESS MEN SUSPECTED IN DEATH OF MAYOR'S FATHER AND PARKCHESTER COMMUNITY ACTIVIST.**

"We can forget that. Now we may have a real case, with two witnesses," the police commissioner said to his chief of detectives, throwing the paper across the room. "That was great work, Terry."

"You'd better call the mayor, boss," Hughes suggested.

"Yeah, he's not going to be happy with this. The 'two homeless men' rumor bought us all a little time. Now we've found them—unfortunately it seems that we've also cleared them as suspects in the homicides—but they could turn out to be key witnesses to the investigation. The press will get the story one way or the other. If not officially from the mayor, they'll get it from somewhere else."

When Russo got him on the phone, McCabe was not impressed.

"There are still no suspects, just 'alleged' witnesses. just as I said in my press release. There were no suspects and that still stands. I never affirmed or denied the homeless men theory, and the fact that the police now have some leads is just part of the ongoing investigation. Nothing that should be commented on by the mayor, or anyone else for that matter. So, there's no need for me, or you, Chris, to make a statement about these two guys you picked up today," the mayor proclaimed.

"Whatever you say, sir."

"In the 41 Precinct, Sector George," the dispatcher barked crisply.

"Sector George, over," the rookie cop had grabbed quickly at the car radio almost cracking the plastic cradle in which it rode. His older partner, seated on the passenger side, said calmly, "For Chris sake, kid, I got it," pulling the mike from the young cop. "Keep driving, keep driving," he ordered.

"Sector George, shots fired near the Hunts Point Sewage Treatment Plant, Ryawa Avenue off Manida Street," she said calmly.

"41 Sergeant, responding, too. I'm just a block away."

"10-4, 41 Sector George and 41 Sergeant," the unwavering voice responded. "Time, zero, zero, fifteen hours," she signed off.

The sergeant's car sped through the entrance to the plant, its floods scanning the piles of empty corrugated boxes, stuffed with newspapers and rags. "Somethin' happened that made them haul ass," the sergeant said to his driver. They leaped from the car, guns drawn and at the ready. Sector George was seconds behind. "Let's go." the sergeant shouted. "You guys, head south, we'll go north." They began walking slowly bending their bodies at the waist so that they were crouching ready to hit the ground if need be.

As one of the cops got to the end of the bulkhead that covered most of the plant's waterfront, he suddenly stood up and turned towards his partner and shouted "Fire, fire."

The flames were only about three feet high but the wind made it look like a rapidly spreading forest fire that the cops saw only on television. The sergeant had quickly discharged the carbon dioxide-charged fire extinguisher they pulled from his cruiser, the cone like nozzle spraying a strong, steady stream on to the small fire and extinguishing it.

"Oh my God," the young cop gasped, stopping abruptly, dropping his gun arm to his side and turning away momentarily from what his flashlight had picked up inside the still smoking remnants of the fire. The older cop had caught up with him by then, gun with barrel facing down, his flashlight joining his partners in illuminating two piles of black ashes. He grabbed the rookie's shoulder as the kid turned away from what they both were seeing and was throwing up.

There were what appeared to be two bodies lying amongst the smoldering soot. They were on their backs, shoulder to shoulder, just beginning to float in huge, bubbling puddles of their own blood. Both had black, smoke-stained plastic bags over their heads tied at their necks with electric extension cord lines—red, black, and green strands of wire sticking out from where the cords had been cut. The insides of the plastic bags were splattered with blood obscuring their faces. The four cops looked at each other.

"Is he OK?" the sergeant asked the cop still consoling his partner. He nodded a yes. The sergeant removed the bags from each of the bodies. Neither of them could have been more than twenty. Their outer jackets, shirts and undershirts had been ripped open by someone who must have grabbed all three layers at once and pulled. Black smoke was rising from charred pieces of clothing clinging to their bare chests. Their underpants were pulled down below their blood-drenched knees.

"Holy shit," one of them exclaimed. At the same time, they all focused their lights on the same body.

"Number One," the sergeant blurted, intuitively. "Number One, facing us to our left, and Number Two, facing us to our right. My God, look at the face." Number One's mouth had been ripped open beyond its normal range—the jawbone split in half. A blood-saturated object was sticking out from the gaping mouth. One of the cops moved closer, "Ugh, ugh, it's his penis. The bastards cut off his cock and jammed it into his mouth." The sergeant shifted his beam to Number Two, "Oh, yeah. Him, too."

"Squealers! *Omerta*! These guys got it because they ratted out somebody," the senior cop turned to his partner who had rejoined them.

"Hey, sarge. Look at this," his driver was still on Number One. "One right through the middle of *la testa*—the head. What a professional job." The other guy got it the same way, someone added.

As the sergeant checked out Number Two, he suddenly exclaimed, "Oh, shit. I know this fuckin' guy. He's a small time hood. What the hell is his name, Danza, Panza—no, no, now I know. Mikey Lanza." He also remembered that Lanza was one of Roger Horan's snitches from the detective's days as a cop in *Fort Apache*.

"Oh, boy. Oh, boy. Sarge, do you know the other guy?" Roger Horan had arrived at the scene after a call from the sergeant. It was almost three in the morning. "No, not yet. Once he's printed at the ME's we may find out. If it was a hit—which it sounds like, right, Roger?—They'll both probably have sheets."

"Well, I may beat you all to it," Horan began.

"What do you mean?"

"Try Johnny Farina."

❀   ❀   ❀

"What the fuck is going on here?" the police commissioner shouted at Hughes and Lombardo. Russo hadn't asked them to sit down. They each stood directly in front of their boss's oversized desk. Chris Russo had been seated, but his anger at them brought him to his feet, and he leaned on the edge of his desk as he asked his question.

"As you know, boss, Lanza was a C.I.—confidential informant—for Horan and this mutt Farina was a suspect in the murders who had been picked up by Horan and Covelli, but they had nothing to hold him on," Hughes explained.

"Terry. Terry. I know all that. What I want to know is where all this shit leaves us. I assume the two so-called witnesses are still stashed somewhere but we have nothing for them to witness. Right?"

"Yes. Yes, sir. That's correct, at this time. I was going to recommend to you——."

"Never mind, Terry. I want those detectives to be reassigned to Chester here and you ride his ass. My riding yours hasn't worked. My God, I haven't heard any progress on this case in a fuckin' month?

"Uh, about three weeks," the chief of detectives corrected.

"Oh, for Chris sake, Terry. The two of you get the hell out of here," Russo directed them.

It was almost impossible for Lombardo to keep his feelings in check.

"OK, *Chester*. I'll expect a plan of action on my desk by four," Hughes mumbled.

"And stay away from that fuckin' candy store or whatever they call that stupid police outpost on Westchester Avenue—I call it a fuckin' coop where the cops can sit on their big fat asses and order in the Dunkin' Donuts instead of being on patrol like they should be," Lombardo was shouting at Horan and Covelli. "That shit has gotten us all into enough trouble already. From here on in, it's good old-fashioned detective work, you *capece*? Call in your snitches, shakedown the dealers, pimps, numbers guys, anybody operating outside the law in the fuckin' Bronx," he snarled.

Their new boss stopped abruptly. He stood up slowly, smiled at them unexpectedly and, leaning over the desk, said softly, "I'm gonna give you guys a nice, cozy office, just down the hall and right near mine here on the 11th floor."

Both soon discovered that the constant noise of the overworked Xerox machine used by every detective assigned to the chief's office and which took up at least a third of their cozy office would force them to keep their telephone conversations brief. On the second day in their new surroundings, Horan got a call from a guy who walked an adjoining beat with him a few years ago. Horan pulled on the phone's stretch line until he was outside the noisy office. "Yeah, go ahead, Eddie, I can hear you now."

"Hey, this guy calls me out of the blue when I haven't heard from him since we graduated and I went on the cops and he got a fancy banking job. Anyhow he ended up working for some outfit that swings big investments in companies. He tried to explain all that stuff to me, but hell, Rog, I can't even balance my damn checkbook."

Horan waited for his friend to get to the point.

"Anyhow, this guy, his name is Wes Reiser, starts getting kinda dramatic. Says there's some bad stuff going on at this place where he works and he doesn't know who to talk to about it."

He heard a muffled laugh on the other end of the phone. "I told him that this sounds like the kinda white collar crime shit that the DAs office gets all excited about. Told him to call up a smart kid that I knew who handled that case back a while where those stock brokers were stealing their customers blind." The caller waited a beat and said, "Then he drops the big shoe."

"Yeah, what?" Horan asked in a bored voice. "He knows where Jimmy Hoffa is buried?"

"Hey listen up, smartass. He lays on me the name of one Gordon Halliday, who I read is a big time buddy of hizzonor the mayor." He paused again and then explained, "I don't like anything about what my old pal, my new-found long-lost buddy is telling me. Sounded like a real shit sandwich. But you got stuck with this murder case, old man McCabe, so I figure you already got your tit in a political wringer."

Horan groaned and said, "Thanks a fuckin' lot, Eddie. OK, where do I reach this guy"?

Wes Reiser sounded relieved when he got Horan's call.

"I understand that you have a degree in accounting, too?" Reiser asked, and went into more details than Roger's friend had supplied. The bank he had worked for was Westport Trust where his father was a senior vice president. He was now with Halliday Associates. His father, Gary, and Gordon Halliday had been classmates at Wharton and had started out together at Westport.

"You know Gordon Halliday? He's a close friend of the mayor's—although I think in today's *Times* they announced he wasn't going to be in charge of the McCabe reelection campaign. My call to Eddie was prompted by some strange stuff, possibly illegal, going on in my office. It's a little complicated, as I'm sure he told you. Could I talk you into having dinner with me?"

Horan hesitated. "First, before we eat, have you told anybody else about your suspicions?" Reiser assured him he hadn't. "Then it's got to be strictly between us. No one else, not your boss, not your family, not your associates, not anyone, understand?" Horan warned.

"No, great, I understand, let's have dinner tonight," Reiser said, obviously determined to unburden himself.

"OK, good,—tonight is OK—as long as you understand," Horan said.

"The *piccat di vitello* was delicious. Now what?" Horan said, lifting the napkin from his lap with both hands and patting the edges of his mouth.

It was Wes Reiser's treat and he picked *Parioli, Romanissimmo*, On East 81st Street, probably New York City's finest—and most expensive—Tuscan dining spot.

"We've got some very prominent, wealthy clients at Halliday—clients, meaning investors. We're always on the outlook for profitable, growing private companies that we can put some money into and get a good return for our investors," Reiser began.

"We still get a lot of our business from Westport Trust. We've developed into a kind of boutique. Here's what we do. We usually look for companies that are doing probably $5 million in pre-tax profits and want to raise money to grow. However, the owners don't want go into debt, so they avoid the banks. They don't want to go to venture capitalists because they'd have to give away too much of their business. Going public may be an option, but then, again, the owners lose control."

Reiser looked closely at Horan to make sure he understood.

"What Halliday Associates offer is A-the opportunity to raise capital, B-retain control of the company, and C-get some 'up front' money for themselves, their partners, and a few family members who were some of the original investors. How do we do that?"

Horan had propped up his chin with his hand and was trying to stay awake as Reiser droned on.

"So, say our due diligence—you remember that term from your accounting courses, right?—shows that the company is worth 20 mil. We usually go to selected investors—those who may have a particular interest or even experience in the business this company is in, and raise the money. But then we tell the owners that out of the proceeds they will 'buy back' 50% of the company. So they get what we call "a little bite of the apple."—We give them $20 million, they put ten back into the business, put the other ten in their pockets and keep control of the company."

Reiser took a big gulp of coffee and plowed ahead. "If we were on the mark, within five years the company will be in a position to go public-or we can sell it at a price at least five times what was originally put in the recapitalization deal. Everybody's happy." He looked around nervously and lowered his voice. "We've done fifteen deals since Gordon Halliday started the firm. The deals are now worth over two billion dollars."

Wes Reiser was in danger of losing his dinner guest, from the wine as well as his long and boring lecture on the intricacies of investment banking. So he cut to the chase.

"About a year ago, Halliday came in with a big deal of his own—new investors and a new company. We didn't get them from Westport Trust or WestVan or anyone that any of us knew about."

Reiser paused for a moment, carefully choosing his words.

"The company was Caribbean Moorings, Ltd. It had been set up in the Cayman Islands, where, I'm sure you know, secrecy laws make it possible to create corporations without disclosing their owners. Halliday handled the transaction himself. The word in the office was 'Ask no questions.' The new investors apparently provided all the capital for the new business. They have an ongoing account with us, which I supervise. We were told CM specializes in providing catering and cleaning services to island resorts and some cruise ships. Money, plenty of it, flows through our firm and into our bank—my father's bank, Westport Trust."

Horan's attention had picked up when he heard Cayman Islands. "Oh, oh. Can I take a guess?" he asked Reiser.

"Yeah, you got it.

"And what about your father?"

"I don't dare ask."

CHAPTER 9

After another month, the McCabe-Velez murders probe was getting little coverage from the media. A series of really nasty breaking and entering jobs by ski-masked perps up in affluent Fieldston filled readers' appetite for the macabre and the titillating. Details were sketchy, but a guy delivering Poland Spring Water in the community thought he spotted them, unmasked—four or five, apparently Latinos, he reported. A week later the same crew was ransacking a home when the owner of one of New York City's biggest commercial real estate companies and his wife, coming in from a party, stumbled in on the burglars. The executive was shot and killed. The media had their replacement for McCabe-Velez.

"Holy shit, he thinks the mayor's former campaign manager, and asshole buddy—Gordon Halliday—is laundering money?" Covelli exclaimed.

"Yeah, yeah, I was a little surprised, too. But I'm not sure how it ties in with the two homicides," Horan replied. "I don't think we should tell you-know-who right now. Do you?"

"Yeah, you're right. If we don't come up with something soon, we'll be back on foot patrol or, worse yet, get assigned here—permanently," Covelli smiled and pointed in the direction of Lombardo's office.

"Yeah, well, I was thinking about the Lanza-Farina killings," he began.

"Yeah, me too, Steve. They must have known more than they told us," Horan replied.

"Exactly. Do you remember when we picked-up Johnny? He said his dealer was Sal. We felt so screwed when the scumbag jumped at the chance to go into a lineup, we just let that go by. Right?" Covelli said, rolling his typing chair along the concrete floor of their cubicle to a point where he was almost shouting into his partner's ear.

Someone was making what seemed to be a couple thousand copies of something on the copying machine. "And don't forget, Mikey said he knew a guy, who knew a guy, who knew a guy. Shit, so far two guys down, literally down, and how many to go. We gotta try them all," Covelli added.

"Yeah, but Farina didn't give us a location. I'd bet it was near where he worked from, on the docks," Horan commented. "Better tell the boss what we're doing," he added, pointing to the wall in the direction of Lombardo's office. Covelli wrinkled his nose and said, "I don't think he's really Italian. Then again, maybe he's too Italian." They both laughed and went to the chief's office.

"Well, you *jabons* have come up with fuckin' air so far, so you might as well take a shot at this small-time dealer," Lombardo told them in a disgusted tone of voice.

"He's supposed to be a supplier, chief, not a dealer," Horan pointed out.

"Whatever. Anything to get you off your fuckin' asses." He didn't see Horan give him the finger as he walked out of the chief's office.

After seven straight days of surveillance they decided that the likeliest place to find Sal was at the ass end of Colgate Avenue at the Bronx River. It was the worst of the Bronx's slum neighborhoods. They positioned themselves in Covelli's old car. The car's heater wasn't working at full capacity so they nearly froze, but their hunch paid off. Sal showed up on time, and had six customers waiting. He palmed a small, white packet to each, and they handed him bills. A couple of his black customers would high-five with him, and one even said, "Thanks, brother."

"What a fuckin' world we're living in," Covelli whispered to Horan, "Where a guy says 'thanks' to a prick who's killing him."

Sal got into his car and drove about six miles to one of Hunts Point's abandoned piers at the foot of Farragut Street, where a line of seven customers were waiting patiently for him, including a kid who looked no more than fourteen and one of the homeless winos from the waterfront area, who must have scrounged up enough deposit cans and bottles to buy a dime bag.

"The cocksucker, let's get him," said Covelli, as they jumped from their car and moved quietly along the fence of a deserted warehouse, until they were directly behind Sal. Covelli jammed his snub-nosed revolver into the drug dealer's right kidney, with a little extra push, while Horan threw his left hand around Sal's neck and, with his right hand, thrust Sal's neck forward into a "death lock"—half hoping that Sal would resist. But he didn't struggle, just a loud "Ouch!"—as his customers scattered.

"Hey, I know you," Horan exclaimed "You're Paulie Conte's kid. Holy shit!" They put him in cuffs and walked him back to their car.

"Goddamnit, I knew I never saw this piece of shit parked here before, but I thought it was dumped by somebody who stripped it for parts," Conte said.

"Thanks, fucko," Covelli snarled. "Just get in the back—you'll find its luxurious interior more to your taste."

"Hey, what about my car? You guys ain't gonna leave it in this fuckin' shithole?" Conte asked.

"What did you say, asshole? I can't hear you," Covelli replied and shoved him into the Mustang.

Horan and Covelli were hoping that once they got to Sal the possible mob connection thing would start to make some sense, or prove to be a dead end. Sal was the son of Paulie Conte, who owned a big trucking company in East Tremont. Daddy would get the best lawyer that dirty money could buy-and Sal would be back on the street before the sun went down.

"Peddling in your old man's community—you're some prick," said Covelli, needling Sal Conte, who just looked back at him passively.

He was chewing on a toothpick, moving it from one side of his mouth to the other. It was driving Covelli crazy. Horan sensed it and playfully slapped his sidekick on the knee to calm him down. But they finally got a rise out of Conte when Horan gave him a quick version of the old man's pedigree. The old man wanted to turn his trucking business over to Salvatore, Horan recalled, but when he found out Sal was fooling around with crack he got agita and turned it over to Sal's younger brother, Augie. The cops knew the old man was "connected" way back, with some of the original Genovese mob in the Bronx, but was never more than a small player. Horan painted a very unflattering picture.

"If you so fuckin' smart, then ya' know I'm not gonna say anything until I talk to my lawyer," Conte said. Like Farina, he had taken Covelli and Horan for narcs. Their act hadn't worked with Johnny Farina, but they figured Conte was even more cocky and belligerent. Maybe it would work.

"We haven't accused you of anything, yet, although we got possession—a misdemeanor, sale—a felony, and we're soon going to be riding around town in your confiscated pride and joy parked back at the pier," Horan said.

"If it's still in one piece," Covelli added, smiling broadly for the first time since picking up Sal Conte.

After rattling Conte's cage for a while they finally gave up and told him they weren't narcs but were investigating a double homicide. He didn't even blink. But he almost swallowed his toothpick when Horan told him there were two eyewitnesses who saw him and an accomplice dragging one victim's body from a car—a Ford, Cavalier, that is—and into the alley of a store on Westchester Avenue, between Pugsley and Olmstead. Then Horan got a little creative and told Conte that the witnesses saw him and another man dump McCabe's body into a chair in the backroom office.

He slumped forward in his chair, took the toothpick from his mouth and closed his eyes. He opened and closed them again. Then Conte sat up straight in the chair and began scanning the room, first the ceiling, the walls, the floor. He then took a deep breath and looked at Horan and then to Covelli and said nothing. He put the toothpick back into his mouth and took his best shot. "Who are your fuckin' witnesses? Numb-nuts Lanza and no-brains Farina?" he asked, with contempt. Horan and Covelli didn't answer him. "You guys ain't got nothin' on me. I know it and you know it, too."

"We'll see, Sal, we'll see," Horan smiled softly, and then suddenly thrust out his right hand and yanked the toothpick out of Conte's big mouth and threw it on the floor.

Berlinger and Adams, to the disgust of Lombardo and McPartland, hadn't blown town but had stayed put at the YMCA at Castle Hill and Zarega Avenues where the Four-three cops had parked them.

"I don't know, as I told ya before, they were wearin' this dark get up—what did you call it again?" Berlinger asked, looking at Joyce.

"Navy pea-jackets and watch caps," Joyce answered.

"Yeah, but we couldn't see their faces, we said that before, right? Adams chimed in.

"No, no, you didn't say that before?" "Horan raised his voice.

"And so, we don't know nothin'," Berlinger said.

"Nothing? How come, when we talked to you last, you knew the car; you knew one guy was bigger than the other. What the hell goes here, guys?" Covelli asked.

"Hey, man, we don't just sleep on fuckin' newspapers—we read 'em too," Adams responded, choking himself with his right hand and throwing out his tongue.

The two cops looked at each other and shook their heads.

"OK, Sal, here's the way it's playing as of right now. The two eye-witnesses we told you about have definitely I.D.'d you as one of the guys they saw carrying the body of old man McCabe out of a Ford—a Cavalier, in fact—into his store. They've given a detailed description of your Co-conspirator and—wait 'till you hear this, Sally my boy—they got the license number of the car and guess what? It was reported stolen the night before you guys hit Morgan McCabe and was found abandoned the next day in Mott Haven," Horan began.

Sal Conte sat motionless.

Covelli looked at his partner in surprise. They hadn't had time to rehearse so they were both improvising, so he jumped in, "Yeah, and we had the lab boys do a test on the car that's been in our pound for the last coupla weeks? They got some beautiful prints, besides McCabe's blood, of course."

"And?" Conte lowered his head and stretched out his neck in a last-ditch attempt at defiance and looked at Covelli.

"We gotcha, Sally," he said quietly.

Sal Conte sat back in his chair. He said nothing for a while, merely sighed a few times and looked around the Xerox room they were sitting in.

"So how do I deal?" Conte finally asked.

"Well, you give us the other guy. Neither your friends Mikey or Johnny had time to tell us about him." Conte began squirming nervously in his chair.

"Hey, wait a minute. Dis deal is for old man McCabe and the other guy, and nobody else, ya understand?" he shouted, a rising note of panic in his voice.

"Yeah, yeah, OK, Sal, don't get excited," Covelli soothed him, looking over at Horan, who sat stone still. It was his partner's turn.

"No fuckin' good, Steve" Horan said flatly. "If it's only for the McCabe murders, the rules change. The best he gets is murder two, no death penalty, but no parole, that's all its worth."

"Nah, nah. I want felony murder and parole," Conte was sweating now.

"Well, Sal, Roger's right in a way. We got you good and if we don't get the other guy, so what? We close the McCabe killings. But we're still carrying the Lanza and Farina hits," Covelli explained. "And let's get real, Sal, you and the dirt bag that helped you hit those two guys, weren't on your own—you're both too fuckin' dumb to have thought it up on your own."

Conte twisted his head nervously from side to side.

"So without ratting out your finger, you got nothin'—nothin' except life with no parole." Horan repeated.

"Unless—unless," Covelli said softly.

"Unless, unless. What, what?" Conte cried out.

"Unless, you were willing to wear a wire, and we get the prick good, not just on you're ratting him out."

Conte shook his head OK.

"So, are we gonna be surprised when we hear who it is?" Horan leaned forward.

"Rossetti. It's Charlie Rossetti."

✤   ✤   ✤

"OK, you *guinea* prick let's hear you spill your fuckin' guts," Lombardo sat behind his desk, twisting a long, narrow cigar that protruded from the side of his mouth. Horan and Covelli worked hard to keep straight faces.

Conte didn't seem to be intimidated. He just sat back against the straight-back, wooden chair the chief had supplied for the occasion, heaved a big sigh and muttered.

"I was asked to whack the old man by Charlie Rossetti."

"Why the mayor's father—and the other guy?" Covelli demanded.

"How the fuck do I know? A hit is a hit, you guys know that," he looked at Horan and then to Lombardo. "Ya neva ask, or you'll never get another one," he added scornfully.

"All right. All right, Sal," Horan said. "So, this Charlie Rossetti. He works for Victor Albanese. Right?"

"I know nothin' like that."

"Yeah, right. So, why you?" Covelli asked, genuinely puzzled.

"Have you done any other hits scumbag?" Lombardo jumped in, before Sal could respond.

"Hey, wait a minute. No fuckin' way am I gonna discuss anything more than I'm supposed to. Right?" Conte exclaimed, looking pleadingly at Horan.

Chief Lombardo grunted, looked at the two detectives with a look of disgust and sat back in his chair.

"Why you?" Horan repeated.

"I got an assignment, *capece*?" he said, looking past Horan at Covelli.

"But, why you? You're a fuckin' drug dealer," Horan wasn't about to give up.

"And Charlie's my supplier. He likes the way I work," he said, with a flash of pride.

"You mean you did hits for him before?" Horan pressed him.

"Hey, that *guinea* prick tried that on me before. Forget it!" Conte replied, pointing at the chief, who chewed harder on his cigar.

"But you knew it was the mayor's father?" Covelli asked.

"Yeah, of course. A lot of plannin' goes into a whack," Conte replied, sliding back a bit on his chair, when he saw the angry expression on Covelli's face.

"OK, so who was your partner?"

"His name is Trevor Burns. That's all I knew about 'im," Conte protested.

"Whatta ya mean, that's all you *knew* about him?" Horan barked.

"I mean just that. I neva met the guy before we got assigned together on this whack," Conte said nonchalantly.

"What I'm saying is that you said, 'knew' not 'know.'" Horan bore in on Conte, as Covelli and Lombardo leaned forward in their chairs, not sure why Horan was following this line of questioning.

"What the fuck you talkin' about?" Conte said, holding his head up erect and then turning it a bit to one side.

"Well, if you had said, 'that's all I know about him' in response to Detective Covelli's question 'who was your partner?' that would mean, at least to me, that was all you knew about him then and that was all you knew about him now. But since you said, 'that's all I *knew* about him' that would mean that was all you knew about him then, but you know more about him now than when you first met him," Horan explained.

"What the fuck is he talkin' about?" Lombardo whispered to Covelli, using his thumb to nudge the detective in his side.

"OK, let me ask you this, Sal. You didn't know Burns before you were assigned together to whack old man McCabe and Ramon Velez. Correct?" Horan began a different tack.

"Yeah. Yeah. That's right. I mean—that's correct?" Conte tried a smile.

"Good. But since the hit, you've met him again. Is that correct?" Horan went on.

"Yeah, correct," Conte stopped smiling.

"In fact you may have gone drinking or something like that and you may have even gone to where he lives. Isn't that correct?" Horan asked. Covelli and Lombardo both saw where this was going and stared intently at Conte.

"Yeah, that's right—corect—oh, fuck it, yeah, that's right. How did you know?" Conte inquired.

"Because you said knew instead of know and that means—" Horan began.

"Stop the fuckin' shit already. We got it. We got it," Lombardo broke in.

Sal Conte folded and told his story.

They tracked Morgan McCabe and Ramon Velez for three weeks, sitting in different cars—supplied by Rossetti—on alternate days, one day down the street from the McCabe home on McGraw and one day down the street from Ramon Velez's tenement on Watson. They watched as Morgan left the house, precisely at six each morning, walked to the newsstand under the stairway leading to the Westchester Avenue elevated subway line at East 177th Street and Parkchester, where he picked up a newspaper, went to Bickford's and got his container of coffee, and finally arrived at the store at 2044 Westchester Avenue at 7:30 a.m., on the dot. They had been inside the store on three different occasions, pretending to look for something to buy.

While sitting on Velez, they were surprised to find that on each of the Wednesdays of the weeks they watched he and Morgan, the young super went to Parchester Paint and Hardware, precisely at eight in the morning. In fact, they timed one of their phony shopping trips when Velez was in the store with old man McCabe. They had seen both men sitting at Morgan's desk in the rear of the store.

Conte and Burns decided they would overpower the old man outside his house, take him to the store, supposedly to rob him, "and then whack them both, you understand?"

They waited down the street from Morgan McCabe's house that morning. He came through the front door exactly at six, picked up *The Times* lying on the welcome mat outside the front door, and threw it inside. He closed the door quietly, and walked down the twenty or so feet from the front of the house to the sidewalk. As Morgan turned right onto White Plains Road, heading towards Westchester Avenue, Conte and Burns made a U-turn with their car—a late-model Chevrolet, this particular morning—and pulled up to the curb next to McCabe.

Conte was driving. Burns opened the passenger side window, and shouted.

"Hey old man, where the fuck is McGraw Avenue?"

McCabe stepped towards the car. Conte jumped out and ran around the car and behind the old man, pinning his arms behind his body. Burns quickly opened the front side door.

"My God, what do you want?" McCabe yelled, as they jerked his arms behind his back.

"Just get in the fuckin' car. We're goin' to your store and clean out the register. That's what we want," Burns had told him.

"I can assure you, there's very little cash in the store," McCabe told them, as Conte pushed the old man's head below the roof of the car and shoved him into the front seat.

No sooner had the car left the curb, than Trevor Burns lunged at McCabe.

"Bye, bye, you old fuck," he shouted as he viciously clutched the old man's neck with both hands and, with an enormous backward thrust of his huge body, began choking him. He temporarily relieved the pressure on McCabe's throat, but only long enough to gather greater strength for a more deadly grip on his victim's neck.

Conte claimed he was shocked and asked Burns why he had killed McCabe in the car instead of at the store, as they intended to do. Burns replied that he had a better plan, but didn't explain it at that time. Conte said he was so upset, he pulled the car to the curb and took a long drink from a bottle of cheap vodka that he always carried with him in the glove compartment of any car he happened to be driving.

They parked in front of a store on Westchester Avenue at Pugsley, down the street and on the opposite side of the street from the McCabe store. They left McCabe, apparently dead, slumped in the seat. Burns pushed the front seat forward, pressing the body against the dashboard so as to squeeze past him as he got out from behind the back seat of the two-door Cavalier. They then crossed the street, and went into the alley separating Parkchester Paint and Hardware and Mantilla's bodega. They took McCabe's keys and opened the back door. They went inside the office and turned on the small lamp that stood on the desk just inside the back entrance of the storeroom. Then they went back to the car, carried McCabe's body to a chair facing the desk, and propped him up in a sitting position.

Conte headed for the large, old cash register in the front of the store, rang up a sale to open it and took out some thirty five-dollar bills and change. That was when Burns suddenly grabbed a plastic bag from the shelves, ripped it open, took out a length of rope and walked over to where McCabe was slumped in the chair. As Conte watched, puzzled, Burns looped the rope over Morgan's head and around his neck. With one enormous motion, he lunged forward and then with a swift backward pull, using all the strength in both arms, brutally garroted Morgan McCabe.

At this point, Conte claimed, he ran into the bathroom and threw up. When he came out, he saw that Burns had apparently cut off a piece of the rope he had taken from one of the store's shelves, and had thrown it on the floor in front of the chair holding McCabe's body.

"Now the fuckin' cops will think he was choked while sittin' at his desk. You know, *ginzo*, to make it look like a real robbery. Wake up for Chris sake!" Burns announced in a satisfied tone of voice.

Conte left the register draw open to simulate a robbery, which was part of the original plan. They planned to leave the rear lights on and the rear door open to give the impression that the store's owner had apparently surprised the robbers. By that time it was just about eight o'clock. And, Ramon Velez was about to become their second victim.

Conte and Burns took up positions behind a stack of wooden crates behind the door, but not so close to the side wall that they couldn't squeeze in between. They watched as Velez approached McCabe's body.

"We, I mean Trevor, the fuckin' Mick, was supposed to choke this guy, too. But then I couldn't believe what I seen. Trevor musta had this long knife, you know, like the old cowboys carried."

"A bowie knife," Horan said, in a voice choked with anger and disgust.

"Yeah, yeah, a long one. He pulled it out from inside his belt. He was like a fuckin' cat—he sprung from where we was hidin' and he was on this guy, without the guy ever knowin' what hit him," Conte said, almost admiringly.

"One in the side, the guy falls to his knees. Another in the back, the guy hits the floor, full of blood. Then, while the guy's layin' in his own blood, on the floor, the fuckin' Mick sticks him one more time," Conte said, concluding his story.

For a long time, no one spoke. Only the noise from the streets surrounding 1 Police Plaza broke the silence in the room as the late winter sun gave way to darkness.

❦   ❦   ❦

It was an unusually subdued group of cops who met in Chris Russo's office that evening. Covelli and Horan had stayed with Conte, while Lombardo and Hughes went to brief the police commissioner. As Lombardo began recounting what he had just heard, Russo interrupted him.

"Wait a minute, hold on. You're telling me that this guy, Rossetti, a member of the Albanese family, was a supplier of drugs to Conte, and the Albanese mob used him—apparently more than once—as a hit man. But what on earth was the reason for putting out a contract on Morgan McCabe and Velez?" Russo seemed stunned. He looked down at his desk and said, "So now you're telling me this animal is willing to wear a wire to make a deal for felony murder instead of a murder one or murder two rap."

"Yes, yes, sir, that's how it's flying as of now."

The police commissioner shook his head.

They should have been elated. They had one of the killers, knew who his partner was, or at least they had a confession from one and could possibly link organized crime to the murders through the use of a wired insider.

"But why in hell would they want to hit the mayor's father? As a warning to the mayor for something? For what?" Russo was totally baffled.

He placed his left elbow on the edge of his desk, raised his arm, rested his chin between the thumb and index finger, and began rubbing his face, lost in thought and oblivious to the two men standing before him. "Rossetti, Rossetti, of course, I know that *guinea* bastard," Russo finally said. "Don't they call him 'Charlie *Potsa*—you know, crazy?"

"Oh, boy, excuse me, commissioner, where did you pick that up?" Lombardo asked, obviously surprised and ignoring, intentionally or otherwise, the politically incorrect remarks of the city's top cop.

"What about the mayor? Should he be brought up to date on the latest developments?" Hughes asked, ignoring Lombardo's comment.

"Yeah, you're right, Terry. Of course, we're still talking about information given to us by a small-time dealer—and yet, on the other hand, he's saying things that would seem to be difficult for him to make up on his own," Russo said cautiously. "And this guy is going to be wearing a wire for awhile. Too dangerous. Too dangerous. Let me think about calling the mayor." He looked up at Hughes. "Terry, what about that other animal, Burns?"

"We've been discussing that situation, commissioner. If we pick him up it would probably be traceable to Conte and blow his cover—not to mention blowing off the top of his head. I think we should wait and see what the wire produces," Hughes responded.

Russo nodded his head and got up from his chair. Hughes and Lombardo left their chairs and headed for the door. Chips Lombardo got there first and stepped aside so that his boss could go ahead of him. He hesitated for a moment, "By the way, Commissioner, you're right, Rossetti is known as Crazy Charlie, but it's really *pazzo*, Charlie *Pazzo*, you know, that's how those of us whose families came from Sicily would pronounce it." Hughes didn't turn around to see the police commissioner's reaction to this inane remark; he just grabbed his aide's arm and pushed him out of the door.

The judge of the 12th Judicial District Supreme Court was sitting at his desk in his chambers on the Grand Concourse—the detectives did not dare sit down. He did not find it amusing that Horan and Covelli were asking for a tap order on a line that went into St. Bernard's R.C. Church, a beleaguered Vatican outpost on Third Avenue in the mostly black Morrisania Section, and leave a message for "Father Maloney." After they explained that the line didn't go into the private part of the rectory but only to an answering machine in the church office, he relented, but warned them against abusing the tap.

"Well, detectives, I'm not too happy with this because I think it could be seen as a fishing expedition having no specific target. Although you state that you believe there is a connection between the activities of this Rossetti and the unsolved murders of the mayor's father and the other gentleman, you don't say anywhere in your affidavit whether or not he, Rossetti, is a suspect or not."

"That's correct, your honor, but we believe that Rossetti may have material knowledge of certain facts pertaining to those homicides," Covelli answered.

"Oh, all right. OK, I'll sign it, but I'm amending your application so that you can only monitor such calls after five p.m., each day, and at no other time. Do you understand that, officers? You are not to listen to any calls coming in or going out of that rectory, except after five each evening," the judge directed. "Raise your right hand, detective," he ordered Covelli.

"Go ahead, Sal, make your call," Horan ordered. The two detectives hovered over Conte in his basement apartment while he made the first call with his bugged phone.

"I'm sorry, St. Bernard's business office is closed for the day. Please wait for the tone and then leave your name, telephone number, the time and date and to whom you would like to leave a message. Thank You," was the recorded message that came through. After the beep Conte said, "Uh, this is Sal, and it's, uh, about ten after seven on February the fourteenth. This call is for Father Maloney. And, uh, he knows my number."

Charlie Rossetti didn't call back for a week. Horan and Covelli removed and listened to the tapes from Conte's tap and the St. Bernard's service each day. Conte seemed to be playing it straight with them. Almost a week to the day after they started the tap, "Father Maloney" called and, in a rasping voice, said he'd meet with Conte the next morning—"You know where."

"Finally, finally. Here we go," Horan said. "Any side bets on who that was, Steve?"

"Tony Soprano?"

"Hey, that's fuckin' cold!" Sal exclaimed as Horan slung the silver, aluminum NAGRA—voice recorder—over the hood's head and on to his broad chest. "And it's too damn heavy, too," he threw in.

"Come on, Sal. It's only about 3 pounds and it'll warm up to your skin. Look the bellyband that goes around your waist is made of Velcro. That's warm right?" Horan smiled as he snapped the band in place after it automatically adjusted to Sal's thirty-six waistline.

Steve Covelli was disentangling the two plastic, tan, less than a penny in diameter, stereo mikes, running from the top of the three by five inch micro-recorder. "Rog, what do you think? On each side of his chest or on the inside of his crotch—right next to his balls!" he asked his partner, looking over at Sal with a clearly malicious chuckle.

"Balls? What's this balls shit," Sal hollered, looking only at Horan.

"Sal, there's always a chance that Rossetti, *the priest*—or somebody—will go through the friendly pat down routine. You know, giving you a playful frisk. I don't think any of your macho *guinea* friends will grab you by the balls. What do you think?

"Nah. Nah. They'd never do that," Conte agreed.

"We want you to wear bulky clothes, particularly loose fitting pants now that we've decided where to put the mikes," Horan went on. "OK, Sal, here's how it works."

There were newer micro-cassette tapes on the market, but the reel-to-reel NAGRA that they used had better transmission quality and the tapes lasted longer, three hours. They opened the cover to the power pack and showed him the two small plastic reels passing through a pair of metal, sensitivity guides. The top of the recorder had four terminals, one each for the mikes or speakers, one permanent on/off switch that could be locked into place, and one terminal attached to a foot-long fiber-covered line of wire connected to a portable on/off button that could be hidden inside the clothing of the wearer and which the wearer could control.

Covelli activated the manual on/off switch:

"This is Detective First Grade Steve Covelli on special assignment in the office of the Special Investigations Division, Police Department of the City of New York. The time is eight p.m., on February 12th. We are monitoring an electronic surveillance device being worn by Salvatore Conte," he recited.

"What the fuck is he doin'?" Conte asked, always to Horan.

"Nothing, Sal, its just some legal stuff. All you gotta do is go to this meet and stay cool."

"So, Sal. What's up? I understan' ya wanted to talk with me," Charlie Rossetti said, sauntering up to Conte in St. Raymond's Cemetery. Conte was leaning against a huge mausoleum that must have contained at least six tombs and with the family name—*Castellano*—emblazoned over the white marble entrance. Covelli and Horan could hear both men's voices clearly over the receiver in their temporary listening post established in a vacant construction shack on Calhoun Avenue near the Bruckner Expressway.

"Lookin' for a new assignment already?" he added, throwing back his huge head and laughing, displaying at least a three-day growth of beard.

"Nah, nothin' like that. I just thought you might want to go out an do a little boozin'—you know like we used to," Conte stood up straight and found himself in an affectionate bear hug suddenly thrown out by Rossetti—who took the opportunity to pat down his good buddy.

"Sure, kid, sure. That'd be good. How about, say, this Friday night in Angelo's about nine. OK?" Rossetti responded.

"Yeah, Yeah, that'll be great, Charlie. See ya then," Conte replied, and gave Rossetti a big *abrazzo*. Just for the hell of it he patted down his friend, too.

Angelo's was a Pelham Parkway Section anachronism. The red-sauce only, Italian bistro had been in the Vallone family for over sixty years. It was also a mob hangout, where in bygone days plenty of cops used to shovel down the pasta and socialize with the local wise guys. The younger generation of cops didn't like either the food or the clientele.

"They got no real taste for home-cooked Italian food," Paddy Vallone would complain, "Even if they're Italian, they come from the suburbs—ya know, Lon*G* Island, Yonk*as* and places like that. What the hell do they know about good, quality, Tuscany cooking?"

Rossetti was late. Conte waited outside *Angelo's*. He didn't mind the cold wind whipping past the store because he had on a few more layers of clothes than he usually wore.

"Sal, baby," Rossetti suddenly materialized from nowhere. He threw his arms around Conte's shoulders, slowly moved them down the outside of the young hoods arms, then under the arms and along both sides of his torso, winding up at Conte's ass, which he patted softly. Conte was glad that the layers of clothing covered the wire. He wasn't so much worried about getting a cold; he was insulating himself from an illness that could prove terminal.

After two hours of serious eating they'd already finished off two bottles of Carlo Rossi, the cheap wine that Paddy Vallone reluctantly agreed to stock at Charlie's request. It was close to midnight and although they were the only ones left in the dining room, the management of Angelo's would never flash the overhead lights, bang dishes or make a move to close. *Un Respecto* for their customers, nothing else was as important.

"So, kid, you need another assignment, right?" Rossetti was slurring his words badly by now.

"Well, ya know, Charlie, the fuckin' money is terrific," Conte answered.

"Yeah. Yeah, you're right. But you must wait, kid. Sometimes there's no one needin' wackin', *espet?*"

Conte looked a little forlorn.

"Hey, kid, come on," Rossetti reached over the table and gave Conte a not very gentle pat on the cheek. "Maybe, just maybe, somethin' will be comin' up soon. There are a couple things happenin.'"

"Like what, Charlie?"

"Come on, kid. You know I can't discuss such things," Rossetti said, taking another gulp of the cheap wine.

"Yeah, I know, Charlie. But I never asked nothin' about the McCabe whackin'" Conte threw out. "And, I did a good job, right? Just what you told me to do."

"Yeah, you're right. But I couldn't tell you anymore then and I can't tell you anymore now."

Horan and Covelli were sitting in the rear of their off green, Chevy, commercial van, Rhode Island Registration 71 RS 5234, with a hand-painted sign that said "Lobsters from Nantucket" on the side, parked on White Plains Road near Morris Park. They both straightened up and listened intently.

"Ya mean, it may involve the mayor, again?" Conte asked.

"Could be, *paisan*. Could be," he reached for his half-full wine glass but knocked it over, the wine spilling onto the table cloth and the glass rolling on its side, to the edge of the table and off and on to the floor, where it shattered.

"Hey, *dov'e Pasquale*. Where's Paddy?" Rossetti shouted.

"I'm sorry, *signore*, he's gone home. Can I help you please," the maitre d' had rushed from behind the reservations desk where he had been dutifully standing since the last guests had left two hours ago.

"Another bottle of your best, ya know Carlo Rossi," Rossetti ordered.

"Coming up, sir. More of our best," he obeyed, turning and rolling his eyes at the remaining waiter and bartender.

"OK, kid. Where was we?" Rossetti slurred.

The next thing Horan and Covelli heard was a loud thud. They jumped up from their seats in the body of the van and were heading for the rear double doors. Suddenly they heard Conte's voice, "Shit. I guess dinner's over. Hey, Charlie wake up, wake up. Ah, shit, hey *paisan* give me a fuckin' hand will ya."

Later, while they removed the wire from Conte they found out that Rossetti had passed out, his head falling loudly on to the table. Apparently someone in Angelo's knew which car service to call and its driver carried out Rossetti to the waiting stretch limo. Angelo's maitre di' and waiter started cleaning up and Conte staggered out into the night.

When Horan and Covelli thought it was safe, they picked him up with their van on Matthews Avenue, about five blocks away.

The next morning Lombardo listened to the tape and told them he wanted them to move on it right away. Covelli and Horan tried to convince him that it might be a good idea to let things play out so that they could determine why McCabe and Velez had been hit. But Lombardo didn't want to hear it.

"We've solved the homicides," he said, quickly turning his attention to Horan's partner. "That's what our assignment was."

When the chief of detectives was briefed Lombardo recommended that they move on Rossetti's statements right away.

"Hey, Chips, we still don't know why McCabe and Velez were hit. Conte says, 'ya mean, it may involve the mayor?'" and Rossetti says, 'Could be *paisan*, could be!' so maybe McCabe was killed because he was the mayor's father. But we still don't know why," Hughes said.

Covelli and Horan just stood there and said nothing. Lombardo squirmed uncomfortably in his chair.

"Besides, what about the possibility of another hit somehow involving the mayor?" Hughes went on. "I think we should hang in there and see if Conte can meet with Rossetti again, pick-up where they left off. But let's see what the boss has to say," he said, standing up and leading the way up to Russo's office.

"Holy shit, so while Rossetti's drunk, he makes a half-assed admission that he was the guy who ordered, or at least passed on the order for, Morgan McCabe to be killed. It's at least circumstantial proof that despite all the mayor's notions that it was a bungled robbery or burglary, it could have been a mob hit. Why we don't know," Russo said thoughtfully and then smiled, "Maybe I'll ask the mayor!"

Hughes and Lombardo wondered if the PC really had the guts to put that kind of question to Tom McCabe.

Russo leaned back in his chair and added, "Let's listen some more. Then maybe I'll call my friend Tommy McCabe."

PART III

And it grew both day and night.
Till it bore an apple bright.
And my foe beheld it shine,
And he knew that it was mine.

—Blake, st. 3

CHAPTER 10

"Hello, this is Cathy Russo. May I speak to Miss Halliday, please?

"Hold on please."

"Thank you."

"I'm sorry, Ms. Russo, can you tell me the purpose of your call? Does Ms. Halliday know you?"

"Would you just tell Ms. Halliday that my husband and I are close friends of Tom McCabe," Cathy Russo said.

After a moment she heard someone else come on the line.

"Hello. Eve Halliday speaking."

"Ms. Halliday, this is Cathy Russo. My husband is the police commissioner and a friend—," she cleared her throat, "of Tom's."

"Oh, yes, you're Chris's wife. I'm sorry, Cathy—Can I call you Cathy?" she said.

"Sure, Eve," Cathy Russo said, and then took in a deep breath. "Tom's a good friend of mine and my family's, and I'm concerned about what's going on between my husband and Tom. You have every right to tell me to mind my own business, but I've got to do something about this problem."

"Well, Cathy, I'm kind of surprised, but flattered, that you think I have that much influence over Tom McCabe, anymore," Eve Halliday said.

"Anymore? Whoa, enlighten me on that, Eve," Cathy Russo asked.

"Well, we don't see each other as much as we did—but hey, who's counting. Right? No just forget that I ever said that, Cathy," Eve Halliday answered.

"Right. Gotcha! In any event, I'm not too sure how much influence I have over Chris Russo. But I sure as hell am going to try to get those two guys back together again," Cathy Russo said.

"Of course. Me, too. Let's get together. When and where would you like to meet?"

"Well, before we decide on that, I want to ask you about inviting Mrs. McCabe, too," Cathy said.

"Ellen? Ellen McCabe?" Eve Halliday repeated, a bit taken aback.

"Yes, I thought she could be helpful. But I understand if you have a problem with that," Cathy followed up.

"No. I really don't have a problem with that," Eve said.

"Good. I'll set it up," Cathy Russo countered.

Sal Conte left two messages a day for a week for "Father Maloney" on St. Bernard's voice mail. "For some reason, he may have been spooked by the first meeting, Sal," Horan speculated. "He was so sloshed that night he doesn't remember what he did say to you, or didn't," Covelli added. What they didn't tell Conte was that other interesting callers were also leaving messages for the non-existent priest.

"Let me see, Roger Horan, being first duly sworn on oath, here deposes and says:

1. I am a Detective, First Grade, with the Special Investigations Division, Police Department of the City of New York and have been so employed since—I see—I see—and finally, based on the information contained herein, and my experience and training, I believe that certain criminal activities are being conducted over the following

telephone instruments—," the judge was mumbling while reading as Roger Horan and Steve Covelli stood in front of his desk inside the magistrate's chambers.

"Hey, wait a minute. You want to monitor all the telephone calls coming in and going out from two businesses and a private residence."

"Yes sir, your honor, that's correct," Horan replied.

"All related to the investigation of the homicides of Morgan McCabe and Ramon Velez. Is that correct?" the judge went on.

"Yes sir," Horan was wondering if the judge was going to blow them off.

"And you believe that the criminal activities that you want to monitor are related to those crimes? I can see probable cause in the application to intercept calls in and out of Maloney Sand and Gravel on Bronx River Avenue and 174th Street, which you allege is used by a Charlie Rossetti, allegedly a member of the Victor Albanese organized crime family, but I fail to see the justification for authorizing you to monitor calls coming in and going out of the other business—let's see, here it is, Halliday Associates, Inc., on Broad Street, no less, nor do I see why you want to monitor calls going to the home of, Mr. Gordon Halliday, in Fieldston."

"But your honor, we believe—," Covelli began.

"Forget it. I'm crossing out the last two instruments. Period." Without looking up from his desk, he crossed out the appropriate sections of the application and signed it. Then he tossed the five-page document back at the two cops.

For the next two weeks Horan and Covelli listened each day to the calls coming in and out of Maloney Sand and Gravel as well as what turned up on the taps on the rectory voice mail and Sal Conte's basement apartment on Fordham Road. They were also hearing some interesting conversations on the lines in Gordon Halliday's office—and the dedicated line in his home.

"Hello, Father Maloney, this is Sister Eve. Are we on for Saturday night or what? Give me a call at the convent. Bless you, Father."

The last two taps could get them in big trouble. Not only were they unauthorized and illegal, but they could also compromise or taint the evidence in whatever this case turned out to be. But as Horan put it when he and Covelli agreed to take the risk, "After all, what they don't know can't hurt us. Like, tapes, what tapes?"

❦   ❦   ❦

"OK, Sallie. I got you're next assignment," Charlie Rossetti almost warbled. He was calling from a public phone to Sal's Arthur Avenue basement apartment.

"Holy shit!" Horan exclaimed in the laundry room, throwing his headset onto the floor and dialing his partner who was home on his night off.

❦   ❦   ❦

"We gotta move fast," Hughes reacted after hearing Lombardo's report of what the detectives had heard an hour ago. They got into to see Chris Russo forthwith.

"Holy shit. They're gonna hit Gordon Halliday?"

"Yes, and there's more, boss," Hughes said cautiously, faltering in his delivery so that the police commissioner squinted strangely at his detective commander. "Horan and Covelli here have some information indicating that Gordon Halliday is into Victor Albanese for a lot of money—gambling, the horses—and Charlie Rossetti, clearly speaking for Victor, has been squeezing him to talk to the mayor about something. We don't know what at this time," he added.

"Information they came across? From where?" Russo asked.

"Don't ask, sir," Hughes responded nervously.

"They also *just* told us that they had picked up something from a guy Horan came across alleging possible money laundering at Halliday Associates—there could be a connection with Rossetti," he added, looking sharply at Horan and Covelli. "What's your friend's name?"

"Wes Reiser," Horan answered.

"OK. We can get the feds on Gordon Halliday if in fact he is screwing around with money and the mob, etc., later on," Russo said to Hughes, Lombardo, Horan and Covelli as they stood in front of his desk. The excitement in the room was so intense no one even thought of sitting down. "But we gotta take everybody at the same time, so there's no tip off. *Capece*?" he inquired. "And, we gotta make sure that we prevent any attempt to hit Gordon Halliday," he added, looking sternly at Hughes.

"Yes. Yes, sir," the relieved chief of detectives responded, "We're going after Trevor Burns and Charlie Rossetti at the same time.

Covelli and Horan, with Sal Conte in tow, would pick up Trevor Burns and Lombardo would assemble a team from the Special Investigations Division to pick up Charlie Rossetti.

🍁　　　🍁　　　🍁

Conte knew exactly where to find Trevor Burns. After the hit on Morgan McCabe and Ramon Velez, Conte and his assigned partner decided to celebrate. It was Trevor Burns who suggested they do some bouncing in the Irish bars in the Norwood Section of the Borough, allegedly an IRA stronghold, although many suspected that the community was intentionally maligned to bring in the tourist trade. They ended up in *The Green Tree on Bainbridge Avenue.*

After five hours of partying, Sal Conte and Trevor Burns had collapsed in the Burns apartment on the top floor of a seedy, rundown brownstone on Hull Street just off East 205th Street, one of the community's main streets. To top off their celebration, Conte's car was towed away from a fire hydrant by the city's Department of Transportation. He spent the next two days with Trevor Burns. It was the last time he saw him, according to Sal Conte.

The two detectives took Conte with them in Covelli's Mustang. "I hate this piece of shit," he groused. Covelli ignored him. Conte kept nervously pulling at the wire he was wearing.

"I hate this fuckin' thing, too" he mumbled.

"Yeah, right. Just keep repeating to yourself—No murder one, no murder two, just felony murder and you'll be surprised how much you'll get to like it," Covelli reminded him.

They parked a block away on Decatur Avenue around the corner from Trevor Burns Hull Street apartment. The description given by Sal Conte made one out of every three males the detectives saw a suspect. For over a half-hour the two cops listened to Sal say, "No, that's not him," to what seemed to be a "couple of hundred of these fuckin' Irish skells," Horan remarked.

"OK, get out of the car," Covelli ordered.

"What?" Conte exclaimed.

"Out. Get outta the fuckin' car," Covelli almost shouted.

"We're goin' to Trevor's apartment and see if he's there," Horan explained.

"Hey wait a minute. I'll point him out to ya, but no way am I gonna let him know that I fingered him," Conte offered, shaking his head from side to side.

"How the hell are you going to tape him, if you don't go face to face with him?" Horan explained. "Don't worry, *paisan*, we're right behind you."

"Yeah, that's what I'm afraid of. You guys are gonna be way behind me."

The two detectives walked on the west side of Hull between 204th and 205th Streets across the street from where Trevor Burns's mangy brownstone was situated while Conte stayed on the east side. As he approached his accomplice's house, and went up the six concrete steps leading to the front door they slowly crossed the street. There were no doorbells in the dark, badly-scarred vestibule nor was the inside door locked, in fact the glass on that door was smashed with slivers still balancing themselves on both the upper and lower frames. Conte went through the inside door and the two cops hurried up the front steps and quickly stationed themselves in the lower hallway of the house. They waited until Conte got to each of the four landings leading to the top floor and then they started walking softly half way up to where he had reached. As Conte got to Burns's floor the detectives motioned for him to wait for them until they were standing next to him.

"OK, Sal. Easy now. Which is his apartment?" Steve Covelli asked in a low voice.

"At the end of that hallway," Conte whispered, pointing to his right. It was about twenty feet away from where the three of them were standing.

"Go," Horan almost mouthed, with a soft wave of his right hand, index finger pointing towards the direction of Trevor Burns's apartment.

The two detectives unholstered their 9mm Glocks and watched him.

Sal Conte moved slowly and somewhat reluctantly as he walked towards the apartment they hoped Burns would be occupying. The two cops started to follow, holding their weapons in a by-the-rules standby position, as Conte got halfway to his destination. After a few more steps, Conte stopped. The cops stepped up their pace until they got to where Conte was still standing. Covelli removed his right hand from the butt of his revolver, switching the weapon to his left hand and pushed Conte forward by digging his right fist into the middle of the pusher's back and pointing in the direction of where they suspected Burns was holed up.

As Conte got to the front door of the apartment he stopped and looked back at the two detectives. Horan arched his eyebrows, freed his right hand from his revolver and threw it out hands palm up. "Well? Knock on the fucking door," he whispered.

"Trevor, are you in there? It's Sal. Sal Conte. I gotta talk to you," he said, in a suddenly hoarse and obviously nervous voice.

No answer from the other side of the door.

Horan went through the same motions. "Knock, again, goddam-nit," he whispered to Conte.

"Trevor. Trevor, it's Sal——." Before Conte could finish speaking or even knock, the door to the apartment burst open with such force that the top hinges burst from the wood molding causing the door to fall on its side, blocking the now open entrance. A huge, hulking creature of a man, long, straggly hair sticking out from under a grubby navy watch cap and a face covered by a wild, red beard, bolted from the inside of the apartment and savagely kicked at the fallen door which flew off its remaining hinge and was heading towards Conte, who was still standing at the door—frozen in place.

The flying door hit against Conte's lower legs. He stumbled back-wards and fell against the wall opposite Burns's apartment. Conte slumped to the ground, but quickly stood up and turned to run.

Conte didn't take more than a few steps, when the occupant of the apartment quickly reached inside what seemed to be a layer of coats, pulled out a small, black object, dropped to one knee, extended his right hand which was holding the weapon and aimed at the fleeing Conte.

"Watch out! He's got a piece," Horan screamed. At that same time the black thing exploded, the first shot hitting Sal Conte in his back. He went down and before Horan and Covelli could start firing back, the hulk spotted the two cops and a second shot tore into the left side of Covelli's neck, just above the vest. The senior partner of the team stumbled back, splattering the walls with blood from the gaping wound and then collapsing across the steps of the landing leading to Burns's floor. His police radio sprung from his belt and bounced down the stairs to the next landing. Horan dove facedown onto the hallway floor and began a series of rapid rolls with his body as the shooter kept blasting away at them. He didn't stop until the gun clicked on an empty chamber. Horan leaped to his feet and raced towards the shadowy figure that seemed momentarily stunned by his weapon's failure to keep firing. As Horan reached the assailant who was still in a kneeling position he dove at him, knocking him on to his back. Horan reached back and with a wide arc of his right arm crashed the butt of his Glock to the side of the shooter's head. Blood began gushing from the deep wound as he rolled over on to his stomach and his immense body stiffened.

"Officer down, 356 Hull Street, top floor. Backup, we need backup and paramedics—forthwith," Horan was screaming as he tore the portable radio from his left front suit pocket, and was now racing to where his partner was stretched out on the stairs, face down.

"Steve, Steve," he yelled.

He gently glided Covelli's body until his partner was on the flat surface of the landing, on his back, face up, but eyes closed. Horan saw blood pouring from his partner's neck. He ripped the handkerchief from his pants pocket and began pressing hard against Covelli's neck, hoping against time to stem the surging tide.

Sal Conte was breathing heavily, but was conscious. He had taken a shot square in the middle of his back but survived compliments of the NYPD-issued flak jacket.

When the paramedics arrived they found Horan still cradling the lifeless body of his partner.

They were all rushed to Montefiore Medical Center at 210th Street.

Russo and Hughes were at the scene within minutes. The mayor was not far behind them.

"Chris, I'm terribly sorry. Will this ever end?"

Russo looked away from the sidewalk where the paramedics had just lifted the gurney holding the body of Steve Covelli into an ambulance, and stared at McCabe. His moist, tired eyes said it all. Terry Hughes briefed the mayor.

Three days later they would be together again at the traditional Inspector's funeral for a fallen cop, this time in Steve's home parish of St. Barnabas in Woodlawn. It was a raw, damp morning, with a steady drizzle of light rain. It always was. The mayor, who never wore a hat, placed his right hand over his heart, as the uniformed pallbearers lifted the highly polished, but simply designed, casket from Mulligan and Reilly's hearse. The small, watery beads trickled down from Tom McCabe's forehead, detouring ever so lightly around his nose, on their way to his chin and onto the roadbed of Martha Avenue. The police commissioner stood to the mayor's right, holding his light tan, felt hat over his heart. The uniforms to their left and right and behind them, saluted smartly. Steve Covelli's young widow and her children walked solemnly behind the pallbearers, Roger Horan gently embracing his partner's wife and the young boy and girl holding the white-gloved hands of Community Police Officers Brian Joyce and Vince Savino from the 43.

❦   ❦   ❦

Every reporter at police headquarters knew that Horan and Covelli were the lead investigators in the McCabe-Velez murders case. The investigation would be back as the lead story in every edition following the usual expansive coverage of Steve Covelli's funeral, Russo had remarked.

Victor Albanese was livid—a cop killing was the worse thing that could have happened to them, he told one of his hoods. "Even the fuckin' horseback cops will be lookin' for us now, for Chris sake."

❦   ❦   ❦

Horan was told to take some time. The Bronx Homicide Task Force guys would take over temporarily, they said. No way. After spending the day of the funeral with Steve Covelli's family, on East 235th Street in Woodlawn, he was the lead interrogator of his partner's killer. Burns said that he shot at some guys whom he thought were "out to get him" for reasons he couldn't explain.

They all had guns, he said, and he was defending himself. He admitted knowing Sal Conte, but nothing else. They did some crack together, that was it.

"Rossetti? The mob" Come on, it was bad enough dealing with one stupid, fuckin' *guinea*—Sal," was the way he put it to Horan and the other detectives.

When both Sal Conte's and Trevor Burns's prints came back from the F.B.I. the detectives discovered that Trevor Burns was a fugitive, a member of the Westies from New York City's tough Hell's Kitchen Section on Manhattan's West Side.

"Westies. Who the hell are they?" someone asked in a quickly assembled meeting in the chief of detectives' office. Horan explained, "They were a bunch of Irish thugs who worked as enforcers for most of the city's Mafia families, carrying out hits and getting rid of the bodies."

Burns had outstanding warrants charging him with murdering five people. Their genitals had been mutilated and the bodies torched and dumped in three of New York's five boroughs. "Mikey and Johnny make seven," Horan said to a guy from the Latent Print Section who handed them a printout of Burns's sheet.

"We got them all," Hughes reported to the police commissioner, "Lombardo just called me on the cellular. They have Charlie Rossetti at headquarters already."

"Ordinarily, I would say, great work," the police commissioner responded, with little enthusiasm. "But what a price we have had to pay, dear lord."

When the sullen top brass reassembled at police headquarters, Chris Russo turned to both Hughes and Lombardo and said, "Why not make the assignment of Savino, Joyce and Sergeant Munro to the detective bureau permanent?"

Both detective commanders were caught off-guard, and showed no reaction to the police commissioner's comment. Lombardo's stomach made a rumbling sound, "It's *tormina*—you know a little colic—from everything that's happened," he volunteered. Neither Russo nor Hughes smiled.

Terry Hughes spoke up. "I think it's a great idea. It'll be a boost all around. For detectives as well as the Community Police Officers. We'll give 'em gold shields tomorrow."

Captain Reynolds couldn't wait to tell the two CPOs and their sergeant.

An hour later he was back on the telephone with Terry Hughes.

"Chief, I'm not too sure how to say this. It is certainly a first for me, if not the department," the 43 commander began.

"What do you mean? What's up?" Terry Hughes interrupted.

"Well, the three of them were grateful for your offer—and in fact asked if they could respond to you in person," Matt Reynolds went on.

Interruption again by the chief of detectives. "Offer? Respond? What the hell are you talking about?"

"They don't want to be detectives, they want to stay where they are. However they're looking forward to working with Roger Horan—and you all—again. Temporarily, that is," the captain's deep swallow was clearly audible to the three-star chief to whom he was talking.

"I'll be a son of a bitch!" Russo exclaimed when Terry Hughes filled him in on the conversation with Matt Reynolds.

"Yes, sir. I felt the same way," Hughes said, while shaking his head in disbelief, too—he thought.

"No, no. I mean those guys are right! The only reward any cop can look forward to is becoming a detective—getting a gold shield. Just being a damn good cop gets them no official recognition," Russo explained as he saw the bewildered expression on Hughes' face.

"As you said earlier, Terry, we'll give 'em the gold shields. Let them help Horan get those two material witnesses—and then we'll give them their shields and send 'em back to the 43," the police commissioner continued. "In fact we should start rewarding more CPOs that way. Do a good job walking your most dangerous of streets—get a gold shield—and go back to those streets. It makes a lot of sense," he said.

"You know guys—these three or any one of them—could be the last cop or cops that we will ever see. They're out of their generation. They're like the cops we worked with many years ago. They're like we used to be," Chris Russo went on to a clearly astonished Terry Hughes.

CHAPTER 11

L ieutenant McPartland from Lombardo's office had led a small
army of Special Investigations Division and Joint Organized
Crime Task Force detectives to pick him up Charlie Rossetti at his
sand and gravel business on the Bronx River.

"This way the press will hear about it and think that it's just
another mob pickup," the chief of detectives had reasoned.

The caravan swept through the front gates of Maloney Sand and
Gravel, and barged into Rossetti's office located in a four-story, brick
building at the far end of the yard, where he was sitting behind his
huge mahogany desk. He was surprised, but not shaken. "Hey, fellas,
what's up, I didn't pay some parkin' tickets, or somethin'?" He got
his rights read to him, and was on his way to the Four-Three within
five minutes. As he got into the rear of the car, precisely in the middle
of the convoy, he looked with a contemptuous glare, first at the
driver who was wearing the usual blue, zip-up jacket with "POLICE-
NYPD" on the back, and then at the two cops he was to be seated
between. He then looked at the cop sitting next to the driver, on the
passenger's side of car, who was the only one wearing a business suit.

"Hey, where's my friend, Horan and his *guinea* buddy, Covelli?"
Rossetti asked, a big grin on his face.

Terry Hughes had read it right. The police reporters at headquarters didn't have a clue. For them it was just another roundup of a prominent wise guy, they thought. Their editors would send photographers and reporters to hang around outside the tall red brick building's gates, waiting for Rossetti to show.

When he finally appeared with his hands cuffed tightly behind him and walking between McPartland and another detective, Charlie Rossetti swaggered past the reporters and their camera crews. His dark blue Brioni business suit, set off by a scarlet, Christian Dior handkerchief folded neatly in his left breast suit pocket and a similarly colored Hermes tie, was partially covered by a full-length cashmere overcoat thrown over his shoulders.

"Hey, Charlie, in for your annual physical?" one of them shouted. Others pushed microphones into Rossetti's face.

"Nah, nothin' like that. It must be just some kind of misunderstanding." McPartland and his partner pushed past the reporters and through the revolving front doors of police headquarters and onto Pearl Street.

"Hey, Horan, what the fuck's goin' on here?" Rossetti protested when he saw the detective in Lombardo's office. Horan ignored him and joined the other detectives with the assembled brass.

Rossetti was confident that he'd be sprung within a few hours. He laughed at the charges of his putting out a hit on old man McCabe.

"Who the hell is this Sal, what's his name?" Rossetti demanded. "I never heard of the prick."

Charlie Rossetti, expecting a call from his lawyer, Gil Strapoli, was getting a little uneasy. "Whew, it's hot in this dump," he complained to one of the detectives who he guessed was Italian, "Don't you feel, it?"

"Na, I'm from Naples—you know Napolitano, we don't sweat as much as Sicilians."

The call finally came. The lawyer did all the talking. Rossetti just listened, nervously looking at his manicured nails, wiping the sweat from his face and glancing at the clock on the wall in front of him. After hanging up the phone, he announced, "Ya' got nothin' on me. My lawyer says I don't have to say nothing."

Then the cops played some selected tapes.

"You have reached the voice mail for 565-7035, the priest at this number (a pause)—'Father Maloney'—(the undisguised, raspy voice interjected) is not available at this time. Please leave your name, the date and time of your call, and a telephone number at which you can be reached. Thank You."

"Hello, Father Maloney, this is Gordon Halliday. Please call me at my office. You know my number."

"Hello, Sallie, I got a new assignment for you."

"OK, kid, here's who ya gonna hit."

"I wanna call Gil Strapoli," Rossetti demanded.

They all waited for the call. Thirty minutes went by. When it came through it wasn't for Rossetti. The caller asked for Detective Horan.

"This is Victor Albanese. That prick was on his own. Ask him about Gordon Holiday," Albanese's bizarre voice wheezed as he coughed into the telephone. Then the line went dead.

Horan hung up the telephone and turned to his two new partners, and finally looked at Rossetti.

"Gordon Halliday."

"Gordon Holiday. Gordon Holiday. Huh?" he started to speak, calmly. "I guess I don't have to guess who the fuck that was on the other end of the phone," he spoke a little louder. "And I'm supposed to cop out on the McCabe murder."

Rossetti glared at the cops surrounding him and shouted, "Forget it, if I gotta go down, everybody's gotta go?"

At that very moment, the phone rang for the second time that day.

"Gaw ahead, answer the fuckin' thing," Lombardo said to a detective seated next to Horan. He picked up the phone, listened for a moment and handed the phone to Rossetti. "It's your lawyer, Charlie."

Rossetti just listened, occasionally mumbling, "I understand." The one-sided conversation lasted less than five minutes.

"OK, Gil, I got it. Thanks. I'll see ya," Rossetti placed the phone down gently.

"OK, here's what I know and what I don't know," he began.

"On the side, ya know, from my sand and gravel business, I had a little "wire room" business. Ya know, horses over the phone. That's how I met Gordon Holiday," he said.

"Halliday, H-A, not O," Horan corrected, as Lombardo glared at the detective for interrupting.

"I know you guys know Holiday's business from the papers and all that shit. But I bet ya didn't know how he got his own business. It was thanks to the rich broad he married—she was a real 'meal ticket', Rossetti said contemptuously. "And I betcha didn't also know that he had a bad habit, that took up a lotta his time.

"Habit, do you mean drugs?" the chief of detectives asked.

"Nah, nah. Nuttin' like that. He was a fuckin' degenerate gambler. I come across guys like that all the time. He was really hooked," Rossetti explained. "After we got to know each other better, he told me that he started it in college. Ya know, horses, craps, high-stakes poker, you name it. Of course I gave him a big line of credit because of his old lady's money and all that, so's he could use the 'wires' as much as he wanted."

"Explain the 'wires' a little more," Horan asked, assuming that the two chiefs weren't as much up on that shit as he.

"Rossetti explained that since Halliday had to spend most of his time tending to business, he often used the telephone services provided by a number of bookmakers, but mostly Rossetti's; "The cops called 'em wire rooms," he stopped and looked at Horan.

Wires were for favored customers with good credit. They were given telephone numbers, which were changed constantly to avoid detection by the cops.

"By the guys we pay in the phone company," Rossetti explained. Like a lot of "easy credit" deals, the wire rooms encouraged a sucker to get in deeper and deeper. While arguably successful in business, Halliday was undeniably a bust at gambling. One began to support the other.

Then one day Gordon Halliday met Charlie Rossetti at Charley's of Hanover Square. "The visit was 'necessary', Rossetti said, emphasizing *necessary* and looking inquisitively at all the cops.

"Because by then Halliday was into you for a bundle," Horan said. "Or was it Victor Albanese that he owed the money?"

"No, no, no. It was strictly me. I don't work for Victor Albanese."

"No, not after that phone call from him today," Horan said in a tone of contempt.

Rossetti glared at him and went on with his story. "So we was meetin' one day at Charley's, you know it's right down the street from Gordon's office on Broad and Wall, you know to collect the vig—he couldn't pay the principal, no way." According to Rossetti, the meeting went extremely well. It was the first of many "necessary" meetings in the months ahead. Rossetti worked out a weekly payment schedule with twenty-five percent interest. Halliday was initially stunned but he needed to spread out his debt so he accepted the deal. He had no choice.

"So, I was out to Gordon's big house once a week. He didn't want his office people to see me. His family didn't know about his problem, so he told anybody was saw me at the house that I was seeing him about business, ya know, my sand and gravel company. Story was that I was gonna become one of his investors—in the deals he's always puttin' together." Rossetti made it clear that it was important for both Halliday's financial interest and his relatively good physical condition and health that payments be made on the exact day that they were due.

One such payday Rossetti was invited to a part at the Halliday home, where he met Gordon Halliday's daughter, Eve, for the first time. He also met her boyfriend.

"Ya know who that turned out to be? The fuckin' mayor."

"That was a surprise to you, Charlie? It's been in the papers for months," Covelli said. Rossetti didn't even flinch.

A few weeks later, Rossetti was scheduled to make a "pickup" on a day that the Hallidays had a full social schedule in Fieldston. Halliday was entertaining clients—former, present, and prospective. He told Rossetti, "Wear your most conservative business suit. Have a few drinks."

Rossetti recalled that Halliday assured him that he would blend in, "After all, you're as good at 'restructuring' debt as any banker I know," Halliday remarked.

"After that party, I started seein' Eve," Rossetti said.

"Seein'? Come on, Charlie. Don't be so modest," Hughes threw in.

Rossetti didn't answer or smile. He went on with his story. According to him this affair went on for at least six months. It led to a break up between Eve Halliday and Tom McCabe, according to Rossetti. "I don't know who dumped who," he threw in.

So Charlie had his lucrative client hooked, thanks to his "restructuring" skills. And Halliday's wife's fortune ensures payment, no matter what—and he was still "seein'" Eve Halliday.

"But then my *pazienza*—ya know, patience with installment payments was runnin' out. I don't like doin' it with nobody, you understand" I started to turn the screws on Gordon. I wanted some up front beside the vig. In the meantime, I thought Eve stopped seein' McCabe, but then I saw in the papers that she was still going around with him. I guess she fooled both of us."

"She turned out to be a real bastard," Rossetti said bitterly. "And I guess I talked too much to her."

"Talked to her about what?" Hughes asked.

"Ya know, I guess I musta told her about my accommodations for her old man's bettin' problems," he answered. "She was surprised." He stopped for a moment, thinking about what he had admitted.

Rossetti explained that while he was still pressuring Halliday, he saw the mayor on television introducing the manager of his reelection campaign. "Who the fuck is standin' next to the guy, but good old Gordon." According to Rossetti, his bookmaking, numbers, and drug businesses had been frustrated for the past three and a half years "with this cops walkin' the streets and talkin' to everybody shit. Ya know, communion policin'," he called it. The mayor had been crowing about it and now, Rossetti thought, Halliday could be his mole inside city hall.

"How could Halliday help?" Horan asked.

Rossetti felt that Halliday could intervene with the mayor to do something "to get the cops off our asses." He suggested that putting them back into their patrol cars would help, emphasizing that the cops themselves felt more comfortable with that arrangement.

"And, did Halliday talk to the mayor, to the best of your knowledge?" Hughes asked.

"Oh, yeah, sure. He told me he was workin' on it."

But then, Rossetti continued, nothing really happened. When Halliday told him that the mayor was not cooperating the way they had planned, Rossetti said if Halliday couldn't convince the mayor to back off, he would.

"So you had the old man whacked, because—?" Covelli was leading Rossetti.

"Because of this stuff with Gordon and the mayor. Ya know, the fuckin' cops still walkin' my streets. I was after the mayor, for Chris sake," Rossetti explained.

"But, why his father?" Hughes asked, puzzled.

"Why not the mayor's old man? It would serve two purposes; it would show McCabe that we wasn't screwin' around and he should start listenin' to Gordon and it told Holiday that we wasn't screwin' around with him and his debt to us, either. Before you ask, the other guy, that spick Perez or somethin' or whatever, like old man McCabe, he was always shootin' off his mouth to the cops about drugs, whores, and stuff like that, ya know, my fuckin' business," he concluded.

"So, you used Conte and threw in this fuckin' Irish hood, Burns, to help with the hit. Right?" Horan asked looking over at one of the other detectives.

"No, I didn't. I never heard of the fuckin' guy," he responded, his indignation almost convincing.

❧   ❧   ❧

Russo called the mayor at about four that afternoon.

"Tom, I think it's important that we meet before the end of the day, in your office, if possible. Alone," the police commissioner emphasized.

"Another cop cloak-and-dagger meeting?" the mayor laughed.

"Maybe. But I believe it's important that we meet," Russo insisted.

"Well, I hope it has nothing to do with that Civilian Complain Committee shit, or something like that."

"No, it's a whole new ballgame," Russo retorted.

When Russo stepped inside the mayor's office at five twenty, he saw that McCabe was not alone. "You know Gordon Halliday, Chris," he said, without getting up from behind his desk. Halliday nodded at Russo who said coldly, "Yeah. Hi, there."

"What's this urgent thing you had to discuss with me—I mean, us?" the mayor began, looking at Halliday, whose facial expressions gave away nothing.

Russo decided to plunge ahead, despite Halliday's inexplicable presence and began to layout what Rossetti had told the police.

McCabe remained strangely calm, almost indifferent, during the briefing. Halliday sat there like a statue. The police commissioner did not give the details about all the players involved in the investigation but went into more detail when he came to the confessions of the two killers. Russo did not reveal their names but made it clear that organized crime may have been involved.

"That Rossetti bullshit, and his getting my father killed because of something to do with community policing and pressuring Gordon here is just that—bullshit," the mayor blurted out.

He was looking at the police commissioner when he said it, but then abruptly sank back into his chair and looked away from Russo's chilling stare. Gordon Halliday was holding his head with the fingertips of his right hand, nervously massaging his temples.

The police commissioner stood up. Nothing else was said between the two once-longtime friends. Russo hadn't mentioned Rossetti's name or Halliday's part in the investigation. He turned and walked to the door. As he put his hand on the doorknob, he hesitated then turned and looked back at the mayor. They stared at each other for a moment—neither was about to back down. Russo opened the door and walked out.

"I was somewhat amazed at McCabe's response to Sam Gershowitz's findings. And then he certainly didn't seem very happy about the news that we had two possible eyewitnesses to what went down at 2044 Westchester," Chris Russo began.

He then went on explaining that he did not mention, by name, of course, the assortment of characters involved in the investigation. That he was very general in discussing the various twists and turns taking place, but went into more detail when discussing the actual confession of one of the "perps,"—although not mentioning names.

"I then hinted at the possibility of organized crime involvement in the investigation, but still no names." He went on, his voice rising, "And you know what my friend Tommy McCabe tells me? He says, 'That Rossetti bullshit, and pressuring Gordon Halliday'. Can you believe that?" Russo asked. "I never mentioned Rossetti or Halliday. Ever! He could only have gotten it from one source. From inside this building," he said almost softly, looking at Coleman and Hughes.

They both leaned back quickly in their chairs, shaking their heads and looking down uncomfortably at the carpeted floor of their boss' office.

"Son of a bitch, son of a bitch. I can't believe it," Terry Hughes finally broke the silence.

All three of them then remained quiet again, but just for a moment.

"Wait a minute. Oh, my God!" Bob Coleman said so loudly that Russo and Hughes both quickly turned towards him.

"Bob, what is it?" Russo asked.

"Do you remember, Chris, about a week ago I told you about the call I got from Harry Garrett?" he asked the police commissioner, while at the same time turning and looking at the chief of detectives. "Terry, I'm sorry, I didn't tell you this, but I should have."

He then explained the significance of his conversation with that caller.

Garrett was one of those cops who had virtually a lifetime job as chauffeurs for the brass. They had to keep a nice balance between getting along with their fellow cops and keeping the confidence of the bosses they drove. What they heard on the job stayed in the car—and as much as other cops would try to pump them, they maintained confidentiality to an extraordinary degree. In part because the job could lead to a gold shield, eventually, and maybe even being loaned out to elected officials, like city commissioners—and the mayor.

Harry Garrett was the most senior of McCabe's three drivers and held the rank of detective, second-grade. While he respected the obligation he had to forget whatever he heard, his first loyalty was always to his fellow cops. The growing strain between his boss, the mayor, and the police department, and the police commissioner in particular, began to worry him, worry him enough so he would reach out to Bob Coleman.

"A few weeks ago, Harry told me, he was driving the mayor to an unscheduled, obviously secret meeting with someone out at the Knights of Columbus Stolzenthaler Council Hall in Staten Island. You know, out in Great Kills, the end of the world," Bob Coleman said.

"Oh, oh. I can see where this is going," Hughes jumped in. "We used to use that same location for many years for 'unofficial' meetings."

All three smiled as they remembered some of the stuff that had gone down in the old days.

"Unfortunately for the mayor, who thought he had taken all necessary precautions to keep his meeting a secret, Harry Garrett had often driven the former chief of detectives, Irv Sackman, to that same location," Coleman said.

"So what did Harry do?" Hughes asked, sliding to the front edge of his chair.

"He goes to the back of the building knowing that one thing you can depend upon finding in the rear of a K of C hall are empty aluminum beer kegs. He puts a couple of them on top of one another, climbs on top of them and peeks through the window, and sees Dan McCourty, big as life."

"Oh shit," the chief of detectives sighed, sliding back to the rear of his chair and slapping his forehead with his open right hand. "Dan McCourty."

"The next morning Harry calls his 'second most successful 'sergeant,'—me—using a pay phone at the foot of the steps of City Hall."

Chris Russo then went on with story. When he was appointed police commissioner and began putting his new team together, he and the newly appointed chief of detectives, Hughes, had discussed the potential risk in keeping some of Dan McCourty's loyalists in top positions in the department. They felt some of them could adjust to an administration far different in management style than that of McCourty's. But some couldn't—and a few of them said so, much to their credit.

Chips Lombardo had been close to McCourty and was, in fact, promoted and put in charge of the Special Investigations Division by him. However, Russo believed that he had shown that he would be a team player by supporting Community Policing and the department's plans to redefine some of the traditional duties of specialized cops, particularly detectives. Coleman and Hughes decided Lombardo could be trusted and recommended that Russo keep him on. Now the three of them realized they had made a major mistake. Lombardo, through McCourty, was the mayor's line into the department.

"Dan McCourty got his hooks into Chips. Real deep," Russo said then added, "That devious old bastard."

The three of them didn't have to discuss what needed to be done. It was obvious. Hughes had told Lombardo and Horan to be in his office for a meeting at 8:00 p.m., that night. "Let's see, that's in just five minutes—they must be waiting for me over there now," he said, looking at his watch. They were supposed to discuss the next move in the McCabe case. They had Sal Conte and Trevor Burns stashed in Hughes's office, one in the training room and one in the conference room—each with cops from Internal Affairs baby-sitting them.

But now Hughes would have to confront Lombardo.

Lombardo was sitting at one of the empty desks outside of the chief of detectives' office. Horan was standing on the opposite side of the room. There was no exchange of pleasantries between the chief and the two detectives.

"Chips. I want to see you first. Alone," Hughes snapped without looking at any one of them, opening the door to his office and going inside.

Lombardo looked puzzled, but merely shrugged his two shoulders, followed Hughes into his office, closing the door behind him.

"So, what's doin', boss?" Lombardo asked, starting to sit down in a chair in front of the chief's desk.

"No, don't bother sitting down. This won't take long," Hughes ordered.

Lombardo was taken aback. He looked at his boss and stood ramrod straight prepared for the worst.

"Chips, when was the last time that you spoke to Dan McCourty?" Hughes asked.

Lombardo leaned forward, twisting his head slightly to the right, his body language suggesting that he didn't understand the question. "Commissioner—I mean, Dan McCourty? What do you mean, sir?"

"Stop the shit. You know exactly what I mean. When did you last speak to him?" the chief shot back.

"Oh, I speak to him, maybe once a month or so. You know for old times sake," Lombardo responded.

Hughes said nothing but sat back in his chair and stared at him.

Lombardo finally broke the silence. With a tremor in his voice, he began to make his plea.

"Chief, you know I just never really believed in this Community Policing shit. I know, I know, before you say it, then why didn't I pack it in when McCourty left and Russo came in, knowing that the department was going to go all the way with it?" Lombardo held his hands out in a gesture of supplication. "But, come on, boss, you know these kids we're getting on the job now are incapable of doing anything for anyone that somehow doesn't do something for them.

They're in the job for the fucking paycheck and that's it. They might as well be working for Kmart," Lombardo was getting up a head of steam.

"Besides, they're scared shitless, they'll shoot at anything that moves and empty their fuckin' pieces besides. They get kinky about almost anyone who looks the slightest bit strange to them. Shit, boss, the cops in our days knew everybody on their beat and——."

Terry Hughes interrupted. "OK, OK. You made your point."

"So you agree with me. Right, chief? You know the mayor feels the same way, too, right?"

Hughes stood up and replied.

"No. No, you silly fuck. Nothing, nothing excuses what you did. Where did you think this would all wind up? You must've known we would have found out about your feeding information to McCourty—sooner or later."

Lombardo retreated a bit. "Yeah. I mean, yes sir. But I was hoping that before that happened, somehow Dan McCourty would make his way back into the job and we'd change things back to the way they were," he said, sheepishly.

Hughes started to move from behind his desk, and headed towards Lombardo.

"Hey, besides, you guys never promoted me in the three and a half years we've been working together," he added, smiling somewhat uncomfortably, as the shorter chief of detectives stood inches from him, staring at Lombardo with a cold rage in his eyes.

"I want your papers on my desk in an hour. I'll have them delivered to the Pension Section the moment they open their doors for business."

Lombardo looked like he was going to be sick. "Do you remember when I was in the Bomb Squad? It was about fifteen years ago?" he said.

Hughes just stared at him and said nothing.

Lombardo went on, his voice full of desperation, "Well, you know there was an incident out near JFK a while ago. We were called in to inspect an old World War II artillery shell some kids found."

Hughes's expression didn't change. He had sat back down and was clenching his fists below his desk, out of Lombardo's sight.

"Well, the artillery shell was harmless, but when I helped lift it into this garbage truck to be carted away, I cracked my back and my balls almost hit the fuckin' ground. I've felt it ever since. Honest, chief," Lombardo concluded.

"Forget it, Chips," Hughes told him. "Get the fuck out." He got up and opened his office door. Lombardo stumbled through it, dazed and oblivious to Horan who jumped to his feet. Neither of the chiefs even looked at him. He watched as the two bosses got to the entrance to the chief's outer office, where Hughes jerked open the door and Lombardo walked out. Hughes slammed the door and beckoned to Horan to follow him back into his office. Horan shrugged his shoulders and murmured to himself, "Some bad shit is going down here."

"So McCourty thinks he can come back as police commissioner?" Gordon Halliday asked in a tone of disbelief. He was sitting with Tom McCabe in the library of the Halliday mansion. The early winter darkness had made the panes of the windows black and they reflected the flames in the room's stone fireplace.

"For services rendered, or something like that," McCabe said.

Halliday frowned and said, "Well, he's one stone we don't need around our necks. Whoever ends up running against you is going to make community policing a big issue, one way or the other. Dan McCourty is history. And his opposition to community policing isn't going to mean much to voters. And we don't know how much mileage we can get out of the issue, despite what that little toady Plotnick tells you."

"Solnich," the mayor wearily corrected him.

"Whatever, he's still no political genius. I can't think of anything worse happening to you than having Community Policing become a racially divisive political consideration. That means Democrats against Republicans—and, theoretically, you're neither," Halliday said. "Besides, the Democrats were the ones who most supported your independent candidacy."

They went at it for over an hour, discussing McCabe's years of friendship with Chris Russo, and predictably, Halliday urging him to stop being sentimental and continue to distance himself from the police commissioner—or even get rid of him. Sure, that course was not without risk, but McCabe might have to take it on, he advised.

"Look, Tom, I don't want to further influence your changing attitude towards your buddy the police commissioner," Halliday went on.

"Oh yeah, right," the mayor said sarcastically.

"But I am concerned that Community Policing and therefore the commissioner, is getting too much good press lately, and that you, particularly in an election year, should be getting more attention for your role in making Community Policing a city wide program after your election." Halliday could still sense that McCabe was resisting his argument.

"I believe that your public displeasure with the way that Russo handled the investigation of your father's murder, your move on the Civilian Complaint Review Board, and now your clear intention to defang these troublesome Police Community Advisory Councils, are all damn good political moves." Halliday kept rolling along, sometimes looking at Tom McCabe and at other times staring into the fire.

"Most of which were your ideas. Right, Gordon?" the mayor reminded him.

Halliday ignored him and kept pushing his agenda. "Let's move on the PACS—get the hearings going. We'll get a lot of support from some influential cops and their unions, and some business people will support us, too."

"Chris Russo may resign. Even at this point, I'm not too sure that I'd be happy with that," the mayor responded.

At that point, Eve Halliday came bouncing into the library. "Hi, honey," she said, kissing McCabe on his cheek, then wrinkling her nose as she took a cigarette from between his fingers.

"I remember when I used to be 'honey' and got that kiss."

"Ah, come on, Daddy," she said. "Hey, you almost made me forget why I cut in on you two guys." She turned to McCabe, "Janet Mullins is on one of our outside lines for you," she smiled.

He took the call in the foyer just outside of the library, speaking in a very low voice, and staying on the phone for no more than a minute. He returned to the library where Halliday and, now, Eve, were seated.

"Janet just got an urgent call from *Virga*—."

"*Virga*? What the hell is *Virga*?" Halliday asked.

"Believe it or not, it's the code name that Dan McCourty chose for himself. Something to do with rain drying up before it hits the ground. I thought he was getting kinda weird on me. 'It's *Latin*, Mr. Mayor,' McCourty says."

Eve laughed nervously, and Halliday suggested the mayor return McCourty's call immediately. McCabe went back to the phone outside the library and called the former P.C.

When he reentered the room, he looked shaken.

"Our contact at Police Plaza has been caught and fired," he said softly.

"I'm sure you know that you let the cat out of the bag in that meeting with Russo," Halliday said. "After that it was just a matter of time."

"Well, thanks a lot, buddy. You just sat there on your ass during the whole meeting," McCabe retorted.

"Well, no use getting upset, Tom. In any event, we'd better watch our asses even more now," Halliday said, glaring at McCabe. "I think you're dangerously underestimating Russo's political skills. Most cops who reach high positions in the department get there because they're shrewd and ferocious politicians."

"You're really worried about my old friend, aren't you, Gordon?" The mayor smiled briefly, obviously refusing to take Halliday too seriously.

"Don't take what I'm saying so lightly, Tom, this is hardball politics, and you'd better start thinking about a strategy to offset Russo's moves," Halliday said.

"Like what?" McCabe asked.

"Hey, what the hell is going on here," Eve asked, jumping up from the chair.

"Eve, for Chris sake, shut up will you," Halliday said.

"Oh, my God, please forgive me. I'm sorry I didn't mean it that way, dear. It's just that the less you know from here on in, the better," her father said.

"I already know, you assholes," Eve Halliday screamed back at them.

It was the middle of March and the magnitude of the criminal conspiracy became more obvious with every passing day.

"Terry, I've decided that we should go for Victor Albanese rather than Rossetti. Let's go for broke. We'll get Charlie one way or the other, but he will become a secondary target from here on in," Chris Russo began.

Hughes sat up in his chair, wrenching his neck in a strategic display of discomfort with the police commissioner's announcement.

Russo smiled and held us his hand, "I know, I know, you'll need additional horsepower to build the case against Albanese."

Russo stood up, walked around his desk and stood directly in front of his chief of detectives. Terry Hughes attempted to stand, but Russo pushed him back down.

"How does this grab you? The possibility of an Albanese-Rossetti-Halliday money-laundering scheme gives us a shot at involving the feds. What do you think?"

Hughes shook his head in a "not bad" gesture.

"Good. I'll call Amanda Stevens, the U.S Attorney. Baby, we're off and running."

Amanda Stevens agreed, but when Russo routinely asked if it would be the FBI, Stevens said she didn't think so. She explained that while the FBI would seem a logical choice, they were usually reluctant to be involved in a case in which they weren't the lead agency. Stevens went on to say that since money laundering would be the reason for federal intervention, she would also have considered criminal investigators from the IRS. But they were somewhat limited in working with the cops, too, because certain information they had at their disposal, gleaned from individual and corporate tax returns, could not, by law, be shared with anyone else. So she called in "the two best federal investigators in town anyway, who happen to be Postal Inspectors," she said, both well known to, and respected by, the detectives heading up the investigation. "I'm sure one of these pricks must have used the mails in some way when they were dealing with that bank in the Caymans," she reasoned.

Postal Inspector Ralph Warfield was a massive man, weighing in at over 200 pounds on his five foot eleven frame but he was surprisingly quick and graceful on his feet, a trait common to many big men. His new partner, Paul Singleton, in sharp contrast, was older than Warfield and his gray hair, placid face behind gold rimmed glasses, and his tendency to wear clothing that was slightly out of style and very conservative made him look more like an insurance salesman or bank officer than the tenacious investigator that he was. Where Warfield stood out in any crowd, Singleton blended into it so quickly and easily that he became virtually invisible. If a tail or a surveillance job was necessary, it was Singleton who did the work. He had amazing street smarts and when he confronted a subject it was invariably a surprise to the target. Warfield was the inside guy. He had superb analytic skills and could follow any paper trail to the ends of the earth. Though very different in every way, the two men had a deadly effectiveness when they worked as a team.

The day following their assignment, Singleton and Warfield, spent over eight hours listening to tapes from Maloney Sand and Gravel and "Father Maloney's" voice mail.

"Where does Rossetti get this 'Maloney' shit?" Singleton asked. "I guess he's getting back at all the Irish cops that must have hassled him over the years."

Horan grinned at him. Then Singleton put his finger on the tender spot in the case.

"Well, it would be better if we could listen in on Halliday's phones, you know, his office and his home."

"Yeah, from what we've heard, he and Rossetti must have spoke often where Rossetti picked up a call from Halliday on his voice mail and then called him at either of those two places and from other than his sand and gravel business," Warfield added. "Of course, our getting a court order for those instruments would be useless at this time, since Rossetti's arrest has alerted all other parties. Oh well!"

Horan looked at them for a moment.

"Uh, we've had some 'overheards' you know," Horan said carefully.

"'Overheards'?" Singleton asked.

"Yeah, you know, picking up bits and pieces of information from conversations you hear in restaurants or bars, or just happen to be standing next to someone in a public place. You know!" Horan elaborated.

"Yeah, I've heard about those conversations that you local cops pick up," Warfield smiled, looking at his partner. "So, officer, you are telling us that you may have overheard certain people conducting or attempting to conduct a financial transaction knowing that the proceeds used in the transaction were from an illegal activity in violation of Title 18 United States Code, 1956: Laundering of Monetary Instruments. Therefore it is your responsibility to report such criminal acts to a federal law enforcement agency that is responsible for enforcement of that statute," Singleton rattled off without taking a breath. "At least if they use the U.S. Mails to do it," he added.

❦   ❦   ❦

"So let me summarize what I believe may have happened here, and which you agree with or don't agree with, which of course you will tell me now," Terry Hughes began after Horan briefed him.

"We have reason to believe that Victor Albanese is behind the murders of Morgan McCabe and Ramon Velez and a planned hit of Gordon Halliday and that Charlie Rossetti was ordered to cop out on the killings because there may be a Halliday-Rossetti-Albanese, and possibly McCabe, connection that we are not being told about. Does that sound correct?" the chief of detectives asked.

"Yes, sir," Horan replied.

"OK, we'll book him, along with Salvatore Conte and Trevor Burns, for Murder One. That fuck Burns gets two counts, of course, because of poor Steve Covelli. The police commissioner will have to be consulted first. There's a damn good chance there will be a political explosion," Hughes warned them.

"We'll keep the administrative bullshit low-key, too," he ordered. "You book Rossetti by phone. Call the Four-Three, get an arrest number, actually three, one each for Conte and Burns, too, and give the desk officer "Doe's" instead of the prisoners' real names."

"They're all your buddies at that precinct by now. Right?" Hughes smiled, looking at Roger Horan.

"Yes, sir. No problem."

Rothman and Hughes, along with Horan, met with Russo in his office at three in the morning. The PC was now sitting alone on his couch waiting for them. He was wearing a jogging outfit.

"The first thing I could grab," Russo explained apologetically.

"But why didn't Eve Halliday come forward after the killing, or why didn't any of her friends, who were ostensibly aware of Rossetti's threats towards the mayor?" Chris Russo began.

"And, if Tom McCabe knew that Eve Halliday was dating Charlie Rossetti and that he had actually threatened the mayor, what did he do about it?" he continued.

"I just can't believe that Tom McCabe knew who—or someone who might have known—who killed his father and didn't give that information to me," Russo said, now fully awake and angry. "What was going on in his mind?"

They decided to hold Rossetti in Hughes' office. It had a couch Rossetti could sleep on. Horan was about to leave but paused and asked if they were on thin ice legally.

"Let us worry about that," Russo said firmly, cutting off any further discussion. "We're gonna take down these three, period."

They agreed that Russo would call the mayor at seven, the mayor's usual arrival time at City Hall, then call the Bronx district attorney, Jules Powell, and ask for a private arraignment of the three prisoners after they were booked. By then the press would pick up on what was going on. A special unit of the Corrections Department trained for that purpose could then detain the three prisoners. Rossetti and the other two would soon hear from their lawyers that their constitutional rights had already been "poked at," if not breached. But they weren't about to complain, Russo guessed.

When Chris Russo arrived at the mayor's office shortly after 7, Janet Mullins looked thoroughly surprised but, seeing the expression on his face, buzzed McCabe and told him that the PC was outside.

McCabe was dressed in exercise clothing, slightly red faced and sweating from his morning workout on a "Nordic" treadmill that he kept tucked in one corner of his office.

"So what's this mystery you couldn't discuss on the phone?" he asked Russo, then looked at Mullins and ordered, "Close the door behind you and no calls until I tell you."

"Mr. Mayor, we believe that we have an excellent suspect in the investigation of your father's murder and that of Ramon Velez. In fact, we're about to book him along with two co-conspirators, one of whom was probably the actual killer," Russo said in a formal tone.

"Good, Chris. It was a robbery, right?" McCabe asked.

"No. I think you should know what's going down before we go any further in processing these arrests," Russo responded.

"You've probably heard the name Charlie Rossetti before." Russo said with an edge to his voice.

"Yeah, he's a mob guy, isn't he? I've seen his name in the papers a couple of times. Why? What's the connection?" the mayor asked.

Russo decided to give McCabe a direct shot to the gut. "It involves a criminal conspiracy that could involve your office."

Russo didn't hold back anything but laid it all out clearly and succinctly.

"How about Eve Halliday?" Russo asked.

No response from McCabe.

"Mr. Mayor, did you hear me? What about Eve?"

McCabe looked aimlessly at the floor or gazed at the ceiling of his office; he kept avoiding eye contact. Russo concluded by telling the mayor that after their meeting he was going to contact Jules Powell, the Bronx DA, who would make the arrangements for the processing of Charlie Rossetti, Sal Conte, and Trevor Burns through the courts and Corrections. "How do you want to handle the press release or releases?" he asked. The mayor knew exactly what his police commissioner was talking about.

"Why involve Eve Halliday at all?" the mayor finally spoke.

Russo just stared at his boss.

"What press release?" McCabe snapped. "So some grease ball gangster takes it upon himself to kill my father because he has some kind of grudge against me. It doesn't make any sense. What's this big conspiracy?"

"The damn mob is involved, and others, probably. For Chris sake, what the hell has happened to you, Tom?" Russo said. He had reached the limits of his patience.

"The courts will decide what the truth is. Not me, and not you, Chris," the mayor responded.

"But they wanted to get back at you, Tom," Russo said, utterly astonished by McCabe's attempt to ignore what was right in front of him.

"Who says so? This guy is just trying to muddy the waters. He's already preparing his defense for the trial," McCabe objected.

"So how and why did they target your father?" Russo inquired.

"I don't know."

"Let me tell you what I think. It wasn't really you that Rossetti wanted to strike out at. Your father was targeted because he was a major pain in the ass for the wise guys. All of his pressure to clean up the entire Westchester Avenue area was raising hell with their business. You know, drugs, numbers, prostitution—all the services they like to furnish the public."

McCabe looked stunned. Now Russo had his full attention.

"And I'll tell you something else, Tom. The second name on their hit parade was Gordon Halliday. Now how do you explain that one?"

※   ※   ※

The same Twelfth Judicial District Grand Jury in the Bronx indicted Charlie Rossetti for Murder l, conspiracy to commit murder, and inducing another to commit murder, and Sal Conte and Trevor Burns for Murder One and conspiracy, plus kidnapping, Robbery One, and Burglary One in the McCabe and Velez murders. Burns was also indicted, and would be tried separately for Murder One in the killing of Steve Covelli. Conte and Burns asked for, and were granted, separate trials from Rossetti in the McCabe-Velez case.

Rossetti was to be defended by a team of six lawyers from the law firm of Wilson, Hayes, Franklin and Hayes, a white-shoe firm that was not often seen representing clients in criminal cases, and certainly not murder cases. WHF&H was best known for its corporate clients, particularly those in investment banking.

"Like Halliday Associates," Russo said to Amanda Stevens, who was excited with the possibility that the state trials could lay the groundwork for a federal trial against Albanese, Halliday and others down the road.

Strangely enough, however, Gil Strapoli was made "Of Counsel" in the firm, just for the duration of the Rossetti trial, of course, and would sit at the defense table. Of all the members of the legal team, Strapoli was the only one who really knew his way around in criminal trials. He would be expected to contribute much to the defense effort, probably by an occasional whisper to one of the WHF&H lawyers.

"And, Victor Albanese would be just as well informed about what's going on as Gordon Halliday," Russo reminded the U.S. Attorney, again.

After two weeks of *voir dire* they got twelve jurors that defense and prosecution could live with.

❧   ❧   ❧

When the case went to trial Rossetti came up with a slightly different story. He got to know Sal Conte through Sal's father, Paulie—"Ya know, I was in sand and gravel and Paulie was in truckin'—we got to know each other," Rossetti said, responding to a question from the Bronx District Attorney Jules Powell, who would be the lead prosecutor in the murder trials. According to Rossetti, young Conte pestered him to become a member of his crew.

"Isn't it true, Mister Rossetti, that your real occupation is performing criminal activities as a member of the Victor Albanese organized crime family?" the DA asked.

"Objection, your honor," a tall, thin, gray haired, impeccably dressed lawyer from WHF&H said softly, but authoritatively. Gil Strapoli immediately resumed whispering into the defense counsel's ear.

"Yes, sustained. Mister Powell, Mr. Albanese is not on trial—at this time," the judge got more than a few smiles.

Rossetti stuck with his story during the remainder of the cross-examination. He claimed he went along with the kid, "Just to get him off my ass."

"Listen," he told the Bronx prosecutor, "I figured old man McCabe and the other guy was making too much trouble for us. They had the cops swarming all over Parkchester, and gotten the people all stirred up. Ya see, that's our turf—*capece*? So I decided to have them hit. And since the kid was so fired up to show he's a stand-up guy, I gave him the job. That's what happened. That's all there is to it."

Then entire courtroom fell silent as Rossetti calmly detailed how easily he had ordered the brutal slaying of one old man, and another troublemaker who had the bad luck to get in the way. It was clear that Rossetti would take the fall.

"Damn it, his testimony closes off our path that would lead to Victor Albanese. At least for the moment," Amanda Stevens commented later to the police commissioner.

"And to Halliday as well." Russo added.

The second planned "hit" on Halliday never came up in the trial. The Bronx District Attorney knew that the evidence was tainted, that

Horan and Covelli's "overhead remarks" would take his case into very troubled legal waters, and since he had Rossetti cold, then his co-conspirators would have to be left for another day.

Salvatore Conte was brought over from his own trial. He would be the prosecution's lead witness.

"Mister Conte, please tell the court what your relationship was with the defendant, Charles Rossetti," Jules Powell began.

"I worked for him."

"Worked? You mean that you were a drug dealer and he was your supplier, is that correct?"

"Objection, your honor."

"Sustained," Judge Cornelia Forde ruled. A former Assistant U.S. Attorney in the Southern District, she was quickly building a reputation for keeping rather complicated trials, along with their ubiquitous overly aggressive and meandering trial lawyers, on track.

"OK, Mister Conte, will you please tell us what you mean when you say you worked for Charlie Rossetti," Powell asked.

"Well, besides him bein' my dealer, I did other jobs for Charlie, too." Conte didn't seem intimidated, slouching against the straight-back, wooden chair.

"Other jobs? Give the court an example, Mister Conte."

"Ya know, roughin up guys and stuff like that."

"Were you asked to rough up the mayor's father and Ramon Velez?"

"Objection, your honor."

"No. I'll allow it. Answer the question, Mister Conte," Forde directed.

"I was asked to whack the old man—and the other guy, too, by Charlie Rossetti."

The courtroom got a bit animated. The judge used her gavel.

"You mean you were asked to kill these two men. Is that correct," Powell was speaking slowly and deliberately.

"Yeah, right. I mean, yes."

"But, why?" Powell insisted.

"I don't know, and I would never ask," Conte said.

"All right, Mister Conte. So, this Charlie Rossetti. He works for Victor Albanese. Is that correct?"

Before the defense could object, Conte quickly retorted, "I know nothin' like that."

"OK. But you knew it was the mayor's father, Morgan McCabe, and Mister Ramon Velez, whom you were going to hit. Is that correct?"

"Yeah, of course. A lot of plannin' goes into these things," Conte replied, sliding a bit uncomfortably in his chair, when he saw the angry expression on Powell's face.

"In your statement to the police, you identified and described the activities of your partner in the hit."

"Yeah, right. I did."

"So?" Powell leaned forward.

"So?" Conte responded.

"Mister Conte, please tell this court the name of your co-conspirator," Powell asked, with a slight hint of impatience.

"His name is Trevor Burns. That's all I knew about him," Conte answered.

"What do you mean, that's all you knew about him?" Powell asked.

"I mean just that. I neva met the guy before we got assigned together on this case," Conte said nonchalantly.

"By Charlie Rossetti. Is that correct?"

"Yeah, right.

"OK, Mister Conte, now let me ask you this. How long did this so-called 'planning' take?" Powell asked.

"We watched the old man, his house, and his store for about three weeks."

"Three weeks? My God, what did you do in that time?" Powell went on.

"We used different cars and watched the old guy leave his house, get his coffee and newspapers and all that stuff. We even went inside the store a coupla times," he explained.

"You mean casing the store."

"Yeah, right. Casin' the place."

"Then what, Mister Conte?"

"We made up our minds to jump him outside his house to make it look like we was gonna rob him, and then we would whack him and the other guy once we got inside the store?" Sal Conte responded.

"So is that the way the murders went down?" Powell asked.

"Nah. I was drivin' and the old man sat in the front next to me. Burns sat in the back, behind the old guy. Half ways to the store, Burns jumps up and strangles the old guy, right in the car, with his hands," Conte was almost excited.

"What did you do then?"

"I asked him what he was doin' and he told me had a better plan."

"A better plan. And, what was that plan?" Powell pressed.

"He said I'd soon find out."

"Go on, Mister Conte. Then what happened?"

"When we got to the store we both lifted the old man from the car into the store and put him in a chair next to a desk in the back of the store. I took money out of the cash register to make it look like it was a robbery that killed the two of them. But then Burns grabs a plastic bag from somewheres, throws it over the old guys head and chokes the guy again."

"You mean he killed Morgan McCabe—again?" Powell looked at the jury. "What did you do when Burns choked poor Mister McCabe with the plastic bag."

"I ran into the bathroom and threw up."

"Right. Now why did Burns do what he did?" Powell asked.

"He said that the cops would think that the old guy was choked while sittin' at the desk. You know, again, to make it look like a real robbery."

"So, when did Mister Velez arrive at the store?"

"As usual, as we knew from watchin' the place, he walked in at eight o'clock. We was waiting for him behind some boxes in the back of the store."

"Then what happened?"

"He was supposed to be choked, too, but Burns pulls out this big, long knife and gives him one in the side, and when the guy falls to his knees another in the back," Conte was shaking his head at this time. "Then while the guys layin' in his blood, on the floor, Burns sticks him one more time."

"No more questions for this—this witness, your honor," Jules Powell looked contemptuously at his star witness, did a military about-face and walked slowly past the twelve jurors.

For a long time, no one spoke. Only the noise from the traffic on the Grand Concourse broke the silence in the courtroom as the late winter sun gave way to darkness.

The Bronx District Attorney neatly packaged the people's case by playing the admissible portions of taped conversations between Conte and Rossetti.

In less than twenty-four hours the four women and eight men jury notified the judge that they had reached a verdict.

As they filed into their respective seats, they avoided looking out into the courtroom, fixing their eyes on Judge Forde.

"Members of the jury, have you reached a verdict in the case before you?" she asked.

"Yes, we have, your honor," the young woman responded.

"Madam Forelady. How do you find the defendant on the charges of murder in the first degree, conspiracy to commit murder, and inducing another to commit murder?"

"We find the defendant, Charles Rossetti, guilty on all counts."

Two days later Judge Forde sentenced Rossetti to life imprisonment with no possibility of parole. He was sent to the state's hard time facility at Attica, in picturesque Wyoming County.

Salvatore Conte and Trevor Burns would be tried by the same judge, Judge Anthony Piscopo, and a new jury, but would sit at separate tables on the defense side of the Grand Concourse courtroom. Young lawyers from Legal Aid would represent them both.

Conte just repeated what he had said at Charlie Rossetti's trial. The taped conversations between him and Rossetti played before a predictably subdued audience.

"Mister Burns what is your occupation?" Jules Powell was still at it.

"I am an unemployed furniture maker."

"I was under the impression that those skills were in great demand. How come you can't find a job?"

"I am a bit down on my luck since coming to the United States."

"Oh, so you are not from this country. Where are you from, Mister Burns?" Powell asked, with some light laughter from the audience, many of whom were already having difficulty with Burns' brogue.

When Burns acknowledged his migration from Northern Ireland, Powell asked if he had applied for citizenship and he replied that he hadn't.

"Mister Burns how do you sustain yourself?"

"Sustain?"

"Yes, you know, housing, eating, washing. Things like that."

"Oh, yes, of course. From time to time I do find an employer who is willing to take me on without reporting my earnings to your government," he smiled, with disdain.

"Come on Mister Burns, isn't it true that you are a long-time member of the Westies Mob, a bunch of Irish hoodlums who specialize in carrying out assassination contracts for the five major organized crime families—the Mafia—in New York City, and—"

"Objection, your honor, objection. How can the prosecution jump from questioning my client on why he can't find a job as a furniture maker to becoming a hit man for the mob," Burns's clearly under-30 legal aid lawyer shouted as he jumped to his feet.

"Your honor, we have four expert witnesses from the combined New York City Police Department and the FBI Task Force on organized crime who will testify and present evidence, not only of the criminal activities of the Westies mob in general, but also the role played by Mister Burns, in particular," Powell enjoined.

"Answer the question, Mister Burns," Judge Piscopo ordered.

Burns narrowed his eyes and hunched his eyebrows in the direction of his attorney and shook his head, no.

"Your honor, my client refuses to answer that question, invoking his right not to incriminate himself, under the fifth amendment to the United States—?"

"Yes, yes, OK, I got your plea. Go on Mister Powell."

"What is your relationship with your co-defendant, Salvatore Conte?" Powell stepped closer to the witness stand, and leaned on the railing.

"Well, I am ashamed to say that with what little money I make working on furniture, I spend on a problem I have." He held up his hand in front of Powell's face, "Before you ask, it is cocaine that I use more than I should."

"What's that got to do with Mister Conte?"

"He's my dealer—and has been for quite a time," Burns replied, seeming to exaggerate his Irish inflection.

"OK, whatever. However, Mister Conte has testified here today, and in a previous criminal trial that it was you and he who were hired to murder Morgan McCabe and Ramon Velez by Charlie Rossetti, a member of the Victor Albanese crime family, here in the Bronx. How do you respond to that, Mister Burns?" Powell was back in Burns's face.

"That is absolutely untrue. I can only guess that he has implicated me because I did fall a bit behind on some payments to him for some drugs I had gotten from him—on credit so to speak."

Jules Powell shook his head in disbelief, "I'm finished with this defendant, your honor."

The trials were over.

The jury wasn't out much longer than the jury that had heard the case against Charlie Rossetti.

Sal Conte was convicted of felony murder and, in line with his plea bargain, was sentenced to twenty-five years, with the possibility of parole after five years. He wouldn't share the same prison as Rossetti; he'd go to a "soft time" facility in upstate Fishkill.

Burns's story was too incredible, the jury decided. He got the same verdict and sentence as Rossetti on the McCabe-Velez murders.

Less than three days after the McCabe-Velez verdicts were read, Burns would be tried separately for Murder One in the killing of Detective Steve Covelli. Burns gave the same story and characterized the killing of Detective Steve Covelli as unfortunate, but an act of self-defense on Burns's part. The state's death penalty law on cop killings required that the perp knew that he was shooting at a police officer. The jury didn't buy Burns's self-defense plea, but decided that there was no way he could have known that Steve Covelli was a cop. Rossetti would be sharing the same mailing address with Burns—at least in Trevor's first twenty-five years.

CHAPTER 12

Chris Russo got up, loosened his tie, it was too warm for late April he thought. He started pacing back and forth in front of his troops. It was possibly symbolic that he had always kept a full change of uniform from his last rank, Assistant Chief, in his closet, and had given it a long look this morning. He apparently wanted to remind himself that he was still a cop, not just an administrator and reluctant political in-fighter.

"I don't fully understand just how we got into this face-off with Tom McCabe. But I think it all started back when the city council gave the green light to reorganizing the entire administrative structure of the major city services—including EMS and our emergency services division reporting to the Fire Department and the fire marshals and traffic departments reporting to us. Everyone got shaken up—social services, building and zoning."

"Yes, but in the same period, remember, the whole PAC thing got approved, once McCourty got out of the way," Rothman reminded him.

"And Tom McCabe backed the program all the way," Russo said, "Until he started catching flak from too many voters, the kind that make huge campaign contributions."

Hughes stared down at the carpet and shifted uneasily in his chair. Looking up he finally said, "Now we know how much influence

McCourty had on him. Meanwhile the old bastard is stirring up the cops, using the PBA and the other union groups covering all the guys on the 'Job'—including the bosses."

Russo nodded in agreement and added, "But the Maynard business might have pushed him over the edge. Back when he was in congress he made a big deal out of his liberal image. But then along comes this 'walking cops' dilemma and he's getting flack from the NAACP and the ACLU and the whole goddamn alphabet, while community policing is getting a big boost from its role in getting things back on track."

They spent nearly two hours discussing how best to head-off the mayor's drive to dismantle the programs. Bob Coleman said very little during the meeting and then said:

"The bottom line is that this isn't just about community policing. It's about the economic and social gaps that continue to grow between many of our neighborhoods—my people's communities, Harlem, BedSty and others—Chris, you know as well as I do that cops in cities all over the country, are handling things that usually accompanied a stable home environment, but now have become, by default, the responsibility of various government family and social services programs, and other private, not-for-profit agencies. But while the family structures continue to collapse in many communities, the fundings for those agencies, here and everywhere else has been cut and staffs reduced. The voters—the ones who vote with their wallets—think that all this welfare crap has to stop, so they don't mind if the cops clean up the wreckage—as long as it just keeps getting swept under the rug."

The others in the room were surprised by Coleman's obviously passionate feelings. It wasn't like him to vent and say, unreservedly, what was on his mind. Russo thought for a moment and then turned to Coleman and said, "Bob, you got it right. This battle for community policing is just one part of something a lot bigger. In a sense, the cops are right—they are being turned into part-time social workers. But with no family support and spotty coverage from government agencies, who else is there to do the job, if not them? Cops should never, ever, say, 'Hey, it's not my job.' It is their damn job, until it's done right. I'm meeting with Linda Wright later today. Maybe she can get together enough votes on the council, and get enough public support going out there where people really desperately need what community policing can give them. Without a lot more help, we're going to lose this one."

Coleman nodded in agreement and slowly walked over to the door. "Chris, it's going to take a real surprise attack to stop the mayor—and everyone else who thinks they can turn the clock back," he said quietly.

Russo looked at him thoughtfully and said, "Well, Bob, if you've got any great ideas, you'd better let me have them soon." Turning to the others, he said, "Before you all leave I want to make a little informal announcement." They all went back to their seats at the conference table.

"As you all know, Chips Lombardo threw in his papers this morning. I will only tell you that it was time for him to do that," he continued.

"But the good news for me, and for all of you, is that I've decided to get rid of that pain in the ass sitting outside my office, Dave Rothman."

No one was more stunned by the PC's words than Dave Rothman. Russo broke out into a big grin and announced, "So that's why I'm jumping Dave two ranks; he will be the new deputy chief in command of the Special Investigations Division."

Linda Wright was still stewing over the mayor's plans to water-down the Civilian Complaint Review Board and legally castrate the local Precinct Community Advisory Councils, and impatient with the police commissioner's slow response to her request to have a meeting on both issues. With the murder investigations over, she finally got her chance to host that meeting at her house on Beach Avenue. Hugh Evers, representing the surrounding Morris Park and Pelham Parkway Sections in the city council, Reverend Curt Bratton, Linda's father Calvin, the old curmudgeon of the Country Democratic Club on Starling Avenue, her husband Bob Lake, who had his own law practice on the Grand Concourse at 159th Street, and a surprise participant, the President of the New York City Council, Rich Everett. Chris Russo sat with them around Linda's dining room table.

"What do you say, Rich? You're a relative newcomer to this group," she smiled, looking around the table.

"Not really—If you mean boosting community policing. Today, there are fifty-one members on the council, about a half dozen of who are not happy with community policing. Three or four are under pressure from their suburban constituents, and another three or four who would support the mayor, no matter what," Everett was guessing.

"So, close to two-thirds of the council like the CPOs," Bob Lake said.

Everett believed he had the votes to stop the council from reviewing the legality of the Police Community Advisory Councils. Getting the council to give the PACs some input into citizen complaints against cops would be much more difficult. They all agreed that the mayor could move against community policing without going to the council or anyone else. What would happen then? They all turned to Chris Russo.

"I'd have to consider resigning," Russo responded.

"Yes, that's a possibility. He could then put in his own acting commissioner and that would probably neutralize a lot of CPO support in the city council. It is clear to all of us that McCabe is going to move ahead with his plans to dilute the CPOs influence in the city, and, in the process, discredit Chris Russo. It is just a question of when and how. Probably be when the mayor requests the city council to look into the PACs," Everett said.

"On the other hand, even if Tom isn't successful with that strategy, he can move against the CPOs in other ways," Russo suggested.

"For example?" the Reverend Barton asked.

"There's a class of four-hundred cops scheduled to graduate from the Police Academy in a month. The mayor could direct that I assign those cops to assignments other than Community Policing duties, and if I refused he could pull the plug on an incoming class scheduled to start the week after the others graduate," Russo explained.

"That's right," Everett agreed. "Since I've been involved in raising city monies for this program, I know for the past three and a half years that all rookies became CPOs. If that policy is changed by the mayor, and not the police commissioner, that would make Chris no more than a figurehead and he'd be forced to resign."

"Or Chris could resign as soon as the mayor asked for the PAC review, successful or not. After all, the mayor is going against his wishes by going to the city council in the first place," Hugh Evers said.

"There is an alternative," the police commissioner said, his voice rising as he stood up at the table.

They all paused, looking at him and then to each other.

"I could resign and announce that I will be a candidate for mayor, come November," Russo said. Bob Coleman's remark about a "surprise attack" had hit home.

"Praise be to God," said the Reverend Barton, looking up to the ceiling. "And beyond," someone suggested.

Because Russo had not had time to talk it over with Cathy and their sons, he was more than a bit apprehensive when he returned to the Russo home late that night. He had impulsively made a decision that would affect their lives dramatically and without consulting them first, something he had never done before. He was relieved with Cathy's enthusiastic support of his decision, when they awoke the next morning.

"I don't see that you had any other choice, Chris. In fact I would have been disappointed if you hadn't come to that kind of a decision." She reached up, embraced him and pulled him close to her. "In fact, the boys and I were discussing the possibility of your doing this."

Russo looked at her in astonishment.

"We all agreed that things are approaching a breaking point, and I don't think that you have any more room to compromise. You've got to fight Tom McCabe, Chris. I don't think he's the same person you agreed to serve under."

Holding her husband's face between her hands, she looked into his eyes and said softly, "I know how hard it is going to be. He's been one of your oldest friends. But he's now made himself your enemy, Chris. Don't ever forget that."

Fortified by the unconditional backing of Cathy, Jack, and Richard, Chris Russo began to prepare for what he knew would be the most unpleasant experience of his life.

Over the next few days, he tried to get some free time from his schedule. He needed some time to think and plan. He tried to get to the office at least an hour earlier than usual and stayed well beyond his regular getaway time. This change drove the headquarters' chiefs, and their staffs, nuts. Their workdays began just before, and ended just after, the PC arrived and left. The last person to leave the police commissioner's office each day would transmit the most important message of the day—"The CLOSE is on" would be the cryptic message that each chief or his most trusted aide would receive each night. It meant the commissioner was about to leave for the day, and it was safe for everyone else to go home.

At 6:00 p.m., on Friday afternoon, with those at police headquarters still awaiting the "Close," Chris Russo used his private line to call Cathy.

"I've decided to do it today. I'll resign. I'll put it in writing and deliver it personally to Tom on Monday morning."

"I see," Cathy said softly. "Thank God it will all come out into the open now."

They then discussed the danger of waiting until Monday. Russo had to make other calls, and he had to tell his staff. There was no way it wouldn't leak and Russo didn't want all the speculation in the media that would follow a rumor that the police commissioner was going to make some kind of announcement on Monday.

"Well, this whole thing is about people and trust. If I don't trust the people with whom I surround myself—at work, and at home—who then?"

"Yes, Chris, it is about trust. But don't make the mistake of trusting the wrong people. If you delay you're going to give somebody the chance to put out some kind of rumor about you or even preempt your announcement and make you look bad," Cathy Russo warned.

Russo realized she was right.

"OK, it's time to bite the bullet. We go now—no waiting around. I will keep it to people I know I have to trust—but I gotta tell my guys and the people putting themselves on the line for me."

In quick succession he called Linda Wright, Rich Everett and everyone else who would support his challenging McCabe. As eight o'clock came and went, it became obvious to everyone at police headquarters that there would be no "close" that night. Then Russo buzzed his new staff chief, Deputy Inspector Matthew Reynolds of Parkchester fame.

"OK, Matt, tell Tom Ford to put out the word," he laughed. He would be the first police commissioner to do that—he, and all his predecessors, weren't supposed to be aware of such a practice as the "Close."

"But, Matt, I want you, Bob Coleman, Terry Hughes, and Dave Rothman to stay behind for awhile. Be in my office in about five minutes," he added.

It wasn't a good meeting. Bob Coleman, who, by law, would be the acting police commissioner until the mayor appointed an interim or new one, insisted he would leave on Monday, too. The others expressed a desire to leave quickly, if not on Monday. They were all mindful of a basic rule for cops: "Don't get carried out on your shield." It meant, "Get out while you're on top. You'll be missed, but the decision to leave will be yours, not someone else's. On the other hand, if you overstay your welcome—you'll probably be told to go, and soon be forgotten."

His senior staff reluctantly accepted Russo's argument against a mass resignation. They all agreed to stay and abide by the mayor's wishes—whatever they might be—but not without great bitterness and animosity towards McCabe. Each of them was apprehensive about what might happen. But each promised to keep quiet until Monday and batten down the hatches for the storm to come.

Russo's ad hoc committee met for over twelve hours, on Saturday and Sunday, first at his house in Riverdale, and then Linda Wright's on Beach Avenue. There were disagreements on strategy. Everett, as the ranking Democrat in elected office, reminded them that McCabe was an independent candidate who would want to get support from the city's Democratic leadership, as would Russo. Russo agreed to run either as an independent candidate, or as a Democrat. It made little difference to him.

"Remember, I'm running so that CPOs won't disappear from our city's streets. Party affiliation isn't that important to me."

That worried Everett. "Look, I've made the mistake of supporting so-called visionary candidates before. You don't have a choice. You need party backing and money, lots of it."

"I don't like that money shit," he argued.

"Well, you don't have to like it, but you must face the realities of running for public office, Chris." Russo's insistence on taking the high road also annoyed Everett.

"My God, Chris, you've got all you need for a devastating attack on the integrity and honesty of an incumbent mayor," he shouted.

Russo stubbornly insisted that he would attack McCabe only for trying to tank Community Policing.

"If you believe, as I do, that Community Policing is only the first step, towards defusing the social and economic time bombs ticking away in our poorest communities, that should be enough to talk about, and to focus our attack on him."

Everett backed off, at least for the time being. "OK, we'll work it out. Let's get set for Monday."

As the police commissioner got about halfway up the eleven marble steps leading to the front entrance of City Hall, one of the two cops from the department's Municipal Security Section ran over to him.

"Good morning, Commissioner. How are you? The mayor's not in yet," the young cop informed him.

"Hi. How are you, uh, Donovan?" the commissioner said, squinting to make out the cop's nameplate on the left breast pocket of his uniform coat. "Yeah, I know that. I'm going to catch him on his way in. Thanks, officer."

He walked slowly towards the west wing, where the mayor's office was located and waited in the deserted outer office.

The first deputy mayor, Stan Brent, was the first to arrive.

"Chris, how are you?" he said. "Pretty early, eh? Wanna see the mayor, I suppose?"

"Yes, Stan. I'm not on his schedule. I just need a few minutes," Russo said.

"I'm sure it's OK. He should be in any minute now." Brent was a seasoned pol, a former state senator who had served with McCabe on the city council; all of his instincts told him that this was no mere social call. He ducked into his office, anticipating the phone call he knew would come soon.

It was another fifteen minutes before McCabe arrived at the three-foot high, wrought-iron railing separating his office from the main corridor running the length of City Hall. The suite of offices housing the mayor and his staff was at one end and the city council's staff offices at the other. He was clearly surprised to see Russo waiting for him.

"Chris, Good Morning. Do we have a meeting this early?" the mayor asked. He knew who he was scheduled to see that day and Russo definitely wasn't one of them.

"No, Mr. Mayor. But it's very important that I see you. It will only take a minute or two," Russo answered.

"OK. Come on in while I hang up my coat and unpack my brief-case," the mayor said, smiling.

He settled behind his desk and asked Russo to sit, but the police commissioner said he wasn't going to stay that long.

"Mr. Mayor, I've decided to resign as your police commissioner," Russo said quickly and without emotion.

"Here it is in writing," he added, handing the mayor a large, white envelope with the police department logo, and police commissioner's five gold stars embossed on the upper left side.

"Needless to say, Chris, I'm sorry to hear this," McCabe said. "Of course, I know that you've been unhappy with some of the decisions I've made lately, affecting your department. But I'm doing what I think is best for all the people of New York City," he continued.

"Yes, you're right. I am unhappy with what you've been doing with the police department. And I don't believe what you're doing is good for the communities of our city," Russo replied.

The mayor was determined to keep his cool.

"Well, who said, 'Even good friends can disagree'?"

"Yes, sir, you're right. I hope we will remain friends," Russo responded sincerely.

"Of course, Chris. And I'll always be accessible to you, if you need me. Do you have any plans?" the mayor asked.

"Yes, Tom. I do," Russo replied.

"Good. What are they?" the mayor asked.

"I'm going after your job, Tom."

McCabe was stunned. He just stared at his police commissioner, saying nothing.

"Well, that's it, Mr. Mayor. Thanks for your time. Bob Coleman will be in charge at 1 Police Plaza. Awaiting your directions, of course," Russo said, walking towards the door. He felt a deep sense of satisfaction at the knowledge that there had been no leaks—and relief at coming out into the open.

"You son of a bitch, Russo, you dirty son of a bitch," the mayor said, finally able to shake himself out of his shock. He jumped up from his chair and stared at Russo. "This time I'm going to kick your ass. You dirty bastard."

Russo stared back at him as a feeling of deep sadness came over him.

"Tom, you forced me to do this. You're trying to trash everything I've worked for, you've forgotten—"

McCabe cut him off, and clenched his fists. "Stop the shit, Russo. You're stepping way out of your league, cop," he snapped, his face flushed with anger. "And if you think you're going to use that Rossetti shit, or drag me or Gordon Halliday through a dirty campaign, forget it."

"Good-bye, Tom, and good luck," Russo called out, as he opened the door.

When it closed behind him he heard the parting shot from his old friend, "Fuck you, Russo."

❧   ❧   ❧

The Committee to Elect James Christopher Russo had to decide where their candidate would simultaneously announce his stepping down as police commissioner and his intention to run for mayor. If he was just saying farewell to the cops and making no other announcement, it would be appropriate to hold a press conference in the auditorium at 1 Police Plaza. On the other hand, if he was not the police commissioner, but someone leaving some other job to run for mayor, it would be appropriate—albeit "tacky," according to Linda Wright—to hold his press conference on the landing halfway up the steps of City Hall. Linda Wright had offered the large. City Council Committee room.—It would have infuriated the mayor—which was probably why she made the suggestion. However, Everett had serious reservations about that.

"There may even be legal problems, using city-owned property for political purposes," he said.

Hugh Evers finally came up with the perfect setting.

"This is all about Community Policing. And where did it all start? The old Laundromat storefront on Westchester Avenue, between Pugsley and Olmstead."

The press conference was at noon. The press took up virtually all the space. Russo went to the front of the room, faced the phalanx of cameras and lights, turned briefly to his right, grinned, and waved to Linda Wright, Charlie Evers, Rich Everett, and the rest of his supporters.

Cathy, Jack, and Richard Russo entered through the rear door. When his wife came to the front, he kissed her and told her to stand directly behind him. Their two sons followed, shaking their father's hand and taking a place next to Cathy.

"Good afternoon," Russo began, smiling and looking at his watch.

"I'm sure that most of you have already written your stories," he said, getting a laugh from the reporters.

"But maybe I can still fill in some of the gaps for you," he continued.

"At about seven-thirty this morning, I met with Mayor McCabe and submitted my resignation."

There was no reaction from the assembled reporters; Russo proceeded to give what was in effect the prototype for the speech he intended to give throughout the campaign, reminding the reporters of the history of community policing and the mayor's attempt to undermine it as well as the civilian complaint review board realignment. For the first time in many months, he was able to talk about the widening gap between those whose dreams were being realized and those who had little hope of achieving theirs in New York City, which was creating explosive conditions in the neighborhoods largely ignored or abandoned by the current administration.

"And, who's out there in the streets, all the time. Who sees the problems, first hand?—Only a cop."

"So, if not him or if not her, who then?"

"I believe that cops have the responsibility, and should have the authority, to report and follow up on anything they see that threatens the well-being of any citizen in this city—rich or poor, black or white. Our seventy-six police stations are all now part of the Community Policing Program. The concept is working, and I can assure you that among the cops there are many more converts each day."

"Just as important as the changing of police attitudes towards the Community Policing Program, is the dramatic transformation of the role of the communities and their leaders towards the police. That Kerner Commission report cited the great need for expanded opportunities for ordinary people to participate in shaping decisions and policies that affect their communities. That's why we established Police Community Advisory Councils, PACs, in each of our seventy-six police stations, along with a Police Community Service Center to get all city government services closer to the people in the streets of those neighborhoods. They've worked extremely well, and each day is becoming more of a force in shaping the strategies to solve community problems. The mayor has decided that these PACs are somehow illegal, or something—I've never really been told what his objections are. It's puzzling to me, since he supported the establishment of the councils in the first place."

"Tom McCabe seems to have withdrawn his past enthusiastic support for the CPOs, too. He and I have had some discussions on this subject, but I'm still not clear on what he's trying to do—or not do—quite frankly. I think he's making a terrible mistake in pulling his support from the Community Policing Program, and I think I can best fight for the program's survival by not working for him."

"That's why I told him this morning that I resigned."

Russo stopped speaking and the questions came at him thick and fast.

"So, you quit. Just like that?" Ben Weinberg shouted out.

"Right," Russo responded.

"But you're supposed to say good things about him, and he's supposed to accept your resignation with great regrets," Weinberg said, and several reporters laughed.

"Does this have anything to do with something other than the Police Community Advisory Councils?" one of the TV newsmen asked.

"No. I'm just not going to stand by and watch the CPOs disappear," Russo explained.

"Yeah, but how is your quitting going to help?" he persisted.

"Because I'm going to run for mayor, against McCabe."

This produced a new outburst of questions from all corners of the room.

"Hold it. I'll spend as much time with you as you want. So, let's start from the right side of the room and then to the left, row by row, alternating front rows with back rows," Russo suggested.

"Do you expect to be endorsed by one of the political parties?" Weinberg asked.

"I hope to run in the Democratic primary. But I'm going to run, in any event—as an independent candidate if I have to," Russo responded.

"How much money have you raised?" a follow-up question.

Everett made his way to the bank of microphones.

"I have put out feelers to some members of my party this morning, after Chris Russo informed the mayor of his plans. The response has been heartening, to say the least. Chris has a lot of support in the legislature, while the mayor has disappointed many of them when he announced his intention to dismantle the local Police Community Advisory Councils, among other things. Many of our constituents feel that, for the first time, they have some influence over public policies affecting their neighborhoods and they're happy as hell with the CPOs. We expect to see an outpouring of campaign contributions to support those views."

Russo broke in at this point and introduced Cathy, John, and Richard to the assembled press. "These three are, of course, the real committee to elect Chris Russo, Mayor of New York City."

Russo motioned for all three to join him so the photographers could get the usual family shots. He was hoping to end the press conference but the questions continued. Reporters tried to open up the Rossetti case and its connections to McCabe. Russo refused to open up the subject and responded to the question with a "no comment."

"Whadda ya' mean, no comment? It's gonna surface in the campaign."

"I don't care. I'm not going to comment on it now or ever. Relevance. Relevance, folks. What's it got to do with family structure, school dropouts, the criminals who peddle drugs in our communities, pigsties that pass for housing, and no jobs?"

"Do you think the cops will support your candidacy?"

"I hope so. They know I believe they are the ones who have to fire up the consciences of us all to get this city back to where it was. I think most of them are willing to assume that responsibility and are committed to pulling it off."

"How about the cop and detective unions?"

"Same answer. They represent the rank and file and most of the cops and detectives support the Community Policing Program."

"What's your reply to those communities that think they are paying more than their fair share of the taxes, and getting less 'bang for the buck' from Community Policing?"

"Well, if, in fact, these poor neighborhoods don't generate their fair share of the tax burden in our city, and yet get the biggest piece of those tax dollars for homelessness, child welfare, public housing—and law enforcement programs, incidentally—there must be a reason. And once we identify those reasons, doesn't it make sense to get rid of those things that are social and economic obstacles to those communities becoming as self-sustaining and independent as those communities that don't have the same problems?"

"Aren't you concerned that the mayor will dismantle everything you've put in place between now and the election?" another reporter asked. Some of the press was leaving to file their stories.

"No. He knows these programs are working, and working well, and the people in the communities are happy with the CPOs. Besides, he was as responsible as I was for expanding the program throughout the city. How could he possibly justify pulling his support now?"

"Besides, he also knows that I'll only put it all back when I take over his job later this year," Russo said, getting some laughs in response.

Ben Weinberg pushed his way to the front again, and asked.

"Will your lack of political experience hinder you in any way during the campaign?"

"No."

"No? Why not?"

"Because this isn't about politics as usual. This campaign is about keeping this city from falling apart."

He looked around the room and chose his words carefully. "What you heard today you're going to hear over and over again. It's what I believe. It is why I'm here. That's the only way I know how to campaign. So, what you see is what you get."

It was over. The press started packing up. A few reporters went after some of the people who had been standing with Russo at the front of the room. Everett and Wright were particularly singled out and Bob Coleman stayed behind to answer questions about the police side of things.

Russo and his family went into the back room of the storefront where coffee and pastries had been put out on a table. Chris Russo picked up a chocolate frosted donut and grinned.

"They ought to get a picture of me eating this. The whole damn force runs on donuts."

❧   ❧   ❧

Russo was back at campaign headquarters, a store that had been vacant up until this morning, and which was next to what was now a newly renovated and busy Laundromat on Westchester Avenue. He was sitting alone for the first time during this hectic day for him, as well as for his family. He was reflecting on what had just taken place. He was now a politician. He had always seen a great difference between using the "delicate art" for a good cause and actually getting paid for it. He despised lobbyists, mostly failed elected officials and bureaucrats who had lost their cushy government jobs. All but a few politicians, in Russo's opinion, sooner or later lost the qualities of realness and sincerity. Some losing it even before they spent the first day in newly decorated, expensively furnished offices.

Some became thieves, corrupt and utterly selfish. But eventually they all lost the ability to be sincere. The first commandment for any politician was "Thou shall not ever lose an election."

Even before Tom McCabe decided to run for Congress from the 16th District, Russo had thought that he might be good at representing his Bronx neighborhood in Washington. But he was quick to see the metamorphosis of his friend as he moved from representing New York City's 18th Councilmanic District to his election to New York State's legislature, and finally Congress. He watched McCabe be consumed by the desire to stay in office—at any cost.

He felt some reassurance when he told himself that worrying about reelection would not inhibit him when he had to speak out on issues. But when he thought about the kinds of questions and problems that would come his way he began to feel a small corner of fear inside himself, a corner, which grew in size as his imagination, took him through all the possibilities. Apart from the social issues related to the community policing program, he would have to address the city's wider fiscal problems, the wisdom of going ahead with a contemplated bond issue to fund major renovations of part of the harbor to make it more efficient for the handling of container ships, and other problems that he was as well informed about as anyone who read the papers, which was to say not very well informed at all, at least for someone who proposed to run the country's biggest, and most complicated city.

Russo decided that he would have to put together a kind of "think tank" made up of people from the city council, even some of the top people in McCabe's administration who he knew were disenchanted with the way McCabe was handling issues that affected their departments. He needed a cram course in city government; to pretend otherwise would only be fooling himself. And he sure as hell wouldn't fool the voters, Russo thought, if he couldn't handle what the press and public was eager to throw at him. It was, he thought, kind of like having a picnic in a minefield. But he tried to assure himself that he could handle it all. While the Community Policing program would be the centerpiece of his campaign, there were many other things he had to be ready to meet head-on during the campaign. Whatever happens, Russo promised himself, I'll run the campaign my way and turn a deaf ear to the kinds of pressures that would surely come from the Gordon Hallidays of this world. And as each day passed, Russo became more confident about dumping Tom McCabe.

McCabe and his staff were ready when the explosion of calls followed Russo's press conference. The official line to the media was, "We'll wait until we have seen the tape of the press conference, and then maybe make an appropriate statement." The strategy was not to act surprised, but react with an air of indifference.

McCabe viewed a videotape of the press conference and then took half dozen calls from selected reporters. He gave the impression, without actually saying it, that he considered Chris Russo a disgruntled police commissioner who, when he couldn't have his way, decided to quit. Someone other than Russo himself, in McCabe's opinion, must have talked him into running against the mayor—because he certainly didn't bring any political experience to his campaign.

"Running the police department is one thing, running the entire city is completely different, experience, skills and talents that I don't think Chris Russo possesses," the mayor said, thereby firing his opening shot in the campaign.

McCabe also decided to play it cool with the cops. He appointed Bob Coleman as Acting Police Commissioner—a popular move—and told him he would be a serious candidate for the position when the mayor conducted a search for a permanent replacement for Russo. However, he also asked that Coleman clear all major decisions affecting the department with the first deputy mayor, Stan Brent. Bruce Solnich wanted that assignment, but Gordon Halliday was adamant about keeping him away from a sensitive and potentially embarrassing situation. The top rank of the police department would accept Brent's role as the mayor's watchdog—at least for a while. It was obvious the mayor wasn't going to do anything to hurt the department or, for that matter, help it in the months before the election. McCabe would attempt to "neutralize" the CPOs as a campaign issue, too. Interestingly, Dan McCourty called Bob Coleman and offered to help in any way he could on that matter. Coleman managed to disguise his contempt for the man when McCourty made his utterly unanticipated approach.

"The prick," Bob said, after hanging up on the ex-police commissioner-turned-spy.

McCabe was most upset by the defection of Rich Everett. He had not expected support from either Linda Wright or Hugh Evers, but Everett was a nasty surprise. While he and the city council president had never been close, they had what McCabe considered a cordial working relationship dating from the time both were serving in the state legislature and throughout their years in city government. McCabe made no secret of his bitterness about being abandoned by the city's highest-ranking Democrat. Everett had received an avalanche of calls from those eager to jump on the Russo bandwagon. He was caught by surprise because he had underestimated the strength of the opposition to McCabe.

Everett had made a quick survey of the fifty-one council members, thirty of whom were Democrats. The first stop for the Russo train would be the primaries, in July. Only five said they were supporting McCabe, come hell or high water, ten were undecided, and fifteen, mostly those representing the less affluent parts of the city, would support Russo in July. It was quite heartening and with little real effort on the "committee's" part. Even the press started to be of much more help than they had expected. The Russo team was as delighted with that as they were with the impressive numbers reported by Rich Everett.

But Bruce Solnich's talents were not wasted. His assignment would be to discredit Chris Russo. His activities ranged from painting the newly announced mayoral candidate as not being a "team player" who had undermined the administrations of the two police commissioners he had last served under, Dan McCourty and then Harold Bartels, to his "covering up" the illegal immigration status of Ramon Velez, to his qualifications to be mayor—"after all, he's just a cop." Solnich got Dan McCourty to speak out on the "loyalty issue." Against the advice of Gordon Halliday. He was convinced that Russo would retaliate by revealing McCourty's—and Solnich's—role in using Lombardo as a spy inside the police department. Russo didn't, and Solnich's tactics were vindicated. But Harold Bartels refused to comment on the entire matter, and the strategy fizzled when a couple of reporters suggested that McCourty wanted to be the police commissioner again and that his undermining of the administration of Mayor Paul Williams was the reason for Williams' defeat by Tom McCabe.

Solnich ultimately got a drubbing on the Velez issue, too. Ellen McCabe held a press conference along with U.S. Attorney Amanda Stevens and Teresa Velez; it turned into a memorial to Velez and his activities on behalf of the Parkchester community. But he really got socked when he used some of Marvelous Marv's old interviews with cops to show that the rank and file of the police department did not solidly support Community Policing. Solnich hadn't asked Marv's permission, and the shock jock was so pissed that he devoted an entire five-hour session talking to, commiserating with, and lauding three of New York City's finest, Munro, Savino and Joyce.

But Solnich, who never knew when to quit, kept plugging away as the countdown on the election ticked away the days.

PART IV

And into my garden stole,
When the night had veiled the pole;
In the morning glad I see;
My foe outstretched beneath the tree.

—**Blake, st. 4**

CHAPTER 13

*B*efore leaving, Russo had warned Bob Coleman and people he would leave behind at 1 Police Plaza, to be extremely careful to avoid doing anything that might be interpreted as supporting their former boss in his run for mayor. He probably didn't have to do that. Discretion was something cop commanders learned very quickly on their way to higher ranks. Nevertheless, they were quickly put to the test when just one week into the Russo campaign, Hughes and Rothman asked to meet with the acting police commissioner on a delicate matter.

About two weeks before, a story appeared in the back pages of *The Post* reporting that Charlie Rossetti, who was doing his time in the state's maximum security prison had been set upon by a couple of inmates who had apparently stabbed him in his chest and stomach. He was reported to be in the prison's hospital ward, and would recover.

Within two days of the assault, Horan, now assigned to the department's Special Investigations Division, had received a telephone call from someone using an obviously disguised voice, claiming to be calling on behalf of Charlie Rossetti. The caller said that he had information which hadn't surfaced in the McCabe-Velez murder trial, and which would, "blow the fuckin' roof off this town."

"So? What are you dealing?" Horan had asked.

"Charlie gets a reduced sentence, gets out a little bit earlier than he's supposed to and goes into that bullshit program—protection for stoolies—or somethin' like that, in exchange for the information," he said.

"That's a big order, *paisan*. What kind of information?" Horan asked.

"It's about this guy, Holiday," the voice said.

Horan had put the call on the speakerphone so a detective at the next desk could hear the conversation. He whispered, "If I didn't know Charlie Rossetti was actually in the slammer, I'd swear this was him."

"Halliday, you mean, Halliday?" Horan shouted into the speaker-phone.

"Whatever. Anyways, this Holiday was dirty and the mayor was, too. Whatta ya' say, are you intri-sted?" he asked.

"What do you mean, the mayor was, too?"

"I'm tellin' you no more. Are ya' intri-sted, or ain't you?"

"We'll talk again," Horan said. "Call me back in two hours."

"No, I'll call ya back, same time, two days from now. You want to hear what I gotta say, be ready to deal."

Horan went to his boss, Deputy Chief Dave Rothman, who took him to see Hughes. Now they were all in Bob Coleman's office.

"Obviously, you guys think this guy is credible or we wouldn't been having this meeting, right?" Coleman said.

"Well, Commissioner, yes—we do think this guy is for real. But there's a chance that he could be pulling our chain. So, we'd like to get some corroboration, if we can," Horan said.

"Corroboration?" the acting police commissioner inquired.

"Yes, sir," Horan said. "I think I could set up a meet with Victor Albanese, and take a shot at confirming or disproving the authentic-ity of this guy's offer."

"But Albanese was Rossetti's boss and he made him cop a plea. I don't see your logic here," Coleman said. "And meeting—talking—or whatever with Albanese would tip him off and screw up a chance to pin the murders on that guinea *fuck*."

Hughes spoke up at this point. "But we're not doing anything about that possibility right now. The feds have been working with us, looking into some possible money laundering involving Gordon Halliday, which may involve Albanese, and then again it might not. But in any event it's moving slowly. Right, guys?" the chief of detectives said, looking at Horan and another detective with him. "We don't know what this guy is dealing. It may involve that aspect of the case, and it might not. But we might learn something. And, if we can make Victor's life more miserable, or even get Charlie Rossetti to give up Victor to us, why not?"

"OK, guys. But let's kick it around a little more before making a decision," Coleman said.

"OK," Hughes quickly followed up. "This is still an anonymous call, so we can handle it in a number of ways." The chief of detectives smiled and held up one finger. "First. We can follow through on the call and try to authenticate it. But, we'd have to consider the downside, if any, of speaking with Albanese about one of his former soldiers."

He raised his middle finger. "Two. If we follow up, does that make it an official complaint—which would mean that we would have to notify the Bronx District Attorney? Would that create a political brouhaha?"

"Oh, shit, yeah," Dave Rothman said. "I don't think any of us know where he stands in the upcoming mayoral race. Talking to him could be political dynamite."

"Right," Hughes said. "Three. If everything checks out, we must deal with the DA, and some judge or judges would have to be involved in order to meet Rossetti's demand for reducing his jail sentence. And four. We could 'shit-can' the whole thing."

"I don't think so, not right now," Coleman said. "But then again, we should never rule it out as an option."

"What about checking with our old boss?" Rothman said.

They all shook their heads from side to side at that one.

"OK, then we keep it to ourselves and play it out. Horan, you lead on this one. Don't screw it up."

❧   ❧   ❧

Horan drove his own car over the Whitestone Bridge to the College Point Auto Pound in Queens to see an old academy classmate. He was the same age as Horan, but looked ten years older. He had never wanted to be a cop, but took the exam under pressure from his father, a sergeant in the old infamous 41—"Fort Apache"—precinct, he passed and was in training before he realized what he had done. He was almost a washout because of his dedication to eating at least three heavy meals a day. After graduating he volunteered for any job that would keep him off the streets. He finally ate himself into a "restricted duty" status and his current post overseeing abandoned vehicles that had been towed off the city's streets. Roger's friend had a way with cars and was able start up some of the near-derelicts that ended up in the auto pound. Horan went to him whenever he needed a nondescript car to use in an investigation. And that meant buying his old buddy large and expensive meals in an expensive restaurant, chosen by the derelict auto specialist.

Horan selected an old Chevy Bel Air. It would never be mistaken for a police vehicle. Even the Narcs wouldn't want to use it. He went back over the bridge and up the Grand Concourse. He pulled into the parking lot of Pasquale Corsentino and Sons Funeral Home just off 186th Street and parked his auto as far away from the main building as possible. He went to the rear building used for embalming and knocked on the steel-plated door.

"Oh, Mr. Horan. *Gizza deech*. I heard you were coming," Anthony Corsentino, seventy-three years old and the grandson of the home's namesake, greeted him. White rubber gloves and a blue stain-resistant full apron, covering him from his shoulders to his kneecaps, did not fully cover the white-on-white shirt, black bow tie, and velour vest he always wore.

"*Gizza deech, bon giorno*, Mr. Corsentino. When can the father see me? *In petto*, of course," Horan asked, bowing gracefully to the old man. Horan was always amazed by how often a meeting with any godfather involved the intercession of a priest.

A few minutes later he was on his way to St. Bernard's R.C. Church on the other side of the Belmont Section. Father Ciccio Felluci, who had been ordained in Sicily and imported to the Bronx many years ago, heard the young detective's "confession," although regular hours for penance were not until six that evening.

"Bless me, Father, for I have sinned. It's been two months since my last confession," Horan began.

"Yes, I know, my son. I ask that you share your thoughts with your friend and mine, by speaking with Mr. Peter Agnello. He will see you at one o'clock this afternoon," the elderly priest said to his penitent.

Horan arrived at the Kingsbridge Cannoli King Bakery precisely at one. He got into a stretch limo parked in the driveway. He sat alone in the rear of the Cadillac for over two hours on a long-distance ride on the Long Island Expressway. They got off the LIE at exit 64 and went North to Route 25 and then east to Middle Island in Suffolk County and a former premier pet cemetery, long abandoned—its former owners had duped a couple hundred pet owners into thinking their loved ones were resting in beautifully carved, ostentatiously-adorned, high-priced, caskets under some fancy and expensive tomb stones. Actually, the father and son team had only one casket, which they sold to each of the bereaved "parents." The dogs were cremated and their remains thrown into the Town of Brookhaven's dump site. Another "stretch" was waiting for him, under a huge elm that despite its obvious loss of leaves still provided shade from the mid-afternoon sun.

A young barrel-chested guy, over six feet six, wearing an obviously expensive suit, "Armani," Horan guessed, jumped from behind the wheel of the parked limo and quickly opened the rear door. A small gray-haired man stepped from the rear of the car. He was stoop-shouldered, his frail body enclosed in a cashmere topcoat, and a homburg sitting on top of what seemed to be a solid head of white hair. He walked haltingly, holding a cigarette in his left hand. As he approached the detective, he began coughing so violently that Horan was about to go to his assistance. He covered his mouth, shooed the cop away, and took a drag on the cigarette. They did not shake hands.

"Hey, Roger. What's doin', *goombah*?" he hissed through the sto-mata in his throat.

"I received a call from someone who said that he was representing the best interests of Charlie Rossetti," Horan said.

"Yeah. So?" he said, coughing, while still sticking the cigarette between his teeth, taking a big draw, and coughing again. "How's he doin'? I hear he got stuck by some crazy niggers."

"I don't know how he's doing and I didn't ask. What I want to know is what is this guy trying to deal us? Do you know anything about it?" Horan asked, as the old man turned his body halfway around while trying to suppress a cough.

He came back to facing Horan and merely shook his head, no. That son of a bitch knows everything about this, the detective thought to himself.

"Charlie Rossetti? Hey, Rog, you know we call him Charlie *Pazzo*, crazy. He's a stupid fuck—a *pantelone*, ya know a fuckin' brag-gart—always he's gettin' in trouble with the broads. An itchy crotch, I told him. But, hey kid, I'm a *Geppetto*, like all bosses; sometimes I make woodenheaded dummies, like Charlie. You know, like that guy in the story, *Finocchio*," Albanese spoke so long, he started to cough up blood.

"I no nothin' about no call, like I never had nothin' to do with the mayor's old man or his spick friend. As you know, Rog, and when I found out about it, I made sure *Pazzo* spilled his guts."

Horan shook his head.

"Hey, and I also don't like this guy, Holiday, and his whole fuckin' family," he said suddenly.

"Halliday, Gordon Halliday—his family?"

Horan started to speak, but Albanese waved him off, turned and headed back to his car.

The "meet" was over.

Horan was dropped off behind the Cannoli King's kitchen. He could smell the panetone baking. "They're getting ready for Easter already?" he said to himself. Someone had reported an abandoned car in the restaurant parking lot. The cops had put a "pick up" sticker on the window on the driver's side, alerting the Sanitation Department to tow it to the pound. Horan drove back to Queens with his head hanging outside the window.

Dave Rothman hadn't liked the idea of no "back up" for Horan. He would not go home until the detective reported back to him at headquarters. He was fidgeting at his desk when Horan knocked softly on his door. It was close to midnight.

"Roger. Good. Come in," a relieved Rothman smiled.

"I think we've got a problem, sir. As usual, Victor Albanese said too much and he didn't say enough," he said.

Horan explained that Albanese denied knowing about the call from Rossetti. The detective also said that he hadn't asked Albanese about the murders of the mayor's father and Ramon Velez, but Albanese brought it up, strange for him since he never initiated a discussion that Horan could remember. Volunteering his dislike of Gordon Halliday was another attempt to muddy the waters even more. Horan told his boss that he believed that Albanese threw in the McCabe case and Halliday's name for a reason, and finding out what that was could be the key to understanding this entire Rossetti rat-out scenario.

It was after one in the morning. Rothman told Horan to meet him in the police commissioner's office at seven-thirty.

Within five minutes, Coleman, Hughes and Reynolds were shaking their heads after hearing Horan's briefing of his meet with Victor Albanese. They went back over their options—go it alone, for a while. Well, they did that with the Horan-Albanese meet. They got more than they bargained for. Next option—call in the Bronx District Attorney.

"What would we tell him at this point?" Coleman inquired. Nothing, they all agreed.

Call Chris Russo?

"But we still may 'shit-can' this thing," Terry Hughes said. "So, why bring in our former boss at this time, if at all?"

They agreed that the next step was to hear about the deal Charlie Rossetti was offering. The caller did not indicate how he could be contacted, of course, but said that he would call Horan exactly forty-eight hours from the time of the first call.

"Just about two and a half hours from now," Dave Rothman said.

The call came in precisely at ten o'clock. Horan indicated he would listen to the offer but couldn't commit to going beyond that. The caller didn't like that.

"But I'm told you can be trusted," he said. "You know, *solo soci.*"

He then set up a rendezvous with Horan; far less furtive than the way the young detective had had to meet with Victor Albanese. In fact, they would meet in the most public of places, the Port Authority Bus Terminal at 625 Eighth Avenue at West 40th Street, which also enjoyed the reputation of being one of New York City's shabbiest sites. On the other hand, for the two actors in this drama, secrecy was ensured—the chance of either of them being seen by someone they knew was rather remote. Many of the "passengers" sitting inside the terminal were homeless and those getting on or off the buses were from the same social strata, except they had somehow cashed in enough deposit cans and bottles to either get to, or get out of, New York City.

While Horan and the caller had a prearranged code to identify each other, it was clearly unneeded. Even though they were dressed to fit in, their wardrobes couldn't possibly have matched those favored by most terminal users. Besides, no one could duplicate the stink that hung over the entire terminal.

"Hey, *paisan*," Horan's new friend acknowledged once the ID was made.

He was in his early thirties, and the detective didn't think he ever saw him before. He probably didn't have a "sheet"—a police record—and could have been from outside New York City. Horan wouldn't try to verify either.

They sat in adjoining telephone booths—very few of the terminal's passengers could afford to call long-distance, or "any distance," Horan was thinking. Besides, half the phones were not working; the constant punching of the coin return button by passing vagrants made fixing them a futile effort by Bell Atlantic. They sat facing each other, legs crossed, leaning half out of their respective booths. Later, after an hour, Horan could hardly uncurl from his position to get up; his legs were so locked into place that he actually had to slam his calves to pry them loose.

His was a tale of horror, not in the traditional sense, but for those who would have to sift through the details. According to his companion—he refused to give Horan his name—it all started with "dis new police shit."

"New police shit?" Horan asked loudly.

Two homeless guys pushing a baby carriage full of old newspapers were momentarily stunned by the shouting coming from a telephone booth. They stopped and looked at the guys causing the commotion. They shrugged their shoulders and went about their business—going to the booths adjoining Horan's and his friend's and punching at the coin return keys. It sounded like they got a couple of returns. They resumed their journey, proudly throwing the coins up and down in the tattered gloves covering their hands.

"Yeah, you know, this foot cop shit. Ya know, they took the pricks out of their cushy fuckin' cars and made them walk the streets. When they were in the cars they didn't know shit what was going on. They just listened to the fuckin' radio and sped off with their lights and horns—"

"Sirens, Sonny" Horan interrupted and smiled.

"Yeah, yeah, sirens. That's good," Sonny said.

"If you won't give me a name, I'll give you one," Horan said. Sonny ignored him.

"Charlie said that he and Victor Albanese and everyone else was always happy to see those fucks so busy, flyin' by and zippin' up and down the streets. They saw nothin'," Sonny went on.

"Then they started to walk and talk—and walk and talk. It was no good for business."

"Business?"

"Come on stop the shit, Rog. You know what I mean, the books, the numbers, whores, crack—and now, this exazee, shit, you name it," he said.

"Ecstasy," Horan said. Sonny didn't flinch.

"Charlie said that it seemed like the cops was always around now, 'the last thing we needed.' Charlie told me. He and Victor thought maybe they coulda put 'em on the 'pad'—ya know take care of them—but it didn't work. 'What kind of fuckin' cops have we got in this city nowadays anyways?' Charlie told me," Sonny laughed.

"You mean, you tried to payoff the cops and they wouldn't go for it. Is that what you're saying, my friend?" Horan said, simultaneously unfurling his right leg from over his left leg and giving that one a shot with his fist in an attempt to bring back some semblance of blood circulation.

"Yeah, Yeah. Charlie said they got a coupla nibbles, but most of the cops walked away, some even grabbed some of Victor's messengers by the throat and threatened to kick the shit out of them," "Sonny said.

"Business—and don't ask me what kinda business, ya fuck—was down all over the Bronx. According to what Charlie told me up at the pen, in some places it was down over half, and in the Parkchester section Charlie and Victor were practically outta business," he went on.

"So that's where you met with Charlie," Horan said.

"Hey, none a that. How Charlie and me get holda each other is none of your fuckin' business, ya *capece!*"

"And, that's why Charlie and Victor had the mayor's father and his friend hit out in Parkchester, they were the ones who were fighting to get more cops into the community policing program, right?" Horan said.

"Wait a minute, wait a minute—geez—I'm gettin' to that. Charlie and Victor were tryin' to figure out what to do about these fuckin' nosy cops. Then they get a break. Some guy who couldn't make the vig payments on his horse wire markers and who Charlie had told he was gonna break his kneecaps, turns out to be buddy buddy with the mayor. Can you imagine this, the fuckin' mayor!"

"So?" Roger said.

"So? So Victor tells Charlie to get this guy to tell the mayor to get the cops off their asses."

"So? How was he supposed to do that?"

"So, so. Will ya stop with the fuckin' SO, already? Who the fuck knows how. Anyways Charlie talks to the guy and he even tries to talk us out of pressurin' the mayor to pull off the cops. Charlie and Victor say no. Then it turns out this guy is a banker or somethin'."

"Do you know his name, Sonny?" Horan asked.

"Nah, nah. But if you go with this deal, Charlie will fill in all the blanks," he said.

Horan nodded.

"Anyways, he comes up with his own deal to let Victor hide his money by sendin' it through this guys bank, in the fuckin' canary islands, or some place like that," Sonny said.

"Money laundering, instead of going to the mayor. Is that what you're saying?" Horan interrupted again.

"Money lauderin'—who the fuck knows? But this guy is stallin' Victor thinks. Yeah, instead a goin' to the mayor. So he takes the deal and they do it for a while, and then Victor finds out that this fuckin' guy is skimmin' from the top of the money Victor's been sendin' through. Can you imagine this fuckin' guy, stealin' from Victor Albanese?"

"And?" Horan asked, with the same blank stare he wore throughout most of their meeting.

"And? So? What a ya some kind of fuckin' heckler or somethin'? So the guy denies it. Victor blows his top, tells the guy he better get his money back, plus goin' to the mayor to get the cops off his ass—or else."

"Or else what? They'll hit somebody—like the mayor's father?" Horan asked.

"Right."

"Did this guy ever say he actually spoke to the mayor about getting the cops off Victor's ass?" Horan said.

"I don't know that. Again, you can ask Charlie at the pen when you see him. Ya know, I don't know everythin'," he said.

"What do you mean, *paisan*, you don't know everythin'? *Boccone del povero*—from the mouths of the poor, *espet*? You're too modest, my friend," Horan said.

Sonny smiled modestly, tilting his head to the right. "OK, so as I said before, everybody's dirty. What's this worth to you? We're lookin' for maybe just one more 'hard' year—and then a transfer to a Club Fed or somethin' like that for Charlie—and into that thing that gives you a new name and puts you up in California or Arizona, or some warm place like that," he went on not waiting for Roger's response.

"The federal witness protection program," Horan started to answer, and was about to keep talking.

"What do you say?" he asked cutting off Horan.

"OK, I'll take your offer back to my bosses. But something is missing, my friend. Why did Charlie Rossetti take the fall in the first place and why is he ratting out Albanese now?" Horan asked.

"I wasn't gonna tell ya this unless you asked. Charlie said so," Sonny said.

Gordon Halliday's gambling addiction was to Victor Albanese what the genie was to Aladdin, bursting from the lamp and granting his fondest wishes. Not only did he have someone who could move some of the *Don's* money around, but someone who could also whisper into the mayor's ear. Albanese wanted both. When he got neither he decided to kill old man McCabe as a message to both McCabe and Halliday. When the cops came up with Charlie Rossetti, on tape no less, Albanese told him that he would take care of him—short stay in prison, early parole, and a bigger role in the family when he got back to New York City.

"So, what's wrong with that?" Horan said.

"So, what's fuckin' wrong with that? Don't you read the fuckin' newspapers? You know about those two big black guys grabbin' Charlie in the toilet and drivin' a shiv between his ribs? Well, now I'm tellin' you that those two mutts ran numbers for Victor."

"Sonny? Who the fuck is 'Sonny?'" Rothman laughed.

"He's Nick Losquadro from Chicago. We got it from one of our snitches out there. He's with the successor to the old Sam Giancana organization, but apparently Charlie Rossetti knew him and did him a big favor some time ago. Rossetti called in his marker," Hughes explained.

They spent almost three hours discussing the Losquadro caper.

"We have information that, if proven, could probably discredit the mayor, depending on whether he knew anything about anything, put Gordon Halliday away for money laundering and Victor Albanese in jail for that plus the murders, if Charlie rats—and we spring that prick," Bob Coleman said.

"And raise a lot of questions about some of the resentment that has been going on with community policing," Dave Rothman said.

"Oh, boy, this is as politically hot as anything can get," Terry Hughes followed up.

"What about the Chris Russo problem?" Dave Rothman inquired.

They all looked at him, shaking their heads in agreement. The possibility of eventually involving the former police commissioner was something they would have to consider.

"On the other hand, we have information that felonies may have been committed and federal laws violated—and possibly some bad judgment, at the very least, on the part of the mayor," Terry Hughes said.

"Which would probably guarantee Chris Russo's election," Matt Reynolds said, as the others quickly turned in their seats to look at the newest member of the inner circle.

Not more than a minute passed as they kept visually polling each other, with no words spoken. Bob Coleman looked around the table one more time.

"I guess we wait until after the primaries, right?" he said.

Horan would continue to work with the feds on the Halliday case based on the information Wes Reiser was continuing to feed them—but officially, it wasn't a case—no number, no records.

CHAPTER 14

With the Democratic primary in June just three months away, The Times's weekly poll showed the incumbent mayor in front by less than eight percent, with just over eighteen percent uncommitted. By all accounts, a spectacular showing for Russo.

Then, Mark Blaine got a phone call. It was a collect call from the State Department of Corrections Facility at Attica—"Charlie Rossetti calling, person-to-person, to Mark Blaine, collect," the Verizon telephone operator dutifully announced.

"Yeah. I'll take the call, operator. Mark Blaine here. Hello?" the reporter answered.

"Yeah, hello. This is Charlie Rossetti," the caller responded.

"Yeah, I know that. Charlie, how ya' doing baby? Blaine asked.

"How am I doin', my ass! I'm not doin' this alone—not anymore," he came back.

"What do you mean, Charlie?"

"I'm not sayin, right now. But I'm callin' you because I want to bring down the mayor, Victor the Wheeze, and that fuck, Holiday—you know the mayor's ass-hole buddy," he raised his voice as he mentioned each name.

"Hey, come on, Charlie. Charlie Rossetti, the loyal soldier is going to drop a dime on his boss Victor, the mayor, and Halliday—not Holiday, Charlie. I can't believe it," Mark repeated back to the mobster. "*Una fasta de respecto*." No respect, that's how you say it, right, Charlie Boy?" he said.

"Yeah, that's right. And fuck you, too, Blaine. You never been in somethin' like this. I'm not takin' this alone, no more," Rossetti said.

"OK. But, why are you calling me, and not the cops or the District Attorney, or someone like that?" Blaine said.

"Fuck those bastards. I trust none of 'em," he screamed so that Blaine had to hold the phone away from his ear. "That's why I'm calling you. When I begin testifying in court, I'm goin' to blow the fuckin' roof off this town. But I want everybody to read about it first, so those fucks, the mayor, Albanese and Holiday can sweat and puke everyday like I been doin' since being here in this fuckin' rat hole."

"So you're going to tell me what you didn't testify to at your trial. Right?

"Nah, ya silly fuck. I'm just going to tell you that I'm going to bring them all down, and that's it."

"But I gotta have more than that to go with a story. You have to tell me more," Blaine said.

Rossetti started from the beginning, like he was almost reading from a script. It was going to be an expensive call for *The Times*. He revealed, at once, how community policing was killing their businesses all over the city, but especially in Kingsbridge. They didn't know what to do until they found this incredible opportunity with Gordon Halliday's gambling debts. He went through the entire story, through the money laundering at Westport Trust, trying to get the cops off Albanese's ass, Halliday's skimming, the murders, Albanese's promise to Rossetti, and a "real fuckin' surprise, which I'm not give you, or anyone else, until the trial."

Blaine could hardly contain his excitement. If true, he had once of the biggest stories the city had seen in years.

"OK, I'll check some of these things out and see what I'm going to do with your story," Blaine said.

"I understand, that's all I ask. Thanks. And remember if you don't do it, I deny we even talked," Rossetti said and hung up.

Blaine forgot to hang up. He threw down the phone after hearing Charlie Rossetti's disconnect and ran to his editor. They went through the various scenarios: Why did he call you and not the authorities? How are you going to verify that what he is saying has some merit? Is his life still in danger at this point? Shouldn't you be reporting this to the cops and others for all those reasons—and more? They decided that Blaine would do a little block building, one block at a time. He started with Chris Russo. The columnist reached him at a Lions Club rally at Manhattan College in Fieldston. A lot of the city's business owners and corporate CEO's lived nearby, many of whom would be leaning towards the incumbent mayor—particularly with Gordon Halliday, one of their prominent neighbors, still the mayor's closest advisor.

Calvin Wright took the call. "Yeah, he, Mr. Blaine. Chris's on the dais and should be finished in about fifteen minutes. He'll call you then."

"It's very, very important that he return my call as quickly as possible," Blaine emphasized.

"Oh, yeah. Yes, sir. Man, everybody says that, but Chris Russo gets back to everybody, important or not."

Blaine smiled and hung up.

"Hi, Mark. Chris Russo, what's up?" It was just under fifteen minutes.

They spoke for more than a half hour, and Candidate Russo couldn't afford to give many people that kind of time.

"Mark, you're right, this is serious stuff. But I can't add anything to it. Why are you calling me?" Russo asked.

"What about the community policing angle. Jesus, that's dynamite. We knew the mayor was trying to rip down the program for some reason. Now we know," Blaine said.

"Come on, Mark. You don't know that for a fact. According to what you just told me, no one has said that the mayor was ever approached on pulling out the cops—because of Victor Albanese and his mob," Russo said.

"What about this guy fingering old Victor the Wheeze?" Blaine asked.

"That surprises me. I always thought that Victor Albanese had an exceptionally loyal following. Compared to the other *goombahs*, that is," Russo said.

"Sammy the bull and John Gotti. Yeah, right," Blaine said.

"But, Halliday, what about Halliday? He's the goddamn campaign manager for your opponent. I know, I know, we carried the story that he wasn't, but we all know he still is."

"I can say that I was shocked with that, too. Particularly the gambling, money laundering and skimming parts of the story," Russo said.

"But come, Commissioner—I mean Mister mayoral candidate—what about the mayor's involvement? You got 'im by the balls, baby."

"I don't know, Mark. From what you're telling me—based on what you got from the prick, Charlie Rossetti—the mayor's part, if any, many turn out to be no more than bad judgment," Russo responded.

"OK, but you're surely going to use—as you say—the "bad judgment thing in the campaign?" Blaine said.

"No, I'm not," Russo insisted.

"Well, my friend, you're crazy. If what is being said by whomever has any merit, I'll bet you a beer at Buddy's (a cop and reporter hangout on Pearl Street near Police Plaza) that the mayor will be discredited, at the very least, and will have to pull out of the race."

"I hope not, Mark. Take it easy," Russo replied, and hung up.

Candidate Russo turned to his campaign aide, Del King—he was on an unpaid leave from New York City's finest. "Del, get me Bob Coleman—forthwith!"

The acting police commissioner had to hold his bright-red, cordless phone at arm's length so that his eardrums would not be shattered. The color of his ears matched perfectly with that of his phone.

They would have to develop a new strategy.

Blaine next put in a call to the mayor's communications director. He was meeting with the Mental Health, Mental Retardation, Alcoholism and Drug Abuse Services Subcommittee of the City Council, she reported, and wouldn't be available for a couple of hours.

"Yes, of course, Mark, I'll tell him it is very important that you speak to him, today," she said. Mark Blaine knew that he would go to press without hearing a word from the mayor.

Gordon Halliday didn't return his call either, but the investment banker's attorney, Richard Kessler, thought by many to be one of the shrewdest criminal lawyers in New York City, did. "His client" had heard "rumors" about this Rossetti thing (he wouldn't reveal the source of those "rumors) and, of course, categorically denied everything.

Mark Blaine didn't try to contact Victor Albanese.

"He'd be busy looking to put out another contract—up in Attica—on Charlie Rossetti. This time, undoubtedly a Colombian necktie party—you know, they slit your throat and pull your tongue out through your neck," the writer smiled while explaining his day's activities to his editor who started gagging and ran for the men's room.

Mark Blaine guessed that it would take him about three days to gather more information and speak to a variety of other sources, including some of Halliday's associates in his office and at Westport Trust. By the second day, he was leaning towards the possibility that, while the bank and some people in Halliday's firm certainly were less than diligent in their dealing with Caribbean Moorings, Ltd.—greed played an overwhelming role in that oversight. Besides, most of them were socially active with Gordon Halliday.

"I can't and won't believe that Gordon Halliday put us into that kind of a deal," said an official at the bank, who spoke to *The Times* reporter only on the condition of anonymity.

Whether that was being said with any degree of sincerity or not, Blaine wasn't sure.

In another day or two, he was convinced he would be ready with his story.

❦   ❦   ❦

Bob Coleman, Terry Hughes, and Dave Rothman met with the U.S. Attorney. They gave her a complete and startlingly frank briefing of the case at hand, beginning with the role of Wes Reiser.

"Now, let me get this straight. You guys are pissers, I'll tell you that already. This guy Reiser is a friend of a friend—a cop—of Detective Roger Horan. He's working for Gordon Halliday, but thought that his boss was laundering money from a business in the Cayman Islands through Westport Trust—where his father, Gary Reiser, works, incidentally. So, he told Horan. Correct?" Amanda Stevens said.

"Right. He's still sending us information and we believe they've gathered enough evidence to show that Gordon Halliday, and possibly the mayor, had lied to detectives during the investigation of Charlie Rossetti's involvement with all of them," Terry Hughes responded.

"Evidence some of which was obtained while Rossetti and the others were on trial, and which the cops did not come forward with," the U.S. Attorney said, causing embarrassed looks around the table.

"Then Charlie Rossetti tried to cut a deal through an intermediary with whom Horan met. This creep now wants to lessen his jail time—and go into the Witness Protection Program, I might add—by implicating everyone, particularly Gordon Halliday, the mayor and Victor Albanese in the money laundering case and Albanese in the McCabe murders," Bob Coleman stated.

"Information that you all were holding until after the primaries," Amanda Stevens said.

She had been sitting upright in her high-back chair, legs crossed, arms folded listening intently to the incredible story that was being told to her by the city's highest-ranking police officials. When they finished, she slumped back into her chair. She said nothing for a few moments, closed her eyes and sighed deeply, with a little more drama than was needed someone noted.

"Oh, boy. I hate to be redundant, but you guys are pissers, let me tell you," she began.

"For Chris sake, first, I did that Title l8, Chapter 13, Section 241, Conspiracy against Rights of Citizens, shit for you guys to 'federalize' those two stupid fucks who actually killed old man McCabe and his friend. Then, I give you my two best investigators to help you unravel all that Halliday money laundering shit," she said, obviously upset with the entire situation.

"And now, surprise, surprise! 'We've known about the possibility of Albanese being involved in both the murders and the money-laundering scheme. But we forgot to tell you, Ms. United States Attorney for New York City's Southern District," she said, in a slow, deliberate, and strangely calm voice.

"Unbelievable!" she said.

"Let me ask this in some kind of orderly fashion."

She picked up a long wooden pointer from the credenza behind her desk and moved stealthily, almost sensually, to the large black-board—it was actually green—in the rear of her office, and stood in front of it. She hit the blackboard with the pointer, breaking the brief spell of intrigue:

"You were sitting on evidence that showed the mayor had met Charlie Rossetti, albeit at a social function, and that the gangster was introduced to him by Gordon Halliday."

She hit the blackboard a second time.

"You knew, that the mayor knew that Rossetti continued to socialize with Halliday."

"You all knew that there was a possibility of money laundering going on among Westport Trust, Halliday Associates, a Cayman Islands dummy, and New York City's Mafioso branch in the Bronx."

The pointer finally shattered into three pieces—one in her hand, two airborne.

"All of this during the trial of Charlie Rossetti and those two assholes who murdered McCabe and Velez."

Whether she was actually finished with her summary, she slumped into a chair at the end of a conference table directly in front of the blackboard.

"We're not excusing ourselves from what we did. However, it was our judgment at the time that the criminal convictions of Charlie Rossetti and those 'two assholes'—as you called them—were more likely if those issues were not introduced," Bob Coleman said. "Realizing that we were way beyond our authority to make that judgment."

Amanda Stevens smiled grimly at that admission.

"We didn't want to muddy the waters of an otherwise straightforward prosecution. The information we had at the time would have inevitably generated the usual 'tabloid-fodder sidebars' that we felt would detract from the murder trial," Terry Hughes added.

"Besides, Chris Russo would not have wanted to unnecessarily embarrass his friend, the mayor," Dave Rothman said.

"Holy shit! Did you give that explanation to Chris Russo?" Amanda Stevens asked.

They all emphatically denied that the police commissioner knew of the additional information gathered by Roger Horan.

"How about your decision to delay until after the primaries, the investigation of the allegations made by Charlie Rossetti from jail?" Stevens asked.

"We had been gathering information all along on the Caribbean Moorings, Ltd. matter via Wes Reiser, and when we had enough evidence we had intended to go to the Bronx District Attorney to move on those crimes that were covered by state laws, and to you, for those violations that were covered by federal statutes," Bob Coleman answered.

"While we didn't think there was a need for speeding up that investigation, we also were of the opinion that our old boss would not have wanted to be elected on anything but the merits of his campaign—Community Policing and its importance to the future of New York City—and not because his opponent was discredited—or went to jail," Terry Hughes said.

Same question from the U.S. Attorney regarding Chris Russo's awareness of their decision—same answer.

"He heard all this from Mark Blaine, when Rossetti called him, after we decided to sit on his first attempt to cut a deal," Bob Coleman answered.

"What did Russo say to you?" Stevens inquired.

"Don't ask. But we're here, right?" Coleman said.

"You guys have broken all the rules in the book. And now I get to clean up the mess, right?" she said, finally breaking into a smile and moving back into her regular chair again, and resting her elbows on the huge mahogany desk, and putting her small, narrow, gently-rouged cheeks between her two, open hands.

"OK, OK, guys, notwithstanding the many reservations I have with how you all have conducted yourselves in this matter, I'm very interested in jumping into this case, particularly since it may, one, involve organized crime—Justice loves that shit—two, it may involve international money laundering—everyone from the United Nations to half the president's cabinet will perk up their ears on that—and three, the possibility of a sitting mayor of the *numero uno* city, up for reelection at that, may be involved, will be of more than passing interest to the national committees of both major political parties," she said.

She paused then slowly looked around at all of them, keeping them on the hook.

"Well, the good news is that I'll do it. The bad news is that time is not on our side," Amanda Stevens said.

"You've got that right! We have no more than a day, possibly two, before Mark Blaine runs his story," Terry Hughes stated.

"We'll have blown our cover by then. All the principals will be on the alert." Dave Rothman added.

"In addition to the embarrassment it would bring to you guys, as well as to me. We did stretch the Constitution a bit with Rossetti, Conte and Burns, and those motel detentions," the U.S. Attorney said.

They quickly assembled the staff that would try to pull off a long-shot chance of successfully sorting out this potential disaster. They decided to form a Super Task Force, which would work out of the basement of 1 St. Andrews Plaza, consisting of the United States Attorney, Chief of Detectives Hughes, Deputy Chief Rothman, Postal Inspectors Paul Singleton and Ralph Warfield, who were working with the cops on the Charlie Rossetti-Gordon Halliday-Westport Trust Money Laundering caper, a third postal inspector, Bill Thomas, and Detective Roger Horan.

"Holy shit, not this guy again," Paul Singleton and Ralph Warfield mimicked exasperation on getting called to the U.S. Attorney's office and coming face-to-face with Horan.

They all started laughing as the handshakes and introductions were made between the police brass and Bill Thomas, the new postal inspector.

"Watch your wallet with this guy, Bill," Ralph said.

Amanda Stevens spent the next hour briefing the postal inspectors. Then it was their turn to recommend the kinds of federal charges most appropriate to the case. After hearing their suggestions, the Task Force members made a decision.

"We believe that your best chance for getting convictions and jail terms for all the actors would be, first, to pursue charges of mail fraud, including SEC violations," Paul Singleton suggested, looking at his fellow postal inspectors, who nodded their agreement.

"Along with invoking the federal antiracketeering law, RICO (Racketeer Influenced and Corrupt Organizations Act)," Ralph Warfield added.

"OK, good," Amanda Stevens responded. "The postal inspectors from the U.S. Postal Inspections Service will be the federal investigators responsible for the probe and they'll head the Task Force that will concentrate on the Halliday-Rossetti-Albanese connections in the Caribbean Moorings, Ltd. case investigation," the U.S. Attorney announced.

"Great. That's fine with us. I think we have complementary talents among these investigators here, and the guys from the NYPD are at your pleasure," Terry Hughes said.

"Good. Thanks, Terry. I think we should start tonight," Amanda Stevens suggested. "I can't overstate the need to move quickly on this matter,"

The Task Force met that night in their basement quarters to go over the public financial filings of Halliday Associates and The Westport Trust bank.

"Oh, boy," Bill Thomas was the first to speak. "These filings clearly show discrepancies between what was filed with the SEC and what's in these financial documents Xeroxed and supplied to them by Roger Horan's buddy. What's his name, again?"

"Wes Reiser," Horan answered.

"He's done a super job, Rog," Ralph Warfield said.

They spent over four hours examining and reexamining the documents. It was after midnight.

"I can issue federal grand jury subpoenas tonight and I think we can get material witness subpoenas—which I think are critical in this matter—from a federal magistrate tonight, too. If the principals could be served tomorrow morning, we could really put time back on our side," Amanda Stevens said, to some surprised looks from the NYPD members of the Task Force.

"After midnight? Boy, those federal magistrates must be a lot more accommodating than our local judges," Terry Hughes said, triggering some light laughter from the participants. It had been a long day.

"Yeah. Not many of them. But we've all got a few that owe us," Paul Singleton said.

It was three in the morning when the Task Force laid out its strategy for the next morning's "flying wedges"—they called it—attack on three fronts. The U.S. Attorney, Paul Singleton, and Dave Rothman would go to City Hall; Hughes and Bill Thomas—they needed a Fed at each location to serve the papers—would go to Halliday's Broad Street office and Horan and Ralph Warfield would attempt to make contact with Victor Albanese.

The mayor wasn't going to avoid even an unscheduled visit from the U.S. Attorney, a deputy chief from the city's police, and a U.S. postal inspector. Besides, with both Stevens and Rothman present they could discuss both local and federal jurisdiction issues.

The city's chief of detectives and two investigators, one from the NYPD and one from the federal government, would similarly not be denied access to the investment banker's office.

And Horan could easily get to see Victor Albanese. He and his partner would have the advantage of surprise since the gangster would still expect to read about Charlie Rossetti's rat out in the papers and would be unnerved by the fact that a Fed would accompany Horan.

It was 7:30 a.m. that morning. None of the Task Force members had gotten any sleep. Stevens, Singleton, and Rothman would be the first ones out. Paul Singleton drove the U.S. Attorney's official, six-passenger, green Lincoln. It wasn't flashy, but had an official aura about it.

"Are those huge red lamps on top of your front bumpers official?" Dave Rothman asked.

"You gotta be kidding? Of course not," Amanda Stevens replied.

They pulled up to City Hall Plaza, which was still calm and uncluttered at that time of the morning. Even the usual picket lines, for whatever cause, didn't go up until nine or ten o'clock in the morning. Singleton pulled the car into the space reserved for the *Executive Assistant to the Mayor*—the unusually large sign read.

"Oh, boy, providence is smiling on us this morning. This parking space belongs to one of the biggest pricks in the mayor's administration, Bruce Solnich," Dave Rothman laughed.

"How come?" asked Amanda Stevens.

"Someday, when we have a lot of time, I'll tell you, Ms. United States Attorney," Dave Rothman said, as all three jumped from the car and headed for the mayor's office.

When they got to the three-foot-high, black, wrought iron railing that separated the cavernous hallway running the full length of the building, from the rabbit warren of offices that made up the "Office of the Mayor," the uniformed cop quickly jumped from his comfortable chair, saluted Chief Rothman, and simultaneously hit the buzzer that swung the gate open.

"Good morning, Chief," said Officer Barnes—his nameplate polished so brightly that the chief could acknowledge him by name.

"Our strategy is working so far," Paul Singleton whispered to his boss.

They went directly to the *Office of the Secretary to the Mayor*. Janet Mullins was startled when they walked into her office—the door was always open—because the cops "at the gate" usually alerted her if someone was heading her way. But not this time. Rothman had given the "keep it quiet" gesture to Officer Barnes.

"Good morning, Janet. I'm Dave Rothman, formerly of Commissioner Russo's office, now chief of the department's Special Investigations Division," Rothman said. Mentioning Russo's name had actually caused her to tremble somewhat. "We've talked a lot on the phone, but have never formally met. How are you?" he added.

"Oh, yes—Dave, I mean, Chief—how are you?"

"Janet, this is United States Attorney Amanda Stevens and Federal Postal Inspector Paul Singleton. I'm sorry for this intrusion, but it's most urgent that we speak to Mayor McCabe as quickly as possible," Rothman said, looking for her reaction, as Mark and Paul nodded and smiled at her.

They offered to shake hands with her, but she ignored them. She turned slowly, and walked into the mayor's office.

She hadn't offered them a seat, so they were left standing and waiting—for someone, they thought. They were right. Mullins didn't come back, but five minutes later the mayor's special counsel, Norman Stansel, walked through the door.

"Gentlemen, how can I help you?" he said, not offering his hand to anyone either.

"Mr. Stansel, I'm the U.S. Attorney, which I'm sure you know. It is a very serious, urgent, and confidential matter that we wish to discuss with the mayor," Amanda Stevens said, not extending her hand. The pleasantries were over.

"Yes. I know who you are, Ms. Stevens. However, the mayor is meeting with the Parks, Recreation, Cultural Affairs and International Group Relations Committee of the City Council right now," Stansel answered.

"Well, Mr. Stansel, if we can't meet with him now, I cannot guarantee the continued 'confidentiality' of this matter, which I can assure you is of the greatest importance to your client," Amanda Stevens said.

"I'll see if I can get him to break away," the mayor's counsel said.

"Thank you, sir," Dave Rothman said.

They remained standing and waiting. Janet Mullins finally reappeared and escorted them to the mayor's inner office, where Tom McCabe was seated behind his desk with Norman Stansel standing to his right.

The federal prosecutor and the investigators held back nothing. Dave Rothman went through the murder investigation culminating with the identification of two individuals as the perpetrators and Charlie Rossetti and now Victor Albanese as the ones behind the killing of the mayor's father and Ramon Velez, and based on information now supplied by him from his prison cell, the involvement of Gordon Halliday with Rossetti and Albanese in a money laundering scheme involving a Caymans Island company, Caribbean Moorings, Ltd. and the Westport Trust bank.

Amanda Stevens then picked up on the investigation that her office had been conducting on the possible irregularities in the finances of Halliday Associates, Inc. and the Westport Trust bank, and Gordon Halliday's involvement with members of the Bronx chancery of one of the city's five organized crime families, namely The Genovese mob. She ended with the role that may or may not have been played, "by you, Mr. Mayor."

"Preposterous. MS. Stevens, I can't believe that you're listening to a known mobster, who is also a recently convicted felon," said an obviously agitated, Tom McCabe.

"C'mon, where are you coming from?" the mayor added.

"Mr. Mayor, the investigators have been looking for a number of things in this case. First, the possibility of mob ties to Halliday's firm and ultimately to an account with one of our major financial institutions, and second, the involvement of Victor Albanese in the murders of your father and Mr. Velez, and finally, the motive behind those killings that are alleged to have something to do with your city's community policing program and the mob's intent to get you to "get the cops off their asses" is the way we've heard it."

"What the hell has that got to do with me?" the mayor said.

Norman Stansel pulled at the mayor's sleeve. Tom McCabe pulled away from his grasp.

"Your name came up in the investigation. It seems you may have been aware that he, Rossetti, had made certain threats to Halliday that you were aware of," Stevens said.

"Rossetti is still a fucking liar by reputation and confirmed by his conviction in a court of law. If you're conducting an unbiased, objective investigation that will prove out again, I'm telling you—"

"Obviously I take exception to that innuendo, Mr. Mayor, and I can assure you that we have sufficient evidence to support that 'fucking liar's' allegations," the U.S. Attorney replied.

"We have proof that Victor Albanese and his bunch along with Gordon Halliday, set up 'dummy' investors to cover the illegal laundering of currency through his firm and the Westport Trust," Amanda Stevens said.

"Bullshit! Pure, absolute, undiluted bullshit!" the mayor said.

"With that information, I'm sure I'll get a conviction," Stevens concluded.

"Well, apparently I can't dissuade you from believing anything this piece of 'shit' Rossetti tells you, but I'm telling you, I'm denying anything about this that concerns me. I don't know anything about all that other nonsense, but Gordon Halliday and I never had any conversations about any community policing or money laundering issues, period," McCabe said angrily. But he obviously recognized that none of this was good news for him, no matter what the outcome.

"No, I never even entertained the thought that you could convince me not to go ahead with this case. I was only looking to give you an opportunity to hear what we're about to make public, and quite frankly I was looking forward to hearing your reaction, and I got it," Stevens said.

"It's all 'bullshit'—that part of the case that involves you? Is that your statement?" Stevens asked. "If so, it will be so reported in my investigation. Obviously, I'll be speaking to other sources."

"You mean Gordon Halliday?" McCabe asked.

"Yes, of course, Mr. Mayor. He's a big player in this, if it's true, wouldn't you think?" the prosecutor said, as the mayor began squirming in his big comfortable chair.

"Yes, if it's true. Which, I repeat, is not the case," the mayor said.

"Well, you'll get your chance to prove your position, Mr. Mayor. We have here a federal grand jury subpoena that I had issued this morning, and a material witness subpoena also issued this afternoon by Federal Judge Marcus Killibrew of the Southern District Court of New York, requiring you to appear in two weeks before a special Grand Jury at Foley Square, impaneled as of this morning, which is looking into the Caribbean Moorings, Ltd-Westport Trust-Gordon Halliday-Charlie Rossetti-Victor Albanese matter," said Amanda Stevens, in a very official manner

"Two subpoenas. Two weeks?" Norman Stansel looked at them with dismay.

"Yes, that's correct, Counselor, two. Paul, give the mayor the sub-poenas," Stevens concluded, as the mayor sat stunned, motionless, letting the subpoenas fall from Singleton's hand to the top of his enormous desk.

"Well, that's it, Mr. Mayor. Thanks, and good luck," said Dave Rothman.

The three visitors were about to close the interview.

"Yeah, sure, good luck—my ass—you bastard."

"You were never much of an assistant DA, LADY, and you were lucky to get what's left of the Democratic machine in this city to get you another job—I'm sure Hillary had something to do with that," said the mayor loudly.

"Your buddy Russo will be rollicking in the aisles with this one, right, Rothman? I'm sure you spoke to him first," the mayor said.

"Hey, I'll bet that son of a bitch had a hand in this. What a ya' say, Dave boy?" Tom McCabe added.

"We have not spoken to former commissioner Russo, because we found no evidence that would indicate he knew about the story Rossetti told us," Stevens said, avoiding a confrontation with the mayor, and without letting Dave Rothman answer—and probably lose his cool.

"Yeah, sure. So long, gentlemen—and LADY. And I'm not wishing you good luck in anything," he said. His special counsel seemed eager to get them all out of the office.

They knew the mayor would call Gordon Halliday, probably the moment the door leading to his outer office closed behind them.

Terry Hughes and Bill Thomas would use a Government car to get them to Gordon Halliday's office at 26 Broad Street. They had left just after Amanda Stevens, Dave Rothman, and Paul Singleton had taken off for the mayor's office. After all, Gordon Halliday was an investment banker, and it would be unusual for him to get to his office much before the markets opened.

Halliday Associates was in one of the more luxurious office buildings in New York City's financial district. Rents ran around two hundred to three hundred dollars a square foot—expensive by any standards. They were located on the seventeenth floor, which was premier space.

They got off the elevator, and were immediately face-to-face with a young receptionist who was talking into the speakerphone at her desk.

"Good morning. Thank you for calling Halliday Associates. This is Tammy. How may I help you?" She was extremely busy and must have answered three calls before she could look up at the two men who were standing, patiently waiting for her to get to them.

"Good morning. Welcome to Halliday Associates. This is Tammy—ah, I mean I'm Tammy. How may I help you?" she asked.

Terry Hughes and Bill Thomas smiled.

"Hi. Hello, Tammy. I'm Chief of Detectives Hughes from the New York City Police Department. This is Federal Postal Inspector Thomas. We'd like to see Mr. Halliday, please," Terry Hughes said.

"Ooh. I think he's busy. But I'll call his secretary," Tammy responded.

The two investigators waited for over fifteen minutes.

A very well groomed, impeccably dressed man, probably in his mid-forties came walking slowly from the suite of offices off the reception area and introduced himself.

"Good morning, Gentlemen. I'm Richard Kessler, Mr. Halliday's attorney. Is there anything I can help you with?" he asked.

"Yes, sir. There is," Hughes responded. "We must see Mr. Halliday on a matter of extreme importance." The chief of detectives also explained that if they couldn't get to see Mr. Halliday they couldn't guarantee the continued confidentiality of what they wanted to discuss with him.

"Gordon, this is Chief of Detectives—uh, Drews, is it?" Richard Kessler began, as they stepped in front of Gordon Halliday's desk. They were not asked to sit down.

"Hughes, Mr. Halliday—Terrance Hughes," the department's top investigator replied. He was sure the mispronouncing of his name was intentional.

"And this is Postal Inspector Thomas from the U.S. Attorney's office," Terry Hughes said, not offering his hand.

"Yes, sir, chief, what's this all about?" Gordon Halliday asked.

"We are conducting an investigation into Caribbean Moorings, Ltd., its dealings with you, Mister Halliday, Halliday Associates, Inc., the Westport Trust, Charlie Rossetti and Victor Albanese and the involvement of Mayor Thomas McCabe," Hughes said, not expecting to get a response from Halliday, who was looking at them with a vacant stare as the chief of detectives had rattled off his opening statement.

He was right. He wasn't going to get a response from Gordon Halliday.

"I'm sorry, chief, Mr. Halliday has nothing to say in this matter. As his attorney, I have so advised him. Write us a letter, if you will," his lawyer responded.

"No. I don't think so, Counselor. We already have put something in writing in anticipation of your response. Bill, serve Mr. Halliday. Or would you, Counselor, like to take the federal grand jury and material witness subpoenas that Postal Inspector Bill Thomas is about to hand your client?" Terry Hughes said.

Bill Thomas flipped the subpoenas onto the desk in front of Gordon Halliday. Kessler grabbed the documents and began reading them.

"Two?" the lawyer was mumbling and shaking his head.

Terry Hughes didn't bother to explain. He nodded his head toward the door and then quickly followed Bill Thomas.

"Hello, Halliday Associates. Good morning, this is Tammy, How may I help you?"

"This is Mayor Tom McCabe. Please put me through to Gordon," the mayor said to a surprised young woman. He was making this call himself from one of the multicolored "hot lines" adorning the wall behind him, probably a red one, he didn't look. The less that Janet Mullins knew about this, the better, he was thinking. Of course, he thought again, it will be all over the papers, if not tomorrow morning, then the Late Day editions, but certainly not later than the following day.

"Oh, yes, sir. Please hold on. I know he has two gentlemen in there with him along with his lawyer Richard Kessler. Oh, hold on, sir.

Here they are now. They must have finished their business with Mr. Halliday and are leaving. I'll put you through to Mr. Halliday now, Mr. Mayor," an obviously unwary Tammy responded, crisply and with obvious excitement. But before she could put her caller on hold, she heard, "Oh, shit," and then a dial tone.

As Terry Hughes and Bill Thomas walked past the receptionist's desk, Tammy was looking at the speakerphone with a bewildered look.

She looked up and watched as they retrieved their coats from the closet at the same time.

Later that evening she would tell her friends, excitedly, "You know who I spoke to today—personally? The mayor!"

Roger Horan and Ralph Warfield would take a circuitous route to meet with Victor Albanese. Ralph would meet Mr. Anthony Corsentino of Pasquale Corsentino and Sons Funeral Home, Father Ciccio Felluci of St. Bernard's, Peter Agnello, the Cannoli King, and finally he would take the long ride out to Long Island and be introduced to the last resting place for many of the metropolitan area's favorite pets. Victor Albanese got out of his car, the usual black stretch limousine.

The old crime boss walked haltingly towards Roger, his artificial voice box gently swaying.

"Hi, Rog. Who the fuck is this?" Victor Albanese said, looking at Ralph Warfield, and actually waving the notorious white square cloth adorning his outside coat. Roger Horan. stepped back a step.

"This is Ralph Warfield, Victor. He's a Federal postal inspector working with the U.S. Attorney for the Southern District, looking into Caribbean Moorings, Ltd. case," Roger Horan said.

"Moorings, what? What the fuck are you talkin' about?" Albanese said, lunging towards his old detective "friend." He couldn't stop coughing, so they all did nothing for a while.

"Yeah. Go ahead. What a you got to say?" Albanese said, looking Warfield up and down.

Ralph Warfield went through the information that they were working on, but not the source, of course. When Victor Albanese heard that the Feds were looking at the SEC filings of Halliday Associates, Inc. and the Westport Trust, along with trying to determine the ownership of the Caymans Island company along with documents they had obtained from Halliday Associates, he stepped back a few paces. Ralph Warfield went into the possible violations of federal rules involved, so far, including the possible applicability of the RICO statutes, which apparently Albanese was well informed about. He started to wipe moisture, first from his face and then from his hands.

Horan then did the Gordon Halliday, Tom McCabe and Charlie Rossetti bit. Albanese started to shuffle back and forth. The coup de grace was delivered when Horan laid out how the community policing program was causing problems for his, Albanese's, "organization" and how they had been exploiting Halliday's gambling problems. They even threw in Halliday's skimming. And, finally, the investigators talked about the attempted hit on Rossetti in prison—ordered by Albanese they added. He stopped walking and swung toward the two investigators.

"It was that fuck, Charlie, right?" he growled. "And I'll be readin' about it in tomorrow's news, right?"

The crime boss got a final jolt when Horan said to Warfield, "Ralph, give Victor his invitation to the party."

Albanese wouldn't accept the subpoena. He snorted at Warfield, "Stick it up your ass. Or if it don't fit, throw it on the fuckin' ground, where maybe I'll pick it up later and rip it up."

Horan tugged at the postal inspector's sleeve and motioned with his head for him to comply with Albanese's request—to throw the two subpoenas on the ground.

They turned and walked towards Horan's car, with Albanese screaming, coughing, and flailing his arms wildly as they moved away.

"A helluva way to act on hallowed ground," Horan said, smiling at his partner.

CHAPTER 15

*T*he rumor mills were grinding relentlessly. The three major news networks were frantic to get some kind of story on the air as quickly as possible, and the print media in a panic to get a headline for their morning editions. Mark Blaine was furious at the sudden burst of activity by the cops.

"Those bastards must have been working on this thing for quite a while, to get subpoenas out as quickly as they did," he said to his boss. "And they never told me about it. Chris Russo must have fucked me."

"Mark, you silly bastard. Just think what we've got," said Sidney Gorshak, *The Time's* City Desk Editor, putting both his hands on the reporter's two shoulders and forcing him to sit down while he explained.

"We've got the complete story. Right?" Gorshak said.

"Yeah, right. But, those bastards—" Blaine started, but his boss put his right index finger in front of his pursed lips in a quieting way.

"Listen, Mark. While the TV, radio, and print news guys are still scrambling, you will have finished your story by this afternoon," he smiled.

"Maybe earlier, Sid," Blaine said.

He'd have the whole thing in the computer within an hour.

It was close to seven o'clock that evening. Members of the Task Force would not go home this night.

"Matt, see if you can get me the Bronx County District Attorney, Jules Powell," Bob Coleman shouted to his aide through the open door of his office. After six o'clock, an air of informality usually overtook police headquarters, strict telephone protocols were generally abandoned, both uniform and civilian coats were hung over the backs of chairs, coffee cups restricted to small kitchens appeared on uncluttered desks, and the doors—those jealously guarded, mysterious, emotional mews—would be swung open as if inviting those who would dare, to bid the occupant the time of day.

"Got 'im, Boss. He's on his car phone, somewhere in the Kingsbridge Section," Deputy Inspector Reynolds shouted.

"Good. Come on in and close the door," the acting police commissioner said. The informality, for tonight at least, was over.

"Jules. Bob Coleman," he said. "Good. Fine. Thanks. How's yours?"

"Listen, we are acting on some information supplied to us by a confidential source that Charlie Rossetti—you remember him. Right?" Bob Coleman said.

"Yeah. Yeah. That sleazebag. We got 'im good. He's doing life for his role in the Morgan McCabe and Ramon Velez murders. Someday the whole story will come out and when it does, we'll get that prick Victor Albanese, too, and get him what he deserves," the District Attorney said.

"That's just it. We may be getting there, and you'll get that chance. Our confidential source says that Charlie Rossetti is looking to supply us with some information in exchange for a deal," the acting police commissioner said.

"A deal. What in hell kind of information can that low-life, numb nuts hood give you that would give him a deal? He's got an I.Q. of about twelve," the DA asked.

"Well, he claims to have evidence about a money laundering deal that would have serious ramifications for some prominent political and business figures in the city."

"Which prominent political and business figures—the mayor?" the prosecutor asked.

"And Victor Albanese's role in the McCabe-Velez murders," Bob Coleman went on overlooking the DA's obviously snide political inquiry.

"*The Times* will have the full story on the news-stands early in the morning."

"I'll do anything you want me to do. What? What?" the D.A. asked.

"Can you break away from the Bronx for a while and come down to Police Plaza or should we all meet on the Concourse," Bob Coleman said.

"We?"

"Yes. We have a City-Fed Task Force that's been looking into this. The 'we' includes the United States Attorney for the Southern District. I think you know her—Amanda Stevens. And some crack investigators from the United States Postal Service."

The Bronx D.A.'s car cut across four lanes of traffic on West 230th Street and was on the Deegan heading south in less than two minutes

Amanda Stevens had to make a call, too.

"Hullo," a voice answered softly, obviously while yawning.

"Alan? This is Amanda Stevens," the U.S. Attorney said.

"Who? What time is it?" the voice inquired.

"Amanda Stevens, the United States Attorney for the Southern District of New York City. I'm sorry about the hour," she said.

"Oh. Ms. Stevens—Amanda. What is it?" the Chairman of the Securities and Exchange Commission in Washington—but who spent most of his time in the. plush surroundings of the Commission's regional office at 7 World Trade Center—acknowledged, quickly sitting up in his bed, as his wife pulled at the covers, turning on her side of the bed away from the phone.

"Yes, I'm sorry about the time. It's—let me see—it's 1:00 a.m." Amanda Stevens said, and heard a groan following that statement. "My office has just completed an investigation into a company from the Cayman Islands called Caribbean Moorings, Ltd. Did you ever hear of them?"

"No, I don't think so. Why do you ask?" the chairman inquired.

"Well, it involves some very well-known business people and political types in the city—I'm talking money laundering—using falsified documents in their submissions to your agency," Stevens replied.

"Well, what's that got to do with me—and at this time of the morning?" he asked.

"We've already served federal grand jury and material witness subpoenas relating to the case, and the jury will be convened later today," Stevens said.

"I am also convinced that The Times will be doing an extensive story on the case in today's edition. Both the Criminal and SEC aspects of the case and why the falsified filings were not uncovered sooner—by your office, for example," she said.

"Oh, oh. I get it. What do you want me to do?" he asked.

"Be in my office within the hour," Amanda Stevens said.

The federal grand jury impaneled by Amanda Stevens opened its hearings two weeks after the last of some thirty subpoenas were served. The U. S. District Courthouse at 40 Foley Square, whose basement would house this special Grand Jury, was surrounded by hundreds of reporters and their television and radio crews. It was rumored that Charlie Rossetti would be the first witness. Precisely at 9:00 a.m., a cortege of fifteen brand new, black Buick New Yorkers, sirens and lights screaming, pulled along the southern end of the court building at Pearl Street. This caused a stampede by the media people from the front to the side entrance. Half of the men and women stepping from the official-looking vehicles could have been taken for business executives; the others wore blue nylon, waist-length, windbreakers, the backs of which were emblazoned with oversized gold lettering that announced each of them as a "U.S. MARSHAL." Each of the occupants of those cars, gold lettering or not, carried a deadly weapon they could hold either with one hand or that had to be cradled across two arms. All the weapons were carried openly. No one would see him, but a passenger in one car wasn't armed. Charlie Rossetti made his entrance without a reporter laying a lens on him. They were told later about his arrival.

The marshals managed to frustrate the news people for the four days Charlie Rossetti needed to spend with the federal grand jury. By design or not, Charlie Rossetti was followed by Victor Albanese and two of his capos who were on their own. After all, it was they who worried the marshals in the first place. The media recouped most of its losses from the Rossetti appearances by surrounding Victor Albanese and the two other guys when they arrived and when they left each day—for the next two days they said nothing.

"I'm sayin' nothin'," Albanese fizzed at the reporters through his ever-present squawk box.

Gil Strapoli, representing the three hoods, was outraged.

"My clients are being harassed by the New York City Police Department, the Bronx County District Attorney and the United States Attorney's Office for the Southern District of New York. They are innocent of any wrongdoing, and that will be clear when the facts are known to the public," Strapoli screamed after each of the two days his clients told their story to the grand jury.

Gordon Halliday and three of his key employees spent two days each before the federal panel. Richard Kessler did all the talking for them.

For five long days, a steady stream of financial types—accountants, analysts, economists—along with high level executives from the Westport Trust, headed by Gary Reiser, and selected members of Halliday Associates, Inc., went in and out of the grand jury room at Foley Square.

After almost three weeks of grand jury proceedings, it was the mayor's turn.

It turned out to be a Monday morning. The sun was just beginning to peek from behind some clouds left over from a weekend of intermittent showers and steady downpours. The press corps had been camped out as early as they had been for Charlie Rossetti. For the witnesses following him they had kept more civilized hours, arriving no more than an hour before those grasping their subpoenas appeared.

They also knew they weren't going to listen to some lawyer. The mayor would talk for himself. He had no choice. Tom McCabe could have walked from his office at City Hall to Foley Square, but the crowd of news people would have brought traffic to a dead halt.

He arrived in NORDIC. Charlie Garrett leaped from behind the wheel and snapped open the rear door of the limousine, before the young detective riding shotgun next to him could unbuckle his seat belt.

"Good luck, Mr. Mayor," Charlie Garrett whispered to his boss as he saw the raucous crowd pushing so tight against the car that the ton-and-a-half vehicle started to rock back and forth.

"Ladies and Gentlemen. Ladies and Gentlemen. Come on, guys. Give me some room," he shouted, as he tried to get out of the car and onto the sidewalk. He finally did make his way to a bank of microphones that had been long in place before he arrived.

"I have a statement that my lawyer asked me to read," he said.

"Come on Mr. Mayor, give us a break," one reporter shouted.

"You're right, folks," he folded the legal-size piece of paper first in half and then in half again and stuffed it into the inside left pocket of his suit jacket. His special counsel Norman Stansel standing next to him looked very unhappy when he saw McCabe ignoring the carefully framed statement.

"OK. You know, fellas, and ladies, of course," he began, "You all know this is a difficult moment for me. Six months ago, the most physically and spiritually painful period of my life began. It began on the day my Dad's life ended."

"I even thought of resigning as Mayor of New York City. How could I possibly carry out my responsibilities to the people of New York City when my life was being totally subsumed by the grief following the realization that my father, Morgan McCabe, would no longer be at my side."

But the press wanted blood.

"Mr. Mayor, what about these community policing and the mob and money laundering things?" someone shouted.

"Ben, Ben, my friend," the mayor sighed, looking at the squat, balding and, as always, disheveled reporter from New York City's NBC Channel 4 Television News.

"I probably know less than you do, Ben. Maybe they should have subpoenaed you."

"But what about all these witnesses we've been watching going into the grand jury? I mean, some well-known and respected business people from the financial firms downtown. You know, Mr. Mayor, friends of your campaign manager, Gordon Halliday." Weinberg was at his ball busting best.

"Gordon Halliday is one of the finest persons I've ever..." the mayor started to shout, but Norman Stansel now grabbed him by both shoulders and wrestled him away from the microphones.

"Thank you, Ladies and Gentlemen. The mayor has nothing more to say," the special counsel said calmly into the forest of microphones while McCabe looked sullenly at the television cameras.

On the Monday following the mayor's appearance before the federal grand jury, Amanda Stevens called a press conference in the spacious conference room adjoining her office at 1 St. Andrew's Plaza, less than a pistol shot from 1 Police Plaza.

"Today, as a result of the investigations I will outline for you, we are announcing the following indictments," Amanda Stevens blazoned calmly.

☙   ☙   ☙

Charlie Rossetti, who had been escorted back to his solitary cell in the state pen, by the U. S. Marshals, and was watching a television set brought in for his private viewing on this day, leaped from the edge of his bed where he had been sitting and began shouting, "Yes-s-s-s-, Yes-s-s-s."

☙   ☙   ☙

Victor Albanese was alone, too, in his modest two-story, frame house on Hoffman Street between 187th and 184th Streets in Belmont. He insisted on watching "the fuckin' circus," he called it, in his home office. "The fucks. I coulda smelled it," that eerie sound coming from his chest managed to wheeze out.

☙   ☙   ☙

"I don't believe it," Richard Kessler said, looking at a despondent Gordon Halliday. They were sipping coffee from nineteenth century teacups, served by a badly shaken Mrs. Halliday and a defiant Eve Halliday, both of whom were seated opposite the sixty-inch television monitor in the library of their stately home on Waldo Avenue in Fieldston.

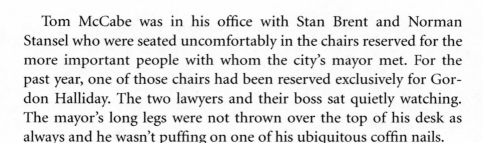

Tom McCabe was in his office with Stan Brent and Norman Stansel who were seated uncomfortably in the chairs reserved for the more important people with whom the city's mayor met. For the past year, one of those chairs had been reserved exclusively for Gordon Halliday. The two lawyers and their boss sat quietly watching. The mayor's long legs were not thrown over the top of his desk as always and he wasn't puffing on one of his ubiquitous coffin nails.

The United States Attorney for New York City's Southern District went on:

"Gordon Maurice Halliday, an investment banker heading his own firm, charged with violating Title 18 of the United States Code, Section 1956—as you all know, that's the R.I.C.O., Racketeer Influenced and Corrupted Organizations statute—in that he knowingly transported, transmitted, transferred money into or out of the United States with the intent to promote a specified unlawful activity or knowing that the money represented the proceeds of an unlawful activity. Mister Halliday is also charged with Title 18, United States Code, Section 371, Conspiracy to Defraud the U. S. Government, and Title 18, United States Code, Section 1341, Mail Fraud, as the financial transactions were sent through the mails. The penalties vary, but no more than $500,000 or twice the value of the property involved in the transactions, whichever is greater, or imprisonment for not more than twenty years, or both."

Some in the crowd gasped audibly as the federal prosecutor nonchalantly threw out those numbers.

She continued. "We also announce the indictment of Messrs. Victor Nicholas Albanese and Charles Peter Rossetti, reputed members of the Victor Albanese organized crime family closely aligned with the Genovese organized crime family, charged with all the federal crimes charged to Mister Halliday."

"Gary Summers Reiser, Senior Executive Vice President for the Westport Trust Bank is also indicted, charged with all the federal crimes charged to Messrs. Halliday, Albanese, and Rossetti, plus Title 18, United States Code, Section 1001, Fraud and False Statements, in that he made either orally or in writing such statements to various federal agencies."

Amanda Stevens stopped for a moment. She took a sip of water from a glass balanced at the edge of the lectern. She picked up what seemed to be the last page of what she had been reading from.

"Finally, we announce the indictment of Thomas Landis McCabe, mayor of the City of New York City charged with violating Title 18 of the United States Code, Section 2, in that he knowingly aided and abetted the actions of Mister Halliday that led to the commission of federal crimes charged to the same Mister Halliday. Under this section Mister McCabe is subject to the same penalties, no more than $500,000, not more than twenty years, etceteras, etceteras, because under the statute Mister McCabe is treated as a principal."

"Thank you, Ladies and Gentlemen. As I said earlier, the postal inspectors and I will be available for your questions," Amanda Stevens concluded, stepping back from the lectern.

A momentarily stunned audience.

Then no more than three hands were raised. All three questions dealt with the mayor's role. What did he know? When did he know it? What did he do or not do and what should he have done or not done? What did he gain from his actions or lack thereof? And Why? Why?

Stevens explained that the mayor knew it all because Gordon Halliday had told him of his dilemma with the mob. He should have tried to convince Halliday to go to the authorities, but didn't. He gained nothing, but was in possession of information about a federal crime. Stevens emphasized the fact that their investigation showed that Tom McCabe was not an unfortunate dupe. He knew what was going down.

"OK, thanks ladies and gentlemen, and now it's my pleasure to introduce the District Attorney of Bronx County, Jules Powell. Jules?" Stevens waved the prosecutor to the podium, shook his hand and slapped him on the back.

"Ladies and gentlemen, the United States Attorney isn't the only one who can move swiftly when justice is at stake. Yesterday we impaneled a blue ribbon grand jury in the Bronx, which I appeared before as well as one of those defendants indicted by the federal grand jury today. As a result of those Grand Jury proceedings, I am pleased to announce the indictment of Victor Nicholas Albanese for murder in the first degree in that he conspired and induced the killing of Morgan McCabe and Ramon Velez on February 10th of this year at 2044 Westchester Avenue in the Borough of the Bronx, City of New York."

"Mister Albanese, it's that fuck, Horan and he's got a fed with him. There at the front door with warrants, subpoenas, or some shit like that."

Victor Albanese slowly got up from his deep, soft, chair and turned off the TV.

The Federal and State indictments were devastating. The federal trial would precede the prosecution of Victor Albanese for the murders of Morgan McCabe and Ramon Velez.

Each of the defendants asked for a separate trial. McCabe's lawyers as well as Gary Reiser's felt that their clients, whom they would present as victims rather than co-conspirators, would be prejudiced by the clear evidence of criminality on the part of Halliday, Albanese and Rossetti that would be presented to the same jury, and at the same trial. The judge denied their motions. All of them, except Rossetti of course, sat at the defense table, extended for this trial, on the left side of the courtroom facing the bench. The first, and possibly the only, defendant to take the stand was Charles Peter Rossetti. His testimony would last three days.

Rossetti's first day of ratting out everybody was nothing more than a repeat of what Mark Blaine had reported in his exclusive story in *The Times* days before. The second day was more interesting. The media had reported the alleged skimming of Albanese's laundered money by Gordon Halliday, but no one knew how the mob boss found out about it. Rossetti roguishly explained that a couple of "our technical experts"—he smiled and panned the crowded courtroom—had bugged Halliday's telephone lines in his office and at home beginning the day the money laundering agreement was reached. Three months into the deal, Rossetti reported, they heard Gary Reiser and Halliday in a discussion in which an obviously nervous Reiser expressed his fear of what would befall them if Albanese found out. Reiser had apparently caught his old business school buddy stealing from Albanese and the bank, and was cut in on the action.

Tom McCabe would be the focus of Rossetti's last day in court. He insisted that he had met the mayor at Halliday's home—"da castle" Charlie Rossetti called it—on more than one occasion. After the mob began squeezing Halliday to talk to McCabe about community policing, and after Halliday reported that the mayor was not as enthusiastic as they all would have liked, Rossetti claimed that he spoke to McCabe himself, who didn't say yes, but he didn't say no either. Rossetti made it clear that this all happened before the killing of the mayor's father and Ramon Velez. With that testimony, true or untrue, whatever lingering support or sympathy Tom McCabe may have had in the city disappeared.

⁂   ⁂   ⁂

At that point, Gil Strapoli, now decidedly no longer representing Rossetti, made his move.

"Charlie, Mister Rossetti," Strapoli smiled, as he approached Attica's latest celebrity. Rossetti half-smiled and wiggled nervously in his chair.

"Mister Rossetti, we all know the kinda deal that you've cut with the U.S. Attorney to lie—I mean testify—here today. Right?

"Objection, your honor."

"Yes. Sustained, Ms. Stevens. Knock it off, Mister Strapoli."

"Yes, your honor. Mister Rossetti, in your criminal court case just a few, short weeks ago you testified that you hired two guys to murder Morgan McCabe and Ramon Velez. Is that correct?"

"Yeah, but only because Victor ordered me to do it," Rossetti moved the back of his right hand under his chin to catch some of the sweat that was already beginning to trickle down from the corners of his mouth.

"No, no, Rossetti. Just answer that question yes or no—Doesn't your state criminal court testimony show that you swore that you were on your own, and in fact, when the Bronx District Attorney pursued the possibility that Mister Albanese may have been involved in the murders, you denied he had anything to do with them. One yes to both questions will be sufficient, Rossetti," Strapoli said, thrusting his right index finger into the air.

"Yeah. I mean, yes."

"Good. So why are you changing your testimony here today?"

"Because I was only doin' what Victor Albanese wanted me to do. It was not my idea. It was his."

"Of course by now falsely implicating Mister Albanese, you're going for soft time as promised by the feds."

"Your honor," Ms. Stevens didn't even stand up.

"Mister Strapoli, get it together. Do you understand what I'm saying," the judge warned.

"Yes, yes, your honor."

"OK. Why did he want you to murder the mayor's father and Mister Velez," Strapoli said, throwing back his head and looking up at the high ceiling of the courtroom.

"I guess, for two reasons," Rossetti began. "First, Victor always had a hard-on—oh, I'm sorry, your honor," he said looking at U.S. District Court Judge Amelia Hart. "He was really pissed off at this new police community shit. You know, the cops were out walking the streets. They was ruining Victor's businesses. As I said before."

"Businesses?" Strapoli said.

"You know, Gil, numbers, drugs, whores. All that shit. Anyways—"

"What did you say, Mister Rossetti?" the judge interrupted.

Rossetti looked first at the judge and then to his lawyer.

"I'll have none of that kind of language in my court. I'm holding you personally responsible for this witness' use of profanity, Mister Strapoli. Do you understand?" Judge Hart said, pointing her right index finger at the lawyer.

"Yes, your honor, I understand. Mister Rossetti, you were describing Victor Albanese's business. Please go on."

"Yeah, numbers, drugs, women and all that stuff. So, Victor had asked me to ask Gordon Halliday to talk to the mayor about pullin' off the cops, especially in Parkchester and the rest of the Bronx," he said.

"And. To the best of your knowledge, did Mister Halliday talk to the mayor?" Strapoli asked.

"I was told yes, but I saw nothin'."

"Who told you 'yes'?"

"Gordon Halliday."

"OK. Then what?"

"Then when we found out that Halliday was skimmin' the money we was sending through his bank, Victor got pissed, and decided that we could kill two birds with one shot," he realized what he had said, and quickly looked down at his shoes."

"So, you decided to send a message to the mayor and put a scare into Mister Halliday. Is that correct?"

"Yeah. I mean, no, not me, it was Victor's idea."

"Yeah, right. OK, Rossetti. Let's go on," Strapoli turned, went back to the defense table, picked up some papers and walked back to his position facing Rossetti.

"Have you ever been to Gordon Halliday's home?" the lawyer asked.

"His what?"

"Mister Halliday's house. You know in Fieldston."

"Oh, yeah, right. I've been there," he realized that Strapoli was on a new path, and Rossetti was twisting and stretching his neck nervously.

"OK. How many times?"

"Times? What do you mean, times?"

"You know. Two times, five times, ten times—every week?" Strapoli emphasized the latter.

"I, ah, I don't know, a few times."

"Again, you testified in your state court trial that you were picking up payments on Mister Halliday's gambling debts every week. Is that correct?"

"Yeah, yeah. I guess so."

"And more often than not—in fact most of the time—you picked up your payments—actually vig, wasn't it Charlie?—At the Halliday house?"

"Yeah, yeah, I guess so."

"And, Mister Rossetti, didn't you become friendly with one of the members of Gordon Halliday's family?"

"Friendly?"

"Yes. Doesn't Mister Halliday have a daughter?"

"Yeah, yes, he does?"

"Will you tell the court her name?"

"Her name is a—is, Eve."

"Ah, Eve Halliday. Good. Mister Rossetti—Charlie—what was your relationship with Eve Halliday?" Strapoli leaned forward, raised his right leg and placed the tip of his shoe on the edge of the platform, which held Rossetti and his chair.

"We was, just what you said, friends." Charlie Rossetti said. He didn't like the imposing figure leaning towards him.

"OK, good. Did she know why you were visiting her home so often."

"No."

"No?" Strapoli said, feigning surprise. "Who did she think you were?"

"She thought, at first, that I was an investor in the old man's business, or somethin' like that."

"At first? Come on, Rossetti, she knew you were a bookmaker and that her father owed you a lot of money. Isn't that correct?" Strapoli said. He was mad, or was doing a great simulation.

"Yeah, yeah, eventually she asked, and I told her."

"What was her reaction?"

"Reaction?"

"Yes, what did she think, what did she say, what did she do?"

"I don't know. Nothing. Nothing, I think."

"She never asked you to take it easy on her father, or anything like that?" Strapoli was become relentless.

"Ah, no, no, she didn't."

"OK. Charlie Rossetti, I want you to look all of us in this courtroom, straight into our eyes, and tell us whether or not you and Eve Halliday were lovers."

"Hey, judge, your honor. Please, do I have to answer that?"

"Answer the question, Mister Rossetti," Judge Hart ordered.

"No, no, I can't. I won't," Rossetti was shaking his head as if he was having an epileptic fit or something. The strain was about to explode.

Judge Hart informed Rossetti that if he didn't answer, he would be held in contempt of court, which would, in fact, affect his agreement with the U.S. Attorney. He shook his head. Rossetti was told to step down and ordered to take a seat at the defense table.

"Your honor, may I call my next witness?" Strapoli asked.

"Yes, of course, Mister Strapoli."

"The defense calls Mister Victor Albanese." The judge had to slam her gavel over and over to stop the spontaneous bedlam that had erupted in her courtroom.

Gil Strapoli went back to the defense table and reached out for his client, who was struggling to get out of his chair. Victor Albanese angrily pulled his arm away from his lawyer's reach and scuffed his way to the witness stand.

In between a series of frightening coughing spells, Albanese, as expected, explained his various businesses, trucking, sand and gravel, carting, and waste disposal—all C Corporations that diligently filed their tax returns on time.

"You could check it out," he said.

Albanese also testified that Charlie Rossetti was an employee, the manager of one of his companies, Maloney Sand and Gravel on the Bronx River.

"Mister Albanese, did Rossetti also have a little business of his own on the side, taking bets over the telephone?" Strapoili asked.

"Yeah."

"How did you know that, Mister Albanese?" Strapoli asked.

Victor Albanese's cough was becoming uncontrollable. He took out a handkerchief and held it over his mouth with one hand, while pressing against his chest with the other.

"That's OK, Mister Albanese. Take it easy. We can wait," his lawyer reassured him.

He put away the handkerchief. "What a ya mean, how do I know that? You know why."

"Yes, yes, but tell the court, Mister Albanese," Strapoli said.

"I helped him out from time to time. You know, when he needed some cash or somethin."

"But it wasn't your business. Is that correct?"

"No, no. He was on his own."

"Good. OK. Now, how did Gordon Halliday get into the picture?" Strapoli said. He knew that a few people in the courtroom would sit up and listen more closely after he said that.

"Charlie came to me because he said that 'Holiday' was into him for a bundle and that when Charlie leaned on him, this guy offered to do some favors for Rossetti so that he wouldn't blow the jerk away. The stupid fuck." It would be the only time that Gil Strapoli would be permitted to apologize to the court for his client's bursts of anger, the judge explained.

The scheme that Halliday offered Rossetti, according to Victor Albanese, was that he, Halliday, could move some of Rossetti's gambling money through an offshore shell company in the Bahamas that Halliday owned.

"What did that have to do with you, sir?" Strapoli asked.

"Charlie was a fuckin' wacko. He said—."

"Mister Strapoli. Do you bring this out in all the people you question? Rossetti wasn't your witness and I held you responsible for his conduct in this court, and now Mister Albanese, your witness, is your responsibility, too. Let's give it one more try" Amelia Hart was not happy.

"Yes, your honor. I'll give it my best shot." Strapoli got a few ripples of light laughter from the crowd.

"So, you've testified, Mister Albanese, that Mister Rossetti told you that Mister Gordon Halliday told him, Rossetti, that he could move some of Rossetti's gambling money through an offshore shell company in the Bahamas that Halliday owned. I repeat my question, what did that have to do with you, sir?" Strapoli asked.

"OK. Charlie was a freakin' wacko. He said that he could do the same for Maloney Sand and Gravel," Victor Albanese responded.

Laughter. Strapoli darted a look at Judge Hart, who shook her hand in despair.

"And?"

"And? I told him to f—freak off. That's what I told him," Albanese was breathing deeply and dabbing at the wet residue coming up from his throat and now dripping from both corners of his mouth.

"Did Charlie Rossetti say anything about his socializing with the Hallidays?" Strapoli was finished with the money laundering issue.

"Yeah, he told me, that he was at the guys big house so often, that he met and started screwin' the guys daughter." Judge Hart had given up, some members of the audience surmised.

"Eve Halliday?"

"Yeah, yeah, I guess that was her name."

"Did he mention anything about Mayor Tom McCabe?" Strapoli inquired.

"Yeah, he said that she was datin' him, too."

Albanese went on to say that he didn't hear anything more about the Halliday caper until one day, while Albanese was sitting with Charlie at the sand and gravel plant, Rossetti casually mentioned to him that the mayor was about to dump Eve Halliday. At the same time, McCabe was turning his back on her father's plea to do something about community policing, as Rossetti had pressured him to do.

"What else did he say, Mister Albanese?" Albanese asked, turning and looking out in to the standing-room only, courtroom.

"He said that he was gonna get even with the mayor, for both himself and this broad, by offin' the mayor's father. I threw the, the, freakin' guy out."

"'This broad' was Eve Halliday. Is that correct?" his lawyer asked.

"Yeah, yeah. Holiday's daughter." Albanese nodded wearily, at this point in his testimony.

Suddenly, Victor Albanese closed his eyes, heaved loudly while grasping his chest and collapsed in the witness chair. Gil Strapoli was the first to get to him. He started shaking his client, but got no response. Two court attendants quickly picked up Victor Albanese and hurried him through the entrance to the courtroom closest to where he had collapsed.

Paramedics rushed Victor Albanese to Bellevue.

❧   ❧   ❧

Eve Halliday had been under subpoena as a possible witness in the federal prosecutor's case against her father, Albanese, and the others. Richard Kessler, who would represent Gordon Halliday, and was considered to be one of the most successful—and most expensive—criminal lawyers in the country, would now represent Eve Halliday, too. In the wake of Victor Albanese's shocking testimony, Judge Hart granted a two-day recess for Kessler to properly prepare his client for her day in court. The lawyer and his new client would use the forty-eight hours to forge testimony that would make it clear to the jury that it would be her word, of denial, against the allegations of a known hoodlum.

Eve Halliday sauntered casually into the courtroom wearing her Tod's flip-flops, with an air of insouciance; if she was worried at all about the testimony she was about to give, she certainly didn't show it.

When she took the stand, Eve Halliday went into great detail of how she watched her father, because of his gambling addiction, get badgered by Charlie Rossetti. Eve Halliday watched and listened as her father, in great desperation, engineered the plot to launder money through a phony company in the Bahamas, in exchange for some relief from the constant threats of Rossetti. Kessler was pleased.

Charlie Rossetti, her lover? She laughed off that by saying that she slept with the mobster only as a pretext to take the heat off her father. Kessler, looked nervously at one of his junior associates seated next to him. But, then she explained that Rossetti came in useful for another reason.

"Another reason?" Richard Kessler said to himself, pinching his chin between his left thumb and index finger. "What the hell is she doing?" he asked his associate counsel.

Eve Halliday explained that she had expected to become the city's first lady—she and Tom McCabe were indeed engaged—for a while. When he started talking about ending their engagement, and also began turning his back on her father, she decided to ask Rossetti for some help.

"Help, Miss Halliday?" Gil Strapoli asked. He was about to finish up the examination of his last witness.

"Yes. Help, Mister Strapoli," Eve Halliday repeated, just short of in your face.

"To do what?" Strapoli asked.

"To get back at Tom McCabe for what he did to me and my father."

"What did Charlie Rossetti suggest?"

"He said that he could arrange for a hit on the mayor's father."

"You mean he was going to contract out the killing of Morgan McCabe?" The courtroom was as quiet as it had been through the entire trial.

"Yes," she replied coldly.

"And, Mister Velez?" Strapoli asked.

"That had something to do with Rossetti's—and, I was told, Albanese's—problems with that community policing thing," she answered.

"Did you ever meet Sal Conte, Jr., and/or Trevor Burns, the convicted killers of Morgan McCabe and Ramon Velez?" Strapoli asked, as the U.S. Attorney and her staff looked at each other with raised eyebrows. By this time, Kessler was slouched in his chair, glaring at his client.

She smiled, and answered, "Sal, I knew because some of my friends and I had been customers of his, in the past."

"Customers? You mean you bought drugs from Sal Conte?"

"Yes."

"And, Trevor Burns?" Strapoli asked.

"I met him in a bar on 9th Avenue, around West 49th or 50th St. you know where the Irish mob hung out. Or so Charlie Rossetti told me. He's the one who took me to the bar," Eve Halliday said.

"Did Charlie Rossetti ask to be paid for the murders?"

"Yes. I paid him one hundred and fifty thousand dollars."

"I'm finished with this witness, your honor," Gil Strapoli smiled.

Pandemonium! Judge Hart was standing, while pounding her gavel.

Eve Halliday began to stand up, but the judge motioned for her to remain seated.

Amanda Stevens jumped to her feet, looked back at the unsettled courtroom, and then began alternating waving her hands in the air and then motioning for the spectators to settle back into their seats.

"Your honor, obviously we ask that the jury be temporarily remanded to their deliberation room."

"Bailiff, see that the jurors are so escorted," the judge ordered.

As soon as the last juror disappeared behind the door leading from the court, Amanda Stevens asked that Eve Halliday be detained awaiting her arrest by local authorities.

Richard Kessler immediately asked that he consult with his client. Judge Hart granted that request.

Eve Halliday had walked into court that morning with a couple of friends and her lawyer at her side. She left with her Burberry thrown over a pair of handcuffs, and was escorted by two U.S. Marshals.

The U.S. Attorney turned to see that Eve Halliday had left the courtroom. She then asked that the jury be brought back into the courtroom. Once they settled in she asked that Charlie Rossetti be called back to the witness stand for redirect examination.

Rossetti was smiling, for some reason, as he settled in the chair for a second time that day.

"You've now heard the testimony of Mister Albanese and Miss Halliday. What is your reaction to what they each said?" the U.S. Attorney began.

"Well, now you know that the idea of killin' old man McCabe came from both of them," Rossetti responded.

"Both of them? Please explain that to the jury, Mister Rossetti," Stevens directed, and then looked out over the crowd.

Mark Blaine leaned over to his editor seated next to him and whispered, "Do you remember I told you that Rossettti said to me, "and a real fuckin' surprise, which I'm not givin' you or anyone else, until the trial'? I think this is it!"

"Yeah. A week after Victor Albanese ordered me to hit McCabe and Velez, Eve Halliday asked me to whack the old man, too."

"Miss Halliday testified that she came to you for help, and that you were the one who suggested the killing of Morgan McCabe," Stevens responded.

"No, no way. She told me exactly what she wanted. She was gonna get even with the mayor. She thought about killing either him or his old man, but she decided that the old man would be like a double-hit on the mayor. His old man would be dead, and he'd have to suffer, too."

Tom McCabe was crying hysterically.

"And, the money?" Amanda Stevens arched her eyebrows in expectation.

"She offered me the money, so I took it. Hey, I got paid a hundred fifty thousand big ones by her for doin' somethin' I was gonna do for my boss, Victor, for nothin'"

Most of the media didn't cover the remainder of the trial. None of the defendants testified, as expected. Convictions all around. Halliday would do five to fifteen at Lewisburg. Reiser got six months soft time at picturesque Allenwood, in White Deer, Pennsylvania, no less.

Tom McCabe was given three years probation and disbarment. He began drinking.

Victor Albanese was DOA at Bellevue. Eve Halliday would sit alone at her criminal trial on the Grand Concourse.

James Christopher Russo ran unopposed in the Democratic primary and would get two extra lines on the ballot in November. One would be on the Community Service Party line, with Ellen McCabe, Linda Wright, Co-chairpersons. They wanted all government services to go the way of Community Policing; grass roots policy-making, they called it. A second line would come from a movement started by former Senator Bill Bradley of New Jersey, calling themselves the Good Government Party, who wanted to make sure that elected officials and their appointed cronies would be held accountable for the achievement of some reasonable goals and objectives, or have their political careers terminated. The communities would take back the city, the way the cops took back the streets for them. "Yeah, right," the Republicans responded.

They would run State Senator Bill Wilson again. He had been a lifelong resident of the Riverdale Section of New York City, having served the city, as a member of the city council, then in the state assembly, and now as a state senator representing that part of the Bronx that included Kingsbridge and Parkchester. He had run four years before on the Republican ticket against an incumbent democratic mayor who eventually lost the election to Tom McCabe, running as an independent candidate. By reputation, he was a real gentleman, but too quiet for what the voters in New York City at that time were gearing up for after listening to the wildly reformist, electrifying programs that the extremely charismatic young congress-man, Tom McCabe, was promising to deliver.

Wilson might have been a gentleman, but this time he came out of his corner with a quick knockout in mind. He immediately latched on to why the electorate had chosen Tom McCabe over him last time out. The tired old liberal view, he called it, of blaming all the problems facing the city on someone other than the people who lived there. Particularly those politicians in Washington, in the state, and in New York City who were not pouring enough money into the social programs to somehow stem the tide of urban disintegration that was taking place. And, community policing, Wilson maintained, was really about diverting the cops into more social responsibilities. Who, he asked, would protect those who didn't need or want such "social services?" He would begin, he promised, as the previous administration did—with the cops. But this time, he'd put them back to work specializing in what they knew and did best—fighting crime. That was a full time job, he insisted, no time for worrying about absentee parents, school truants, negligent landlords, late garbage pick-ups, or delayed welfare checks. Those are serious problems that need to be taken care of—but not by cops. The responsible city agencies will get off their asses and be held accountable for what they're supposed to be doing.

And the people who vote with their pocketbooks seemed pleased.

The candidates had agreed to three debates. The first would be in early September at Manhattan College in the Fieldston Section of the Bronx. Tony Guida, a savvy and respected TV anchor would be the moderator.

Tony asked first about garbage.

"Gentlemen, New Yorkers throw out 10,000 tons of garbage each day. Most of it ends up in the Fresh Kills landfill on Staten Island, which is groaning with the overload. There have been a number of proposals to address this problem, all of which are weighted down with political ramifications for the sponsors."

"Senator Wilson you lost the toss and therefore go first."

"Thanks a lot, Tony," Bill Wilson smiled. "Tony, there's no question in my mind that we must step up the recycling program on which the McCabe administration has been dragging its feet. Once I get that back on track, I would consider sending the remaining tonnage out of the city to distant landfills."

"Commissioner—I'm sorry, Mister Russo?"

"Yeah, thanks a lot from me, too, Tony," Chris Russo laughed. "Well, I assume that the senator doesn't mean distant places such as Greenpoint in Brooklyn or, heaven's to Betsy, our own Hunts Point in his district, because that's where some of the commercial trash is being diverted right now. I know it's politically unpopular, if not suicidal, to suggest that we have some serious discussions about incinerating our waste in New York City, but there are many examples of successful programs in other major cities. I'd give it a good look as mayor of this city."

As the night went on, the discussion covered public assistance programs—centering on the city's "Workfare" program—overcrowded and poorly maintained schools, the future of the city-owned hospitals, traffic gridlock in Manhattan, the homeless, the battered, the abused, business incentives to keep jobs in the city, and, finally, how much or how little effect the city's community policing program has had on the precipitous drop in crime in the city.

The State Senator and the former cop answered these questions as most of the viewers sitting in front of their TVs and those crammed in to the small auditorium at the Christian Brothers' school would have expected.

Bill Wilson would go after the phantom fathers of kids on welfare, replace the Board of Education with a new mayoral agency, sell off the hospitals, ban private cars in Manhattan and toll the East River bridges, institutionalize the homeless, contract out the city's social services, increase financial incentives to businesses to stay in or move into the city, and make the cops enforcers of criminal law once again, not social workers.

Loud applause from the live audience.

Chris Russo was for more educational programs for the young and poor, would give the local school boards the financial and political support they need, move the city's hospitals into the outpatient care business, use cops to move cross-town traffic more expeditiously, upgrade and increase the number of city-sponsored shelters for the homeless, and treat them at the city's new outpatient centers, ditto for battered women, abused kids, and others needing such care, and entice businesses to stay and come by providing a pool of trained, talented, and enthusiastic workers from special programs at City University's many colleges. Finally, he said:

"As for the cops?"

Bill Wilson interrupted his opponent.

"Yes, yes, commissioner, I'm sure we're all breathlessly awaiting your comments in that area. I've heard from some former and present high-ranking police officials that community policing as envisioned by you will never work for a number of reasons."

"Why don't you start with number one, Senator," Russo smiled.

"OK, fine. In their opinion, and mine, I might add, the kinds of problems you and I are debating here today, abused, neglected and abandoned children, the absence of badly-needed health care, poor housing, lousy schools, low-paying or no jobs, drugs and violent crimes would be best addressed starting with the family structure—or the lack of it." Wilson began.

"I agree, but in the meantime, Senator—"

"No, no, Commissioner. Let me finish."

"By holding those responsible for providing wholesome, family surroundings, we begin to address the myriad of issues facing those in our city who suffer more than anyone else—our children. We, in turn, will free up those city agencies, including your cops, who can direct their resources and talent to accomplishing what they do best—health services for all, affordable and decent housing, attractive schools and accountable teachers, better jobs for better educated city residents, and fighting drugs and crimes on a full-time basis. No overlaps. Damn it, Commissioner, cops can't do what only a loving mother or father can."

Another round of applause for Wilson.

"I hate to ask you what your number two reason is," Russo replied.

"You don't have to, it's reality, my friend, reality," Wilson began. "Community policing as I understand it is successful only to the extent that police officers have experienced and can therefore understand and can share the problems facing the most needy in our communities. Is that true, sir?"

"I know where you're going with this, Senator. In fact, my former friend, Tom McCabe, feels the same way. I gave him my answer and I'll give you the same one—after you finish, of course."

"Thank you. So, therefore, isn't it true Commissioner Russo, that the vast majority of the men and women in the New York City Police Department come from our suburbs, having been weaned by two caring parents, either or both of whom had good paying jobs, lived in comfortable one-family homes, gone to some of the best financed schools in the country, have had unlimited access to health care since birth, have never been hassled by a drug dealer, or had their favorite and only school jacket ripped from their backs by some local scum. Not like you or me, Chris, both born and raised in the South Bronx. We've seen it all, right? God help us, Commissioner Russo, but we here tonight and those watching in front of their TV sets may be looking at New York City's Last Cop."

"I don't think so, sir," Russo began, wistfully. "You see we've all changed. I'm no more the 'Last Cop' than you are the last State Senator. And, the young people who are today becoming cops—or becoming doctors, lawyers, teachers, and state senators, I might add—have changed, too. They are no more, or no less, prepared to take on a new and changing world than you and I were—and our parents, and theirs before them were. Most of us were willing to learn. Most of the young women and men of today are eager to learn. I've seen them, I've talked with them, and I've listened to them, and I've learned from them, too. They can do the job that has to be done, Senator. Sometimes, the very factors that you laid out, the loving parents, the great schools, the kinds of health care available to them growing up, make them even more anxious to help those who weren't so fortunate. Have no fear, Bill Wilson, whatever you and I may accomplish in our lives, those who follow us will accomplish more."

The debate went on until the late hours of this mild, uneventful day of 9/10, 2001.

About the Author

Joe Hoffman is a former First Deputy Police Commissioner in New York City, past President of the New York City Health and Hospitals Corporation, and held senior executive positions with St. Vincent's Medical Center and W. R. Grace.

He lives in East Williston on Long Island with his wife, Kitty. They have two sons, a daughter-in-law and four grandchildren. He has B.Sc. and M.P.A. degrees from John Jay College. An adjunct professor at Adelphi University, he is working on a sequel to *"Acts and Omissions."*

0-595-22524-1